EXITUS

FRANKIE JAMES

CONTENTS

FOREWORD

If you're here, that means you've come a long way—through magic, mayhem, questionable decisions, and at least one character you definitely said, "Kick his ass to the curb" about. Well done.

Before we dive in, one quick, promise-it's-important note: this series is meant to be read in order, and yes... that includes the novella.

EMBERHOLD ACADEMY READING ORDER
Exordium
Inter
Primitus (An Emberhold Academy Novella)
Exitus
Primitus isn't a detour—it's more like the scenic route with important information and a few "ohhh, that's why" moments. You can skip it, but some connections in this final book will feel extra satisfying if you don't. Think of

it as bonus insight into Adelaide (Reverie's mother) and her Faction.

If you've already read it—excellent choice. If you haven't—this is me gently sliding a Post-it across the table that says, *trust me.*

Now, back to Emberhold.

Let's finish what we started.

Glossary

Bellator- warrior.

Draxon- dragon-like creatures.

Gerendel- a bigfoot-like creature that considers Aurathions a food source.

Cryptfiends- towering, grey-skinned beings with long arms and clawed hands. Restless corpses, cursed by their past misdeeds.

La' u alo fagia- My darling.

Aegisseal- is the act of sealing with protective force, or creating an impenetrable barrier that not only closes but safeguards what lies within.

Aegisseer- an elite confidant bound by the ability of.

Aegisseal-never to betray a secret.

Aegisworn- mystical, strong, bound to serve the Queen.

Varruk- monster from the wilds of Aurathia with wolf-like facial features.

DF- Dark Faction.

WARNING

This book contains sexual situations and other adult themes. Recommended for age 18+. Trigger warnings include (but not limited to): Dubious consent, Non-Consent (rape), Profanity, Sexual situations, Violance, Death, Blood Play, Extreme torture. If you have any specific questions please email me at frankie-james153027@gmail.com.

PROLOGUE

UNKNOWN

She was *fucking* magnificent.

I hadn't missed a performance since I'd been notified of her arrival.

Before she appeared, I couldn't remember the last time I had attended these events; my interest had faded years ago.

Some never tire of the battles fought here. They thrive on the blood and gore, as well as the desperation of the warriors involved. I had enjoyed it just as much as anyone when it all began. However, I eventually grew bored, as I often did.

Nothing held my attention for long...until now... until her.

My little Bellator.

Whether I wanted to love her or kill her was still unclear.

I was home, sitting in my study by a roaring fire and sipping a brandy that had been part of the spoils from one of our recent victories. When Ubel walked in. My tolerance for the man was growing thin, but for now, he was still needed.

"Do you assume you're not required to knock?" I raised my brow in question.

"Your house staff let me in." He removed his jacket and fixed himself a drink.

His actions demonstrated that he believed he was entirely safe from my anger. For the moment, he was, but that wouldn't last forever.

"I'll need a name. Whoever it was needs to be punished." I waited for his answer, but he changed the subject.

I knew the little bitch had let himself in.

"When was the last time you left this house and went out into Aurathia? Or visited the coliseum?" He eyed my clothes in distaste. "Have you even changed your clothes in the last week? It seems to the rest of us that you've become somewhat of a recluse."

I narrowed my eyes. "Why do any of you think that your opinions matter to me?" He hesitated, subtly shifting back in the face of my annoyance. "If there's a purpose to this visit, please get to it. I have important matters to attend to, and you're interrupting."

"Things like getting blind drunk?" Ubel casually walked around the room, picking up items from the shelf and putting them back, but never quite in the same position.

Apparently, he was braver with a little distance between us; what a fool.

My blood began to heat, and the familiar need to kill began to overtake me at the sight of him touching my things. The man was clever and manipulative, but never stupid; he usually handled me with kid gloves.

Sanity was not my strong suit, and he knew that.

Today, he was almost cocky; now my curiosity was piqued.

"Cut the bullshit. Why are you here?" I growled, determined to find out what he was up to.

"You need to make an appearance at the coliseum. We have a new warrior that I think will interest you." Ubel smirked, then took a seat on my couch, spreading both arms on the back as if he lived here.

"Why the hell would I give a shit?" I was fighting the need to rip his throat out. "I was over the fuckery that takes place there years ago."

"I get that you believe you have more pressing matters, but you'll want to be there for this." He flashed that crocodile grin of his, which made me grind my teeth.

"I'm growing tired of your company, so if you have something to tell me, get to it. I hate the way you dance around things." I cocked a single brow. "One day I'm going to lose patience." I stared at him, letting him see the murderous rage in my eyes that I usually kept hidden and sending my shadows to cover the floor like a heavy fog.

Ubel flinched but then sat up straighter, finding the balls to continue as if he wasn't staring death in the face. "This ennui that's affected you the last few years has really grown tiresome." When I gave him no reaction, he huffed out a breath in exasper-

ation. *"Fine. Her name, the warrior's name, is Reverie, and she's the daughter of Adelaide."*

I sat up straight. "Adelaide Hawthorne?"

"Is there another?" He raised one eyebrow in question.

"I'll be there. Now leave." I couldn't stand looking at his face one more moment.

Ubel hesitated, clearly wanting to say more, but he did as I asked. He recognized he'd pushed me as far as was wise today. He sped up his departure when one of my shadows wrapped around his neck like a noose.

I was pissed that I hadn't been notified the moment she arrived. These little power plays of his and Selene's were ridiculous. Was Hayes also back? Damien?

⌒☙⌒

R everie was beautiful; I'd expect nothing less from Adelaide's daughter. But it wasn't her beauty that held me captive.

It was her fierceness in battle.

I could tell by looking at her that she'd been through some shit since she arrived here. Fresh bruises and cuts covered every exposed part of her skin. One cut on the side of her forehead looked deep enough to scar. For an Aurathion, the damage had to be severe to leave that kind of mark.

I'll have to interrogate Ubel and find out who was responsible. I'd already decided that I alone was permitted to mark that beautiful body.

I turned my attention back to the battle as Reverie cut

through the enemy as if she were born to do it. Every swing of her twin blades hit a spot on the body that would cause the most damage possible.

The two Gerendels she fought were huge, but she'd already incapacitated one. And it looked like she was going to dispatch the other in short order.

Almost as soon as I had the thought, Reverie vaulted off the body of the first monster and stabbed her remaining foe simultaneously in both eyes, killing him instantly. She landed in a crouch, then stood and wiped the blood from her face with the back of her hand.

A true Bellator. A warrior among warriors.

No expression whatsoever on her face, even as the crowd went wild.

Reverie Hawthorne fascinated me. I needed to get closer.

I sat up straight. I had a brilliant idea.

A grin spread across my face. I stood and leaned against a pillar on my private balcony, watching my warrior princess until she left the colosseum.

I had plans to make.

Prepare yourself, Reverie Hawthorne, because ready or not, here I come.

CHAPTER 1
ZEKE

I silently moved down the hallway, looking for my twin. The last time I saw him, he was questioning a prisoner we had captured during the recent battle outside Atlanta.

I pushed open the large door that led down to the dungeon.

Emberhold had rearranged itself since the attack on our world from the Dark Factions. A dungeon was just one of many changes. Every day, it seemed we woke up to more. Sometimes it felt like the academy was grieving my Treasures' absence, too.

When I reached the bottom of the long flight of stairs, I began to hear the screaming.

I smiled.

Since Reverie had been abducted, I'd become a different person. Every scream was like music to my ears, as it gave me hope that we were closer to finding a way to open a portal to reach her. I'd let my dark side take over, not trying to hide that part of myself anymore.

The awakening of my abilities helped with that. The monster inside and I would stop at nothing to get our Nexus back.

My smile faded when I thought back to the day Reverie disappeared; a day that would live in my memory forever. It went from extreme joy when Jet was marked, and our Faction was complete, to extreme pain when suddenly we were attacked, and I felt Reverie leave this world.

The door had burst open, and several members of the DF (Dark Factions) entered, accompanied by some of the most fearsome creatures I'd ever seen.

Later, John informed us of what they were and emphasized the danger they represented: The Cryptfiends were towering, grey-skinned beings with long arms and clawed hands. He explained that they were restless corpses, cursed by their past misdeeds. Drawn to life's warmth, they fed on more than just flesh—they consumed memories and breath, leaving victims hollow-eyed and soulless. They had lived in the dark corners of Aurathia, waiting to hunt any who were foolish enough to wander into their territory.

Those of us unfamiliar with the giant, zombie-like creatures had frozen at the horrifying sight. Luckily, the older Aurathions knew precisely what we were dealing with and, after a gruesome battle, were able to dispose of them.

Somehow, the DF managed to control these creatures and use them to attack us. One of many horrors at their disposal, all in an effort to try and kill the earthbound Aurathions and take over this world.

We'd managed to capture several of our Aurathion enemies, hoping to get information from them… unfortunately, when Jet returned, he was in the frenzy of a killing rage, and no hostages survived.

Chloe and Oliver came in immediately after and explained everything that had happened while we'd been distracted by our attackers.

Another consequence of that horrible day was that our existence was revealed to humans. The council has been very busy trying to smooth things over and reassure Earth's leaders that we weren't here to take over.

That wasn't an easy task with the DF attacking at every opportunity. Some major cities had been nearly destroyed, and countless lives had been lost.

Jet had been invaluable to the council in dealing with human and Aurathion relations. Who would have thought that his spying would give us an advantage? The reports he had submitted before the attacks showed that we wanted to live peacefully with humans and trained daily to protect this world.

Truly, we were their only hope, and the powers that be knew it.

"Where are you going?" A deep voice startled me out of my thoughts.

Nathan was standing in front of me, covered in blood. "I'm looking for Zane."

"He's cleaning up." Nathan nodded toward the door he'd just come out of.

"Did you get any new information?" I asked as I walked toward the room.

"No, but we have a lead on another attack they have planned." He smiled, but it didn't reach his eyes.

"Where?" I stopped, waiting for his answer.

Oren had surmised that if they could be caught just as they entered our world, we might be able to commandeer their portal and reach Reverie. It was the best idea we'd come up with so far, and everyone agreed on this plan of action.

Getting all of us to *agree* on anything these days was nearly impossible. Reverie was the glue that held us together, and without her, everything was falling apart. The only thing uniting us now was our grief and determination to get her back.

Nathan's expression was smug. "The town where I grew up. Jesse was right, they're trying to find Adelaide. *Finally*, they seem to be taking the bait."

It felt like my heart was going to leap right out of my chest. "Do any of the other guys know yet?"

"No, I'm on my way to tell them. We need to finalize all of our plans and be ready to go in two weeks." He pulled a rag from his pocket and wiped his face—smearing the blood around more than anything else.

"Shit! Two *fucking* weeks?" I knew this was good news, but we'd been without our Nexus for months now—two more weeks seemed like an eternity.

"I know. I'm not happy about the wait either, but it is what it is." His face took on a sinister expression. "What helps me deal is fantasizing about what I'm going to do to the people who've held my Nexi all this time. You should try it."

I dreamed of that on a regular basis myself. My methods of vengeance changed nightly, but they always ended the same. With the claws of my beast buried deep in their guts, and blood covering everything.

Nathan smirked. "I can see by the expression on your face that you've already tried it." He slapped my back. "Tell Zane to hurry it up. We all need to plan for this one together." Nathan turned and started up the stairs.

I pushed the door open just in time to see Zane open his mouth and incinerate the guy sitting in the chair. We'd both learned to embrace our abilities because we knew they'd be vital in rescuing our Nexus.

Since Reverie had been taken, we expected our abilities to fade or at least weaken. However, it seemed the opposite had happened. They'd actually grown stronger, and we'd even gained a few more.

Zane's fire abruptly cut off, and he turned to me, "Zane's mobile body disposal, you ax'em I ash'em."

I didn't acknowledge his morbid joke; he covered his pain with humor, and it had progressively gotten darker as the months had passed. "Nathan told me the good news —great job getting him to talk."

"Yep. If the guy weren't on the wrong side of all this, I'd have admired the son of a bitch. He didn't give in until Nathan cut off his last finger." Zane went to the sink and washed his hands and face.

"I came down here to tell you that Chloe and Oliver are back from their assignment." I pulled the hose from the wall and washed the ashes down the drain in the floor.

"Are Jet and Deshawn back?" He asked, walking to the sink, splashing water on his face.

"No, but Oren believes they'll arrive in a few hours. Likely sooner if he tells Jet about the new information you found." I followed Zane out of the room and up the stairs.

The hallways were busy with everyone dressed in their battle gear. Classes were still taking place, but only for first years. No one had been initiated since the war had resumed. Dean Mathews was now allowing Potentials and their prospective Nexus to perform the ritual.

There had been no shortage mentioned of D's wine, but I knew it was only a matter of time. For now, we needed strong, trained Factions, and we needed them as soon as possible.

Zane and I left the main building and headed to our house at the edge of the forest. After we returned, we applied for Faction housing, no longer willing to keep our relationship with Reverie a secret.

The details of how it happened were still under wraps, of course.

With Damien's help, we convinced the dean that we had performed the ritual at our parents' home before the attack. Damien and Hayes hinted to him that they'd brought a small supply of D's wine just in case they needed it to reaffirm the bond with their Nexus.

I'm not sure he was thoroughly convinced. And even though forming the bond that way was against our laws without a council witness, he let it go.

Approaching our home, I pictured Reverie lounging in one of the overstuffed chairs surrounding the fireplace, waiting for me to prepare a delicious meal; knowing that wasn't even a possibility was like a knife to the heart. Every day I spent on this earth without my Treasure made me realize that without her, life was pointless.

The only thing keeping me from total insanity was the knowledge that we *would* get her back—no matter the cost. Our people, this world... nothing mattered but getting her back.

We entered, and Zane went straight to the cabinet, pulling out a bottle of whiskey, pouring a shot, and downing it in one swallow. "Do you want one, brother?"

I shook my head and leaned into the fridge to make some sandwiches for everyone. None of us had been eating enough. I knew we needed to be at full strength to retrieve Reverie, so I tried to fix that when I could.

"I'm going to head upstairs and shower before everyone gets here." Zane downed another shot.

"Okay, I'll have food ready when you get back." He nodded, and reaching the top of the stairs, he didn't enter his room but headed down the hall to Reverie's.

All of us spent more time there than we did in our own rooms. As soon as our housing had been approved, we moved Reverie's things in here with us. Chloe didn't protest because she knew we were all on the edge of losing ourselves. We needed to feel close to her, even if it was an illusion.

I heard Reverie's shower start up just as the front door opened.

"Is Nathan here yet?" Oren strode in, carrying multiple scrolls and large codices.

"Nope," I said, finishing the sandwiches and stacking them on a plate in the center of the island.

He dropped everything onto the large table that divided the kitchen and living room, then sat down and grabbed a sandwich.

The housing provided to Factions was more than sufficient. Emberhold designed and modified them as it pleased. Fortunately, the home Emberhold created for our Faction suited us perfectly. It was a completely open-concept space; when you entered through the front door, you had a clear view of the dining and kitchen areas. All the bedrooms were upstairs, with one for each of us.

Reveries was at the end of the long hallway, and it was by far the biggest, with a bathroom that would be any woman's dream.

I couldn't wait for the day that I'd be able to run her a bubble bath in the giant tub. My Treasure's feet probably wouldn't touch the ground for months after her return. I'd see to it personally.

Oren spoke with his mouth full. "Damn, I knew I should have made him walk over with me."

I poured him a glass of tea, and he downed it much like Zane had the whiskey earlier.

"Thanks, man. I can't remember the last time I ate." He rubbed a hand down his face.

"That needs to change. We're not going to be able to help Reverie if we're not at our best." He nodded in agreement. Then I asked, "What's going on with Nathan?"

"He's been torturing anyone who had the smallest relationship with Kristine. I told him I'd already investigated everyone thoroughly, but that hasn't stopped him." Oren sighed and poured another glass of tea from the pitcher I'd sat near him.

"Good thing you locked Sophie away where he can't find her." I had no sympathy for the little bitch, but we needed to get everything out of her that we could before we disposed of her.

Nathan materialized next to me. "I'll find her, and when I do, she'll sing like a canary. You can bet your ass on that."

I didn't even startle at his appearance; he popped in and out so much I'd grown used to it.

"The girl is so terrified now that she hardly speaks since Jet got hold of her when we first returned. The last thing we need is you questioning her." Oren frowned at Nathan. "I'm still hoping that Kristine will contact her. Leave the dead girl walking alone until then."

"What took you so long to get here?" I asked the Psycho, as my Treasure called him.

"I had people to see and torture to inflict." He grabbed a sandwich and stuffed it into his mouth, almost swallowing it whole, not bothering to clean the dried blood from his hands first.

"Fuck, Nathan, what kind of mess do I have to clean up now?" Oren dragged a hand through his hair.

"Why do you give a shit? All that should matter is getting my Nexi back!" He slapped both hands down hard in front of Oren.

"I care because we need the help of some of the families you're pissing off!" Oren yelled. "Don't you think I want to go on a fucking killing spree too? I hate every single motherfucker that even looked at Reverie wrong, but I know it's going to take more than just the five of us to get her back."

I frowned at Nathan, "And she's not just *your* Nexi. We all belong to her. You tend to forget that."

"Fuck… *fine*, she belongs to all of us." He directed at me, then scowled at Oren. "I'll try to hold back, but when she returns, I'm going to make sure that none of the people who even caused her the slightest inconvenience still draw breath." He grabbed another sandwich, then found the bottle of whiskey Zane had drunk from and poured himself a shot.

"I truly hope you mean that. I could use the extra time spent trying to get you out of trouble to recover our Nexus." Oren stood, grabbed another glass from the cabinet, and motioned for Nathan to fill it.

Zane came down the stairs and grabbed the bottle, just as Nathan finished pouring Oren a shot.

Nathan roughly slapped him on the back and clinked his glass to the bottle. "To the silence after the screams."

Those two had become closer since Reverie had been taken. It didn't surprise me; both of them were more than a little crazy and had become more so over the last few months.

Oren followed with, "To mercy… may it die screaming." He threw his shot back.

"So, what's the plan, Boss?" Zane grabbed two sandwiches at once and began eating.

I was glad to see it after all the whiskey he'd consumed. It took a tremendous amount of alcohol to affect an Aurathion, so he wasn't in danger of getting drunk. For me, it was knowing he was on the edge and in danger of falling. I needed him—no, I needed *all* of them—to be whole when we found our Nexus. I was going to take it upon myself to make sure it was so.

"Let's wait for Jet and Deshawn to arrive, then we'll sort it out. I want to find out what his contact has planned and see if it will benefit us," Oren ran a hand through his hair and sat back down, the mantle of leadership heavy on his shoulders.

I nodded, recognizing the importance of that. I understood that Oren was barely holding on, just like all of us. His family's involvement with Reverie's disappearance must have been tearing him apart, but he refused to let it stop him. In fact, it seemed to drive him—sometimes he wouldn't get home until early morning and would sleep on the couch in his clothes, working nonstop to get our Nexus back. I knew he had contacts with the resistance in Aurathia, but he kept his information tight—knowing there were many ears in the academy that would kill for it.

Before I could reply, Jet and Deshawn walked in with Chloe and Oliver following right behind. Jet had a thunderous look on his face.

"What the fuck has happened now?" Nathan asked Jet, already scowling in preparation for his answer.

"The damn council has decided to use someone more experienced in Aurathion culture to represent them with the humans," Chloe spoke up before Jet could.

"Why the fuck would they do that?" Oren stood and began pacing.

"That's what I was going to ask you." Jet plopped into Oren's chair and began stuffing a sandwich into his mouth.

I'm glad I made them. Apparently, everyone was starving to death.

Oren kept pacing and muttering to himself. By now, we all knew his routine and understood it could take anywhere from a few minutes to several hours before he decided to involve us. We usually remained patient with him because we'd come to understand that he was a genius at the workings of the council and the other leaders of the Aurathion people.

"La'u alofagia, can I get you a sandwich? You haven't eaten at all today." Oliver began fixing a plate, not waiting for her answer.

Even in the midst of my personal heartache, it was truly a wonder to see my sister cared for with such love. She was almost as devastated as we were and sometimes forgot to take care of herself. Oliver had been a big help to us in our search for Reverie, but his first responsibility was to his Nexus, as it should be.

And yes, we knew she was Nexus now because everyone, except Chloe, acknowledged that Deshawn was hers too. She was denying it because I believed, subconsciously, that she wouldn't allow herself to take that step without Reverie here.

Oren had been sending her out to the war-torn cities and towns to help with the recovery effort. It was just one of the ways we tried to keep her busy and away from the majority of the fighting.

Chloe took a seat next to Jet. "I'm not really hungry."

"Hungry or not, you need to eat." Deshawn sauntered over, standing so close to her that his chest was touching her back.

Deshawn wasn't willing to wait. He was getting impatient for Chloe to admit who he was to her. The poor guy had been through a lot, discovering he was Aurathion the way he did.

Chloe ignored him, but I noticed her leaning into him just the slightest bit.

Oliver smirked and repeated exactly what Deshawn said: "Hungry or not, you need to eat."

"Okay, since you insist." She took the plate and began eating.

Deshawn laughed, "Ignore me all you want, Firefly. I'm not going anywhere."

I couldn't help but laugh, "She's hardheaded like that."

Zane held his knuckles up to me for a fist bump, "Hell yes, she is. Our little booger can be a handful."

"Booger?" Oliver and Deshawn repeated simultaneously.

Chloe's face turned an alarming shade of red, and I knew that an explosion was imminent.

Before she could kill my brother, and by the look on her face, I thought his death was a real possibility, Oren stopped his pacing and yelled, "I've got it!"

"What do you have?" Nathan asked, sinking back onto the couch, his clothes covered in dried blood and who knows what else.

"The reason the council wanted a change." Oren walked over to the sink and splashed cold water on his face.

Jet stood and leaned against the counter next to Oren. "And just what would their reason be?"

The man was huge. After Reverie was taken, his focus

was solely on searching for her and working out. Now his muscles had muscles. If he kept it up, his head would be swallowed up by his pecks… I wasn't dumb enough to tell him that, though.

"I believe it's power. They're scared that with a foot in both worlds, your power will surpass theirs. And that is something they'll never allow." Oren leaned back against the sink, staring into space.

"I don't care about power; I just want to find a way to bring Reverie back." Jet rubbed his face, visibly frustrated with the political obstacles we had to deal with.

"We have a lead on that," I spoke up, realizing we hadn't let him in on the information Nathan and Zane had collected.

Oren straightened, giving me his full attention. "What would that be? And I'm going to need someone to explain why that wasn't the first fucking thing I was told as soon as I got here."

"Maybe, because you busted in here with something else we needed to deal with," Zane said, clearly having a death wish. He was on a roll today.

Jet glowered at him. "Reverie is more important than *anything* else." He turned that anger toward me. "Tell me exactly what you found out."

I ignored his anger because I understood it. "They're going to attack Copper Creek."

He slowly grinned. "Jesse's plan worked." He started pacing, then stopped suddenly. "When?"

"In two weeks." Nathan strolled back into the kitchen. "We need to have a foolproof plan for commandeering their portal. I can't take being away from her much longer."

"None of us can." I scowled at him. I could feel my Draxon growing irritated with my Faction brother. Nathan's human upbringing sometimes hindered his ability to remember that he wasn't in this alone.

I took deep breaths, trying to calm him.

Not long after Reverie was taken, mine and Zane's creatures revealed themselves. We hadn't shifted yet, but I knew that it was only a matter of time. We used our flames and frost, respectively, and our beasts made their opinions known all day, every day. It was a lot to manage, especially when we needed to keep them hidden.

"We'll make sure we're prepared for all scenarios. I've already informed the Hawthornes of the information we collected, and they want to meet tonight to finalize our plans. They'll want input, especially since Adelaide is the bait." Oren headed for his office. "In the meantime, I'll work on what to do about the council."

Jet frowned, impatient to start planning, but he kept his mouth shut. Oren had a lot on his plate, and we all knew it. Without his knowledge and contacts, we would be fucked.

Reverie's parents would play a big part in the success of our plans, so waiting for their input was the right move.

CHAPTER 2
REVERIE

After the battle in the coliseum with the two Gerendel, I was allowed back to my room.

I took off my battle leathers and headed to the shower after using my new ability to seal the door. Oren had used it several times, but I hadn't remembered its name. Then I remembered my mother teaching me about some of the more common abilities, and this one I'd gained was called Aegisseal.

If I closed my eyes, I could recall just how she sounded, her beloved voice echoing in my mind: *"Aegisseal is the act of sealing with protective force, or creating an impenetrable barrier that not only closes but safeguards what lies within."*

Unfortunately, the duration depends on the wielder's strength, and mine was uncertain at the moment. It wasn't only my body that was tired; my spirit was too.

I took a quick shower, carefully avoiding glancing in the small mirror above the sink, then collapsed onto my bed and buried my face in the pillow. I swear I could still smell Nathan's scent. The terrible, no-good assholes in charge here made sure I knew this was his room.

They believed it would hurt me to learn this.

They were mistaken.

Knowing I lay my head at night exactly where Nathan's had lain brought me comfort instead of the pain it was meant to cause. It was the only comfort I was likely to get. Every day, I faced some form of torture, whether physical or mental. It all depended on Selene's mood and, in some cases, the Brummond himself.

I sighed. No matter how intense the physical pain was, it couldn't compare to the mental torture. That was the most challenging part to deal with. Knowing my dad had made it through this hell was one of the things that kept me going. There was no way I'd shame him by letting these evil bastards break me.

Fighting in the coliseum was another way I released some of the poison from my soul. Without that outlet, I would be much closer to breaking. If Ubel or Selene knew how much I needed to fight, they'd see to it that I never entered another battle.

One of the most essential skills I learned for my survival was to compartmentalize. I had to mentally pack certain experiences into boxes, some sealed and wrapped in orange caution tape with "DO NOT OPEN" written on top. Those would never be unpacked. I wouldn't give my tormentors the satisfaction of revisiting those experiences, nor would I allow my Faction to be tortured by discovering what was done to me.

Selene was a demon from hell.

Her preferred form of mental torture was to tell

stories about what happened to my dad in her tender care, and her plans for my mother and Faction when the DF captured them. I couldn't even *think* about the things she'd described, or I'd never stop screaming—those were kept in a few of the caution tape boxes.

Sometimes, she was in the mood to torture me physically. You'd think that would be what I hated most, but in those moments, I'd managed to let myself drift away; sometimes I was with one of my Faction, and in others, I was safe at home with my parents. I preferred it over listening to her talk about how she was going to dispose of the people I loved.

I had no idea how I would regain what I'd lost here.

I sighed, then got up and dressed in a clean pair of pants and a shirt. It was late, but I knew the dining hall would still be serving food for a few more hours. Pulling on my boots, I made sure to tuck my knife inside. I'd learned quickly that danger lurks around every corner here. It was highly frowned upon for me to defend myself —Selene had made that clear in several of her sessions, but old habits die hard, and I was determined to survive this place.

Dead bodies couldn't tell tales.

I braided my hair tightly against my scalp from memory. I'd cut it off if I thought I could get away with it. It had been used against me too many times to count. I couldn't bear to look at my reflection anymore. The scar on the side of my forehead was still ugly and red, bringing back memories I couldn't handle right now.

On the bright side, since I had arrived, I'd acquired several new abilities. I thought all that I had gained while at Emberhold would fade because of the separation from my Faction. To my surprise, the opposite happened. I actually continued to gain abilities as the months went on, and I wondered if my Faction had experienced this, too.

I needed to keep this hidden from Selene and Ubel at all costs. She liked to take me to her apartment and torture me at least a couple of times a week. Not defending myself was beyond difficult, but I knew even with the new abilities, I was nowhere near as strong as she was… *yet.*

The loss of Beatrice had left her more unhinged than ever, according to the few acquaintances I'd made since arriving here. I used the word "acquaintance" because no one wanted to be a friend. Most were too afraid to associate with me, worried it would draw her attention.

The isolation didn't help me acclimate to this new world; I'm sure that was Selene's intent. Of course, she wasn't my only tormentor.

If Selene were a demon, then Ubel Brummond was Lucifer himself.

I never forgot the sadistic bastard was Selene's boss. He allowed everything that was done to me. Ubel also enjoyed keeping me informed about what the guys were doing, apparently having spies deep inside Emberhold. He tried convincing me they'd moved on and found another Nexus, hoping to bring me to tears.

Of course, he was unaware that our bonds hadn't weakened. Aside from losing our ability to communicate, I could still feel their grief and rage at my absence. I had no doubt they were doing everything they could to find me.

I couldn't doubt their love and devotion to me—that would be the one thing that might break me.

Leaving the room, I headed to the dining hall to eat. It was hard to get anything down, but I had no choice. Keeping up my strength was paramount to surviving.

It helped to imagine Zeke's voice, *"Eat my Treasure, I need you healthy."*

I'd gotten good at pretending what each one of my men would say to encourage me, and "heard" their voice at the time it was most needed.

It helped me do what I needed to do to survive and not just give up.

I shook myself out of my thoughts. I couldn't afford to get lost in my head. Kristine would love nothing more than to catch me unawares. I'd taken several beatings from her and her men until Selene made it clear that I was not Kristine's to torture.

Sometimes that kept me safe—sometimes it didn't.

Entering the hall, I took in everyone's positions. Most were insignificant to me. But I did notice Evan was sitting at a table, being his usual loud and obnoxious self. He was one of Kristine's men. I was shocked to find out she already had a well-established Faction here. Of course, she was Nexus; I suspected the serum played a significant role in that.

Approaching the buffet, I grabbed a plate and filled it with whatever was nearby. Everything tasted the same to me; it was all just fuel I needed to survive.

I felt a hard bump on my right shoulder. "Move over, bitch. Let your betters eat."

Great, Kristine was here to brighten up my evening.

I didn't acknowledge her and turned, making my way to a table far away from the one she usually sat at. I'd learned quickly after I was approved to fight in the coliseum, not to allow her to provoke me.

The one time I did, I couldn't lie on my back for a week. Selene punished Kristine, too, but her punishment was just a slap on the wrist. Strangely enough, I thought it was more about possession than anything else. Whether she loved or hated you, she was tightfisted with her things.

When it came to Selene, either emotion could get you killed.

The one thing I had on my side was that Ubel didn't take kindly to losing money, and even Selene didn't want to irritate him.

I'd hate to meet Trent Storm if he were Ubel's boss. But he was only seen from a distance, lately at the coliseum, and I was told that was rare—so high up that only his silhouette was visible. Otherwise, he remained a mystery to everyone here.

It was ironic that Selene didn't see that her punishment kept me out longer than fighting with Kristine did. I sighed. There were many ways to punish that left no mark, and Selene was skilled in all of them. If I ever gained enough power to kill the bitch, I might challenge my mother for the opportunity.

"We decided to sit with you. I wouldn't want you to feel lonely, way over here by yourself." Kristine, along with Evan, sat down at my table. "I'm sure my company is better than that redhead bitch you sat with back at Emberhold."

I winced at the mention of Chloe. Her friendship had been priceless to me, and even though I wouldn't want her near here, I missed her every day.

Evan leaned over and kissed Kristine on the cheek. "I can guarantee that. No one can compete with your greatness."

Her relationship with Evan upset me on a different level. Not that I wanted anything to do with the evil bastard, but because he resembled Jet to a disturbing degree. He was much smaller, and he had green eyes instead of Jet's beautiful, soft brown, but other than that, he could've been his brother.

Kristine smiled briefly but then returned her attention to me. "Don't think just because you're winning in the coliseum that Selene or the Brummond are going to suddenly go easy on you."

"I don't think that." I lowered my eyes to my plate and started eating as quickly as I could. Using every bit of willpower I had not to slap a bitch. Being meek didn't suit me, but I'd learned to swallow what pride I had left. I trusted that my time was coming; I just had to be patient.

Evan used his ability to tip his glass of milk, spilling it all over my tray and covering everything. I kept eating as if nothing had happened. Worse things had been done to me. Milk mixed with my food was the least of it. And his weak-ass telekinetic powers didn't impress me either.

"Gross." Kristine wrinkled her nose in disgust. "I bet if your men saw you now, they'd break the bond right away. You're not fit to be a Nexus for anyone."

What she thought didn't matter, but her words stung just a little. The things I'd done and been forced to do truly might horrify them if they ever found out. At the very least, they'd lose respect for me.

"Let's get out of here. I can't stand to watch her eat that disgusting mess one more second." Kristine stood and said, "You'll throw my trash away, won't you?"

I didn't look up.

"Hey, I know you heard her talking to you," Evan said, as my tray went flying from the table and onto the floor.

I glanced up, wishing I could annihilate this asshole. I'd burn him alive if I could, but in the end, I just nodded my head. There was no point in resistance... *at the moment.* There would come a day when I'd unleash on them, and you better believe that I was keeping score.

"Come on, baby. She's almost too pitiful to even bother with." Kristine slipped her arm through his and shot one last smirk at me before heading out of the dining hall.

I ran my hands down my face and took a deep breath. Just a few months ago, I wouldn't have been able to take her shit. Now I knew that her taunts couldn't hurt me, but Selene's cat-o'-nine tails would.

I heaved my tired body up and, using *my* telekinetic ability, started cleaning the mess. (Another new ability I'd mastered since coming here.) I didn't mind revealing this ability because it was relatively common and one of the last to be severed when a bond was broken.

I wish that I could say swallowing my pride had gotten easier over time, but it hadn't. Kowtowing to that bitch and her men never got any easier. I thought I hated her back at the academy, but that was nothing compared to how I felt about her now.

As I left the dining hall to head back to my room, I

caught a few looks of sympathy thrown my way. I'd been shocked to find out that most of the Aurathions had voluntarily come here, hoping to catch the eye of a Nexus. The serum allowed them to pick and choose whom they wanted, rather than letting their Faction form organically. The competition was fierce, causing fighters to turn against each other regularly.

I understood their reasoning; it was the cause of the war, after all, but I hated that it had come to that. Nothing could replace the feeling of a true bonding—absolutely nothing.

It seemed that using the serum corrupted their character over time, resulting in a loss of sanity. At least that's what I'd come to believe through my observations. Even the Aurathions that were part of a Faction seemed "off". If I hadn't had the privilege of growing up in a true Faction and observing many others, I might not have noticed.

Turning the corner into the hallway where my room was, I sensed a shift in the atmosphere. A dark figure suddenly lunged at me. I narrowly dodged and dropped into a low crouch, kicking the attacker's legs out from under them to bring them to the ground. Before they could recover, I was on top of them. I reached down to retrieve my knife from my boot, but was suddenly grabbed from behind by both arms.

I dropped, letting all my weight fall unexpectedly, and managed to break free of their hold long enough to throw a punch. Cartilage and bone snapped under my fist, and I felt warm blood splatter my face. I kicked the body on the floor that was trying to stand and leaned again to grab my knife out of my boot, but a searing pain shot through my head.

Damn, that *hurt.* I grabbed my head with both hands.

I recognized this ability because it had been used on me before. I briefly resisted the command to surrender, then realized I couldn't expose my strength and, as difficult as it was, let it take hold. I felt something hard hit my head, and it was lights out.

⁓ ☖ ⁓

The first thing I heard as I began to wake up was the sound of slow dripping water. My eyes opened, but I quickly shut them again when the pale light worsened the pain in my head. I could feel the cold stone beneath me and dampness seeping through my clothes.

Forcing my eyes open, I found myself sprawled on the floor in a small room that looked like an old cell. I hadn't explored every corner of the building, but I wasn't surprised to find a dungeon somewhere in the massive structure. I knew there were cells used to hold the creatures we fought in the coliseum, but I didn't hear any sounds that would indicate I was anywhere near there.

I slowly sat up, holding my head with both hands. Turning around, I was surprised to see that the door to the cell I was in was wide open, unlike the locked door I had expected.

It didn't look like this dungeon had been used for decades. There were cobwebs in the corners, and the hinges on the door looked rusty. I suppose it shouldn't surprise me; most defiers were likely dealt with immediately, rather than imprisoned.

Pushing myself up with my hand, I rose to my knees and then slowly stood. I leaned against the wall for a moment, waiting for the dizziness to fade, then made my way out of the room and into the hallway.

At the end of the long corridor, a set of rickety stairs led up to a large wooden door. I cautiously made my way up, grateful for my small stature, then pushed the door open. I didn't recognize the area I found myself in. It was another long hallway, lit by torchlight, with no windows in sight. At least that told me it was an interior hallway, which—*really didn't help me at all.*

I heard a chitter and looked down to see a tiny grey mouse. My head hurt something fierce, but I focused on the little guy and knew he wanted me to go left. My ability to understand animals had grown in leaps and bounds over the last few months. I had several rodents that helped me steer clear of Kristine and her Faction. Too bad they hadn't been around last night.

Not wanting to stay here longer than necessary in case my attackers returned, I took a chance and followed him, hoping it would lead me somewhere more familiar. The little guy (Murrey, he'd informed me, was his name) led me through many twists and turns and several long flights of stairs. I realized the dungeon must have been located under the coliseum. I soon recognized where I was and proceeded to my room with a thank you to my rescuer. Pushing open the door, I collapsed onto my bed, damp clothes and all.

Curling up around my pillow, I imagined it still

smelled like Nathan. Tears started to flow, and I realized I needed the release of emotion. I was determined not to break, but I also knew that sometimes, just bending a little could help you get through another day.

I knew Kristine was behind my incident; the head pain and the command to lie down and surrender came from her. I guess I should be thankful that my only injury was a bump on the head and waking up in a dungeon.

How crazy was it to realize I probably owed Selene a thank you? If it weren't for her threats to Kristine, I'm sure the damage would be a lot more extensive.

I pressed the pillow against my face and took a few more moments to cry. I'd never show this vulnerability outside of my room. One hint of weakness would be blood in the water.

I'd been left alone by my fellow warriors to this point. Even though they'd seen me take Kristine's shit on numerous occasions, they knew that I wasn't to be fucked with. My performance in the coliseum alone proved that.

I wasn't even sure why Kristine was here unless it was to torment me. She wasn't required to train or fight in the coliseum. So, what other reason could there be for her presence here?

"That's enough feeling sorry for yourself, baby. You've had your moment of weakness. Now get up, take a shower, and get some rest. Tomorrow is another day, and you need to be strong. I will find you, don't lose hope." I heard Oren's bossy voice in my head this time.

My tears slowly dried, and I dragged my exhausted body into the shower. I needed his strength and wisdom more than anything right now, and this was as good as it was going to get.

I examined my body thoroughly in the shower, avoiding my Nexus mark, and found some additional bruises and cuts, but those were already starting to heal. I finished washing, then crawled back into my bed and closed my eyes. I figured I would have trouble falling asleep, but I was out almost as soon as my head hit the pillow.

CHAPTER 3
REVERIE

T he corridor was quiet, the kind of quiet that makes every footstep sound loud. I slipped into the deserted classroom, closing the door behind me with a soft click. Chalk dust hung in the air, catching the moonlight that streamed through the high windows. I just needed a moment alone—a long breath after everything.

The door creaked again.

I turned, and there he was. Zane. Leaning against the frame like he'd been waiting for me to wander right into his snare. His shirt collar was loose, red hair damp from training, and that smirk—Ancestors help me—was pure trouble.

"This room's off-limits after curfew," I said.

"Then it's a good thing you broke the rules first."

"I needed space."

"So did I." He pushed off the door and started toward me, slow and deliberate.

I stepped back without meaning to, boots scuffing the floor.

My spine hit the edge of a desk, and I realized too late he'd maneuvered me there—no hands, just his considerable presence.

He didn't stop coming until he was close. Too close. One hand braced against the chalkboard behind me, the other planted on the desk beside my hip. I was boxed in before I could think of an exit.

"Zane," I warned.

"Reverie," he countered, voice low and steady. "Why do you always say my name like it's a threat?"

"Because you're always causing trouble."

He leaned in, not touching me, but close enough that the heat of him slid over my skin like a dare. His scent—cedar, sweat, leather—filled the air between us.

"And what if," he murmured, "I like the way you threaten me?"

My pulse quickened. The moonlight outlined his jaw in silver and highlighted the spark in his eyes. I could feel the desk pressing into the backs of my thighs. My hands clenched against the wood, nails digging into the surface.

"You should move," I whispered.

"Should I?" He tilted his head, just enough that his breath brushed my cheek. "Or do you just want me to?"

I lifted my chin, defiant. "You're in the way."

His smile was slow, dangerous. "Exactly where I want to be."

Then he closed the distance.

It wasn't rushed. It was inevitable. One sure step, and suddenly his chest pressed against mine, heat radiating through our clothes. His hand slid from the chalkboard to the desk, caging me in completely. My breath caught, and so did his—just for a heartbeat.

"Zane..." I started, but it came out softer than I intended.

"Yeah," he whispered, and then his mouth was on mine.

The kiss hit like a spark to kindling—sharp, hungry, alive. His hand found the small of my back, pulling me in like he couldn't stand even an inch between us. My fingers tangled in his shirt, brushing warm skin beneath the loose collar.

The desk creaked under our weight as I tilted my head and deepened the kiss, the clash of tongue and teeth just this side of painful. Somewhere, dimly, I knew this was reckless; a classroom after curfew, a door that wasn't locked. But Zane kissed like consequences didn't exist—almost like he had an animal inside.

His hand slid up my spine, sending shivers racing across my skin. I arched into him before I could stop myself. When we finally broke apart, both of us were breathing hard, foreheads resting together in the thin strip of moonlight.

"Still think I should move?" He murmured, his voice rough.

I swallowed, pulse hammering. "Ask me again later."

"Lean back and let me taste you." Demand strong in his voice, not waiting for my consent as he slowly slid my skirt up to my waist, revealing the sheer black panties I was wearing.

I moaned as he worked them down my legs, then put them in his pocket. "I'll be keeping these. I've decided to start a collection."

I couldn't speak as I felt his warm breath on my belly—he licked and kissed his way down to my clit, sucking it into his mouth abruptly. "Fuck." I breathed, sitting halfway up to watch what he was doing.

He tilted his head sideways as he nipped gently down my slit and gave me a cocky wink right before he plunged two fingers into my pussy, pumping in and out, then began licking my clit with the flat of his tongue.

I felt my orgasm build, and when his fingers repeatedly hit the small bundle of nerves deep inside, I stiffened. "Zane!" I came with his name on my lips, the pleasure so intense it bordered on pain.

He kissed his way up my body, his lips glistening with the evidence of my bliss. "Do you hear that?" Zane whispered in my ear.

"Hear what?" I couldn't concentrate on anything other than the aftershocks of pleasure coursing through my system.

"You'd better wake up, precious girl." Zane stroked my cheek with regret.

"What?" I answered in confusion.

"NOW!"

I shot up in bed, the flush of desire still in my system, and my heart pounding a mile a minute. "Get your lazy asses out of bed and report to the training field. Your performances yesterday left a lot to be desired, and Selene is pissed." Seamus, the douche, yelled. Beating on all the doors in the hall.

I groaned and rolled over.

Fuck.

That dream had been beyond realistic. I was still pulsing, and my panties were definitely wet with my release. I breathed deeply; my nose filled with our combined scents. I needed that, even if it wasn't real. I missed each of my guys with a pain that was beyond description.

I took one more moment to bask in the closeness I'd felt with Zane, then heaved myself up, dressed quickly, and headed to breakfast. Today was going to suck, but I wanted to get it over with as soon as possible.

Hopefully, my day would be filled only with the rigors

of training, not torture from Kristine, Selene, or Ubel the bastard. I had serious doubts that I'd be that lucky after I punched one of Kristine's men, but there was no harm in dreaming.

I went to the dining hall and ate breakfast without any interference, then headed to the field.

As I did a few stretches to loosen up, I was relieved to see that neither Kristine nor her Faction was present at the moment. Since she wasn't required to train and didn't participate in fights, she was rarely here this early, if she ever came at all. That provided me with some much-needed relief from her bullshit.

I headed to the armory to retrieve the short swords that I had become proficient at fighting with. I was allowed to practice with them and take them into the coliseum, but I had to return them immediately after. There's no way that I would be allowed to carry them on me all the time.

Instructor Razor was handing out weapons, "You had an excellent match yesterday, Hawthorne."

Apparently, he was promoted after he raised the alarm when Dad and Damien escaped with Nathan... there were no witnesses to say otherwise.

He was one of the few people whom I knew I could trust. "Yes, and most of that is thanks to you."

Razor handed the large guy in front of me a broadsword, then turned to grab my babies. "I'd love to take all the credit, but you've been an excellent student." He winked, "Your previous instructors must have been very talented."

I smiled a little sadly. "They were the best."

"Go through your warm-ups, and I'll be by soon to help with anything you're having trouble with." Razor looked at me in sympathy, then turned to answer a question from another warrior.

I headed to my usual spot to start, when out of the corner of my eye, I saw a tall, muscular man stop nearby and begin a warm-up similar to mine. He was wielding a rare stormcutter sword. The only people able to use this specific weapon were those who could control lightning.

I paused, unable to begin my own warm-up, mesmerized by how smoothly each movement flowed into the next. This man was incredibly talented; his movements were so fluid that it seemed the sword was an extension of his body. I knew I'd never seen him before, but something about the way he moved felt familiar.

He noticed me watching and smiled, but he didn't pause in his warm-up. I couldn't tear my eyes away. His talent was incredible. I hope I never have to face him in the coliseum. I knew I was good, but I wasn't confident about who would come out on top.

He finished with a flourish, then slipping his sword into the scabbard on his back, he approached, "Hi, beautiful, did you enjoy the performance?"

If he expected me to blush and deny that I was watching, he was going to be disappointed. "I did. You're amazing with that Stormcutter you carry. Are you new here? I've never seen you before."

He flashed me a cocky grin, "I am. I just arrived late last night." He bowed with a flourish. "Torren at your service."

I returned his smile. "I'm Reverie."

"It's a pleasure to make your acquaintance... *Reverie*." He breathed my name, saying it slowly as though he savored the taste of it rolling off his tongue. He gazed at me for several seconds longer than was appropriate, and I found it hard to look away.

The moment was broken when I heard Razor yelling at a couple of guys practicing near us. "You two are handling those swords like you probably handle your tiny dicks. Inadequately and with zero finesse."

I grinned, but my attention was drawn back to Torren when he pulled a band from his pocket and swept his shoulder-length blonde hair back out of his face. "Those short swords you use look deadly. Are they the only weapons you use in battle?"

I could only nod because I was momentarily struck dumb at how stunning he was. The sun shining on his head turned his hair golden, and his hazel eyes were captivating, leaning more toward green than blue. He had a strong Roman nose that was almost too large, but it added character and kept him from appearing overly feminine. All of that was complemented by a strong jaw with a cleft in his chin.

Many handsome men were competing for a Faction, but he was far above them in looks and skill. My men were the only ones who could compare, but if the Ancestors were kind, they'd stay far from this place. He would be a member of a powerful Faction within the week, or my name wasn't Reverie.

Torren winked at me, grinning, clearly pleased by my attention.

This was ridiculous. "Well, I'd better get back to it." I

walked a few feet away to make some room and began my warm-up. I'd been distracted long enough—I had another battle to prepare for. Torren seemed like a nice guy, but as soon as he found out who I was, he would keep his distance like all the others.

Time to get my head back in the game.

These short swords were fun to fight with, but I'd love to practice refining my fire ability. I knew it wasn't possible at the moment and that I had to keep it hidden unless absolutely necessary. The only way I'd show my hand was if my life was at stake.

Selene and Ubel knew how powerful my parents were. Still, they didn't know anything about me, and I wanted to keep it that way, mainly because being away from my Faction hadn't lessened my abilities.

No one could find out about that.

So far, I had only used common abilities most Aurathions possessed. I made sure even those didn't seem too powerful. I relied heavily on my physical training in all my matches so far, and luckily, it was enough to get me through.

I heard a sound to my left and saw that Torren had stayed to watch me. I'd blocked out all the noise around me and hadn't noticed that he was still there. He watched me with a critical eye, but I managed to ignore his presence long enough to finish strong.

"You're good. But if you're interested, I think there are a few things I could help you with that would make you even better." He cocked his head to the side and waited for my answer.

I knew I'd better warn him about Selene and Ubel. I

didn't want to be the cause of anyone losing their position or even their life because of me.

"That would be great, but I'm sort of persona non grata around here." I rubbed the back of my neck awkwardly, "You don't want to draw the attention of the Brummond or Selene. Helping me in any way will definitely do that."

Torren stared at me for so long that it began to feel like a weight, pressing against my skin. "I'll take my chances." He turned and walked away.

Well then. I guess that settled that.

CHAPTER 4
CHLOE

I woke up sweating and realized I'd rolled partly under Oliver in my sleep. My big guy ran hot, but I couldn't sleep without his comforting presence.

Lately, even that wasn't helping curb my restlessness, and I knew why… but I wasn't going to think about *him* before my first cup of coffee.

I carefully slipped out of bed and headed to the kitchenette to turn on the machine. This used to be my favorite part of the day. Reverie and I would meet in the kitchen before class and catch up. It's incredible how close we became in such a short time.

Sometimes in life, you meet people who immediately feel like family. Reverie was that from the moment I met her.

Really, she's become a sister to me, and I miss her every day.

I knew enough about myself to realize that some of my

feelings, at least initially, stemmed from hero worship for Adelaide and her Faction. They sacrificed so much in an effort to keep Aurathia safe and a home for all Aurathions. Their efforts obviously failed, but the fact that they persevered and kept going through all the past and upcoming trials showed I was right in my admiration.

Nothing else had felt *right* since Reverie was taken.

Seeing the pain my brothers were in, along with her other men, was agony for those of us who loved them.

Zeke had become a completely different man, and I barely recognized him anymore. He was no longer the quiet, thoughtful person he used to be. Now, he demanded action and would use any means necessary to get it. From the things Oliver had shared with me, there were no lengths he wouldn't go to further his search.

Zane, on the other hand, had always been a little thrown off. (I say that with complete affection. I, too, could be considered the same at times.) But now it was more than that; he'd become quieter and leaned more into the darkness he'd at least tried to keep at bay before. His jokes had become so dark that they leaned more toward the macabre than the humorous.

The rest of Reverie's Faction had followed them down the same path.

Granted, Nathan and Jet forged the path long before she actually disappeared. Both would rather cut your throat than speak to you if you had no valuable information in helping them get to Reverie. There had even been a few foolish girls who tried to garner their attention in her absence.

That was a mistake.

Those two didn't give a shit if you were male or female. They would gladly dole out punishment either way. Friends of Kristine tried to make themselves scarce because both men looked for any excuse to rain down punishment on them.

Now, everyone avoided those two like the plague.

Oren had become immersed in his scrolls and tablets. Often disappearing for long periods, I assume to locate information from outside sources. He'd not shown up to train any of the incoming students since her disappearance. Not trying to hide the fact that he didn't give two shits about any of their survival. Always looking for a way to open a portal and get Reverie back.

That's assuming she's still alive…

I couldn't think like that.

I looked down at the mark on my wrist and ran my finger across it. The only people who knew about it were in our immediate circle. And that's the way it had to stay.

This was beyond rare.

Not since Queen Lilibet had an Aurathion developed the ability to mark anyone outside of their Faction.

None of us knew what to make of it, and with the DF's attacks ramping up, research time was limited.

One thing I did know was that I now felt a strange connection to Reverie. Oliver and I had discussed it at length. Ever since we'd been marked, it was almost like we could feel when she was in distress.

The feeling was distant, like knowing you'd forgotten something, but the memory was just beyond reach. Like an itch you couldn't scratch.

It was beyond frustrating, and the guys weren't helping relieve those feelings *at all*. They wouldn't let me participate in any of the skirmishes that had occurred lately. The main explanation being that I wasn't part of a fully formed Faction.

Of course, Oliver and Deshawn agreed with them. Not that Deshawn had a say in the matter, because, well, he wasn't my… my… nope, I couldn't even lie to myself.

My shoulders fell in dejection. I *knew* what Deshawn was to me, but finding joy in completing my Faction felt so wrong without my bestie. Not to mention the agony my brothers were in.

I was selfish enough to know it was only a matter of time before I gave in… probably hours, if I was honest. The guy was gorgeous, a little over six feet of mocha skin, muscles, and dark green eyes.

I should get an award for lasting this long.

There was so much frustration in my life right now that I felt like I was going to explode.

Oren and my brothers were throwing excuses right and left about why I needed to stay safe—claiming that possible harm could come to Reverie through our connection. It might be true; we didn't know anything about our connection, but I was an excellent researcher, dammit! And I wasn't even being utilized in that sense.

I was tired of the excuses and being sheltered like a princess when Reverie was out there facing who knew what.

The desire to be useful was riding me hard. Whether it was due to the marks or just because I loved Reverie so much, I didn't know. But I *needed* to help.

I'd told Oren as much; if fighting was out, then at least let me help more with research. If not about opening a portal, then at least trying to learn more about the marks.

Both Oliver and I felt driven to do something. We had to do *something*.

"What are you thinking about so hard, Aegisseer?" Pantar popped in suddenly, scaring me half to death.

He'd begun calling me that after Reverie marked me. I didn't know what it meant, and he refused to explain.

I hadn't gotten used to hearing him in my head yet, either. "Damn, you've got to quit doing that!" I held a hand to my fast-beating heart. "And where have you been for the last few days?"

Reverie's mark had allowed both Oliver and me to hear the large Fellat… among other things.

He gave his creepy grin, showing all of those shark-like teeth. *"Mira and I have been busy continuing to try to open a portal into Aurathia."*

"I thought you gave up on that." The coffee machine beeped, and I poured a large cup of the delicious brew.

Pantar looked at me in disapproval. *"We never gave it up. I find it insulting that you would think as much."*

"What my La' u alofagia meant was that we hadn't heard anything from you about it, so we assumed you'd moved on to looking for other solutions." Oliver walked in with bare feet and no shirt, only those sexy as fuck grey sweatpants of his.

He was well aware of what they did to me.

I poured him a cup of coffee and licked my lips at the sight he made. "That's exactly what I meant. I'm just not as good at wording things as my sexy man."

Oliver blushed under his tan complexion. "Your talents lie in other things."

I walked over and stood on tiptoes for a kiss. "Is that so?"

"Yes… it… is." He said, spacing each word between kisses.

This man had become my everything, along with Deshawn— dammit—he who shall not be named.

Step Brothers wasn't the only movie franchise I loved.

Pantar prowled into the living room and shrank his size to lie on the back of the couch. *"There are no other solutions. I have tried to tell Storm that, but he does not want to believe me."* He licked his paw, *"Mira thinks that with a little more time, I will be able to get to my Nexus."*

I frowned, "You said 'I', not 'we'. Does that mean you won't be able to bring the rest of us?"

"I am not sure yet. If bringing everyone is not possible, then I will join her alone and work on a solution from Aurathia to get the rest of you there. Our connection isn't completely broken. I can still sense her emotions."

I raised my eyebrows, "You've never mentioned still having that connection."

"I have not, and I do not wish you to either." Pantar turned his head toward the door. *"The denied one is here."*

"Denied one?" I was confused. Then there was a knock on the door.

Oliver went to answer, and Deshawn barged in before the door was completely opened.

"Well, come on in," Oliver smirked, happy to see him. They'd both become good friends since Deshawn had become a part of our community.

Of course, not much bothered my big guy. He was the most even-tempered person I'd ever met.

Until he wasn't.

"I brought donuts." He leaned down to kiss me, and I turned my head, the kiss landing on my cheek.

Oliver looked at me in disapproval, but I just shrugged.

I knew I was being an asshole, but I felt like a stick of dynamite with a very short fuse. One kiss on the lips, and I might throw him down on the floor and mount him immediately.

At least that would clear up one of my frustrations.

Deshawn didn't let my action bother him in the least, "Come eat, Firefly. It's from Java and Jam, your favorite."

I realized I couldn't go on like this much longer, and I understood how important it was for us to complete our Faction. I just had to find a way to move past my irrational feelings.

Taking a donut, I hopped up on the counter and faced both of my guys, "Thank you, to what do we owe this early morning visit?"

Oliver and Deshawn glanced guiltily at each other, but then Oliver seemed to come to a decision.

"We've reached our limit," he growled in his deep voice.

"You're limit?" I felt my temper rising.

"That's right, *we* have." Deshawn stepped close enough to me that my leg was touching his.

"And just what limit have you reached?" The nerve of them to discuss me behind my back.

"Your need to punish yourself because your friend was

taken. I was there, La' u alofagia, there was nothing either of us could do." Oliver stepped up to my other side.

"It's about time. I will be back to discuss my information with you when this problem is resolved." Pantar disappeared from the room.

None of us acknowledged his departure.

I jumped down off the counter and turned to them both in fury. "I can't believe you two are ganging up on me!"

Oliver was starting to get mad now, "That's not what this is, and you know it! I've let this go on as long as I'm going to."

"Oh, really. You think it's *your* decision?" I knew I was being irrational, but I'd gone too far to back down now.

"Firefly, you're only hurting us both. If you can look me in the eye and honestly say you don't want me, I swear I'll leave you alone. But if you feel the same way about me as I do about you, then you need to stop running so fast and let me catch you already." Deshawn looked at me with a pleading expression.

Oliver pulled me into his arms and hugged me. Saying he spoiled me and tolerated my theatrics is an understatement. So, for him to stage this intervention, he must be fed up with me denying Deshawn.

I struggled for a moment, infuriated that they were making me face this now.

"You've denied him long enough. It's time to come to terms with this." My gentle giant said firmly.

I looked into his beautiful eyes and felt my anger draining away. It *was* time, and I knew with my very soul that Reverie would want me to be happy.

I nodded, then kissed his chest, taking comfort in his arms for a few minutes.

I pulled away reluctantly, then approached Deshawn. "Are you sure this is what you want?"

"With everything that I am," Deshawn spoke solemnly.

"Okay then. I'm done running." I stepped closer to him.

"It's about fucking time!" He pulled me into his arms and began spinning me around.

"Stop! I'm going to be sick, you crazy fool!" I couldn't hold back my laughter.

He stopped spinning and squeezed me tightly. "You know what this calls for?"

"What?" Oliver asked, grinning.

"Sunday snuggles." He lifted me and carried me over his shoulder back to my room, leaping onto my bed with me in his arms.

Oliver was right behind us and cuddled me from behind.

For the first time since Reverie left, I felt whole.

Before guilt could sneak in again, I felt Oliver kiss the back of my neck. "How about we take our Sunday Fun Day to the next level?"

"What did you have in mind?" Deshawn grinned.

"Maybe a little Faction bonding time?" Oliver asked, teasingly.

I turned onto my back, where I could look into both of their faces. I could feel Oliver's breath on my neck and Deshawn's hand brush mine in a silent claim. Their gazes pinned me in place, different but equally consuming-one fire, one storm.

No one moved. Not yet.

My heartbeat stuttered, caught between them, every second pulling the air tighter, heavier, until it felt like the world itself was holding its breath.

"Look at me," Deshawn said finally, voice low, deep, threaded with something dangerous.

I obeyed-not because I wanted to, but because resisting him had always been a losing battle. His eyes caught mine and held, heavy with heat and promise, the kind of look that unraveled walls brick by brick.

From behind, Oliver shifted-a subtle movement, but it made my breath hitch. His heat brushing my spine, his presence coiled tight like a predator waiting for the right moment to strike.

"You know what this means," Oliver whispered darkly.

My lips parted, but no sound came out. I could feel the storm gathering around me.

"There is no turning back," Deshawn finished Oliver's thought, then continued. "You belong to neither of us..." he paused, just long enough for his words to sink in. Then his gaze sharpened, "...we belong to you."

And in that instant, I understood; this wasn't about choice.

It was about surrender.

I nod in agreement just as their hands began to move simultaneously, undressing me like they'd worked together a million times before.

Deshawn's hand slowly trailed from my shoulder to my stomach, the tip of his finger just barely brushing my nipple. At the same time, Oliver began to kiss and bite at my neck and the curve of my shoulder.

Deshawn whispered, softly, "Your skin is like silk."

My breathing became erratic as their hands continued to explore my body.

Deshawn touched his lips to mine.

The kiss wasn't rushed.

It wasn't desperate.

It was reverent—like he was offering something fragile and sacred with every touch of his mouth. There was no urgency in it, only a quiet devotion that unraveled my carefully built walls one heartbeat at a time.

When the kiss ended, I was done.

My body ached, and I needed them both at a level that couldn't possibly be healthy.

Oliver smiled knowingly, and his hands followed the curve of my stomach, and then lower.

I spread my thighs just as Deshawn's hand trailed behind Oliver's until he spread my pink lips with two fingers.

I gasped and arched my back when Oliver pushed one of his large fingers in my opening… then another joined the first.

"That's it, Firefly. Let us make you feel good." Deshawn murmured, biting the shell of my ear.

I was past answering, and when he began to flick my clit, I thought I was going to die of pleasure.

Oliver continued to fuck me with his fingers, slowly moving in and out of my body. "Come for us, La' u alofagia."

I had no choice but to obey.

My orgasm tore through me, a loud moan falling from my lips. I might have even blacked out for a moment; the pleasure was so intense.

Before I could catch my breath, Oliver flipped me over and demanded in his deep, rough voice, "Spread your legs."

I did as he said, knowing my pleasure was far from over.

Oliver entered me abruptly.

"Oh, fuck." I arch my back, taking him as deep as possible.

Oliver moaned darkly, "Our Nexus feels divine, brother."

I gasp as his strokes become quicker and so deep I swear I could feel him in my throat.

I felt a hand tip my chin up, and Deshawn was kneeling in front of me, holding his massive cock to my lips. "Can you take me too, Firefly?"

I nodded, not knowing if it was true, but wanting him so badly, I was willing to try.

"Get me good and wet first." He panted as I began to lick up the side of his dick, pressing my tongue firmly to the veins bulging under the delicate skin.

Oliver pulled out, and Deshawn slid down under me, holding his cock up in a silent invitation.

I gasped as I slowly lowered myself, enjoying the feeling of him being inside me for the first time.

I felt Oliver push me down onto Deshawn's chest, then a warm tongue licking around my back hole. I startled and looked over my shoulder, surprised by the unexpected, taboo pleasure of his actions.

Oliver raised his head; the heat in his eyes was scorching. "Are you ready?"

I nodded slightly, then gasped out in pleasure-pain

when he began to enter me slowly. "Breathe, sweet girl." He moaned, "Fuck, you're so tight. I'm not going to last."

The feeling of both of them inside me was insane. The stretch was almost more than I could take.

They both paused, giving me a moment to adjust. Then they started to move.

Deshawn began moaning and cursing as they both found their rhythm. Both of my men growling filthy things that intensified our desire.

The pain was completely gone now, and nothing but pleasure was coursing through my body. They fucked me like I was their salvation, owning my body in a way that wrecked me.

The room was filled with gasps and moans; each one of us was lost to the intensity of the moment.

I felt Deshawn stiffen. "Cum for us, Firefly."

At his words, I shattered. The pleasure was so intense that I thought I would die, my entire body shaking with the force of my orgasm.

"Fuck!" Oliver growled in a voice that didn't sound human, right before I felt both men stiffen, finding their pleasure, and filling me with their warm cum.

We lay wrapped together, shivering in the aftermath of our bonding. My only regret was that it wouldn't be official until we could perform the ritual.

Oliver stepped away, then went to the bathroom to get a rag. He started gently cleaning me as Deshawn went to wash up in the bathroom.

When we were finished, we all lay back down to cuddle...for real this time.

I hated that my bestie wasn't here to talk to. But at the end of the day, I had to do what was right for my men and me.

Hopefully, Pantar and Mira would have the answers we needed to find her soon.

CHAPTER 5

NATHAN

I prowled the hallways looking for Jet.

We'd just returned to Emberhold around one in the morning. Deshawn had gotten information about a small group of DF moving near Copper Creek. Likely scoping things out for the bigger force they were going to be bringing through the portal.

Jet and I had managed to capture all five of them… with a bit of help from Hayes— dammit, Sly. It was tough to get used to the name change.

Sly had been punishing the DF's forces since my Nexi was taken. He, along with John and Jesse, had shown us the reason their Faction's reputation had become legendary after the first war.

Sly and Damien had planned out every operation we'd been part of so far. Their expertise in strategy and the DF's capabilities were invaluable.

Adelaide hadn't participated in the fighting for several reasons. The first being that her abilities weren't stable.

She'd lost most of them before Sly returned and, even after their re-bonding, hadn't regained them all. She probably wouldn't unless her entire Faction was recovered.

The second reason was to make her even more elusive to the DF, increasing their desperation to capture her. Selene wanted Adelaide more than anything else. We hoped that if a rumor were spread implying that Adelaide would be in Copper Creek at a specific time and date, she would become reckless and open a portal directly into town, giving us the chance to take control and reach Reverie.

Especially if she believed her information came from a trusted ally.

That was the advantage we had now that Jet was a part of this Faction. His contacts had been involved in Aurathion politics even more than we were aware and had planted a spy among them.

None of us knew this person's identity, but we had come to believe they were completely loyal to our side. Oren had tried his best to find out because the bastard didn't like being kept out of the loop, but up to this point, it had been impossible.

I didn't care who it was.

All I wanted was Reverie back in my arms.

Imagining what she was going through kept me up most nights. I'd survived it and knew she could too. But Reverie was the daughter of Selene's most hated enemy, and there was no telling how she was treating her.

I saw Zane coming towards me, mumbling and laughing to himself. What the fuck was the crazy bastard doing now?

"Hey fuckwit, who the hell are you talking to?" I grinned, anticipating his answer.

He tilted his head and just stared at me for a few moments, then a huge grin overtook his face. "Drakk says to tend to your own business."

"Who the fuck is Drakk?" This dude was losing it. There was no one here but us. The Passives roaming the hallway around us didn't even register with me. They were completely insignificant.

"My Draxon." He mumbled under his breath, then grinned once again. "Drakk the most incredible Draxon ever to grace us with his presence... to be exact." Zane smirked. "He likes a more elaborate introduction."

I shook my head but couldn't contain my grin. "Sounds like someone I'd like to meet." I raised my brows, "Just when does he think he's going to make an appearance?"

Zane tilted his head, listening to a voice only he could hear, "In good time."

"That's it...in good time, really?" I rolled my eyes.

Zane just shrugged. "That's what Drakk the Incredible said, so I guess that's all the answer you're going to get."

"Well, I think the first meet-cute between us should be a ride. We'd both look amazing flying through the air, charring our enemies to ash."

"Fuck no—and that comes from both of us," Zane growled at me. "No one is riding us but my precious girl... no one."

"No need to answer in haste, both of you take your time, mull it over." I slapped him on the back.

"There's no—"

"I've got places to be… talk to you both later!" I rushed off before he could deny me again.

I was determined to ride a Draxon, and if my Faction brothers weren't willing, I might have to find my own in Aurathia. The idea of riding into battle and leaving our enemies a pile of blackened ash appealed to me greatly.

I decided the most likely place to find Jet was in the dungeons, so I headed in that direction. When I got to the bottom of the steps, that's when the smell hit me.

"What the fuck?" I gagged.

The smell of shit and puke mixed with copper was so strong I could actually taste it. I'd have to brush my teeth immediately upon leaving.

I followed the terrible smell to a room at the very end of the long corridor. When I opened the door, surprise-surprise, that's where I found Jet. He was standing in front of an enormous fireplace, heating a branding iron in the hot coals.

Two men were hanging from shackles that were attached to the high ceiling. Both were naked and covered in burns that were red and bleeding, and in some cases, actually smoking. One word branded into their skin over and over.

I squinted my eyes and tilted my head to the side… what was the word? Was that an R, E, … holy shit… Reverie? The crazy fool had covered them in our Nexus' name.

Vomit and shit covered the area under both men, and I was pretty sure they were both dead.

Before I could pull myself from my astonishment at

what I was seeing, Jet had pushed the brand into the closest man's forehead.

The sizzle, along with the smell, almost made me lose what little I'd eaten today. "Damn man..." I gagged, "I think you've gotten everything from them you're going to."

Jet just shrugged and returned the iron in his hand to the coals, presumedly to brand the other man's forehead next. "You never know for sure—until you've made damn sure."

I blinked, then looked back at the two men hanging from the ceiling. "I don't think either one of them can tell you anything more... and I'm pretty *damn sure*."

"How can you know?" Jet walked to the second man and stuck the brand to his forehead. When he removed the iron, 'Reverie' appeared clear as day.

"The fact that neither has moved since I entered this room, even when a hot brand was stuck to their foreheads, is one clue." I eyed him with caution. "And if that's not enough, the fact that they're not breathing is your second."

Jet slowly examined both bodies. "I guess you're right." He calmly returned the iron to its stand, then moved to the sink and began washing his hands. "Did you need something?"

"I wanted to know if you found out any more information." I grabbed the hose from the wall and started washing the mess down the drain in the floor.

"Actually, I did." He splashed water on his face, then turned, taking off his shirt and throwing it into the fire.

I glanced from his over-the-top muscles to my chest

and made a vow to triple my workouts. "Well, no need to build the tension. What was it?"

"Reverie is being kept at the coliseum, as we suspected, and has been participating in the battles regularly." He walked back to the sink and grabbed a rag, wiping the blood and gore off his chest.

I felt my knees weaken with this new information. I'd known instinctively that we would've felt if Reverie had been killed, but confirming she was alive through an eyewitness was everything.

"He also confirmed that they will be opening a portal into Copper Creek to try and capture Adelaide. The only disappointment is that Selene herself won't be coming through." He headed out of the room with me following close behind.

"Where are you headed now?" I asked, my mind busy with plans I needed to make, but finding it hard to focus, knowing it was only a matter of time until my Nexi was back where she belonged.

"To let Oren know. The man really gets pissy if he doesn't have all of the information we've collected as soon as possible." Jet took the stairs two at a time.

I smirked. He wasn't wrong. Oren could even scare the psychos in this Faction at times. The man was highly organized, with charts and shit hanging on every wall in his room. He was a big hypocrite though because I seriously doubted that he kept us informed of everything he knew.

When Jet entered the hallway, everyone gave him a wide berth. Some of them had learned the hard way that he wasn't to be fucked with. Others had been smart enough to recognize the predator in their midst.

Oren was leaving the house when we caught up with him. "What do you have for me?"

"Reverie is alive and being kept at the coliseum," Jet said, with no preamble.

Oren reacted just as I had. "Thank the Ancestors." He took a deep breath and slowly exhaled. "Now that we know exactly where she is, we can finalize our plans." He headed quickly toward the academy.

Jet entered the house, presumably to clean up, but I kept pace with Oren. "What do you need from me?"

He glanced at me, "I need you to contact Reverie's parents and let them know what we've learned. They'll all want in on finalizing our plans. Also, see if you can locate Pantar. I've called for him numerous times in the last few days and haven't heard anything." This last was said in annoyance.

"Will do. He's probably still prowling Copper Creek looking for more of the DF," I shrugged. The giant Fellat didn't keep us updated on his plans. I wasn't as butthurt about it as Oren was. I wanted her returned immediately; how it was accomplished was irrelevant.

"Also, find Zeke and Zane and let them know what's going on. I want everyone back at the house in two hours. We need to make sure everyone is on the same page." He shoved open the doors to Emberhold and headed in the direction of the dean's office.

I stopped turning in the opposite direction and headed for the forge. The forge was a new addition, like the dungeon. It had appeared a few weeks after Reverie had been taken, along with an ironsmith named Berrick Farrowe.

Oren had questioned him extensively as to how and why he'd appeared, and all he would say was that the Ancestors had come to him in a dream and directed him to help us in any way we needed.

Of course, Oren had thoroughly researched him and found him above reproach. His talent with crafting blades was unparalleled, so we allowed him to stay.

Zeke had started hanging out there regularly, learning whatever Berrick was willing to teach him. I found it pretty ironic since Zeke's Draxon breathes ice. You'd think Zane would be drawn here instead, but that crazy bastard hardly ever left the dungeons.

As I approached the building, I marveled at how it seemed to have stood here for thousands of years instead of just a few months. It looked like a forgotten chapel, its arched windows barred with soot-darkened iron, and its stonework streaked with what appeared to be centuries of smoke. Moss crept between the flagstones, soaking up the water that constantly dripped from a cracked gargoyle spout above the entry.

I pushed open the massive door and entered the forge, where blackened beams groaned overhead, and from them hung chains and hooks that swayed faintly. The great anvil rested upon a cracked dais like an altar, its edges worn smooth by countless blows, its surface etched with the ghost of every blade and chain that ever passed beneath the hammer. The air surrounding it, thick and coppery, as if the stones themselves had drunk too much blood.

Just as I suspected, Zeke stood next to Berrick, admiring their latest creation, a set of short swords.

"What do you have there?" Neither man was startled by my presence.

"Proof that the student may have surpassed the teacher." Berrick spat on the stone floor; it sizzled briefly in the heat before dissipating.

He was nearly as tall as Jet and Hayes, but he was hunched from age. His hair was entirely white, and a full beard covered his face, braided into a long plait that nearly reached his chest. The man must have been ancient, as Aurathions are known to look young for hundreds of years.

"I doubt that's the case," Zeke said, even as his chest puffed out in pride.

I stepped closer to examine the blades more thoroughly. They were both about 22 inches long and slightly curved, but that's where the similarities ended.

The first appeared to be made of smoke-stained steel that absorbed the light. Faint crimson veins ran along the blade, as if there were embers trapped inside the metal.

The second blade shimmered with a pale, silvery glow as if a thin layer of frost covered it. Faint, jagged patterns resembling ice fractals were etched along the edge.

"I call them Ashfang and Frostbane." Zeke muttered to himself, "I felt duty-bound to make them."

Berrick grunted, "Always follow your instincts. A true ironsmith lets the Ancestors guide him."

"Seems like a representation of you and Zane." I narrowed my eyes. "If those are intended for my Nexi, I think a dagger to represent me should be your next project."

"I'm sure you do," Zeke smirked. "I'm not surprised you'd request she wear a phallic symbol on her person to remind her of you."

"No need to make it true to size. It wouldn't be practical for her if it drags on the ground." I was designing it in my head when a loud bark of laughter startled me out of my musings.

"Damn boy, you don't lack in self-confidence." Berrick guffawed, slapping his thigh in amusement.

"He definitely doesn't." Zeke rolled his eyes. "Was there a reason you tracked me down?"

"Yes. Jet got the information we've been waiting for. My Nexi is alive and being kept at the coliseum."

Zeke dropped to one knee and bowed his head. "Thank the Ancestors. She's alive." He stayed still for a few moments, then got to his feet. "Now let's figure out what kind of hell we're going to unleash on those motherfuckers that took her when we find a way into Aurathia."

"Fuck yeah, brother. Now you're talking my language."

CHAPTER 6
REVERIE

I was startled awake by a banging on my door. I rubbed my hands down my face, then stumbled to my feet. "Who is it?"

"It's Seamus, get your ass dressed. Selene wants to see you in her apartment." I heard him stomp away, likely off to brighten someone else's day.

Fuck.

I sank back onto the bed, knowing this was inevitable after the hall incident. I rested my head in my hands, questioning how much longer I could endure this.

I missed Oren, Jet, Nathan, Zeke, and Zane.

I missed my Mom.

I missed my Grumpy.

I missed Pops and Dad.

I missed Pantar.

I missed safety.

I missed laughter.

I missed not being afraid.

I missed Chloe and everything she represented.

I missed living my life on my own terms.

Until I arrived in Aurathia, I hadn't faced any real hardships. Yes, I lost two of my fathers, but I was loved so deeply by my remaining parents that the only sorrow I'd felt had been through their experience. I hadn't even been born yet when their tragedy occurred.

My parents had been preparing me for Emberhold Academy and initiation, and yes... it was dangerous. But with my training, I expected to survive, and if I was honest, I hadn't been *that* worried about it.

The Faction I was building was another layer in the charmed life I had been living. Each man, remarkable in their own right, but together they are more than any one woman deserves… and they were *mine*.

No real trials or tribulations. Nothing to test my true metal... until now.

Tears rolled down my face as I wrapped my arms around myself—the only person in this cold world who could or *would* give me comfort.

"I love you more than life, my Nexi. You are my every breath. When you laugh, it's like every lungful of air becomes joyful, and when you hurt, it feels as if my own chest is splitting open. I could lose everything else in my life—home, name, pride —and still keep crawling forward, as long as I have you." Nathan's deep voice whispered in my ear, helping me to find the strength to move forward, if only in my imagination.

I took in his words — a mixture of different moments from our past, spoken at various times — and dropped my arms, wrapping myself in them instead.

I stood wearily and got dressed, shedding each bit of emotion inside with every article of clothing I put on.

I left all weapons behind, knowing it was better not to have them on my person when visiting Selene.

When I was ready, I paused briefly before opening my door and took a deep breath, briefly placing a hand over my Nexus mark. Its presence on my skin comforted me. I took another deep breath, wiped any expression off my face, then pushed my door open and walked briskly down the hallway.

I'd made this journey so many times in the last few months that I could do it with my eyes closed. Selene's apartment was quite a long way from my quarters, but it felt like I was standing in front of the large black doors in seconds.

I knocked quietly and savored my last few pain-free moments.

The door opened, and a maid bid me to come in with a brief look of sympathy. "Mistress will be with you momentarily. You're welcome to have a drink while you wait."

My feet sank into the plush red carpet as I made my way over to the bar and poured a shot of Bloodmead. It was similar in proof to Everclear, but colored a deep red, like blood.

I thought it appropriate.

I downed a couple of shots and then stood leaning against the bar. I'd seen so many disgusting things here that I preferred to stand; there was no telling what bodily fluids covered the furniture.

I heard footsteps coming from the kitchen and braced myself, but it was only Fabien.

He walked behind the bar and fixed himself a drink. "How have you been holding up, kid?"

"About as well as someone in my position can." I didn't trust Fabien, per se, but I knew that as long as his safety wasn't in question, he'd play straight with me.

"What are you in for?" He took a sip of his drink, then sat on one of the black stools lining the bar.

"You know, the usual—one of Kristine's Faction hits—I hit back. She tattles—then a couple of rounds of torture—and everything resets." I tried to sound blasé, but I couldn't hide the slight tremble in my voice.

"Tough breaks." He said nonchalantly, but his eyes held genuine sympathy. He took another long sip of his drink. "Selene's been busy lately, running around in a tizzy."

"That's odd. Do you know what's going on?" I knew I was taking a risk even asking; there were ears everywhere. But information was power and could be bartered if need be.

Fabien looked around cautiously before speaking. "I'm not sure yet. That's actually why I'm hanging around." He grimaced, "The unexpected can be bad for your health around here."

I nodded in agreement, but before I could reply, Selene walked out of her office. "Hello, spawn of Adelaide. I'm glad you could fit me into your busy schedule."

"I'm never too busy to visit *you*, Selene." I tried to sound sincere, but I'm reasonably sure I missed the mark.

She gave a tinkling laugh. "Don't be absurd. We both

know that's nonsense. I, on the other hand, enjoy your visits quite thoroughly."

Selene walked over to Fabien and gave him a long and thorough kiss. "I'm so happy you've taken to hanging out here more." She pouted, "I don't know why so many of you want to stay in those disgusting barracks."

Fabien kissed the top of her head. "I like to keep an eye on the warriors and make sure everything is running smoothly. Serving you and our Faction is extremely important to me."

"That's so sweet." She giggled like a child. "Unfortunately, before we can spend some quality time together, I have to take care of a little business." Selene glanced at me briefly. "Lucky for you, I'm sure I'll be good and worked up when I'm done." She gave him one more short kiss. "I'll send for you when I'm ready."

I saw Fabien wince slightly, but only because I was observing him closely. "I'll await your invitation with eagerness." He gave a slight bow and left the apartment.

Selene poured herself a drink, then gracefully sat on the large sofa. "So, why in the world would you believe it was okay to hit poor Evan?"

I *knew* that was why I was here. Fuck Kristine right to hell. "I wasn't sure it was Evan, ma'am. I was attacked as I was leaving the dining hall and defended myself. I didn't have time to identify my attacker."

"Blah…blah…blah, I truly don't give two shits for your excuses. The fact I had to endure a visit from that whiny brat Kristine is enough to make me want to punish you." She drummed her long red nails on the arm of the sofa.

My hatred for Kristine was hotter than the fires of

Hell, but I knew Selene would've found one reason or another to get me here.

"I won in the coliseum again, and I dedicated the fight to your Faction." I *hated* how timid and fearful I sounded, but I would say anything to get out of what I knew was coming.

When I first arrived, I was almost cocky, but it didn't take long for me to realize that swallowing my pride hurt a lot less than Selene's torture did.

She gave a chilling smile. "That's sweet of you, child, but I'm afraid that we both know what has to happen here."

I hung my head for a moment, then headed for her room. I'd tried to avoid this and was disgusted with myself for the effort. I knew any further pleas would be pointless.

I entered, took off my vest and shirt, folded them neatly, and set them on the desk in the corner. Then, I walked over to the manacles hanging from the ceiling and waited.

Selene walked in, not bothering to shut the door. She pointed her finger at me and made an upward movement. My arms jerked up, and the manacles clasped around my wrists.

That's the kind of control I needed to take on this bitch. I didn't have it yet, but I was getting there. Every day, I grew stronger. I just needed time, and I'd do what I had to do to get it.

Selene opened the large black cabinet that held all of her favorite devices of torture and bypassed the cat-o'- nine tails for my least favorite, the flagrum. It was composed of three leather thongs, tipped with bone shards for maximum damage.

"It seems my previous punishments may not have emphasized the level of obedience you are expected to show." She walked up to me and dragged a single finger over my left nipple. "It's a genuine pity that I see so much of Adelaide in you, and not enough of my Hayes." Her eyes heated with lust. "I'd never consider making you a part of my Faction, but it would be fun to play."

I shuddered internally at the horrible thought of what that would look like. I was never so grateful for the resemblance to my mother.

Selene lifted my chin and looked into my eyes, "Unfortunately, those amber orbs of yours are identical to hers and leave me cold."

She dropped my chin and trailed the cold leather of the flagrum around my torso until she reached my back.

I closed my eyes and tried to prepare myself for the first strike.

The whistle of the leather as it traveled through the air was the only warning I received before the first lash stole the breath from my lungs. A sound like tearing cloth cracked across my back, and then fire seared through me, hot and blinding. The bone weights bit deep, dragging skin with them as they tore free.

The second blow jerked my body forward, my arms straining in their bindings as if they might tear free. The pain from the first hit hadn't subsided, and now it intensified—doubling, tripling—until I couldn't tell where one wound ended and the next began. My breath came in ragged gasps; my body shivered violently.

By the third lash, I could feel blood trickling down my sides, warm against the cold air. My shoulders screamed from being bound overhead, every muscle burning. The cords kissed me again and again, each kiss a theft... of skin, of breath, of strength. The world shrank to leather, bone, and pain. And still the shackles held me upright, forcing me to endure when all I wanted was to collapse in the welcome darkness.

"Come, my dear girl, your father handled way more than this. Don't shame him by collapsing under this bit of light torture." She drew back to hit me again.

I lifted my chin at her words.

I knew she meant them to taunt me, but they gave me the courage to endure the rest of the lashes without losing consciousness. Just barely.

"You know, I've been thinking of the best way to let your parents know how much I'm enjoying your visit, and I think I've come up with the perfect plan." She went to her cabinet and replaced the flagrum.

I managed to raise my head long enough to see her grab a hyde hook from her macabre collection. A knife named for its curved, claw-like shape, carried by hunters who used it to skin their kill.

My consciousness wavered in and out for a moment, the pain on my back excruciating.

"No, none of that, little Adelaide. I want you awake for this." Selene laughed, "though I doubt it'll be for long."

I opened my eyes at the sensation of cold metal on my skin and saw her circling my Nexus mark with the tip of the blade. "So fragile," she whispers, voice full of velvet and venom. "One stroke, and you are nothing. Your mother's legacy erased."

The blade kisses my skin, then presses in. Heat flared sharply. I bit the inside of my cheek until blood filled my mouth.

She hummed at the twitching flesh. "It parts so sweetly. Layers, that's all you are."

Ancestors, please, don't let her... "Fuuuuck!!! No... *Please*, no!" I threw my head back and screamed.

The pain was more than I could bear, but no matter how much I begged, it didn't stop. My voice had grown hoarse from the screaming, and I knew I was seconds away from passing out.

I feel our bond jolt. For a breath, I saw one of them—stumbling, his knees hitting stone. Another clutched at his chest as if struck, rage curling bright in his eyes—a third doubled over, breath gone, knuckles white against his thighs. Then, a fourth gripped steel in his hand, snapping the hilt in two, his fury uncontrollable. And the last—I feel his roar, silent but raw, his throat ragged as he screams my name.

Then they vanish, leaving only the queen's knife, slicing deeper. Fat glistens pale, fascia clings like a cobweb, and muscle shudders alive under her hand.

Selene leans close, her whisper hot against my ear. "Without this, you are nothing to them. No mark, no bond. Only ruin."

Through blurry eyes, I see her holding up my Nexus mark, blood running down her arm in rivulets.

I tremble, choking on pain, unsure if the visions were

truth or lies, fever-dreams conjured by agony. I can't call out. I can't know for sure. Perhaps I imagined them all.

But still, the thought clings to me like blood to steel: what if every cut she makes is branding them too? What if they bleed with me?

～△～

When I wake up, I'm lying on the bed in my room, bandages covering my chest and back. I feel like my entire torso is on fire. The pain is near unbearable.

I staggered to my feet. I had to know.

I made it to the bathroom and looked in the mirror. My face was swollen and covered in red splotches; dried tear tracks were still discernible.

But that was the least of my concerns.

I hesitated to look down and took a few moments to build up my courage. When my eyes dropped, I saw a bandage soaked through with blood covering the place where my mark was located. I bowed my head as tears once again rolled down my face.

Randomly, I wondered if there was a quota on the amount of tears a person was allowed on any given day. I'm surprised at this point that mine hadn't dried up completely.

I took a deep, painful breath, then raised my head and pulled the bandage loose. Only a corner peeled down, but that was enough to confirm my fears.

I braced my hands on the sink and sobbed. Where my mark used to be— where it meant something— it's just...

gone. What's left is ugly. Torn skin, red and swollen, edges jagged where her knife dug too deep. Dried blood clings like cracks in old paint, and underneath, it looks raw, like meat left out in the sun.

My hand lifts on its own, shaking, hovering just over it. I can't touch. I don't want to. It feels wrong—like pressing on the hole where my heart used to be.

Tears blur everything, but the reflection doesn't change. I'm not me anymore. I look like a stranger, like someone hollowed out.

A sound slips out of me, broken, ugly. I lean into the mirror, forehead pressed to the cold glass, and sob until my whole body shakes.

Selene took it.

She tried to take them.

Her voice echoes in my head, smug and cruel; *Without this, you are nothing. No mark. No bond.*

And yet... when I reach inward, past the pain, past the hollow place where the mark used to sit, I still feel them.

The well of power that is now a mix of all of us, amber, green, red, purple, yellow, and crimson, is stronger than ever. I let out a shuddering breath, pressing my palm flat to the mirror, over my reflection's wound. Tears slide hot down my cheeks. Grief still burns sharp—but underneath it, something steadier grows.

Selene failed. She just doesn't know it yet.

CHAPTER 7

OREN

"What the fuck, Oren? What did we just feel?" Nathan paced my office, pulling at his hair with both hands.

None of the others were in any better shape, including myself. Everyone had rushed here from wherever they were, in a panic.

"I wish I knew, brother." I wiped my hand down my face. Ever since we'd felt the searing pain on our chests, exactly where Reverie's Nexus mark was located, I'd been frantic, contacting everyone I could think of that might have contacts still in Bellona. I'd had no luck so far, and that was tearing us all apart.

"She was in agony. I could feel it," Jet said without any emotion on his face or in his voice. To anyone other than Faction, he may seem cold, but I could feel his emotions as well as my own. The guy was a mass of anger and hatred, just waiting for a target.

Zeke and Zane hadn't said ten words to anyone since

the incident. I knew it was taking every bit of control they had to keep their Draxon from taking over and destroying the world.

At this point, I was all for it, starting with the Council. Those bastards hadn't been helpful at all. Reverie's fathers, along with myself, had tried several times to get them to take action to prepare us for what was to come, but they failed. Now, with the attacks, they'd been forced to at least pretend to rally the troops. From what I'd seen, Sly and Damien had organized most of the Aurathion forces so far. Jesse and John, along with our Faction, were helping to train those inexperienced in battle. I was waiting for concrete proof that they were conspiring with the DF. When I had it in hand, the days of them drawing breath would be over.

"I need to get to her now!" Nathan collapsed into the chair in front of my desk and buried his face in his hands. "How the hell did this happen? Five men, and none of us prevented her capture. What kind of Faction are we?"

"It was my fault." Jet scowled. "I was the only one there." He walked to Nathan and laid his hand on his shoulder. "I swear on my life, brother, I will get her back. And when I do, I'm going to rain hell down on the motherfuckers that took her."

Zeke spoke in a voice that was so deep and gruff it wasn't even recognizable as his. "There were mistakes made by us all."

When I made eye contact with him, I saw that his pupils had retracted into slits. I tensed and prepared to contain him if need be. This wasn't Zeke; it was his Draxon talking.

"They will not be made again. I'll see to it." He looked at Jet, his head turned too slowly, too smoothly, like oil poured over glass. The motion was silent, but it carried the weight of something coiled and patient, the stillness of a predator before the strike. "You won't be the only one raining hell on my Treasure's enemies."

Before I could form a reply, I heard the door slam, and everyone in the room assumed a defensive stance that relaxed when Chloe, Oliver, and Deshawn entered.

"What's going on? I felt an indescribable pain that I know came from Reverie," Chloe said breathlessly, clearly having run all the way here.

When Zeke turned to look at her, Oliver and Deshawn stepped in front of her protectively.

Zeke growled low at their actions, and Chloe pushed between them. "For fuck's sake, that's my brother, and he'd never hurt me in any form he chose to take." I heard her mumble under her breath about overprotective men. "Now what the hell is going on? The marks on mine and Oliver's arms lit up, and we both felt the call to aid Reverie."

"We aren't sure." I stood and walked around my desk. "I've tried reaching out to contacts that might have spies in Aurathia, but so far I've got nothing."

Jet straightened. "What about the spy my military contact has planted? Fuck! Why didn't we call them immediately?" He rushed out of the room.

"Firefly, I'm going to help him get the info you all need." Deshawn kissed Chloe briefly, then followed Jet.

"What can we do while we wait?" Nathan had a look of hope on his face that I'm sure mirrored mine.

"We need to finalize our plans to hijack the portal when the DF attacks Copper Creek. If Jet's contact doesn't come through, that may be our only hope." I ran both hands through my hair, needing to kill something more than I needed to draw my next breath.

"Not according to Pantar." Chloe started pacing the room, obviously having a hard time sitting still. Oliver pulled her into his arms as she walked near him. When she tried to pull away, he whispered something in her ear. She stayed in his arms, but a single tear rolled down her cheek, unchecked.

"What do you mean?" Zane growled low, his Draxon at the forefront as well.

"Pantar still believes he holds the only hope of opening a portal. He can also still…" Chloe slapped her hand over her mouth and looked around guiltily.

"Still what?" I demanded. What was she hiding? Pantar had been scarce ever since Reverie was taken. Popping in less and less as the days went by. I'd been busy trying to get to my Nexus, so I hadn't paid as much attention as I should have, apparently.

"He didn't want me to say anything." Chloe hung her head. "I don't want to break his confidence, but with what just happened, I feel like I should tell you."

"Tell us *what??!!*" Nathan yelled, losing his patience. Nothing was left of the man he used to be—once easy to smile with Reverie by his side.

Oliver stood, "Don't speak to my Nexus like that, 'ula vale!"

Both men stood chest to chest, with Oliver, a full head taller than Nathan… not that Nathan was intimidated.

The damn fool — which ironically was what Oliver called him in Samoan — wasn't afraid of anything if it stood between him and his Nexi.

The tension eased when my cell phone rang. Most staff and students didn't bother with their phones because, typically, they were useless here. Mine was not. I didn't want to be unreachable when waiting on information, so I'd found a way to remedy that.

I looked at the screen. "It's Jesse." I answered and put it on speaker.

"Get over here now!" Jesse yelled into the phone and hung up immediately.

Before we could recover from that abrupt command, Mira popped into the room.

"I'm here to open a portal to my Faction." Without delay, she did so, and we stood to step through, alarmed by the urgency in Jesse's voice.

Before Chloe could enter, Mira stopped her. *"I'm afraid, Aegisseer, that you must stay here."*

"What?!" Why?" Chloe asked, more than a little upset.

"All will be revealed soon. For now, I need you to trust me." Mira stared deep into her eyes.

Something Chloe saw in those deep pools of wisdom must have eased her because when she spoke, she was much calmer. "I do trust you." She turned to Oliver. "Let's train. I feel the need to work off some of this stress."

～☩～

The warehouse that the Hawthorne Faction was staying in was vast. Mira brought us to the lowest level, where all their vehicles were kept. They moved here shortly after Reverie was abducted. We needed a safe place for Adelaide to lie low while we made plans to rescue Reverie. To say she argued fiercely when her men refused her the chance to fight would be an understatement. She only relented when Damien explained the strategy he had devised to gain entrance into Aurathia.

Only Sly and John were present; no sign of Adelaide or Jesse.

Both men were standing in front of a table with a small box on it. The box was unremarkable to the eye—small, square, fashioned of pale wood rubbed smooth by careful hands. No carvings, no inlays, no lock. It could have been mistaken for a jewelry case left on a bedside table.

I couldn't explain my sense of dread at seeing it. But nothing in me wanted them to open that box.

"What's the emergency?" I asked, dreading the answer.

"This box was delivered to our condo this morning." John's expression was grim.

"It's from Selene. We didn't want Adelaide to know about it until we could determine what was inside." Sly rumbled, not taking his eyes off the box. "She's upstairs and Jesse is keeping her busy."

"Do you think it has something to do with Reverie?" Nathan asked with obvious reluctance.

John nodded. "It actually says 'from Reverie,' but Sly recognized the box as Selene's."

"Fuck." Zane began pacing but never took his eyes off the box, much like Sly.

Jet approached the box. He had arrived at the warehouse separately, brought by Pantar, when he was unable to contact the military's spy. "Do you want me to open it?"

"I'll do it," Sly growled, then squeezed his eyes shut. "I know how evil Selene is. You need to prepare yourselves because nothing good resides inside this box."

I nodded and prayed to every Ancestor I could think of, asking for the strength to endure whatever it was.

Zeke stepped beside Jet, and that seemed to be our cue. We each stepped up, so we were standing shoulder to shoulder, drawing strength from one another.

Sly slowly opened the box, and I wanted to yell at him to hurry it up. But I knew why he didn't fling the lid back quickly. Once we saw what was inside, we couldn't *unsee* it.

When he finally lifted the lid enough to gaze inside, his chest sank. "There's something wrapped in black satin." He frowned. "The note on top is addressed to Adelaide."

"Adelaide is not opening that," John stated emphatically.

"I can smell Reverie," Zeke growled, pupils slitted.

Mira and Pantar began growling low from near the entrance to the warehouse. Clearly upset, not of Zeke's Draxon, but from the smell of Reverie that shouldn't be coming from such a small box.

We definitely weren't dealing with Zeke anymore. Maybe we could use this. "What else do you smell?"

"I smell evil, and a bitch that I mean to kill." Smoke came out of Zeke's nostrils.

He'd have to wait his turn. If I ever got my hands on Selene, she'd beg me to use my abilities to kill her because I was planning to go old-fashioned on her ass and use my hands.

"He is correct. There is a smell of wrongness and evil coming from the box." Pantar spoke in our heads in a voice filled with more rage than I'd ever heard from him.

"What's going on down here?" Adelaide marched down the stairs with Jesse close on her heels.

"Nothing, angel, go back upstairs. We'll be there in a few minutes," Sly said, scowling at Jesse.

"Hell no. I can sense that you're all hiding something from me. I'm not stupid." She stomped to the bottom of the stairs and pushed in between the two men. "Where did that box come from?" She leaned closer and gasped, "That's my name on the letter in Selene's handwriting."

She would recognize it because she had been roommates with Selene for a few weeks while at Emberhold, before moving into Faction housing.

John put his arm around her waist. "Baby, please go back upstairs and let us handle this."

Adelaide leaned into him for a moment, then stood straight and pushed his arm away. "If my baby can go through whatever this is, then the least I can do as her mother is deal with it." She reached into the box and pulled out the letter.

Dearest Adelaide,

I've had the pleasure of hosting your daughter these last few months. I can't tell you how much joy she's brought me. She's really something special.

I'd love for you to share my gift with her men; I'm sure they'll enjoy it.

Give my love to Sly— or Hayes, as he preferred to be called while in my loving care. I hope to see him soon.

Until Reverie is in your gentle arms again, I sent a small piece of her to offer you comfort in these trying times.

All of my love,
Selene

Adelaide's knees went weak. Sly and John both grabbed her around the waist with Jesse at her back. All four of them stood like that for a few brief moments, wrapped in each other, drawing strength. Then Adelaide stood tall, shook her men off, and slowly unwrapped the black silk to reveal what it held.

My chest constricted as if a vice had closed around it.

There it was.

Reverie's Nexus mark.

Wax-sealed.

Pale.

Laid out on the silk like a prize. My vision blurred at the edges, breath hitching sharply. That mark was supposed to be decorating my baby's glowing skin, alive and thrumming, not carved from her, a piece of butchered flesh.

The bond inside me recoiled, snapping taut, dragging me under. My fists clenched until my knuckles split, blood dripping down my palm, sparks flaring at the end of my fingertips.

Around me, the others buckled in their own way—wood cracked under a slammed fist, curses hissed between clenched teeth, a strangled sob choked off into silence.

Reverie's fathers were no better. John pressed himself to the wall, face bloodless. Jesse mouthed words of prayer silently, and Sly's stare was empty, fixed, and hollow.

And Adelaide… she stood at the center, her grief pressing into my bones, heavier than stone. Her hands shook, her eyes shone wet, but her spine stayed rigid. Rage simmered under her grief—cold, steady, lethal.

I couldn't take it. Couldn't bear the silence, the weight of it. My throat scraped raw as the words forced themselves out.

"They cut her… like she's *nothing*." My voice cracked, low and ragged, fury scraping against grief. I swallowed the copper taste of blood, then lifted my head, meeting every eye in the room. "Selene did this—" My voice hardened. "The bitch will pay with her life."

The words hung there, not a threat, not a promise— just truth. And in the silence that followed, I knew even her death wouldn't be enough.

CHAPTER 8
REVERIE

I dragged my injured body out of bed and then into the shower. No healer had been sent. Razor had come to check on me when I didn't show for training and managed to find enough supplies to treat my wounds.

This was the fifth day, and my back was almost completely healed. The skin had returned to its pale shade, with only light red marks where the worst of the damage had occurred.

This type of healing was unusual. It's true that Aurathions recover from injuries faster than humans, especially when we are part of a Faction. But my Faction was far away, so I shouldn't be able to do this kind of healing.

Unfortunately, my skin had healed where my Nexus mark had previously been, but the mark itself hadn't returned. I wasn't really expecting it, but I had hoped the Ancestors might see fit to restore it.

I was heartbroken, but the fact that deep inside, where it really counted, our connection was still strong helped me survive the pain. As long as that wasn't lost, I could deal with anything.

In fact, I was almost 100% sure I could hear my men now. I even caught the sound of Pantar whispering in my head… so faint that I couldn't understand the words spoken, but I had faith our connection would strengthen.

Maybe Selene did me a favor. The trauma of her actions may have let me get past the barrier that being here had put between me and my Faction.

I smiled at the thought.

Today, I was on my way to the dining hall for a meal, and then to training. I had rested in my room for as long as possible. I needed to train, but I also had to keep my healed back and front concealed for at least a few more days.

I stepped out of the shower but froze again at the sight of my chest, bare of my mark. I paused, clenching my eyes shut tightly to send a prayer to the Ancestors, hoping that somehow my mark would return to where it belongs. Suddenly, a gentle breeze lifted the dark, wet strands of my hair, and I felt a wave of peace and comfort.

I opened my eyes, and my skin shimmered, illuminating all the dark corners of the small bathroom. I stared in the mirror in amazement as my mark appeared briefly before seeming to sink deep into my skin.

I sank to my knees on the cold bathroom floor and bowed my head in gratitude. I didn't fully understand what it all meant, but I knew at that moment that no matter what lay ahead, I would face it, and I wasn't alone.

Walking down the hallway toward the dining hall, I saw Torren approaching me. "Hey, stranger. I haven't seen you in training or the dining hall for several days. I was beginning to worry."

I smiled warmly, "No worries, I had a small injury from sparring. It really wasn't a big deal."

"Must have been pretty serious to keep you down for so long." For a second, I thought I caught a flicker of rage in his eyes, but it was there and gone so fast I couldn't be sure. "Are you headed to the dining hall?"

"Yes, I planned to grab a quick bite and then do a light workout to get me back on track." I needed to ensure that I kept my training limited until my recovery reached a speed that would be considered normal.

"Why don't I come with? Then we can train together afterward," Torren said, then looped his arm through mine and started heading in that direction without waiting for my approval of his plan.

We entered the room, and everyone paused in what they were doing. I believe it was partly because of my appearance after days of absence, and also because of the man beside me. In all the months I'd been here, no one had dared to befriend me openly.

"Why don't you take a seat, and I'll fix us a plate?" Torren led me to a table smack dab in the middle of everyone.

"It might be better if we sat over there." I pointed to a table in the back corner.

He frowned, "What's wrong with this table?"

"Nothing. But it would cut down on the bullshit if we were a little more isolated." I shrugged my shoulders. "I told you that I'm not well-liked around here."

"And I don't care." He raised his brow. "Anyone who doesn't like where you sit can take it up with me."

"Well, okay then, big man." I shrugged. "Don't complain to me when you get heartburn from all the shit they feed you about me. Carry on and bring my food, garçon." I waved him on with my hand.

"As you wish, my Queen." Torren bowed deeply before turning and heading to the buffet laden with food.

I smiled. This guy was something else. I admired his bravery —or maybe it was just pure arrogance — that made him think he was untouchable. Either way, I was happy to have his company. After everything that happened, I needed some lightness and humor in my life, or at the very least a distraction.

I hadn't been completely honest; it was only Kristine and her Faction that caused trouble. I didn't think everyone here hated me. They would've probably befriended me if it weren't for all of her bullshit. Most were so busy trying to stay alive and find a Faction they wanted no part in whatever was going on with *me*... I understood that, but it was lonely.

I was pulled out of my thoughts when a large plate of food was placed in front of me.

"This should put some meat on those bones," Torren smirked as he sat across from me with a plate even more loaded down than mine.

I laughed, "I have a large appetite, but there is no way I

can eat everything on this plate." He'd brought me a large steak, a mound of scrambled eggs, and a small stack of pancakes.

He motioned at me with his fork. "Eat what you can, then I'll finish the rest."

As I watched him dig into his food, it reminded me of my guys; every one of them ate as if it were their last meal.

"Why the sad face?" Torren asked around a mouthful of food.

"Just thinking about some people I miss from home." I smiled faintly, then started to eat.

"What people?" He gave me his full attention.

There was no way I was going to tell him my story. He'd probably find out soon enough, but until then, I was keeping it to myself. "I don't want to go into all of that right now."

Torren eyed me in annoyance for a moment but nodded his head and began eating again.

I heard Kristine's whiny voice talking to Hugo, another member of her Faction. I winced, waiting for her to walk over, but she just scowled in my direction and sat at another table on the other side of the room.

"Who's the uppity bitch?" He motioned to Kristine.

"Don't point." I panicked and pushed his finger down.

We looked at each other in shock when I felt a jolt run up my arm. I was utterly speechless, and he must have felt the same way because he didn't say anything either.

When the silence had lasted so long that it grew uncomfortable, I laughed awkwardly, "I guess we're Potentials."

He didn't answer for several long moments. "Maybe."

He cleared his throat. "Are you almost finished? I just remembered something I have to do." Without waiting for an answer, he stood and headed out of the dining hall, leaving his plate and everything.

Well, that was awkward. I guess he wasn't looking for a lowly warrior as Faction. Fortunately for him, I wasn't seeking another Faction member—especially without any of my men here to agree to adding someone new to our group.

I took a deep breath and stood, then disposed of both our plates. I'd lost my appetite after that startling development. I didn't have the headspace to deal with this right now.

When I exited the hall, I thought Kristine would make a rude remark, but, to my surprise, she didn't acknowledge me at all, nor did Hugo. Selene likely ensured I was left alone, at least until after my upcoming battles.

Instead of training, I went back to my room. The quick healing I experienced had drained me, and I needed extra rest. With a few days until my next fight, I hoped to recover fully by then. Honestly, I saw only two choices: fight or die... and dying was not an option. I desired a long life with my men, and I would fight for it with all my strength for as long as necessary.

I pushed open my door and sealed it behind me, then took off my clothes, plopped down on my bed, and sighed in exhaustion. The last few days, my body hadn't felt like my own. Changes were happening that I couldn't explain, and the previous nights, I'd had strange dreams.

Snuggling under my bedraggled blanket, my final

thought before I drifted off to sleep was of my men and what they would think of this latest development.

I was on the bank of a beautiful river. The wind was blowing gently, and I felt a deep sense of anticipation. I leaned back against the trunk of a tree with a book in my lap and dozed lightly. Feeling an insect tickle my ear, I swatted at it in irritation, then began to drift back into sleep. Before I was completely submerged, the bug landed on the tip of my nose. I swatted at it again, and my eyes flew open at the sound of deep masculine laughter.

The reason for my anticipation was kneeling beside me, holding a long piece of grass. "Ambrose!" I squealed, "When did you return?"

"Just now. I came straight here instead of the castle because I knew it was where you'd be." He gave me his hand, then pulled me to my feet.

For a moment, I didn't speak—I just let my eyes drink in the sight of him, whole and safe. Then his arms opened, and I was in them, held so tightly it hurt in the sweetest way.

"I didn't expect you back until tomorrow, but I hoped I was wrong." I grinned, unable to contain my joy, then pulled him in for a soft kiss.

"Queen Lilibet, you frightened us. We heard you scream and thought you'd been attacked," my Aegisseer, Lexith, said as she rushed to me, closely followed by her Faction and my Aegisworn, Cassian, Viktar, and Soren.

"Looks like she was attacked, but it wasn't unwelcome." Cassian laughed.

Lexith swatted him on the arm, "That's our Queen you're talking about."

"Oh, really? Didn't I hear you two talking about sexual

positions yesterday?" Viktar smirked as mine and Lexith's faces burned with embarrassment.

"I'm sure you were mistaken." Lexith narrowed her eyes at him. "Let's leave our queen and her consort alone."

Soren put his arm around Lexith. "I'm sure he wasn't, but we can discuss that back at the castle." He smiled widely. "Good to have you home, Ambrose."

I smiled as I watched the four of them walk down the hill and through the castle gates.

"Is that all the welcome home I get?" Ambrose picked me up and held me in his arms bridal style.

I held his precious face in my hands and said, "I think a bigger celebration could be arranged."

"Is this celebration only going to have two participants?" He looked into my eyes with all the love anyone could ask for.

"If that is what you wish." I felt my blood heat up in anticipation of what was to come. I'd been without him for too long, and I missed him so much.

His lips found mine slowly, not rushed or ravenous, but reverent, as if he was afraid I might shatter if he pressed too hard. The kiss carried weeks of absence, yet it was gentle—like a promise whispered against my mouth. I melted into him, my hands buried themselves in his hair tightly, but not out of desperation.

More out of relief for his safe return.

He tasted like rain and warmth, familiar as home. The slow press of his mouth softened something that had been wound tight inside me, loosening the ache I hadn't let myself feel until now. I breathed him in between kisses, tears burning at the corners of my eyes, and he brushed them away with the lightest *touch of his thumb, never breaking the fragile rhythm of our kiss.*

When he finally pulled back just enough to look at me, his forehead resting against mine, his smile was small but steady. And in that soft, unhurried kiss, I felt it—the ache of parting, the relief of return, the quiet certainty that whatever storms waited, he was here.

He was mine.

I woke breathing hard with a warmth that still lingered on my lips and a single tear rolling down my cheek. As I lay there trembling, caught in the bittersweet knowing: that kiss wasn't mine to keep, yet it had always belonged to me.

As I drifted back into sleep, I knew one thing: the kiss had been real.

Not in this life, not *here*—but somewhere long ago.

CHAPTER 9
REVERIE

I spent the rest of the day dozing on and off, then half the night trying to understand what I'd seen, staying awake to avoid the nightmare of reliving Selene taking my mark and the real possibility she had sent it to my Faction.

That last part was too horrific to dwell on. Although I believe the glimpse I had of each of them feeling my pain was real. As horrible as that possibility was, did that mean our ability to communicate was returning? So many questions that needed answers...Was I truly Queen Lilibet, reincarnated? Could that really be possible? Her name kept surfacing in connection with the rare abilities I had acquired. And the dream that didn't feel like a dream was beyond strange.

These questions had made for a fitful sleep, and now I was rushing to the dining hall to grab breakfast before heading out to train. I wanted to dwell more on the dream and what it could mean, but I had a battle at the coliseum this weekend. If I knew anything about Selene, it was that my next fight would be the most difficult yet. I'd defeated everyone they'd thrown at me so far, and I knew it pissed her off as much as it had pleased her. She was a person full of contradictions, and none of them were pleasant.

Honestly, I could use the distraction of pushing my body to the point of exhaustion. Maybe if I were tired enough, I could return to the place I visited last night in my dreams and find more answers. It may be the key to getting out of this place.

My gut warned me that my time was running out; I had to hope that either my abilities grew stronger at a faster pace or that I would find a way to leave as soon as possible.

"Hey, fancy meeting you here again." Torren was smiling as we both entered the hall, coming from opposite directions.

"Fancy that." His presence rattled me, but I returned his smile, trying to shake off my thoughts enough to engage in everyday conversation.

"You look better today." I saw an emotion in his eyes that I wasn't able to identify before he looked away. "Do you want to train together?" He grabbed a plate and handed it to me as we approached the buffet.

"Sure, if you have time." Neither of us mentioned how he'd booked it out of here the other day. I grabbed several pieces of bacon and a large spoonful of potatoes and eggs. I was starving after spending the whole day in my room yesterday.

"Absolutely, I've been thinking of some moves that

would really help you with those short swords you favor." He filled his plate, and we sat down.

We both reached for the salt, and he jerked his hand back before our fingers touched. That was a little insulting; I guess I was right, and he was looking for bigger fish than me to bond with. Which was *totally* fine...I had more than enough on my plate to deal with at the moment.

I knew I was only lying to myself.

"Do you have any abilities you use when fighting?" He paused with his spoon halfway to his mouth, waiting for my answer.

I took a moment to think about how to reply. Since I didn't know much about Torren, I couldn't trust him. I only used the simplest abilities, because using my stronger ones would draw attention—especially from Selene and Ubel, since they knew I hadn't taken any serum, and my Faction was far away.

A whole world, in fact.

The only thing that would force me to reveal my hand would be a life-or-death situation, and only as a last resort. I had to depend on my physical abilities and skills to keep me alive, and so far, that had been enough.

"Only the most common, levitating, strength, and teleporting for small distances." None of the things I'd named would lead to the scrutiny I was hoping to avoid.

Torren looked at me with narrowed eyes, seeming slightly irritated with my answer, then his expression cleared as he nodded. "I can work with that. Maybe when you've taken a few more doses of the serum, you'll develop some major abilities."

I shoved a whole piece of bacon in my mouth, then mumbled, "I can only hope."

Over my dead body would I ever take the serum.

"Are you hoping to find a Faction?" he tilted his head in inquiry. I guess I understood his curiosity after we touched yesterday.

I just shrugged my shoulders and took a large bite of eggs. Hopefully, he'd get the hint and stop asking questions.

"She fucking wishes." Kristine's whiny voice came from over my shoulder. "Reverie already has a Faction." She sneered, "She'd have a better chance of finding a new one than getting back to them." Kristine laughed, and Evan, Thomas, and Hugo joined in.

When I first arrived and found out Kristine had a Faction, I couldn't imagine anyone tying themselves to her for life. When I met her three men, everything became clear. They were as messed up as she was. And Evan's resemblance to Jet was beyond freaky.

Torren frowned in confusion, "What do you mean she has a Faction?"

"Just what I said, handsome, she has a Faction back on Earth… a big one." Kristine sidled a little closer to him. "They're all traitors to our cause, including Reverie herself." She smiled in satisfaction, proud of herself, assuming she'd ruined another friendship.

Torren appeared to ponder the information for a few moments, then said, "Well, she's here now, fighting in the coliseum like the rest of us. That has to mean something."

"All it *means* is that she's accepting her punishment like

a good girl. It doesn't change her traitor status." Kristine smirked at me.

"Why, of all the traitors on earth, was *she* brought here?" He turned to me. "Were you Nexus to your Faction on earth?"

I understood why he wanted to know. "I was Nex—"

Kristine interrupted, "She was Nexus, but it's a mystery to me how the Ancestors could have chosen her for that role."

"It's not a mystery to me." Torren smoldered my way. "You're a strong, beautiful woman with amazing fighting skills. There is no doubt you could handle more than a few men."

I hated that my body responded to that look. I missed my men to the depths of my soul, and somehow it felt like a betrayal to have feelings for anyone else, even if he was a Potential.

Kristine glowered at him. "Haven't you been listening? She's a traitor to her people; her looks are inconsequential. You wouldn't even have abilities now if it were up to her."

"Maybe, maybe not." He smiled slightly at me. "I guess we'll never know." For some reason, that last statement seemed to sadden him.

"I don't understand why Ubel and Selene are even keeping her alive." Thomas glowered in my direction, needing to put his two cents in.

I was surprised he'd stayed quiet this long. He had an opinion on everything and, unfortunately, rarely kept it to himself.

"Probably because Ubel and Selene don't have the final

say, unless something has changed, and I'm not aware of it?" Torren tilted his head in question.

"Are you talking about Trent Storm?" Kristine asked, frowning slightly. "Everyone knows that he's Ubel's puppet."

Torren threw back his head and laughed, "Is that so? I hadn't heard that rumor." His laughter faded, and an expression crossed his face that made Kristine put some distance between herself and him. "I wonder if anyone has informed Trent Storm of this."

"I very much doubt that." I smirked, "If he's anything like his nephew, the thought of being considered anyone's puppet would enrage him."

"And what do you know of his nephew?" Torren frowned in question.

"I can answer that," Kristine smirked. "He's a part of her Faction. I guess that makes her my sister." She tilted her head, and a lecherous gleam entered her eyes. "Although, if I were completely truthful, Oren has never felt like my brother."

The look on her face made me sick to my stomach. I'd thought there were a few times when the way she looked at him was less than sisterly.

"I'm sorry, but we'll have to postpone our plans again. I've got to retrieve something from my room." Torren stood up but paused before he left and glowered at Kristine and her men. "You four need to mind your own business and allow Reverie to finish her breakfast in peace."

"Who the fuck are you to give us orders?" Evan scowled at Torren and took a step in his direction.

Torren smiled sweetly... then his hand made a slashing

motion so fast that I almost missed it, and a cut appeared on Evans' cheek. Blood welled instantly, streaming down his face as the gash split wide, nearly to the bone, and he dropped to his knees.

"What the fuck?!!!" Evan screamed as he held his hand to the bleeding flesh, trying to keep the hunk of his torn cheek from flopping down.

"Now you know just a touch of what will happen to you if you disobey me." Torren watched the blood flow down Evans' arm in fascination and with a kind of hunger that I didn't understand.

Kristine motioned to Thomas and Hugo to help Evan to his feet, "That was uncalled for! We were trying to warn you away from her. Ubel and Selene won't take kindly to what just happened here." They left, headed to the infirmary, I was sure.

"I truly appreciate you defending me, but you've put a target on your back now. Believe me when I say that you don't want Selene or Ubel's attention." I stood and picked up my plate.

He stared at me for a few minutes. "That was more about asserting my dominance over them than anything else. Don't take it to mean more than that." He turned and walked away.

Well, fuck you very much. I frowned at his back as he walked away. Now I was glad he avoided my touch because we were definitely on the same page. I didn't need any more obstinate bastards to deal with. My Faction was bursting at the seams with men that filled that position.

R azor met me as I approached the armory to get my short swords. "I'm glad to see you here. You have a battle tomorrow, and so far I haven't been able to find out who or what you'll be fighting."

"I know that it's probably going to be my toughest battle yet. Selene wasn't happy with me, and even after her punishment, I'm sure there will be consequences in the coliseum too."

He leaned in closer. "I'm so sorry I haven't been able to help you more. Just know if the opportunity presents itself, I'll get you out of here."

I touched his arm. "I don't want you to help at the risk of something happening to your Faction. You've been a real friend and ally, and I truly appreciate it."

Razor let out a small cry of distress and wavered on his feet. He dropped his head and took several deep breaths, then grabbed my arm and led me deep into the armory. "What the hell was that?" He asked as he undid his shirt to examine his shoulder.

I gasped when I saw a mark on his arm: the tree of life inside a perfect circle, just like Chloe's and Oliver's.

"I'm so sorry! I didn't do it on purpose." I honestly didn't know how or why this was happening.

Razor looked from his shoulder to me in shock, "Do you know what this is?"

I shook my head, "No."

"Has this happened before?"

I nodded, "Yes."

"Can you give more than a one-word answer?" He asked, seeming annoyed and amused all at once.

"Right. Before Kristine pulled me here, it happened to two of my closest friends after I touched them." I couldn't tear my eyes away from his shoulder.

Razor stared at me in amazement. "This was a mark given centuries ago by Queen Lilibet to mark her Aegisworn."

Lilibet again —this was starting to freak me out a little. Then my eyes widened. "Someone in a dream I had recently used that word in reference to a friend."

"Who?" He led me further back into the building when Aurathions began entering to grab weapons.

I really didn't want to answer him or say it out loud, but I knew I could trust him, and the mark reinforced that feeling. "Queen Lilibet."

"Fuck." He bowed his head for a moment and took several deep breaths. "I've got to inform Tanya of this." He grabbed my arm so tightly it hurt. "Don't whisper a word of this to anyone."

I jerked my arm out of his grip. "Who the hell would I tell? I don't have friends, and I'm a little insulted you'd think I'd be that stupid."

"I'm sorry." He apologized quickly. "I'm feeling a little protective, and I know how much danger surrounds you here." Razor looked thoughtful for a moment. "I'm going to arrange a meeting with you and the rest of my Faction. I'll let you know the time and place."

I nodded. That sounded like a good idea.

"Good. I want you to meet Tanya. In fact, I feel like it's essential that you do." Razor started walking back toward the entrance. "Get your swords and begin your exercises. I'll be out shortly to check on you."

I nodded, then grabbed my short swords and left. Maybe I'd finally find out more information about Lilibet and what an Aegisworn was.

The practice field was crowded today, as it usually was the day before we performed in the coliseum. Every warrior hoped for victory and for a powerful Nexus would choose them, getting them that much closer to leaving this hellhole.

I find a clearing and take my stance, resting both blades against my thighs for a moment to feel their weight anchoring me. Then I move... My feet slide smoothly over the packed earth in an ancient rhythm—step, pivot, glide. One sword swings high, slicing through the air with a hiss, while the other strikes low, quick as a serpent's strike. My movements are well-practiced; each sequence perfected until I'm satisfied.

My muscles warm quickly, heat spreading beneath my skin as I transition between drills. Slash, spin, parry, thrust—my body moves in sync with an internal rhythm like music only I can hear. I observe every detail: the whisper of steel, the flex of my wrists, the sting of sweat sliding down my temple.

There's power in control, a quiet thrill in knowing that if anyone entered my orbit, these graceful arcs could become deadly strikes. This is where everything comes together—where each elegant line ensures my survival.

A bell clangs twice—sharp and grating. The sound slices through the clash of steel like a knife. Around me, men and women stumble. Blades lower. Boots scrape over packed dirt as every warrior heads toward the posting board. The evening air is thick—sweat, dust, anticipation—and beneath it all, that low, hungry murmur that always precedes match announcements.

Seamus arrives with his usual swagger, a hammer slung over one shoulder as if he's marching to a throne. His assistant, Marvin, scurries behind him, clutching the parchments as if they were sacred scripture. Together, they move slowly, capturing the crowd's attention. I grit my teeth, wishing Razor were here. Seamus isn't a commander—he's a shriveled little ballsack in nice clothes.

The first blow of the hammer strikes the board with a sharp THUNK. The iron nail sinks in deeply—and I have a feeling of impending doom. Seamus smoothly reads the names with his characteristic theatrical flair, pausing to let whispers ripple through the crowd. His little shadow giggles after each name, as if on cue.

One by one, names are called out. Some warriors grin, others curse under their breath. My heartbeat remains steady, even as the crowd presses in closer, bodies slick with sweat from drills.

Then Seamus finds *mine*.

"Ahhh," he drawls, lips curling in a smile that makes my knuckles itch. "Reverie. How *thrilling*."

He raises the second parchment high, making sure everyone can see it. The ink isn't still—it moves, as if it's alive, swirling across the page. My stomach tightens. He slams the nail home.

CRACK.

The board shudders. A pulse of blood-red magic

ripples out, hot enough that the hair on my arms stands up. The name beside mine unfurls like a nightmare:

The Varruk.

The crowd reacts as one—ripples of movement, sharp gasps. Even the veterans stiffen. The Varruk isn't just a creature; it's a nightmare with bones. A hulking monstrosity dragged from the wilds of Aurathia, with broad shoulders hunched, powerful limbs, and a thick hide that is nearly impervious to weapons. Its elongated muzzle is filled with rows of sharp teeth, and the strangest part of the creature is the horns arching back, forming a strange crown-like pattern.

Grumpy had told me about them. He'd said that hundreds of years ago, they used to be considered honorable warriors, but now they were little more than predators.

Seamus turns to face the crowd, soaking in the tension as if it were sunlight.

"Try not to die too quickly," he says loudly with a malicious smile on his face. "The spectators do so love a good show."

Laughter spreads—some cruel, some nervous. I don't give him the satisfaction of looking away. Instead, I meet his gaze squarely, steady and sharp. The smile that curls my lips is purposeful, thin, and sharp.

"Don't worry," I say, ensuring they hear me in the back. "I'll make it scream just for you."

Marvin is the first to stop laughing. Seamus's grin flickers—just for a moment.

I hold his gaze like a promise.

I will not die tomorrow, but *they* might.

CHAPTER 10

CHLOE

The guys had been gone all night, and I was drinking coffee with Oliver in the cafeteria, having slept maybe thirty minutes in the last twenty-four hours. I hadn't been able to go to Java and Jam since Reverie had been taken. My guys had brought it to me several times, but I couldn't get through the doors without breaking down in tears.

"When is Deshawn getting back?" I took a big sip of my coffee and grimaced at the strong taste.

"I'm not sure, La'u alofagia. I talked to him about an hour ago, and he's still trying to locate their contact in Aurathia." Oliver kissed my cheek, then drank his coffee down like it was nectar.

"How in the hell do you drink this stuff like it's actually good?" I took another small sip of the hot brew, needing the caffeine.

Oliver shrugged his large shoulders, "It's all the same to me. Nothing compares to the blend I can get on my island."

"It's *your* island?" I bumped my shoulder into his side.

He grinned, revealing bright white teeth shining against his beautiful skin, which I envied. It looked like sun-dappled honey, making me want to lick him all over.

"It is. Soon, after this all ends, I'll take you there. I want to see that beautiful body laid out on the golden sand, with only me covering it." His eyes gleamed with desire, and I felt my nipples stiffen at the look.

I tilted my head back, and he leaned down, pressing those plush lips to mine in a kiss that made my head spin.

"Hey, I'm feeling left out, firefly." Deshawn's voice broke into our moment.

I jerked out of Oliver's embrace and stood, throwing myself into his arms. "Did you find him? Does he have any information about Reverie? Can he get us to Aurathia?"

Deshawn's big, booming laugh filled the room. "Slow down. Let's go somewhere a little more private, and I'll fill you in."

We left quickly and headed to my dorm. They'd both practically moved in, Oliver right after Reverie was taken, and Deshawn the night we all christened my bed with throuple sex. I shivered at the thought of that extraordinary experience. It wasn't the last time it had happened, but it marked the beginning of our relationship, so it was special to me.

We hadn't performed the ritual yet; I'd hoped to get it done this weekend. I wanted these men tied to me in every way possible.

As soon as we entered, Deshawn sat on the couch with me in his lap, while Oliver sat across from us on the coffee table. I hoped the table held up; he wasn't a petite guy by any stretch of the imagination.

"To answer your first question, I did manage to contact him, but our connection wasn't great." He frowned and said, "The important thing is he let me know that Reverie was in the training yard this morning after a few days of absence."

"OMG!! He actually saw her!" The joy I was experiencing was off the chain. "I have to tell the guys… this is *huge!*" I stood and began pacing, rubbing my hands together in excitement. "Maybe he can get a message to her?" I glanced hopefully at Deshawn.

"I'm sorry, firefly. We can't take the risk. If he's caught, our chance of getting information is gone, not to mention his life being forfeit." Deshawn stood and pulled me into his arms, hugging me tightly.

I inhaled his scent. He always smelled like cedarwood and clean soap—steady, warm, the kind of smell that made my shoulders relax without me even noticing. But there was a subtle undercurrent of spice too, distracting but gentle, like heat hiding beneath a calm surface. It wasn't just comforting; it drew me in effortlessly.

"I know you're right. I just want her to know that we haven't given up and we're coming for her." I felt a tear trickle down my cheek. "I can't imagine what she's going through, and it's killing me."

Oliver stood, and I felt his warmth right before he pulled both of us into his massive body. We all just stood there, soaking in the comfort of being together.

The moment was broken abruptly when Pantar popped into the room. *"There is no time to explain. Grab a small bag and come with me immediately. We have a small window to leave, and it's closing rapidly."*

"Where are we going?" Deshawn went from the man I knew to the soldier he'd always been.

"There isn't time to explain, as I've told you. Grab the essentials, and we'll locate the rest when we get to Aurathia." The giant Fellat growled, seeming almost frantic.

I gasped, "You've found a way in?"

"Yes, that's why Mira wanted you to stay behind." Pantar snapped impatiently.

Oliver hadn't asked questions and hurried back into the room with a large backpack. "I've packed a couple of changes of clothes and a few weapons. We're ready when you are."

Deshawn hurried back to the bedroom and returned shortly with a small case that I knew held a Glock 29. We had been practicing with it since we hadn't bonded yet and had no abilities, and Deshawn insisted that even after we did, it would still be a useful skill to have.

"Good choice." Oliver smirked. "I packed my Smith & Wesson 360."

Deshawn nodded in approval, "Reliable little rattlesnake. If anyone fucks with us, the bite will be deadly."

"That it will." Oliver agreed with a grin.

"Enough, it's now or never." Pantar was out of patience. *"I will not miss the chance to get to my bonded Nexus."*

"What about her men? They're going to be livid." I grabbed the boots Deshawn had brought me from our room and pulled them on. I had no idea where we would be when we emerged from the portal.

"They are needed here. There will be a way for them to come when the time is right." Pantar turned and began forming a portal that led to the barn on Reverie's farm.

I knew my brothers would be pissed, and I didn't blame them, but I had a strong need to get to Reverie, and I wouldn't miss this opportunity. I had to trust that Pantar had access to information we didn't possess. Reverie always trusted the giant Fellat, so I would too.

We stepped through, and Mira was waiting on the other side. *"Come, we need to hurry."*

We followed both the Fellats into a small area on the edge of the Hawthornes' property. The morning lay heavy over the clearing, the kind of silence that seemed to hold its breath. Pantar prowled to the center, each step deliberate, panther muscles rolling beneath ink-black fur. Mira joined him without a sound, her golden eyes catching the fractured sunlight as her tentacles unfurled in a slow, deliberate arc.

❧ ⟁ ☙

MIRA

We chose this spot carefully—an old ley-crossing long forgotten by most Aurathions. When portal travel briefly flickered back to life with my return, I'd felt it—a pulse through the ley lines like a heartbeat. And just as quickly, Aurathia sealed it again, unless it was for the DF to enter and leave this world at will.

But we weren't alone.

"*Are you ready?*" I sent the thought to Pantar.

"*Always.*" His mental growl rumbled low. "*Signal him.*"

I closed my eyes, reaching across the void—far beyond the clearing, beyond the sealed skies—to the unbonded Fellat who had answered our silent call. No one in Aurathia knew this connection existed; we'd buried our presence deep, threading our minds through cracks in the wards too small for any watcher to notice.

The reply came faint but sure. "*I'm here. Quickly. Before we are discovered.*"

He would disappear after we accomplished our goal, but I wouldn't expect him to stay.

Pantar thrust his claws into the ground, with tentacles extending downward like deep roots. The earth responded, glowing with silver-blue lines that spread out to reveal ancient sigils. I echoed his gesture, and our combined power intensified, pushing against the unseen barrier Aurathia had created.

The air quivered. A thin slit of light appeared—a crack no wider than a hand-span. Right away, the wards pushed back, sensing pressure but not what was causing it.

"*They can't sense where the breach is.*" I hissed, breathless with effort.

"*Then let's keep it that way,*" Pantar growled back.

We operated in perfect sync; a rhythm refined through months of shared hunts. The unbonded Fellat on the other side poured energy into the breach, carefully threading it to avoid triggering the ward alarms. The fissure widened stubbornly, inch by inch, edges sparking like hot metal.

Pantar's tentacle split, spilling deep red blood, but he

didn't falter. My claws gouged furrows in the dirt as I held the portal's edges with raw determination.

The portal suddenly opened with a sound resembling a gasp dragged through broken glass.

It was unstable, jagged, thrumming with stolen energy —but it was open. And no one on the Aurathion side had the slightest idea.

The portal wasn't meant to exist.

It hissed and crackled at the edges like fragmented lightning, struggling to collapse even as Pantar and I held it open with claw, tentacle, and sheer willpower. The clearing thrummed with unstable energy, silver-blue light tracing ghostly patterns across the grass.

Oliver stood just beyond the glowing sigils, his jaw tight and hands clenched at his sides. I was sure he'd seen portals before, but this? This looked more like a wound than a true portal.

"Is it supposed to look like that?" Deshawn asked, voice low.

Chloe gave a short, humorless laugh. "Does it matter? It's our only way to Reverie." Her curls whipped around her face in the magic-heavy wind, eyes darting between the portal and him.

Pantar's growl rolled through the ground like distant thunder. *"Hurry."* The word wasn't spoken, but it filled our heads, dark and resonant.

My tentacles were braced against the portal's edges like living anchors, my muscles shaking with the effort of keeping the rift stable. *"I can't hold this forever,"* I ground out, sending the urgency I felt to them all.

The three Aurathions exchanged a quick look—no

hesitation, just shared determination. Reverie was trapped in Aurathia. No one else knew this breach existed. If they didn't act now, there might not be another chance.

Oliver's face showed grim determination. Deshawn flanked him, restless energy emanating from him in waves, not feeling the same urgency as the other two since he wasn't Aegisworn—*yet*. Chloe held her ground beside them—face pale in the eerie light but eyes sharp and steady.

The cub of my bonded had chosen well for her Aegisseal.

Pantar moved up behind them, his presence like a silent storm. The massive Fellat's fur shimmered like liquid shadow, amber eyes blazing as he slowly withdrew his tentacles from the ley lines. When he finally pulled free, I bore the full weight of the breach alone. I let out a low, guttural snarl but didn't falter. I would sacrifice everything to bring Adelaide's cub back, even my own life.

"Go now," I sent my voice ripping through their minds, taut with strain. *"All at once."*

Oliver inhaled and nodded to the others. Deshawn cracked a grin that was more malicious than amused. Chloe exhaled through her nose, steadying herself. And Pantar stepped forward, muscles tensing like a spring.

They moved as one.

Oliver was the first to step through the rift, his silhouette shining against the light. Chloe and Deshawn followed closely, swallowed by swirling energy that smelled of ozone and ancient origins. Pantar thundered after them, launching his massive body through the unstable opening with a smooth, flowing leap. The ground trembled beneath him as he vanished into the breach, amber eyes being the last to disappear.

The moment they crossed, I roared. I tightened my tentacles with brutal precision, ripping my connection free and snapping the portal shut before the DF could trace it. The sigils flared, then faded, leaving the clearing silent and dark once again.

No one had detected them. And in my mind's eye I saw four figures—three Aurathions, one Fellat—now on the other side, racing into hostile territory to reach Reverie.

CHAPTER II

REVERIE

The air in the lower hallways clung to me like a damp shroud—cold, heavy, and faintly humming with the old energies of the Ancestors buried in these stones. My fingers brushed the wall as I moved forward, torchlight flickering unevenly ahead. I wasn't supposed to be here. If Selene found out, I didn't want to imagine the punishment I'd face. But the thought of tomorrow's match had wrapped around my ribs like a vise, and curiosity—reckless and persistent—had won over sleep.

I knew where the creatures were being held until our battles started tomorrow, and I had to find out what I was up against. I needed to see if I stood even the slightest chance of winning without using the abilities I had to keep hidden.

I passed through several cells filled with all kinds of nightmare creatures. Some I knew about; others I'd never heard of before. The Varruk's cell was at the end of the long corridor, barred with iron so old it had fused with the stone. Strange runes were carved deeply into the walls, emitting a faint blue glow. This was no ordinary holding cell.

It was a cage for something dangerous.

Something ancient.

He crouched inside like a great beast carved from black stone. Broad shoulders hunched, powerful limbs coiled, thick hide glimmering with the faint oily sheen they were known for. His elongated muzzle rested on his folded arms; horns curved back from his head like a crown forged from darkness. Those ember-bright eyes burned steadily in the shadows.

Chains as thick as my arm wrapped his torso, etched with runes that dug deep. But he wasn't thrashing or snarling.

He was waiting patiently.

My heartbeat quickened as I approached. I'd come here to study him, to gain the upper hand before tomorrow's fight in the coliseum. But the moment his head lifted—slowly, deliberately—that illusion shattered.

His ember eyes found mine through the bars.

I froze.

It wasn't the gaze of a beast spotting prey; it was sharp.

Knowledgeable.

Measured.

He inhaled slowly, chains creaking, and tilted his head. The gesture was subtle but oddly intentional—like a thought made physical. Then, in a fluid motion, he stood up to his full, imposing height.

The runes flared in protest as the chains strained, but

he didn't fight them. Instead, he crossed his massive fore-arms over his chest, dipped his head, and dragged one claw slowly down the center of his sternum—a clean, deliberate stroke that made the hairs on the back of my neck rise.

I didn't know what it meant. But it meant something.

The sound that followed was deep and resonant, echoing from his chest like distant thunder. It wasn't a growl or anything resembling speech, but something that caused the torches to flicker.

I swallowed hard, fingers tightening on the cold iron. "What does that mean?" The question slipped out, shaky and small.

He didn't reply—of course, he didn't—but his eyes gleamed more intensely, and in that moment, something changed. It wasn't hostility or surrender. It was... recognition.

Of me.

Of something *in* me.

But I didn't understand why.

I instinctively took a step back, confusion tightening in my chest. Tomorrow, I was supposed to fight him in the coliseum for my survival. But here, in the dim corridors, I felt like I'd stepped into someone else's story—someone who this creature already knew.

And the way he watched me... it wasn't like he'd just recognized an opponent.

It was like he'd recognized a *queen.*

I stumbled back from the bars, heart slamming against my ribs so hard it hurt. His eyes followed me the whole time—steady, unblinking, as if he'd expected my reaction. As if *this* had happened before.

The sound of that deep, resonant growl still vibrated through my bones when I turned and ran.

The corridor stretched out ahead in a blur of torch-light and shadow. My boots slapped against the damp stone as I sprinted, my breath sharp in my chest. The air felt too thick, too close, pressing in on me like the walls themselves knew something I didn't.

That gesture. The way he had risen, crossed his arms, and dragged his claw down his chest— it wasn't random. It felt... ceremonial. And the way he looked at me— not like prey, not like I was his enemy.

Like a warrior standing before someone they owed allegiance to.

"That's ridiculous," I muttered under my breath, rounding the last corner toward my room. My voice sounded shaky, too loud in the empty halls. "He doesn't know me. He can't."

But the image wouldn't leave my mind—the ember-bright eyes, the flare of the runes, the almost reverent tilt of his head. No creature acts like that toward their opponent before a coliseum match.

They snarl.

They posture.

They try to frighten you.

He hadn't tried to frighten me. He'd *acknowledged* me.

The word lodged in my chest like a thorn. I shoved through the door to my quarters, slammed it shut behind me, and leaned against it, breath ragged. My palms were damp. My pulse still hadn't slowed.

"I'm imagining things," I whispered. But the part of me that had gone still when he looked at me—the part that had *recognized* the recognition—knew I wasn't.

Why had he done that? What did that gesture mean? And why had it felt like something deep inside me understood, even if my mind didn't?

I crossed the room after sealing my door and splashed cold water on my face, trying to clear the fog of adrenaline. The reflection that stared back at me in the mirror looked the same—wild amber eyes, flushed pale skin, midnight tangled hair—but something in my expression had shifted.

He'd looked at me like I was someone else.

Someone he recognized on instinct.

I pressed my palms flat against the sink to steady myself. Tomorrow, the coliseum would roar for blood. The fight would be real. And yet, for the first time, I wasn't just thinking about survival.

I was thinking about those ember eyes... and the way my name—my title—had seemed to echo in them.

Sleep finally dragged me under like a slow, relentless tide. But it wasn't the restless kind I'd expected.

The darkness cracked open. Warm, golden light spilled through towering windows, draping the throne room in brilliance. The air smelled of steel and smoke, cut with something sweet—like crushed flowers. I stood at the center of it all, at once disoriented and entirely home.

Banners of deep crimson trimmed in gold hung from vaulted beams, their embroidered sigils pulsing faintly, infused with my power. My fingertips grazed the arm of a throne I didn't remember but somehow knew. —

And seated upon it—no, I was seated upon it—my body settled with the practiced ease of someone who'd ruled for years. My spine straightened, my chin lifted, and my hands rested lightly on the armrests. A crown's weight—unseen but unmistakable—rested against my temples like a whisper of authority.

To my right, a Fellat stood sentinel.

Graceful and formidable, its panther-like form glinted under the golden light. Two tentacles extended from its shoulders, swaying slowly and smoothly as they sampled the air for danger. Its head was raised confidently, with golden eyes sweeping the throne room. Authority emanated from it—controlled and purposeful. The loyalty it had for me was unmistakable.

I didn't need to look at it to know it was mine.

The heavy doors at the far end of the hall opened with a resonant boom.

They entered.

Six men strode down the long aisle, armor scarred from battle, cloaks stained with dirt and blood. The sight of them hit me in the chest—familiar in a way that hurt.

Ambrose led them, helm tucked under his arm, his presence slicing through the room like a blade. Merritt walked beside him, sharp eyes softening when they landed on me.

Bren followed with that irrepressible glimmer in his eyes, tempered but not extinguished. Zenon's icy precision softened into quiet devotion when our gazes met.

Larkin's movements maintained the cadence of the battlefield—steadfast and rooted—while Kratos moved like a formidable storm—fierce, protective, and unstoppable.

My lovers.

My Faction.

My six.

When they reached the base of the dais, they dropped to one knee in perfect unison. The sound of armor striking marble echoed through the hall like a shared heartbeat.

I opened my mouth to speak or ask a question, but the words that came out weren't mine, even though the voice was.

"You've returned."

The Fellat beside me lowered its head slightly, tentacles curling inward in what felt like a gesture of approval, as if recognizing their return as much as I did.

Emerging from the shadows behind them, the Varruk appeared—unshackled.

Majestic.

Whole.

His ember-bright eyes locked onto mine, and an ancient, unspoken connection seemed to unfold between us, reminiscent of the bond I share with my Fellat. He folded his arms across his chest, traced a claw down his sternum, and then knelt beside the six men.

The sight of everyone kneeling—my Faction, my lovers, this ancient creature, and the Fellat standing tall beside me—made something inside me ache.

I rose from the throne, moving with a grace that wasn't learned but remembered. Ambrose lifted his head first, his sharp gaze softening completely under mine. One by one, the others followed—devotion, love, and the bond shining in each of their faces.

The Fellat beside me gave a low, approving rumble that vibrated through the floor.

A voice echoed through the hall, not from any one mouth, but from the air itself.

"All hail our beloved Queen Lilibet."

The words hit me deeply, resonating within places I hadn't realized existed.

The golden light fractured, then the hall dissolved as if someone had thrown a stone through a reflection. I gasped awake, sitting bolt upright in the darkness of my room, breath ragged.

Their faces.

The Varruk's gesture. The Fellat by my side.

It hadn't felt like a dream.

It had felt like *remembering*.

❧ ☙

The first pale light of dawn slipped through the narrow window, painting faint lines across the floorboards. I hadn't really slept after the dream—if it even was a dream. My eyes were gritty, my body restless, my mind replaying every second of that golden hall on a loop.

When I finally pushed myself upright, something felt… different.

Not wrong, but not exactly right, either. Just *changed*.

The air in the room felt sharper, somehow clearer. I could hear the drip of water in the distant halls as if it were right beside me. My heartbeat sounded louder, as if the world had turned up its volume and forgotten to tell me.

I swung my legs over the side of the bed, rubbing at my temples. A faint warmth pulsed there, lingering from the crown that had faded hours ago. When I exhaled, the flame in the small wall sconce across the room wavered—even though no breeze had touched it.

My chest tightened. "That's new."

I stretched out a hesitant hand toward the flame. Not close enough to touch it—just... toward it. And the strangest thing happened.

The space between us shimmered faintly, as heat rising from stone. For a brief moment, the flame leaned toward me, reacting as if it sensed my call.

My breath caught, and the shimmer snapped back. The flame steadied.

I stared at my hand. I could use fire as a weapon, and I could move objects from a distance, but I'd never thought to control a flame that already existed with my telekinesis.

I slowly stood, every sense heightened. Something was humming inside me now—soft yet persistent. I pressed my palms against the cool stone wall, still trying to understand the flickering flame and the strange thrum beneath my skin. Fire was familiar—it was the bond, the Faction, the wild, fierce part of me that shared Oren's flame.

But this... this wasn't *that*.

It wasn't loud. It was quiet. Ancient. A thread pulling somewhere beneath the surface, like something was calling from deep inside my soul.

I closed my eyes and focused. It felt like all of Aurathia was holding its breath.

And then—faintly—I heard it.

Not quite a voice. More like a whisper pressed against my bones, a time I didn't recognize but somehow felt part of, slipping through the edges of my mind like smoke through a keyhole.

A presence.

My heart stuttered. "Who's there?"

The air shifted—warmer and more loaded. I sensed the presence more clearly. Not menacing, just watching. Familiar in a way that made my chest hurt.

I stumbled back toward the bed, pulse hammering. "Okay. Nope. This is… creepy as hell."

But the whisper followed. Not so much a sound, but from *inside*. It brushed along my consciousness with the lightest touch, like fingers trailing ice along my spine. One word rose clear, carrying a weight that made gooseflesh race up my arms:

"Child."

I froze.

The word wasn't threatening or questioning; it was knowing—similar to a voice from a dream you recognize but can't quite place when you wake up.

Images flickered in my mind: a line of women standing beneath starlight, their silhouettes wreathed in flames; ancient Fellat padding silently at their sides; a crown being passed from hand to hand, generation after generation.

And then, a voice—Clearer now, feminine, strong, threaded with that same authority I'd heard in my dream.

"You are not the first."

My breath hitched. "Who… are you?" I whispered into the empty room.

Silence answered.

Then the presence dimmed, fading like mist in the

morning sun. The humming inside me quieted but didn't vanish. It settled somewhere beneath my ribs—waiting.

I pressed a hand to my chest, the echo of that single word still reverberating in my bones.

This wasn't fire. This wasn't an ability I'd gained through my Faction.

This was blood-deep. A door I hadn't even known existed had opened, and on the other side were the voices of those who'd come before me.

Ancestors.

Queen Lilibet hadn't just ruled. She'd carried the weight of a lineage. And now, somehow, that *lineage* had found me.

CHAPTER 12
JET

We'd returned to the house at Emberhold. Zeke and Zane went to find Chloe, Oliver, and Deshawn to update them on everything that had happened.

I went to the basement, where Emberhold had seen fit to put a full workout room for our benefit. It seemed that every day I came home to a new addition of some kind or another. Growing up human, it was hard to get used to some of this shit.

I needed to relieve some stress, and for now, this was all I had. There were no new DF to torture, and I needed an outlet badly. If we didn't find a way to Reverie soon, I was afraid I was going to lose my mind. Seeing a piece of her in a box left me in a murderous rage. If I ever got my hands on that bitch Selene, I would pluck her eyes out and shove them up her ass.

I'd just started running on the treadmill when I heard

shouting from upstairs. "What the fuck now?" I muttered, stopping the treadmill and heading upstairs.

Oren stood frowning at the twins, "What are you yelling about?"

"Chloe and the guys are G-O-N-E!" Zane spelled the last word, obnoxiously.

Oren frowned at him. "Maybe they went to help out at one of the relief stations."

Zeke started pacing. "We checked, Mom hasn't heard from them, and neither has Adelaide."

"They could be anywhere. There's no reason to panic," Oren said with little inflection in his tone. He'd been mostly unresponsive since we got back from the Hawthorne's. I knew his mind was working overtime trying to find a way to reach our Nexus.

I hated seeing Zeke and Zane become so agitated. Both were dangerously close to losing control, and with the Draxon inside them, we were concerned about what might happen if they didn't keep a firm grip on themselves. Transforming now wasn't a good idea.

Well, everybody but Nathan was concerned. He was constantly fucking with the two men, hoping they *would* change.

"We're not panicking without reason; it's not like Chloe to disappear without leaving at least a note. She knows, ever since Reverie was taken, that we've been on edge about her safety." Zeke continued more calmly. "And with Mom and Adelaide not knowing where she is, we're both understandably worried."

Oren's cell rang. I don't know how he managed to have

a working phone, but at this point, I'd come to realize Oren was more powerful than he let on.

"What the fuck?!" We all came to attention at Oren's tone. "Mira said WHAT?!" Oren was near screaming at this point.

Before he could say another word, a portal appeared in our living room, and Mira stepped out. The Fellat looked a little bedraggled, and the expression in her eyes was more than weary.

"Don't shout at my Nexus, Storm. It wasn't her decision to send them; it was mine." She sent the message out so forcefully that I winced in pain.

Oren narrowed his eyes at her. "Why?"

"I don't have to explain myself to you, but since I understand what it means to be separated from your Nexus, I'll excuse this behavior and tell you." She lowered herself to her haunches and shrank her size down to that of a large bobcat.

"Why is the door wide open?" Nathan walked in with blood on his shirt.

I guess he needed to blow off some steam, too. I narrowed my eyes. Was that bastard hiding DF from me?

"I'm not completely sure, but it has something to do with my sister and her guys not being here," Zane growled low, never taking his eyes off of Mira.

Once again, his pupils had narrowed to slits, and his Draxon was in control. I didn't know who would win in a fight, but if Mira's explanation didn't satisfy the animal inside him, we might find out.

"Chloe, Oliver, and Deshawn were needed there now. *You*

are needed here *for the time being.*" Mira stared into Oren's eyes and slowly blinked.

"What do you know that you're not telling me?" Oren gritted out.

"Wait, are you telling us that you found a way to send Chloe to Aurathia?" Nathan asked in a voice almost devoid of life.

Mira just looked at him and nodded.

Nathan went off like a bomb.

One heartbeat, he was standing there, trembling with tension. Next, the cabinet door burst off its hinges and slammed into the wall with a crack that shook the entire house. Then the chair. He shattered it into splinters, flames flickering along his arms as the air grew hot and sharp, heavy with the threat of disaster.

None of us moved.

Zeke leaned against the counter, eyes slitted, radiating cold that had ice forming on the walls near him. Zane stood near the couch, a deep, guttural growl rolling through his chest. Oren's shadows slid across the floor like a living thing, coiling around his boots.

"She—" Nathan's voice broke before turning jagged. "You sent *Chloe*?" He punched through the drywall with a sickening thud, dragging his hand downward and leaving a smear of blood and scorch marks. Fire seemed to consume him completely.

Zeke muttered softly, with a hint of Draxon, "This is new. He's going to torch the place."

"Let him," I said, feeling the need to join my Faction brother in his destruction. "Better the walls than one of us."

Nathan turned on us, flames flickering across his skin. His gaze locked on Zeke. Zeke's Draxon flared, pupils narrowing, cold rippling off him.

Zane's growl grew deeper as he saw Nathan's focus on his brother. The room seemed on the verge of an explosion.

And then the shadows shifted.

Mira had stood once again, at her full size. Her sleek gold fur glimmered in the light, only outshone by her golden eyes burning with something older than time. From each shoulder, a tentacle flexed slowly, alive and tasting the air.

The temperature dropped. Even Nathan's fire hesitated.

Her fierce roar slammed into my head like a physical blow.

"Enough."

Nathan froze—not because he wanted to, but because none of us were capable of ignoring that voice.

"She was needed. You all need to stay. You're not finished with the tasks that are vital to saving this world."

Nathan's fire sputtered around the edges, caught between fury and confusion. His chest heaved, heat bleeding off him in waves.

Zeke's Draxon energy rippled beneath his skin, but he didn't challenge her. Zane's growl faded to an uneasy hum. Oren's shadows withdrew like loyal hounds, giving her space.

Mira prowled closer to Nathan. One tentacle brushed his cheek, with what looked like affection. *"You will get to your Nexus when the time is right. This I vow to you."*

Nathan didn't raise his voice or escalate further. He simply remained there, trembling amidst the wreckage, with his rage no longer raging intensely but instead smoldering quietly, no less dangerous.

Mira scanned the rest of us—a look that held each of us in place. Then, she slipped back into a portal and disappeared.

The silence left behind in her wake was deafening.

The quiet lingered for a few seconds more, then Zane blew out a breath, shoulders rolling like he was shaking off the Draxon's control. "Well," he muttered, "that wasn't even a little fucked up."

Zeke let out a sharp exhale through his nose. "She knows more than she's prepared to say. What are we going to do?" His voice was low and careful, as if he were trying to wrestle back control from his beast.

Oren stayed by the wall, shadows still coiled tight. His eyes were locked on Nathan.

Nathan hadn't moved. He stood in the wreckage, hands bloodied, shoulders heaving. The flames were gone, but the heat lingered, clinging to him like a second skin.

I stepped closer, slowly, like approaching a cornered animal. "I want to be with our Nexus as badly as you do, brother."

He looked up at me, eyes still burning faintly, something raw behind them. "I can't go on without her for much longer."

I didn't have an answer to that. I didn't think any of us did. I hoped we could face whatever challenge awaited us and reach Reverie before we all imploded.

I woke up the next morning and had an urge to check in with Josh. He'd been invaluable in helping me stay up to date with all of the military operations. We'd even been involved in planning several counterattacks when we received information about DF encampments. Unfortunately, after most attacks, the opposing forces returned to Aurathia through a portal, preventing us from returning the favor.

I got dressed quickly and found Oren already at his desk, working. Zane was in the kitchen rummaging through the cabinets. "Can I use your phone? I need to contact Josh."

"Is something going on I need to know about?" Oren retrieved his phone and handed it to me.

"No, I just felt the need to talk to him." I took the phone and dialed Josh.

Oren raised his brow. "This might be an ability."

Zane walked over to us, chewing on a chicken leg. "It's about time something showed up. I was beginning to think his ability was being a giant dickhole."

I listened to the phone ring from the other side and flipped Zane off. "No. I've always had feelings about certain things. That's what made me a good soldier." I smirked. "Dickhole comes naturally."

"What the fuck?! Did he make a joke?" Zane laughed in disbelief.

"Hey brother, good to hear from you." Josh's cheery

voice came across the line. "I was just about to contact you."

"What's up?" The man was happy in the middle of a gun battle, so just because he sounded cheerful didn't mean we weren't thirty seconds away from an apocalypse.

"I found out about an attack on one of our last two air bases, Joint Base Langley in Virginia. If they destroy that base, it'll be over for us, and we'll lose the capital." He snorted, "Our leaders don't like to give credit to your friends, but we'd already be done if it weren't for them."

"How can I help?" The man took forever to get to the point.

"You know, sometimes a man likes to be romanced. Not just jump straight into the action." Josh sighed in exasperation.

"I'm not that kind of guy. Now what do you need?" It was my turn to sigh.

"Could you, Deshawn, and the rest of the Fantastic Five head this way to help us plan the base's defense? It might be a chance for you to save the capital and get a ride through a portal into Aurathia a week before Copper Creek." I could hear the pleading in his voice. "Also, you still owe me for saving your life."

My heart started beating faster. This would get us into Aurathia much sooner than anticipated. And maybe the attack was the reason we needed to stay behind.

"Let me talk to Oren." I sighed. "And you most definitely didn't save my life." He was still talking when I hung up. The man could go on for hours, and I didn't have that kind of time.

Oren was watching me closely. "What's got you looking positively giddy?"

Zane snorted, "How can you tell? Looks like resting bitch face to me."

I ignored him. "Josh has heard word of an attack coming on an air base in Virginia and wants our help deterring the DF." I saw his eyes light up with the same excitement as mine.

"Maybe that's why we needed to stay behind. If we stop the attack, we can use their portal to get to Reverie." He was reaching for his phone even before he stopped speaking.

"Gather the guys and let's head to the Hawthorne's. We can get to Virginia and Josh and start making plans." He began speaking into the phone, and I knew I was dismissed.

That's part of the reason I liked the guy, straight to the point and on a mission. None of the bullshitting everyone else around me so enjoyed.

Hold on, Angel. We're coming.

CHAPTER 13

REVERIE

The fight in the coliseum was less than an hour away, and I still hadn't decided how to escape this predicament. I paced nervously in the designated warm-up area. Defeating the Varruk seemed impossible, and I sensed it might not even be necessary. His respectful attitude suggested he might choose not to fight me at all.

"So, you're fighting the Varruk?" I turned and saw Torren standing there with a frown on his face.

"Seems that way." I smiled. "You don't think I can take him?" I joked to keep from crying.

He frowned in disapproval, "You shouldn't make light of this. I've seen them fight, and they are basically undefeatable."

"Do I have a choice? Better to get through it with humor than to cry." I smirked, "Can you imagine me bawling on the floor? That would really tank my street cred."

"What the hell is street cred?" He asked, tilting his head to the side like a questioning puppy.

"It doesn't matter. I need to warm up, maybe for the last time." I tried to laugh, but it fell flat.

"When do you go on?" He grabbed one of my short swords and checked it for sharpness. Then he handed it back to me and motioned for me to give him the other one.

"In a little less than an hour." I raised one brow. "Do you want to help me escape?" I joked.

"There's no time for that." Torren pulled me into an alcove to give us some privacy away from the other warriors. "Listen closely. The Varruk does have one weakness. Their hide is incredibly thick, but directly under their chin is a spot that's thin enough for a sword to penetrate." Torren grabbed my arm and pulled me closer as a couple of men walked near the alcove, bringing his mouth to my ear. "You'll have to work to get him to expose it, but I have faith you'll be successful." I shivered at the feeling of his warm breath on my ear. He startled me when he grabbed my chin to stare directly into my eyes. "You will survive. I won't accept any other outcome." He pressed his lips to mine, kissing me so hard that it was almost painful.

I was so stunned by his actions that it took me a moment to recover from the shock, and by then he had already disappeared. "What the actual fuck?" I whispered, touching a finger to my lips that were still tingling.

I didn't know what to think, but right now, I needed to get my head in the game. I walked out of the alcove and started my warm-up. I remembered Grumpy telling me that sometimes, when things are out of your control, all you can do is handle each thing as it comes. This was definitely one of those times.

Hopefully, a solution will present itself; if not, I'll do what I've always done and find a way to survive.

Long before I was ready, I heard Seamus calling me to the front to prepare for my entrance. "Come, Reverie, it's your time to die." He laughed at what he thought was witty banter. The only one who laughed with him was, of course, Marvin the toady.

With all emotion gone from my face, I stepped toward the doorway, waiting to hear my name. I had participated in many of these battles, yet the butterflies fluttering in my stomach made it hard to believe.

I heard the announcer say in a dramatic voice, "Now we have a special treat for you. Our current undefeated warrior, Reverie Hawthorne, will fight the dreaded *Varruk!*" The crowd roared. He spread his arms wide. "Wait, wait, there's more, my lovies."

What the fuck? How could there be more? Seamus glanced over at me before heading to the stands with an evil smirk on his face. "That can't be good," I mumbled under my breath.

The announcer continued, "A surprise guest will join the Varruk...*Cryptfiends*!!!!" The roar of the crowd was so loud at this point that it drowned out the rest of what the announcer was saying. Then I heard, "Come out, Reverie of the Hawthorne Faction, show us what you're really made of!"

The air was alive—pulsing, searing—like the entire coliseum breathed as one massive beast waiting for blood.

My blood.

Sand hissed beneath my boots as the sun burned mercilessly overhead. I stared up at the cloud-filled sky, and I wondered if it would be the last thing I ever saw.

Then the gate groaned.

The Varruk stepped through the iron maw.

Caged, he'd looked monstrous—but out here, under the sun, he was something else entirely. His skin caught the light like weathered bronze, scars mapped stories I didn't want to know. His eyes found me immediately.

No rage.

No bloodlust.

Just… awareness.

Recognition.

He dragged the weapon they'd allotted him on the ground, heavy steel scraping across the sand. When the gate clanged shut, he didn't lift it. Didn't move.

I braced myself.

Waiting for the charge.

For the roar.

But the sound that ripped through the coliseum wasn't his.

The earth split open—*literally split*—and three Cryptfiends clawed their way out, all teeth and sinew, dripping rot, followed closely by dozens more. The crowd went feral, chanting for a kill.

Unfortunately, I didn't think it was in my support. I felt a moment of desperation and then… *acceptance*. No way I could win against the Varruk and dozens of Cryptfiends.

I locked eyes with the Varruk, and to my surprise, he made that same strange gesture to me as he had in the cell and in my dream the previous night. Then turned his back on me and roared—not at me, *for* me. A sound that vibrated in my bones, older than memory. Before I could react, he swung his blade and split a Cryptfiend in half. Black ichor hit my cheek, hot and reeking of death.

The second creature lunged straight for me. I met it halfway, steel flashing in an arc. My right blade buried deep in its jaw; my left tore across its throat. Black blood hit my chest like rain.

The Varruk was beside me before the body hit the ground. We fought in sync—his brute strength breaking through armor, my blades finding every gap and soft spot —a rhythm built between us—violent, perfect. I didn't think; I just moved, reacting to him as if we'd fought together for years.

The last Cryptfiends tried to flank me, but the Varruk intercepted. His weapon shattered both of their skulls with one clean strike.

Silence fell.

Then he dropped to his knees in front of me and tilted his head back—exposing the kill spot under his chin.

A gesture of surrender. Or allegiance.

My grip on the swords tightened. I could end him. End all of this. But my body refused to move. My pulse roared louder than the crowd. The place on my wrist that Pantar had bitten to bond us together, thrummed, hot and bright, like it recognized something in him.

The air between us shifted—heavy, electric.

I met his eyes. "Why?"

No answer. Just that look, steady and unflinching, like he'd been waiting for me long before I was ever born.

The crowd screamed for blood, but I barely heard them. Strangely, I thought I heard a Fellat, *my* Fellat, roar somewhere in the distance.

I stepped forward, blades slick and trembling in my hands, and whispered, "Please, stand with me."

He did. Slowly. Then gave me a regal nod of approval.

The crowd erupted—chaos and fury and disbelief—but I only heard my heartbeat. And I knew the coliseum would never see a fight like this again. Never would a supposed enemy fight alongside their foe the way the Varruk and I had.

For one breathless moment, there was nothing but the echo of his weapon hitting the ground. The Varruk stood by my side proudly, blood and dust streaking both of us from head to toe.

Then—chaos.

"Finish him, girl!" Seamus's voice split the silence like a whip.

He stood in the upper tier of the stands, his face flushed from wine and fury. I could see the veins pulsing in his neck even from here.

I didn't move.

His sneer deepened. "Do it, or I'll have you dragged in front of your betters and punished!"

The crowd fed on his rage, chanting for a kill. But I could feel something else moving under the surface—a tension, an awareness. The Varruk hadn't just surrendered; he'd chosen. And whatever he'd chosen, it terrified Seamus.

He shouted again, "Guards!"

I heard the click of crossbows from the platform above the gate. Four soldiers aimed down at the Varruk's head.

My body moved before my mind caught up. I stepped between them.

Gasps rippled through the stands. The guards hesitated, uncertain.

Seamus's expression twisted from fury to disbelief. "You insolent little—"

"Try it, and you'll regret it." I slid my swords into their sheaths and prepared to reveal my hidden abilities. I wouldn't… no, I couldn't let them hurt him if I could stop it.

The Varuk turned his gaze to me, and in his eyes, I saw respect for me and his allegiance.

Seamus screamed in rage, "You'll regret this, Reverie Hawth—"

The Varruk's growl cut him off. The sound was deep enough to rattle the sand under my boots.

Seamus flinched. Just slightly—but enough that I saw it.

I took another step forward, pulling my blades from their sheaths and raising both so they caught the sunlight.

"The crowd came for blood," I said, voice carrying across the arena. "And they got it. Dozens of monsters down." I tilted my head, eyes locking on Seamus.

Before he could respond, a voice that sent chills down my spine spoke. "Finish him."

Her voice alone raised the temperature in the arena. Selene appeared at the edge of the observation box; black silk clothing that revealed the menace she carried, hair like gold, her tight smile filled with evil—the kind of control that hides madness.

Seamus tried to match her authority and failed miserably. "You heard her!" He bellowed. "*End it!*"

The crowd took up the chant again, bloodthirsty and eager.

I didn't move.

The Varruk's breath was heavy and deliberate. He wasn't begging—it was almost as if he was giving me permission to sacrifice him to save myself. And something in me refused to obey.

"No," I said softly. Hoping my voice didn't carry the terror I was feeling at this moment.

It was almost a whisper, but the word landed *hard*. The crowd wavered. Seamus blinked. And Selene's lips froze halfway through another command.

"What did you say?" She whispered in disbelief.

"I said *no.*" This time, much firmer than before.

Her composure shattered. The mask cracked from one heartbeat to the next. "You dare defy me?" The sweetness vanished from her tone—what came out was pure venom. "You think *mercy* makes you noble? You think it makes you a *hero?*" Her eyes went wild, bright with rage. The air around her seemed to bend with it, silk fluttering though there was no wind. "Kill him," she hissed again, "or I'll—"

"Enough."

The word rolled through the arena like thunder.

It came from above.

The sound of it silenced everything—even the crowd's roar died mid-breath. The air itself seemed to hold still.

Selene stiffened. Her head turned upward in disbelief. Her fury faltered, if only for a second.

High above the stands, past the golden glare of sunlight and the dust drifting through it, I saw him—a silhouette framed in shadow. The light hit just behind him, leaving his features lost, only the hard lines of a tall figure standing on a private balcony far above the crowd.

His voice carried again, smooth, deep, and unyielding. "Stand. Down."

The words weren't shouted. They didn't need to be. They carried weight—Not the kind born of fear, but command so absolute it could not be denied.

Selene's shoulders went rigid. Her mouth opened, then closed again. "Tr—" she started, voice trembling between reverence and panic.

"I said," the man interrupted, each word precise as a strike. "*stand down.*"

For the first time in my memory, Selene looked small. Her jaw clenched; her hand trembled as she gripped the rail. Seamus shrank beside her, suddenly eager to be invisible.

The shadowed man turned his head slightly, not toward Selene, but toward *me*.

Even from that distance, I sensed it. The urge to follow whatever he commanded. The strange awareness rooted me to the spot. My fingers clenched around my hilts, the metal slick with sweat and blood.

The Varruk stood beside me, his massive frame blocking part of the sun. He didn't bow. Didn't look away. He just watched that silhouette with something close to recognition and *hate*.

Selene's fury simmered beneath her silence. "You can't mean to let her—"

"I can," the man said quietly, "and I do."

A hush rippled through the crowd. The balance of power had shifted—and everyone could feel it.

Selene's glare fell on me, her voice low and shaking with contained rage. "This isn't over."

I only nodded, my voice too thick with fear to speak.

Her eyes held mine for a moment more, then she turned and bowed her head to the man.

The man's silhouette lingered a moment longer, then he turned, cloak catching the light as he disappeared back into the shadows.

For a long heartbeat, the coliseum held its breath. Then, slowly, the crowd erupted. Fear and awe were clearly displayed in the sound.

Suddenly, I heard in my head, *"I've been waiting for you for a long time, my Queen."*

I exhaled, still in shock, and narrowed my eyes at the Varruk. "Lucy, you have some 'splaining to do." As comebacks went, it was weak, but it was the best I could do right then. Besides, I'd watched the old black-and-white television series with Grumpy on many occasions, and I always loved that line.

The place where the silhouette had stood still gleamed with sunlight—but all I could feel was the weight of eyes I couldn't see, and the certainty that whoever he was… he'd have a part in my fate here on out.

CHAPTER 14

REVERIE

After the fight concluded, I was instructed to stay in my room until further notice. The Varruk, whom I was calling Vee in my head (since he hadn't revealed his real name), was once again confined to his cage.

I tilted my head back and let the water wash away the blood and guts until it ran clear, then took the chance to try and sort through everything I was feeling.

On one hand, I was thrilled that I had stood up to Selene and actually won. Vee would live to fight another day, and the connection I felt to him was safe for now.

I stepped out of the shower and dried off. Pulling a clean pair of pants and a shirt on, I loosely braided my hair and sat on my bed.

On the other hand, who knew what the consequences would be for everything that happened? Selene was probably going to tear my spleen out of my asshole or something just as gruesome. The bitch never ran out of ideas when it came to torture.

And who was that man in the coliseum who had no fear of Selene? Was it Trent Storm? I've seen even Ubel hesitate to contradict her. She looked pissed at his interference but still deferred to him with little argument.

I flopped back and curled up with Nathan's pillow. After the day I'd had, sending me to my room without supper wasn't that horrible. I was exhausted anyway.

My eyes fluttered closed, and I drifted off.

"Oooh, my Ancestors, that feels amazing." I breathe as Kratos's mouth moves slowly down my stomach to the apex of my thighs. He nips and licks up and down my slit before sucking my clit into his mouth.

I arched my back and then opened my eyes when I felt a mouth on each of my breasts. Ambrose gently flicks his tongue over one nipple as Merritt sucks on my other breast feverishly. The dual sensations force an orgasm out of me that's almost painful in its intensity.

Before I even have time to recover, Bren is shoving Kratos out of the way, flipping me over, and entering me in one savage thrust. He's enormous, and even though we've done this more times than I can count, the stretch is still a little painful. That is soon forgotten when he starts thrusting into me.

Zenon kneels in front of me, and I take his cock into my mouth. He begins to pump in and out roughly, groaning as I open my throat, taking him deep. Bren's movements become more savage as he grabs me around the waist with his huge hands, using the leverage to pound even further into me. When I clamp down on him, he stiffens and groans out his release.

Zenon takes his place as Kratos lies under me and begins to suckle on my breasts while running his hand up and down his velvet shaft.

I mentally send out my shadows, and they curl around Ambrose and Merritt. Both of them fall to their backs and arch and moan as the shadows move over their cocks gently squeezing then releasing, mimicking the feel of my pussy contracting around them.

All that can be heard are moans and gasps as we all get closer to our release. Zenon's movements become savage, and my shadows pulse and release on my men's cocks in time with our movements.

I see Ambrose stiffen as cum erupts out of his cock. "Fuuuck!"

The sight of that causes my pussy to pulse. Kratos pinches my clit, and immediately another orgasm rips through me. I hear multiple groans and filthy words as the rest of my men follow right behind.

We clean up, then the guys cuddle around me in our giant bed, holding me close as we start to fall asleep.

"I love you, Lil," Kratos whispers in my ear. "Never forget that."

I smile and whisper before drifting off, "I love you too."

Too bad I didn't recognize the desperation in his voice for what it was.

I awoke gasping and felt more aroused than I'd been in a long time. "What in the hell was that?" I whispered into the dark room.

"Watch and learn, child. All is not what it seems."

Well shit! I guess the voice I'd heard wasn't my imagination after all. I'd known it *wasn't*, but I had hoped I was wrong.

I thought that I'd never be able to go back to sleep, but I was mistaken and drifted off within minutes. This time, there were no dreams, only peace.

～⚛～

I left my room early the next morning to head to breakfast. I hadn't made it ten steps down the corridor before the air shifted. That damp, metallic tang —the scent of blood baked into stone —still clung to the walls. It reminded me of yesterday's match, and I shivered at the memory.

It was at that moment that Seamus found me. He was leaning against a pillar, arms folded, the smirk already waiting for me, sharp, like a knife he wanted to twist in my gut. "Morning, little champion," he drawled. "Sleep well after your *grand* act of mercy?"

I kept walking. If I looked at him, I'd lose the thin thread of calm I had left.

"You know," he went on, matching my pace, "it's funny. The creature you spared—spent the night screaming in agony."

I stopped, just for a heartbeat. It was enough for him to see the crack.

"It turns out a Varruk is as tough as it's reported to be," Seamus added, voice low now, almost gleeful. "They said it nearly broke its bindings. Took six men and the drugging ability of one of the guards to keep it down. One poor bastard lost his arm. But eventually the creature did scream. Over and over."

The corridor blurred for a second. My throat went tight, my hands useless at my sides.

"You're lying," I said, though my voice betrayed me.

He chuckled, brushing past, close enough that his shoulder grazed mine. "Believe what you want, Hawthorne *bitch*. Just know that whatever bond you started in that arena—you won't be able to finish it."

He left me standing there, breath shaking, heart pounding like a drum in my ribs. The smell of spiced oatmeal and bacon wafted faintly from the hall ahead, but my appetite was gone.

Several floors below where I was standing, Vee was caged, probably in terrible pain, regretting saving my life against the Cryptfiends.

❧ ◬ ☙

The tunnels under the coliseum always carried a musty smell of rust and decay—like the very air was spoiled. I told myself I just needed to verify Seamus's words—that Vee had been badly hurt. I didn't want to disturb him if he was resting, but I needed to be certain he was alright. I descended the stone steps until the torchlight faded and the silence grew heavy.

Then I saw him.

The cell was half-collapsed from his earlier frenzy, bars twisted as if something enormous had pressed out from within. He crouched near the center, much larger than a man—shoulders bowed, head hung low, the shape of a snout catching the flicker of the torch.

Not human. Not entirely a monster either.

The sound reached me first—not a voice, but a vibration that settled behind my eyes.

"You shouldn't be down here."

I froze. His lips didn't move, but the growl threaded straight through my skull much like Pantar communicated with me.

"They'll know."

"I had to make sure you were okay," I whispered, though the words felt absurd in the damp air. "Seamus said you were injured."

A low rumble rolled from his chest, not laughter—something much rougher, like the growl of a lion. The sound made the torch gutter.

"These weak Aurathions with their perverted abilities couldn't kill one such as myself." There was a hint of amusement in his voice.

He moved closer, dragging his shackles, claws gouging the stone. The faint torchlight highlighted the edges of his teeth—too many, too sharp, meant for tearing, not talking.

"You carry the old fire," he said, his words scraping like claws on bone, "the scent of queens long gone."

My breath hitched. "You mean Lilibet?"

At her name, the air shifted. The tension between us hummed, a delicate high note that quivered through the cage bars. I watched him turn his wrist—the Aegisseal mark—the tree of life within a circle.

He stared at me intently through the bars. *"Blood remembers blood."*

The words hit, and a shiver went up my spine.

"Go, little heir. Before they make you watch me die."

The chains rattled as he stepped back, fading into the darkness, with all signs of sentience gone from his stance. Only the beast remained.

I ran back up the stairs to my room. The shock of seeing the mark that Chloe and Oliver wore on his wrist, tearing through my mind. I had to get him out of here—there was no other choice.

By morning, the entire place was buzzing with the same rumor—that the Varruk had paid for his defense of me in the coliseum.

Kristine and her Faction mocked me with it during breakfast, with Evan screaming in pretend agony and collapsing on the floor.

I still hadn't heard anything from Selene, and I was beyond grateful. I needed to focus all of my attention on Vee. I had to admit it was nice to have my focus on someone else, other than my own shitty situation.

A plan was beginning to take shape.

All day, the thought nagged at me—what if I could stop the next round of torture? Vee's eyes had haunted me through every corridor. He hadn't been pleading for his life. He'd been more concerned for my safety.

By dusk, I'd memorized the guards' rotations outside the coliseum: four posted at each gate, two at the stairwell that led down to his cage. They changed shifts every hour, the schedule precise.

I spent the afternoon in the training yard, no sign of Torren, and for that I was glad. I needed my mind on the mission with no distractions. And after that kiss, he *was* a distraction.

My plan wasn't perfect, but it was the only one I had, and Vee's life depended on me making it happen.

By the time night fell again, the plan had teeth. I'd slip down to the section of the building where I'd awoken after Kristine's attack. My mouse friends had led me to an old door that opened into a network of tunnels deep under the dungeon, where the Vee and the other creatures were being held. From there, it was an easy climb through a trapdoor at the end of the corridor where Vee's cell was located.

He was awake when I reached the cage this time. *"You came back."*

"You said they'd kill you," I whispered. "They'll kill me, too, if they know I'm here."

"Then why are you here?"

"Because I can't watch another thing die in that arena for someone else's amusement."

Something like admiration shown in his eyes. *"Mercy is dangerous, little heir."*

"Good," I said. "So am I."

"More than you know." His voice was so faint in my head that I almost didn't catch it.

I crouched at the base of the cage. The lock was sealed, but my Aegisseal ability was much stronger. I pressed my palm against the iron, and it sizzled, my ability fighting against the one who had sealed it. Energy surged up my arm, white and scalding, and my ability rushed to meet it.

"You can undo what others have sealed?"

"We'll soon find out." My voice shook, but I didn't let go.

The lock gave with a metallic crack that echoed

through the tunnels. Vee surged forward, stopping just short of me. Torchlight danced across his snout, those predator's teeth glinting inches from my face.

"I owe you a death."

My breath caught. "A death?"

"Not yours."

He turned, claws gouging deep into the stone, and with a single strike, ripped the door off the cage next to his. The sound thundered through the corridor.

"Run." He sent the word a snarl in my skull. *"They'll come."*

"I'm not done," I frantically looked around. "We need a distraction."

He tilted his head, a low growl vibrating through the floor. His thoughts brushed mine again—gritty, savage, but curious. *"What do you intend, little heir?"*

I pointed across the corridor. Rows of cages lined the walls— lesser creatures used for training or blood sport. Hybrids. Things that had been alive too long in the dark.

"They deserve out," I said. "Or at least a chance to run."

Vee's nostrils flared, that low thunder rumbling again —amusement? Approval? Hard to tell. *"Then break their chains."*

Together, we moved. I used my ability to break the sealed locks; he tore through bars with raw strength. The moment the third cage gave, a shriek ripped through the tunnels—part bird, part nightmare. Then another. And another.

Soon, the corridor seethed with movement—scaled bodies, fur, wings, claws scraping stone as the freed creatures surged toward the stairwell.

The alarm bells hadn't even started ringing yet.

Vee turned toward the sound of approaching guards, the glow of his eyes catching the torchlight. *"You should run now."*

"I'm not leaving until you're out of here." I was filled with adrenaline as I searched for our way out.

"You already have." He lunged forward, slamming his claws into the ceiling arch. The stone cracked, collapsing into the passage just as shouts echoed above.

The impact threw me to the ground—dust choking the air. When I looked up, he was gone, vanished into the shadows beyond the rubble.

Screams rose through the tunnels—the freed beasts tearing through the guards' ranks.

I staggered to my feet, heart hammering. I'd done it.

My friend was free. Now I needed to get out of here before I was discovered.

I couldn't imagine my punishment for this level of destruction if Selene found out what I'd done.

CHAPTER 15

OREN

"Shut the fuck up!" Nathan yelled at everyone sitting at the large table.

Sylvester, one of the longest-running council members, narrowed his eyes at him. "You can't speak to us like that."

Nathan's entire body lit up with flames, "Why the fuck not?"

Ever since his ability had leveled up, he never missed an opportunity to "flame up", as he liked to call it. It was a cool look, but I'd never admit it out loud to the idiot.

I blew out an exasperated breath. "What my Faction brother is trying to say is that none of this is productive."

"That's not what I was trying to say at all," Nathan muttered.

I narrowed my eyes at him, then turned back to Sylvester. "You can understand his frustration. We're trying to explain that we need to get organized so we'll be ready for the attack on Langley. It might be a chance for us to jump through a portal earlier and get to our Nexus."

"Langley isn't our concern," Claudia Louting, another long-standing councilwoman, spouted. "We have enough on our plates keeping Aurathion towns safe from attack. And frankly, your Nexus isn't on our list of priorities."

My jaw flexed, hand curling against the stone of the table. "Rescuing our Nexus aside, if Langley falls, your towns won't matter. The country most of us were born in will be no more." I scowled. "Where do you think they'll strike next?"

A few eyes flicked toward me—disapproval emanating from their faces. But I saw the flicker of truth there, too. They knew I was right. I was beginning to wonder just how many of these council members were actually on our side.

"The council will deliberate and get back to you promptly." Randell Hunter said, trying to keep the peace.

I leaned forward, voice low and dangerous. "Then take this as a warning. My Faction will not miss this portal, and we won't leave our allies to defend themselves." I curled my lip at Councilwoman Louting. "My Nexus is at the top of *all* our lists, and if this council doesn't see fit to help us get her back, then the next time it reaches out for help, we'll be unavailable." Put that in your pipe and smoke it, bitch.

I pushed back from the table, the chair screeching against the floor. Shadows curled instinctively at my boots —my power responding to the urgency building in my chest. The council members flinched as the air dimmed around me, lights blinking on and off. I usually kept the extent of my abilities hidden, but I felt like a show of power was needed here.

"I'll see to it that you get a response from us within the hour." Randell nodded respectfully to me. "I give you my word of honor."

Sly spoke up from where he'd been propped up in the corner, "You damn well better. My patience is at an end, and I won't lose this opportunity to get my daughter back."

"Are you all threatening us?" George Handston asked, his face turning a bright shade of red. He'd refrained from speaking until now because he was a coward.

"Take it as you will," Jesse growled. "The time for action is *now*, and so far, this council has thoroughly screwed the pooch."

"This insubordination can't be tolerated!" Claudia screeched. The other three members had kept their mouths shut this entire time, perhaps wiser than their counterparts.

"You'll not only tolerate it, but do it smiling, or I'll make sure this council is no more." She gasped, "You can count on that." John stalked over to the table and leaned down in Randell's face. "You've got one hour. Make the right fucking decision."

As a group, we filed out of the room, and Nathan teleported us to the Hawthorne warehouse. All of his abilities had leveled up since the flame up incident.

"So, what did the windbags have to say?" Adelaide met us in the garage.

"The usual bullshit." Jesse stomped up the stairs and disappeared inside.

"I assume things didn't go well?" She looked to Sly for answers.

"Randell promised to have an answer for us in an hour." He followed Jesse, and the rest of us fell in line.

Delicious smells were coming from the kitchen, and, of course, Zane headed in that direction.

"Everyone, fix a plate. I made a pot of chili, and all the fixings are on the counter." Adelaide entered, and Jesse handed her a bowl full to the top.

"I'm not really hungry right now. I'll eat later." She tried to hand the chili back to him.

"You have to eat." John frowned at her, taking the bowl and guiding her to the table. "I know it's hard, but we *are* going to get our baby back."

"I know we are. I won't accept anything else." Adelaide sat and began eating. "What are we going to do if the council won't help us?"

"We're going to defend the base without them." I took a seat beside her and dug into the delicious food.

She looked at Sly and John. "Can we win without their help?"

They both took a moment, then Sly nodded. "I think so. Between the nine of us and our friends and family, we have enough to put up a hell of a battle."

John nodded. "Our abilities are strong, and the four-legged allies at our disposal aren't to be overlooked either."

"We have my flame-up ability. That's worth ten ordinary abilities, at least." Nathan's eyes gleamed. "I can't wait to add to my collection." He scooped a heaping spoonful of chili into his mouth.

"What are you collecting?" Zane raised a brow at him.

I rolled my eyes. Would these fools never learn to ignore comments like that from Nathan?

"Eyeballs and ballsacks." He continued to eat, as if what he'd just said was completely normal.

"What the *fuck*? Where the hell are you keeping them?" Zeke looked a little green. He pushed his bowl of chili away.

"In my room. I'm going to make Reverie a purse and a necklace out of the ones that are the highest quality." Nathan looked up when Zane started gagging. "What?" he asked in confusion.

"Son, surely you can see how disgusting that is?" Jesse looked at him in amazement.

All of us ignored the quality comment, but I was more curious than I'd like to admit. What constituted *quality* in a ballsack? I subtly glanced down at my lap.

At this point, nothing Nathan did shocked me anymore. He was completely deranged, and Reverie's absence had only added to his insanity.

"Only if you don't dry them properly. I've watched *Mountain Men* for years, so I know what I'm doing," he said, frowning at Jesse, as if feeling insulted.

Sly cleared his throat. "This is getting off topic." He walked up behind Adelaide and leaned down, kissing her neck. "We'll be ready with or without the council. I'm going to get our daughter back from that *bitch* no matter what it takes."

"No matter what it takes," I repeated vehemently.

True to his word, Randell contacted us exactly an hour later. The news was surprising because they had decided to help us defend the base.

"Maybe Randell isn't on the side of the DF after all," Adelaide said after we got the news.

"As far as I'm concerned, everyone is suspect until proven otherwise." I turned to my brothers. "Jet, can you contact Josh and have him meet us?"

"Yes."

Always a man of few words. I liked that about him.

"I'll get Damien and Jasmine over here, too. We need to let them know that Deshawn is in Aurathia." Sly ran a hand down his face. "Jasmine will be thrilled with that situation."

After Damien escaped Aurathia and reunited with his family, it was quite a scene. Jasmin had assumed he was dead, and Damien still believed his son was missing or had perished with Jasmin's sister, Rose. Saying they were all pleasantly surprised is an understatement.

Poor Deshawn was confused by everything. Jasmine thought it was best to hide his heritage from him, even going so far as to change his name. Damien still referred to him as Blaze most of the time. After all that had happened, she just wanted to keep him safe. I can't imagine the scene she caused when he joined the military.

Deshawn, for his part, adjusted pretty well. Jet helped with that, but when he met Chloe, his fate was sealed, and he became more concerned with wooing her than giving his mother shit for lying to him.

⁓ ⚜ ⁓

It took several days to coordinate everyone, but I felt we were ready for anything the DF threw at us.

At least I hoped we were.

Our Faction had used the time wisely and trained extensively with our new abilities.

Well, *they* had. I hadn't gained anything new, but my abilities had grown stronger.

Exponentially stronger.

Our ability to communicate with animals had been seriously underused, and tonight we were determined to change that. John generously offered us tips on developing this skill, and with his help, it could become the secret weapon that turns the tide in our favor.

We hadn't been using everything at our disposal, and that changed tonight. In the past few months, I had held back, trying to be diplomatic and handle things the way my family has for generations—but that was over.

Behind-the-scenes plotting worked well for my father, but he was evil, and evil thrived in the dark. My love for Reverie was meant to be in the light, and from now on, that's where it would live.

I needed my Nexus back *yesterday*.

The council had sent several strong Factions, but they'd been less than cooperative. I was afraid that this would be the case when they agreed to help. I felt Randell was truly on our side, but I knew of at least three who couldn't be trusted.

"I'm in place, but so far there is no sign of the enemy." Mira's voice sounded in my head.

"None here either," I replied, using my invisibility to hide from anyone who could see the ridge I was on. I heard each of my brothers respond similarly.

Sly had suggested that they stay behind to protect the Aurathion towns near the base in case the DF attacked. It made me proud that he trusted us to find and bring Reverie back. I knew the decision was difficult for them, but ultimately, it was the right one. Even without their fifth member, Adelaide's Faction was still one of the strongest in this realm, missing abilities or not, and would guard our people well.

Our Faction *was* the strongest, and as much as they loved Reverie, we lived for her. If she were to die, none of us would remain in this world for long.

There was a flash of lightning, and I saw a large shape in its light. "Is that a relay tower?" I mumbled in confusion. "What the fuck?"

CHAPTER 16

JET

The base was *too* quiet.

Even the wind held its breath.

We'd killed the lights an hour ago, grounded the jets, sealed the gates—waiting for an attack we were supposed to start.

But something was off. The night didn't just feel heavy; it seemed as if it was watching us.

A low whine came from the north gate. The shepherds stationed there were restless, hackles up, eyes fixed on the tree line. A pair of crows circled above the hangar, cawing sharp warnings into the storm.

The animals always felt it first.

Nathan stood beside me, flame flickering around his hand like it couldn't decide whether to burn or not. He murmured to the kestrel perched on his shoulder—a creature that shouldn't have been this calm in thunder like this. It had attached itself to Nathan during our practice with John and hadn't left his side since. Nathan had even named the bird Dale in honor of Reverie's love of *Step Brothers.*

Zane and Zeke watched the fence line, both motionless except for the twitch of their fingers. The wolves they'd befriended days ago were pacing at the edge of the woods, uneasy. Oren had been gone twenty minutes, cloaked and invisible, scouting the ridge.

"No movement yet," I murmured. "Either they're smarter than we thought or—"

"—or we've already been found." Oren's voice cut through like a blade.

"There's a relay tower up here," he said. "Not ours. Council encryption. They're broadcasting our coordinates through dimensional frequency."

My stomach dropped. "You're sure?"

A flash of lightning cracked the sky. For half a second, I saw him hovering over the ridge, lightning crawling over his arms like veins of light.

"They sold us out," Oren said, voice low and shaking with fury. "The Dark Faction know precisely where we are."

The shepherds at the gate started to howl.

And then the ground split open. A portal coming from underground was rare and something we hadn't prepared for.

The first pulse hit hard enough to throw me to my knees. The air twisted, heat and cold clashing as a massive circle of violet energy ripped open across the runway.

A *second* fucking portal!

Mira's voice slammed through my head like a thunderclap. *"The ground opens beneath you! Brace yourselves!"*

The wolves lunged forward with Zane and Zeke, their growls matching the rising roar of the breach. Ravens dove into the swirling black, vanishing into the light.

I shot into the air without thinking—what the *fuck*?! I'd been able to move objects, but I had never even considered lifting my entire body. Adrenaline hit, and I flew even higher. Like gravity had given up on me entirely.

Cryptfiends poured out of the rift, shrieking through broken jaws. Oren streaked across the sky beside me, fire and lightning trailing behind him in a storm of gold. Nathan teleported into the heart of the horde, flames erupting in all directions.

"Hold the line!" I shouted. "Protect Mira and block their escape!"

The moment I got close to the portal, everything faltered—the Cryptfiends' power, the shadows they threw, even Mira's psychic energy wavered. I didn't understand it at first; I just knew their magic died near me.

Oren's voice rang out. "Jet—you're nulling them! They can't use their abilities near you!"

I didn't answer. Couldn't. The realization hit too fast.

They couldn't use power near me.

Not them.

Not even Mira.

Suddenly, I heard a *roar* tear through the rain. I looked down and saw Zane stagger, hands clawed, eyes molten gold. Zeke grabbed him, but his own control shattered—and in a blinding flash, the brothers exploded outward, bodies giving way to something ancient and wild.

Twin Draxons unfurled in the storm—wings splitting the clouds, scales gleaming with fire and frost.

Mira's voice thundered through every skull on base. *"I can't hold both portals! Anchor them, or the bridge will collapse and our chance to rescue the cub with it!"*

Oren shot upward again, lightning splitting the sky. I followed—the air bending around me as if the storm itself obeyed. Nathan burned through the ground forces, a living wildfire, as Mira planted herself between the two portals, psychic tendrils digging into the earth.

Every animal on base howled, screamed, or shrieked—the sound of nature itself tearing as reality began to fold.

"Mira!" I shouted, hovering above the chaos. "Pull back!"

"No!" Her voice cracked through my mind. *"I will not fail!"*

The second portal exploded outward, light swallowing everything.

For a heartbeat, I saw Mira and the two Draxon through the glare—wings spread, power colliding—and then they were gone.

We had saved the base, but only two of our Faction had made it through to Aurathia.

When the light died, silence fell hard. The rain hissed on scorched asphalt. The wolves whimpered at the tree line, tails tucked.

Oren landed hard beside me, smoke curling off him. "They're alive," he rasped. "I can hear them—through the portal. Every creature in this hemisphere just felt them cross."

Nathan stared at the empty air where the portal had been, flames still licking his hands. "Then we go after them. I'm not going to be left behind this time." The kestrel landed on his shoulder and cawed in response to his statement.

I holstered my weapon, throat raw. "We will."

Lightning forked overhead, and it looked like the world was burning.

The hangars were gone, the sky a storm of flame and screaming wind. Mira was standing near the first portal. The light dimmed inside, but it was still open. Our brothers—Zeke and Zane—vanished into light.

And yet, I could still feel them. Not see. *Feel.* The bond between us humming in my chest.

Oren was right. "They're still alive," I said. My voice didn't sound like my own.

"Then we follow," Nathan snapped, repeating his earlier statement.

Oren didn't hesitate. Lightning rippled over his shoulders as he floated above the cracked tarmac. "We don't have a complete portal anymore. It's raw, unstable—"

I stepped closer to the fading portal. "Then we make it stable."

Mira's voice whispered through my skull, *"The tether remains open... if you dare."*

I didn't think. None of us did. When family burns, you run into the fire. There is no other option.

Nathan reached out, clasping my shoulder, his skin hot enough to sear. They still echoed faintly through the bond. Oren hovered beside us, eyes bright with electricity.

"On my mark, I said.

"One," Nathan growled.

"Two." Oren's hands sparked.

"Three," Mira growled, and she dug both tentacles into the ground and opened the portal as wide as she could.

We stepped into the light.

ZEKE (IMMEDIATELY AFTER STEPPING THROUGH THE PORTAL)

Heat.

That was the first thing. It wasn't the sunlight—it was alive, pulsing, invasive.

It crawled over my skin, as if it wanted to erase me.

When I opened my eyes, the world was red and gold, an endless horizon of volcanic peaks bleeding rivers of light. The air shimmered, thick with smoke and the metallic taste of ash.

I rolled to my side, coughing, and frost ghosted across the black sand where my hands touched it. Steam hissed up around me in angry plumes.

Zane was already standing, smoke rising from his shoulders. His eyes gleamed like molten gold, the heat loving him—claiming him. He grinned when he saw the frost. "Brother, the natives aren't going to love that Jack Frost thing you've got going on."

"Good," I rasped, forcing myself upright. My chest ached like I'd swallowed lightning. "Might as well start as I intend to go on." The atmosphere wasn't that different than Berrick's forge.

The ground beneath us thrummed—not with tremors, but with breath. The whole land was alive, and it didn't like what it felt in me.

"What the hell is that?" I muttered to myself.

From the haze beyond the molten ridges, shadows unfurled—massive shapes with wings like stormfronts. Scales glittering, eyes molten and knowing.

Draxon.

The sight hit like a memory from another life. My blood responded, roaring in my veins—fire and frost fighting to coexist.

The largest of them landed with an earth-splitting boom, its wings folding in a cascade of sparks. Its scales burned like living bronze, and its eyes pinned us both where we stood. *"Halflings."*

The voice filled my skull, deep as a cathedral bell. *"You reek of mortal air and stolen flame. Speak, or burn."*

Zane straightened. "We came to find our Nexus. Reverie Hawthorne, she's being kept in Bellona."

"There is no Nexus in Nyberie. Only Draxon and ash." The huge Draxon sneered in my direction. *"There also is no frost Draxon in existence."*

Something inside me broke loose—a cold fury that cut through the heat. Frost bled down my arms, spilling over my fingers until the sand froze solid beneath my feet. "Then you've forgotten your history," my voice deepening until it echoed with something not human. "Because I remember the truth. I *am* the truth."

The Draxon tilted its massive head, studying me. Steam curled where my ice met its heat, neither willing to yield. *"You carry cold where there should be fire,"* it rumbled. *"An abomination of the flame."*

Zane stepped closer to me, his hand sparking with heat that didn't burn. "He's no abomination. He's my brother. Zeke's twice the Draxon any of you will ever be." Then he flipped them off… with both hands.

The creature's eyes narrowed, amused. And if I'm being frank, I also detected a little confusion. *"Then prove it."*

The volcano behind it roared to life—rivers of molten gold spilling down its sides.

"Enter the Welcoming Flame. Survive the fire that rejects you."

The heat surged, a living wave that rolled toward me, bright enough to blind.

I didn't move, nor did I flinch.

Zane's hand landed hard on my shoulder. "You can do this—" He waggled his brows, "or I'll be the only ginger in Reverie's bed."

I smirked, frost billowing from my mouth as I spoke, "That will never happen. Get ready to be amazed."

The fire hit—and I heard Zane roar my name.

Frost exploded outward, colliding with the inferno, and for one heartbeat, Nyberie froze.

Then fire swallowed everything.

I heard a voice saying, *"Frost in our cradle. Ice in our bloodline. You don't belong here."*

The world around me blurred—the cliffs, the volcano, even Zane's shout—all dissolved into a sea of molten gold. The flame rose higher, pressing against my skin like judgment.

Then another voice cut through the inferno, low and ancient, curling through my thought like smoke. *"Let me through, boy."*

Frynn.

I'd talked to him many times, but he'd never been this close to the surface. I suppose with the complete change, I'd better get used to it. "They'll burn me alive," I muttered through gritted teeth.

"You're already burning," he answered, his tone almost amused. *"But you've forgotten—frost is just heat in reverse."*

What the fuck did that mean? The Flame struck again, a tidal wave of molten energy that should've erased me. Instead, Frynn roared. The sound wasn't in my ears—it was in *everything*.

Then I let the change swallow me whole.

Ice bloomed outward in fractal patterns, dazzling against the fire. The Welcoming Flame hesitated, confused—then tried to consume it.

But the frost didn't die.

It fought back.

The fire froze midair—a storm of glass and light—and I realized what Frynn was doing. He wasn't rejecting the flame. He was teaching it balance.

Zane shouted from somewhere beyond the haze, his voice rough and fierce. "Zeke!"

Through the glow, I saw him—wings flared, his own Draxon form breaking through. Drakk was an immense shape of burning bronze and fury. His roar joined the storm, shaking Nyberie to its core.

"Hold your ground, brother," Drakk's voice thundered through the flames. *"Show them your strength."*

I spread my wings wide, calling every shard of cold left in me. Frost split the ground, climbing like veins up the volcano's side. "You want to see what doesn't belong?" I growled.

Frynn laughed inside me—the sound sharp, wild, and proud. *"Now you remember who you are."*

The fire surged one final time, and I didn't fight it. I embraced it—let it mix with the frost until steam and lightning burst outward in a shockwave that tore through the clouds.

When it cleared, the flame was gone.

The volcano had gone silent.

The Draxon who had summoned the trial now bowed his massive head. *"Frost-born who conquered flame,"* it rumbled. *"You are no longer half. You are whole."*

Zane landed beside me, smoke rising from his shoulders, eyes blazing gold. "Well," he said, grinning. "Looks like Nyberie just got colder."

I exhaled, steam curling from my lips. "Let's hope it's ready for what's coming."

Behind us, the ground trembled again—not from the trial, but from something answering it. Something far older than any Draxon we'd seen.

Frynn stirred inside me, his tone suddenly sharp. "They've felt us. The true elders. And they're waking up."

CHAPTER 17
OREN

I hit the ground hard enough to rattle my bones. The sand here wasn't *really* sand—it was glass ground fine by fire. It hissed under me, hot enough to burn through the layers of my gear.

I rolled to my feet, every nerve alive with static. The air was thick, metallic, charged—like the moment before a storm breaks.

Nathan emerged from the smoke, coughing and smoldering. "If I ever do that again," he rasped, "knock me out first." Then he frowned and said in a low, threatening tone, "Don't tell my Nexi I said that."

"Noted," I smirked. My voice came out raw, still buzzing from the portal. I could taste ozone, feel lightning under my skin like something alive and impatient.

Jet floated a few feet off the ground, scanning the horizon—calm, *too* calm. That was his tell, I'd learned that over these past few months.

Everything about this place felt wrong. The sky was bleeding light, rivers of molten gold running through black peaks, and the ground beneath us vibrated as if it were breathing.

And underneath it all—a sound.

A rhythm.

A heartbeat.

I closed my eyes and listened.

Zeke.

Zane.

The bond was unspoken; it was a pulse running through the wild—wolves howling somewhere far off, the sharp cry of a hawk echoing through fire and stone. "They're here," I said. "North ridge. And something's with them."

Jet turned sharply toward the glowing horizon. "You feel it too?"

"Hard not to," I muttered.

No sooner than the words left my mouth, a shockwave of power slammed through us—half flame, half frost, pure chaos. The horizon erupted in white-blue light that froze the air itself, then shattered it in fire.

I barely threw my shield up in time, electricity bursting from my hands to deflect the wave. Nathan braced beside me, flames coiling like armor. Jet didn't move—he just *absorbed* it. The energy hit him and vanished, snuffed out like smoke.

When the wind finally died, the landscape was... changed.

The volcanoes had quieted. The sand had fused into

black glass. And far off, two Draxon shapes loomed against the red sky—vast and glowing, one wreathed in fire, the other in frost.

Zane and Zeke.

"What the fuck?" Nathan breathed. "They actually—"

"Awakened something," I finished for him. My voice dropped lower. "And not just themselves."

Because above the twins, shadows moved—enormous, slow, deliberate. The air vibrated under the weight of their presence. Eyes opened in the clouds.

Ancient.

Hungry.

"Ancestors," Jet said quietly, almost to himself.

A crack of thunder answered him—except there were no clouds left to make it—just the beating of colossal wings.

Nathan's kestrel squawked loudly in warning as it landed on his shoulder. I contacted the other animals that came through and warned them to lie low until we came to retrieve them. There were monsters in this world that would consider them prey.

I lifted off the ground slightly, letting the lightning hum through me. My skin tingled, my bones humming with power I couldn't contain. "We need to move before we're seen."

Nathan smirked. "Too late." The crazy bastard stroked the kestrel and seemed to anticipate the fight to come.

The air split open behind us—a roar that held such power it felt like the very foundation of Aurathia trembled.

I turned just in time to see a shape dive from the haze —a Draxon, smaller but fast, its scales reflecting the firelight like molten mirrors. No way this was the one that had made that sound.

It must be a hunter.

"Contact," I hissed. "We've got company."

Jet rose higher beside me, eyes narrowing. "Maybe we need to see how well these things handle our abilities."

Nathan's smirk grew into a grin. "As my precious Nexi would say, let's get western on their ass!"

The beast roared again, shaking the air. I vanished— pure instinct—slipping into invisibility as the storm built inside my chest.

Apparently, this land ran on fire and fury.

Good thing I brought both.

The beast landed hard—claws sinking into molten glass, wings folding with a hiss. Its eyes were molten amber, too sharp to be anything but intelligent. The ground around it steamed where its breath touched.

"Big bastard," Nathan muttered under his breath, sounding hopeful. "You think it's hostile?"

"Everything here's hostile," I murmured back, floating a few feet above the ground, trying to get a clean angle. "Question is, how *intelligent* is he?"

I reached out with my ability, lightning threading silently through the air—a net of static to read its movements. What came back wasn't instinct. It was *thought*.

"Trespassers. Unforged flame. The air reeks of Aurathions." The voice wasn't sound—it was pressure in my skull, old and heavy. The creature tilted its head as if scenting us

through the air. Its gaze passed right over where I hovered.

Jet stayed still, levitating a foot off the ground, calm as always. Taking to this new ability as if he'd always had it. Nathan crouched behind a glass outcrop, fire flickering low, his body coiled for attack, Dale sticking close to him.

"We're not your enemy," I said carefully, sending the thought back, slow and deliberate. "We came for our brothers."

The Draxon's head turned sharply toward my invisible position. Its nostrils flared. *Brothers? No kin of mine would hide like a coward.*

Lightning rippled across my skin—involuntarily. And my shadows writhed on the ground. "Copy that," I muttered. "I'm going to fuck him up."

I barely finished the sentence before the air detonated —a blast of heat and shock that sent sand and shards of glass whipping past. The Draxon inhaled, chest expanding, a glow building in its throat.

It was about to breathe fire.

"Jet!" I shouted, even though I knew he'd already read the signs.

He raised one hand. And the fire stopped.

Not slowed—stopped—frozen mid-exhale, suspended between the creature's fangs like liquid amber.

The Draxon blinked, confused.

Growled.

Tried again.

Nothing.

Its flames simply refused to exist in Jet's presence.

"Well," Nathan said, stepping out of cover. "That's going to come in handy."

Jet's eyes glowed faintly—not with power, but with control. "Yes, it will."

The Draxon snarled, pacing in frustration—until the sky itself answered.

A cry, deep and rolling, split the air. Then two shadows dropped from the red clouds—vast, glowing shapes that made the hunter recoil.

When they landed, the shockwave nearly threw me out of the air.

Zeke and Zane.

Their forms towered over the hunter, wings still steaming from the cold and fire that bled off them. The frost steaming from Zeke's scales made the ground hiss and crack, while Zane's molten glow pulsed in rhythm with Nyberie's heartbeat.

The smaller Draxon lowered its head instantly—not in submission, or fear, but in recognition of their dominance.

Zeke's voice echoed like thunder inside every skull on the plain. "*Stand down. They're ours.*"

The hunter hesitated—then backed away, folding its wings.

Nathan let out a slow whistle. "What the actual fuck. We're only behind them for a few minutes, and they become king of the Draxon."

Zane's human form stepped forward from within the fading glow of his Draxon form, eyes still molten. "That's what real men do." He fluttered his lashes at Nathan.

"What the fuck?" He yelled as a glob of birdshit dropped from the sky onto his head.

Dale screeched from high above, and it almost sounded like laughter.

"I'm going to fry that fucking chicken of yours," Zane growled as he wiped the mess from his hair.

"You do, and I'll clip your balls off and add them to my collection." Nathan made a snipping motion with his hand.

I dropped the invisibility, static snapping off my shoulders. "That's enough, you two." I glanced in Zeke's direction. "Maybe next time, inform the welcoming party of our arrival."

Zeke smiled faintly—cold mist spilling from his breath. "Nyberie doesn't welcome anyone. At least as far as we can tell."

"Yeah?" Nathan said, wiping sweat from his forehead. "Well, it almost ate us…and not in a good way."

The hunter rumbled low—almost a laugh—before spreading its wings and vanishing into the haze.

Zane clapped me on the shoulder, the heat radiating through the leather of my jacket. "You did good, exalted leader. They don't let just anyone talk and live."

I smirked, shadows dancing between my fingers. "I guess *Shitstorm* doesn't fit me now that I've charmed a Draxon."

"I wouldn't go that far." His smile turned melancholy. "We'll let Reverie decide that."

Jet finally lowered to the ground, still unreadable, but I could see it—the faint hum of energy around him, the silence where Nyberie's magic refused to exist.

And the Draxon? They felt it.

Every single one of them turned their gaze toward him.

Curious.

Cautious.

Because even in a world of monsters, something is unsettling about a man who can silence them all.

I couldn't wait until the Dark Faction tasted his ability for themselves.

We were trying to get our bearings and decide on our course of action when the wind shifted. A shadow moved through the crackling light—massive, deliberate, ancient.

The elder Draxon. The one that had roared earlier.

He was larger than any I'd ever seen, scales glinting like tempered steel, eyes molten gold, and older than time. He landed between us and the portal, the ground shattering beneath his weight.

"You trespass on sacred ground," he said, voice so deep it made the air vibrate.

Zane's Draxon stirred within him, his tone low and reverent. "Elder."

The ancient creature's gaze swept across us. *"You rip open what was meant to stay sealed. Why?"*

Zeke stepped forward, frost curling from his skin. "Because our Nexus was captured and brought here by the Dark Faction."

At that, the elder stilled. His eyes glowed brighter. *"The Nexus... Reverie..."* He inhaled deeply, the sound like a gale wind moving through a canyon. Then his wings unfurled, casting us in shadow. *"She stirs."*

My pulse spiked. "Reverie?"

His gaze flicked to me—seeing too much, knowing too much. *"Her call reaches even here, though she knows it not. She wakes in what is now known as Bellona."*

Nathan looked almost feral. "You can feel her?"

The elder's talons flexed. *"We all can. She is Aurathia."*

I couldn't catch my breath. I knew what this meant. Everything that I had believed about my Nexus was true.

The elder slammed his claw into the ground, runes lining his wings blazing beneath us in a spiral of light. *"Then go, Faction of the Queen,"* he intoned. *"Find her. Restore what was broken. We will be waiting for your signal."*

There was no time to find out what he meant. The ground vanished beneath our feet.

Light. Sound. Nothing.

When I could breathe again, the world had changed.

We lay sprawled across a cracked plain beneath a copper sky. The air buzzed with energy, and I could almost feel Reverie's heartbeat. My body hummed with it —an ache that wasn't pain but pure joy.

Zeke was the first to speak, voice low. "It's… her."

I froze. Then felt it too—a *pulse*.

Warmth flooded through the bond, faint but steady. The emptiness that had haunted us since she was taken snapped, replaced by something fierce and alive.

Jet's breath hitched. "It's back. The bond."

Nathan pressed a hand to his chest, eyes wide. "I can *feel* her."

Zane looked toward the distant city of Bellona, with the giant Colosseum stark against the sky. "No," he said. "She's more than alive. She's calling to us."

The air shimmered as her pulse echoed through us again, bright and unyielding.

I clenched my fists, fire flickering at my fingertips. "Then we find her."

The five of us turned toward Bellona—toward the coliseum, where our Nexus waited.

And for the first time since this nightmare began, I was able to draw a full breath.

CHAPTER 18

REVERIE

I dreamed of voices.

They rose like wind through the ruins of memory— soft at first, then layered, dozens upon dozens, old and echoing. Some were familiar, like lullabies half-remembered from childhood. Others spoke in tongues my mind shouldn't have understood, but my blood did.

The air in the dream glowed amber, smoke curling through the dark. I stood barefoot on marble streaked with gold veins— the same throne room I'd seen before, but broken now, overtaken by flame and shadow.

"Child of all of us," the voices murmured together. "The line endures."

"Who are you?" My voice was barely a whisper.

"We are the echoes that built you. The Ancestors who carried the crown before you."

Their words thrummed through me like a second heartbeat. The floor cracked beneath my feet, splitting to reveal light—raw and pulsing.

"Yes." Their tone deepened—neither kind nor cruel, but absolute. "The queen was but one of many. We are all that remains of what was once whole."

I took a hesitant step forward. "Why now?"

Because the veil thins. Your Faction rises. And past betrayals must be atoned for.

The marble shattered. A brilliant flare of gold and white light burst upward, engulfing me.

They reach for you, child of our blood. Five lights through the shadow. Five hearts bound by oath and love. Feel them. Call them. Remember.

Beware the sixth.

The light swallowed everything.

And I woke gasping.

My body jerked upright, heart pounding so hard I was scared it would beat right out of my chest. I knew it must be morning, but with the stress from helping with the Varruk's escape and my strange dreams, it felt like I'd barely slept at all.

Then I felt them.

A pulse of warmth, no longer just a vague feeling.

Jet.

Oren.

Nathan.

Zeke.

Zane.

They weren't just names but pieces of me snapping back into place.

I stumbled out of bed, my breath catching. My hands trembled as light flickered beneath my skin. The Nexus mark burning—still invisible to the naked eye—the bond pulsed like a living thing, each thread connecting, weaving, calling.

It was overwhelming—heat and ice and static all at once—but beneath it was something steady, achingly familiar: *them.*

I pressed my palm to my mark, tears spilling freely now. "You're alive," I breathed. "You're really—"

"Here." Oren breathed into my mind. *"And we're coming."*

The pulse of their energy faded back into my bones, leaving me trembling but alive in a way I hadn't been since I was torn from them.

Outside, Bellona's dawn bells tolled—a cruel, mocking sound over the city of blood and spectacle.

I thought of everything that stood in their way and the danger we all faced. *"Don't come to the coliseum, wait for word from me, and above all, stay safe."*

"I love you, my Nexi." Nathan's voice felt like a caress.

"We'll see you soon," the deep voice of Jet sounded in my head.

I noticed that *no one* agreed to wait until further notice.

"I love you all to the depths of my soul, but you have to wait until it's safe." I pleaded with them.

"Trust us." The twins spoke in unison in voices that didn't seem wholly human.

I felt them cut off the connection before I could respond. "Those hard-headed bastards better not get themselves killed," I murmured to myself.

The whispers of my Ancestors lingered faintly, wrapping around me like smoke.

The blood remembers. The bond endures.

And for the first time since being here, I believed them.

～☘～

I could barely contain my excitement as I went to breakfast. So far, there hadn't been any consequences from the Varruk's escape. He was so powerful that it wasn't surprising at all that he managed to escape on his own.

I knew that I would probably still be punished for what had taken place in the arena, but if the Ancestors were with me, then I'd be gone before that happened.

"You five better be safe." I waited a moment, but no one responded. My heart beat a little faster knowing it wouldn't be long until I saw them again.

"Can you believe that all of the creatures escaped last night? Including your new best friend." Torren came up from behind me, startling me with his question.

I ignored the best friend comment, "That's what all the alarms were about? He should never have been locked down there to begin with."

"I can't imagine why not. They're just creatures after all, some of whom should be eradicated." He narrowed his eyes at me in challenge.

"Maybe," I said, noncommittally.

"Maybe? That's all you have to say on the subject?" Torren grabbed my arm and pulled me to a stop.

I jerked my arm out of his hold. "What's your problem?" It's like the kiss never happened. This man blew hot and cold like no other.

"I just find it annoying that some of us are here to find a Faction and some of us are here to be some kind of hero." He growled in my face.

"Are you *fucking* kidding me? I didn't come here voluntarily, so no, I'm not looking for a Faction. I already have one *after all*." I pushed his chest with both hands and tried to shove him backwards, but even with my strength, he didn't budge. "And I would have surely died if the Varruk hadn't stepped in to help. So, *no*, I didn't want to kill a being who helped me live to fight another day!"

"I've heard about the guys in your Faction, and I'm not impressed. You'd better get with the program, or you're going to find your stay here increasingly difficult." He growled, then turned and stomped back the way he'd come from.

"What the hell?" I mumbled under my breath.

Where the crap did that come from? He'd been mostly kind since I'd met him, but it was like he took my actions personally. He could go fuck himself for all I cared. I had no regrets concerning Vee.

I entered the dining hall, filled a plate, and then sat in the back corner. The room was mostly empty because it was very late and the day after the coliseum battles.

"Who were you talking to earlier, you felt upset?" Zane's voice startled me, and I dropped the eggs I was scooping into my mouth.

"It was nothing. I can't believe you could feel that." I ducked my head to hide the wide smile that overtook my face.

"There's a lot that's changed since we bonded. Also, I wanted to let you know I enjoyed the meal you provided the other night." I could hear the heat in his voice.

"What are you talking about?"

"The tasty snack I had in the classroom." I felt him smirk. *"I had no idea that was a fantasy of yours."*

He couldn't be referring to the sex dream I'd had about him… could he?

He laughed huskily, *"I've always wanted to desecrate an instructor's desk."*

Holy shit, he was. I suddenly felt shy because it had been so long since we'd seen each other. *"We weren't even able to communicate then."*

"At the time, I thought it was my dream, but there was always a little doubt. I wanted to believe I'd been able to visit you, but I didn't know it was possible. Seems you found a way to visit me instead." I could hear the smugness in his voice. *"Shit, Oren is giving me his pay-the-fuck-attention look. Sexiest twin, out!"*

I couldn't contain my laughter, and the few people who were in here gave me strange looks. I just waggled my brows at them and continued eating. There wasn't much that could ruin my good mood today.

A warrior I was unfamiliar with entered the room and kept glancing furtively at me. He filled a plate and then headed in my direction. "Is this chair taken?"

"No."

I didn't elaborate because after everything that happened yesterday, I was short on trust. It would be just like Selene to send an unknown to collect intel. Trying to find out if I had anything to do with the Varruk's escape.

He sat and began eating, but was obviously casing the room. I took the opportunity to study him. Green eyes and mocha skin, complemented by lots and lots of muscle.

He was a beautiful man, but I wasn't attracted to him in the least. There was something familiar about him, too, but I couldn't put my finger on what it was.

"I don't think I've ever seen you here before." I wasn't able to contain my curiosity.

He turned to me and grinned. "You wouldn't have. I just arrived last night in the middle of all the chaos."

"You weren't involved, were you?" I asked the question, hoping that if Selene did send him, it would throw him off.

He leaned closer. "Nope, I was too busy planning a trip to the Catalina Wine Mixer."

I blinked. "*Excuse me?*" Did I hear him right?

He grinned, "I'll be in touch. Someone I'm close to wants to plan some *activities* for later." Giving me a wink, he left the table.

I was too stunned to move. Only Chloe would use *Step Brothers* to let me know I could trust someone. Was that crazy redhead here? Did her brothers know?

We weren't required to train the day after coliseum battles, but I usually did a quick workout, anyway. Today, I really needed to move. I needed the focus. Knowing my guys were here and that Chloe might be had me on edge.

I walked out to the training yard and retrieved my short swords from the armory. The air still smelled of blood and ozone from yesterday's fights. Every muscle in my body demanded to be stretched—I needed movement.

I took my swords into my hands and began slowly.

Breathe. Step. Pivot.

Each movement bled into the next. My wrists remembered the weight, my shoulders the rhythm of survival.

But this morning wasn't about fighting—it was about listening.

The whispers came softly at first. The same voices that had guided me in dreams the last few days—Ancestors whose names I didn't yet know. They wove through my mind like threads of smoke.

"Balance is forged, not found.
The blood remembers."

My blades glimmered faintly as if the steel itself pulsed with their words. I sank into a low stance, exhaling fire. It licked across the edges, not burning but purifying.

Sweat mixed with something else: energy—a hum beneath my skin, answering the call of every soul who came before me. My movements grew sharper, faster, no longer mine alone. I could feel several others add to the precision in my strikes, another Ancestor's grace in the turn of my wrist.

I felt Pantar watching approvingly from the shadows, his eyes unblinking, tail sweeping slowly. The connection between him and me snapped back into place.

I stopped my movements abruptly, trying to find him with my eyes, not just with my mind. *"Pantar, are you here?"*

"I never left you, Nexus." I heard his voice in my head.

Then, I felt him leave abruptly. It seemed like everyone had shown up to rescue me.

Suddenly, the training yard blurred, colors bleeding at the edges. The dawn haze fractured into shards of light and shadow until I wasn't standing on packed dirt anymore. I was in marble halls.

A throne room.

Marble stretched beneath my feet, white streaked with gold and ash. The throne room was heavy with smoke and ruin. Queen Lilibet, I, stood at its heart—armor split at the shoulder, crown cracked but gleaming through blood and dust.

Before her/me six men knelt. Ambrose, Merritt, Bren, Zenon, Larkin... and Kratos.

Their loyalty was a living thing in the air, electric and fierce. Five of them held their heads bowed, devotion carved in every line of their faces. But one—Kratos—kept his eyes lifted. They burned not with reverence, but with conflict.

"Don't," she whispered. "Not you."

Kratos stood and stepped closer. His expression was raw, almost pleading. His lips moved, but I couldn't hear the words— only the tremor of them, thick with pain.

Lilibet shook her head once, tears tracing paths through the grime on her cheeks. Then the light around them erupted.

Golden sigils flared across the marble, searing symbols I couldn't read. A deafening roar split the vision, part grief, part fury—and then everything shattered into shards of sound and light.

I hit the ground hard, the training yard rushing back in fragments of color and breath. My palms burned. Faint lines of gold still lingered beneath the skin, pulsing like a heartbeat that wasn't mine.

"I saw him," I whispered. "Kratos... and her." The words caught in my throat. "Something happened between them. Something that broke everything."

The voices of the Ancestors stirred, but none spoke. Only the wind answered—carrying the ghost scent of smoke and salt, like Aurathia was remembering a heartbreak older than itself.

"Reverie!" Seamus's voice broke into my musings.

"Prepare yourself. You've got another match tonight." He smirked evilly.

"What?!" We never fight two consecutive days in a row. I pushed myself slowly to my feet.

He laughed. "Today is special. You are much in demand after your last performance."

Fuck! I knew that yesterday wouldn't go unpunished, but I never thought it would take place in front of everyone and possibly mean my death.

There's no way I can let the guys know. They'd get themselves killed trying to rush my rescue.

Seamus was still laughing as he left. I saw the guy from earlier in the dining hall slip into the shadows behind him, giving me a slight nod of his head before he disappeared.

Shit. What the fuck was I going to do now?

"Survive." I heard the ghostly whisper of one of the voices that had plagued me lately.

CHAPTER 19
ZANE

Bellona was louder than sin. Even at dawn, the city roared with life—vendors shouting, soldiers barking orders, the coliseum gates still slick with yesterday's blood.

Word traveled fast here. Everyone wanted to talk about the girl who refused to kill her monster.

Our girl. Our Nexus.

I leaned against the crumbling edge of a market wall, scanning the towers above the arena. The whole place pulsed with energy—auras layered like storm clouds. Reverie's presence brushed my mind again, soft but steady, like a heartbeat trying to sync with mine.

"Zane?"

"Still here, precious girl."

"You shouldn't be. It's way too dangerous." I could hear the concern in her voice.

"Danger is my middle name."

"I happen to know that's bullshit."

A low growl from behind me snapped the smile off my face.

Oren. Better known as Shitstorm.

I understood him more after all these months and all the time we'd spent together. He'd definitely changed since our younger years, and there were reasons for that. Still, he was *Shitstorm* until Reverie said otherwise.

"*Focus,*" he said, voice like thunder. "*She's near the upper part of the compound.*"

"*The training yard,*" Nathan grunted.

Oren nodded. "*We move when Jet gives the all-clear.*"

I raised a brow at him. "*You're sure you're not ceding control of this mission to Jet?*"

Nathan snorted, "*He'd sooner give Selene oral.*"

Oren shot him a look that would've roasted a lesser man. "You talking to her mid-mission is exactly how people end up dead."

"*Boys,*" Reverie's voice cut through, warm yet tired and sharp all at once. "*Maybe save the arguing until after you aren't surrounded by danger from all sides.*"

Jet chuckled quietly, his tone calm even as his eyes flickered from place to place. "*She has a point.*"

I noticed he only smiled like that for our Nexus.

Zeke crouched beside him, drawing a map of the tunnels Damien had described to him from memory. Frost hissed from his fingertips. "*The main tunnel is beneath the east barracks.*"

"*Meaning?*" I asked.

"*Meaning we don't charge the front gate like idiots,*" Zeke looked at me in exasperation.

Nathan elbowed me. "Your brother thinks you're an idiot."

"Yeah," I said, grinning. *"But my dick's bigger."*

"Less than a quarter inch, fuckface!" Zeke growled.

Oren sighed, a sound that said he was reconsidering every life choice that led to this moment. *"We move at dusk. No mistakes. No noise. Reverie, you stay where you are until we reach the coliseum wall."*

"You're assuming I'm not going to try to get out of here and meet y'all before you get yourselves killed."

Sassy girl. I smiled at her defiance of Oren.

Zeke muttered under his breath, "Of course, she wants to do it on her own."

Frynn stirred inside me, scales rippling beneath my skin. The Draxon's voice slipped through my thoughts like smoke. "She burns brighter today. The bond grows stronger."

I straightened, glancing toward the coliseum's towering form. *"We're coming for you, Nexus. Be ready."*

～☖～

We moved in shadows—Oren leading, Jet watching our backs, Nathan and me doing our usual brand of subtle chaos.

Nathan sent Dale away for now. He would've been helpful, but we had grown fond of him and didn't want him injured unnecessarily. Besides, my twin and I had the most superior animals of all inside us.

"*I am far from an animal, boy,*" Frynn growled, not pleased with the comparison.

"Feels too quiet," Nathan muttered.

"Quiet's good." I checked the knife at my belt. "Means nobody is trying to fuck with us yet."

Oren shot me a look. "*Yet* being the keyword."

Then I froze.

A flicker of movement at the edge of an alley—too deliberate to be a rat, too cautious to be a drunk. Frynn stirred beneath my skin, scales itching with instinct.

Oren motioned for silence, and we fanned out.

That's when a voice whispered, "If you're planning to attack me, then I'm telling Mom when we get back."

I'd know that voice anywhere. "Chloe?"

She stepped out of the shadows like a ghost. Mud-streaked, exhausted, but alive. Her red hair was pulled back in a rough braid, and two men flanked her—one broad-shouldered with a blade still dripping something that wasn't water (Oliver, clearly), the other leaner and cool-eyed, scanning the rooftops (Deshawn, protective and calm).

Zeke moved before I could. He had her wrapped in a crushing hug in a blink. "You absolute menace," he muttered into her hair. "Do you have any idea—"

Chloe's smile wobbled, equal parts relief and irritation. "Nice to see you too, brother."

"Aw, look at that—Booger and the Draxon. Sounds like a movie title. Anyone else feeling the need for popcorn?" I mimicked eating popcorn, smirking at my two siblings.

Chloe glared. "*Don't* be a dick."

I snickered, "Just fucking with you."

Nathan elbowed me. "You'd better watch yourself. My Nexi would totally approve of me holding you down so Chloe could kick your ass."

Chloe grinned, "Yes, she would."

I grinned back, truly happy to see my sister. "So, wanna tell us why you're strolling around Bellona like you're on holiday?"

Deshawn answered before Chloe could. "Because she didn't listen to me." His voice was smooth, low, with the kind of lethal calm that came from killing more people than he wanted to count. "I've been in the coliseum posing as one of their warriors. Trying to get close to Reverie."

My stomach clenched. "And?"

"I saw her, spoke to her." He said simply. "Seems that she's fighting again tonight."

Oren's jaw tightened. "Then we move sooner than planned."

Deshawn's gaze swept the street, calculating. "You'll need the eastern tunnels. Less patrol coverage, and the old arena channels still run power from before the war."

Jet nodded slowly. "That's good. The distraction of the crowd will mask our approach."

Chloe's voice cracked as she said, "I'm happy you're all here."

Zeke sighed. "You realize Mom is shitting a brick about you being here."

Chloe winced. "I figured."

"Zane?" Reverie's voice brushed my mind, soft and unaware. *"Everything all right?"*

"Everything's fine, precious, how about on your end?"

"All good." The connection broke abruptly.

"Liar," I murmured out loud.

Oren frowned, "She didn't mention anything about being put in the arena again tonight."

"Nope." Nathan scowled.

"I'm going to spank her ass." Jet growled.

"Get in line." I waggled my brows and grinned.

Chloe huffed, "Fantasize on your own time. We have to rescue my bestie before she gets her ass killed. The fight in the coliseum will start in just a few hours."

My grin vanished. "Then we stop the show."

Before anyone could respond, the air shifted—thick, heavy, wrong. The sound was almost a growl, but too deep, too intelligent.

A shadow peeled itself out of the alley behind Chloe. Four paws the size of dinner plates hit the cobblestone, claws whispering against stone. Quieter than anyone his size had the right to be.

Pantar.

He seemed bigger than he'd been just a few days ago. Sleek black fur rippling like smoke, amber eyes glowing like twin suns. The tentacles along his shoulders moved with eerie precision, tasting the air.

Pantar's voice rolled through our heads like thunder. *"I tracked her to the compound. The time to move is now."*

Frynn stirred inside me, snarling back. *"Watch your tone, beast."*

I swallowed hard at Pantar's unamused look, forcing a smirk. "He was just joking."

Pantar flicked his tail. *"Your Draxon will come in handy."*

Oren spoke quietly. "Stay out of sight. The guards won't hesitate to kill you."

Pantar rolled his eyes. *"I go where my Nexus is."*

"Can't you just order him to remain invisible? He was yours before he was Reverie's." Nathan smirked.

"He doesn't take orders. He listens only to Reverie, and *that's* not even guaranteed." Oren flipped him off.

"Great," Nathan grinned. "Just like Zane."

"Hey, dickhead," I growled.

For a moment, no one spoke. Then Jet broke the silence, his tone cutting through the night. "We need to move."

"They change rotations every six hours. Next shift's in less than one. Once it flips, the eastern tunnel will be half-guarded for maybe ten minutes." Deshawn looked to Jet.

Oren nodded, "That's our window."

Deshawn knelt, sketching quick lines in the dirt with a broken blade tip—clean, efficient. "Two entrances. North gate is suicide. The East tunnel connects to the fighter prep hall. If we move then, we can reach Reverie before the next round begins."

Jet crouched beside him, his null energy pulsing faintly. "If I dampen our signatures, we can slip through the barrier wards without tripping alarms. But it won't be easy. I haven't truly mastered this new ability yet."

"Do it," said Oren.

Zeke crossed his arms, frost curling from his finger-tips. "What about the spectators? Hundreds of them. Even if we get in, getting *out* will—"

"We won't get out the same way," Oliver interrupted. "There's an old drainage channel beneath the arena floor. It was sealed off decades ago, but Deshawn was able to find the schematics."

Deshawn gave a single nod. "Runs all the way to the southern cliffs. Flooded, dark, but navigable."

Nathan grinned. "So, we break in, steal my Nexi, and surf out through a sewer." He waggled his brows, "Romantic."

"Only you," I gagged, "could describe escaping through ancient piles of shit as romantic."

He shrugged. "I can make anything romantic. It's a gift."

Chloe cut in, voice shaking with tension. "Selene isn't going to let her walk out alive, not after everything."

Oren's eyes flared with heat. "I hope that bitch tries stopping us. I'm going to skin her alive."

"I'm going to help." Nathan's face lost all humor.

None of us mentioned what Selene had done to our Nexus. It felt like something only we should know, like her pain was sacred and belonged only to us.

Oliver stood, brushing dirt from his hands. "All right. We strike on the shift change. Zeke and Jet cover the rear. Deshawn leads us through the fighter's hall. Oren, you and I clear the eastern corridor. Nathan, Zane—"

"Chaos squad." Nathan said instantly.

I saluted. "Damn straight."

Jet's mouth twitched—the closest thing he ever got to a smile, unless Reverie was involved. "Just try to leave some for the rest of us to kill."

Pantar's tail flicked. *"If they die, I will finish their work."*

"Wow, thanks for caring," I muttered.

Nathan looked delighted. "I knew he loved me."

Pantar growled at him.

Oren straightened, voice going hard and sure. "We

move at first bell. No mistakes. We get in, get her, and get out before the city even realizes she's gone."

Everyone nodded, faces serious.

Oren's shadows wound around his fists, Zeke's frost shimmered blue across his palms, Jet levitated several inches off the ground, and Nathan cracked his knuckles with a sound like distant thunder as his palms lit up with fire.

I looked around at the group—my brothers, her protectors, her chaos—and felt that sharp, dangerous thrill roll through me.

"Let's fuck shit up."

CHAPTER 20
REVERIE

I'm given zero time to prepare.

And *no* weapons.

The stands are packed shoulder-to-shoulder, every Aurathion who loves a spectacle perched on the edge of their seat. Today's entertainment? The traitor who wouldn't kill the Varruk at their demand.

I'm also pretty sure that his escape and the escape of the creatures kept for the amusement of the DF are being blamed directly on me. A surge of pride takes over, and my spine stiffens. I might die here today, but I've accomplished at least one thing.

Selene leans over the upper balcony, dressed in metal the color of spilled wine, smiling at me as if she's already cut my throat. Seamus stands beside her, smirking, fingers curled around the railing as if he can already taste the kill. And fucking Kristine is sitting below them in the front row with the rest of her Faction, smiling like it's Christmas.

Then I see Torren.

Tall, armor dented from training, jaw clenched. He stands with the other warriors, but his eyes never leave me—not once. Concern? Curiosity? Something darker? I can't tell. But when my gaze meets his, he gives the slightest nod.

You've got this.

Maybe.

Maybe not.

Without weapons, my only option is to use my abilities. Keeping them a secret at this point isn't feasible. I hope my guys have a plan because once Selene sees how powerful I really am, I'll be executed.

The gate lifts.

Metal shrieks.

Something snarls.

The Cryptfiends spill out like nightmares skinned and stitched back together wrong—elongated limbs, long fingers that end in curved claws—smelling like death and bad decisions. Several Gerendel followed behind them.

The crowd cheers.

I hear the whisper of chains behind me—guards stepping back, sealing the exit.

They want a show.

They want death.

Preferably mine.

The Cryptfiends move first. Not a charge…a slow stalk. They test the air, tasting me, hissing low and rumbling. Their movements are coordinated—wolves on two legs.

The nearest one clicks its jaw open so wide I hear the bone pop.

I could try to outrun it. Hide. Beg. That's what they want, what they expect.

Instead, I stand perfectly still.

My pulse hammers. My blood heats. But something inside me rises—sharp, electric, ancient.

And then I hear a voice.

"It is time."

The voice doesn't come from the stands. It comes from everywhere and nowhere, whispered in a language that hasn't been spoken in centuries.

The Cryptfiends heard it too. Their heads snapped toward me in unison. Strangely, the Gerendel stumbled back into the tunnel they had come from. Maybe they sensed that something wasn't right.

My palms burned, and I couldn't hold back. Suddenly, they ignited.

I curled my fingers to try and hide the shimmer, but sparks leaked between them.

Looks like the cat is out of the bag.

Selene leaned forward in her seat, her face showing the realization. Panic gripped her features.

Did she really believe that the daughter of Adelaide Hawthorne would be powerless? If the expression on her face is any indicator, then the answer is… yes.

The first Cryptfiend lunged.

My body moved on instinct without conscious thought. Heat roared up my arm, light flared, and when my palm met its chest, fire erupted—not wild—controlled. Directed. Like I've done it a thousand times.

The beast shrieked, flipping backward in the sand, chest smoldering.

The crowd goes completely silent.

I glance over at Torren, and he looks stunned—like he's watching someone he's seen a thousand times suddenly become a stranger.

Two more rush me. One bites me viciously as I burn the first, but I barely feel the pain.

I pivot, blast sand into glass beneath my heel, slide under a swinging claw, and slam a wall of heat between us. Fire arcs outward, burning him into ash.

Whispers break out in the stands.

Selene stands.

Seamus swears.

Ubel, whom I hadn't noticed before, whispers something to Selene, and she smirks.

And then, with a single signal from Selene's hand, three more gates slam open.

Six more Cryptfiends flood the arena—bigger, faster, starving.

The crowd roars.

My stomach drops.

I'm still dripping fire from my palms, breathing like my lungs are full of coals. I can barely hold myself upright, and the monsters are coming again—twice the number, twice the size.

One leaps.

I raise my arm, but I'm too slow—and something slams into the sand between us.

A blast of invisible force ripples outward, hurling Cryptfiends back like ragdolls.

The dust clears.

Oren stands there—dark hair whipping in the wind, palm still raised, that dangerous calm in his eyes.

"Sorry, we're late." He says. "Traffic."

Before the crowd realizes what's happening, two massive shadows drop from the coliseum walls.

Zeke.

Zane.

The twins hit the sand in perfect sync—ice crackling across Zeke's skin, fire igniting along Zane's arms. Blue-white frost races across the ground, freezing Cryptfiend limbs mid-lunge. Zane's flames explode outward, searing the sand into glass.

The arena screams.

Guards panic.

Archers aim.

The crowd scrambles backward.

The final two appear like two demons straight from hell itself.

Nathan flickers into existence beside me—flames covering his arms. Jet emerges from behind a pillar, knife dripping blood, and eyes burning with fury.

Five men.

My men.

My heart nearly caves in.

Oren reaches me first. His hands cup my face, voice raw and fierce. "We're here. We are *finally* here."

A Cryptfiend lunges forward.

Oren doesn't look away from me. He flicks two fingers toward it. Shadows spear upward from the sand, ripping the beast off its feet and dragging it into the darkness.

Another leaps for us—Jet raises his hand, and its power dies. It slams into the ground, limp and shocked, unable to regenerate or shift.

I stare at them in awe—their abilities are beyond amazing.

Zane and Zeke join hands—fire and ice colliding in a violent whirl. Flames spiral outward, encasing the beasts in cylinders of heat, while ice locks their limbs in place.

Nathan teleports behind a Cryptfiend mid-pounce, grabs its head, and fire-teleports—reappearing fifteen feet away as the beast turns to ash in the air.

The crowd is in chaos.

I'm in shock because these men… this Faction is ten times more powerful than it was when I was taken.

Selene screams for archers with their own brand of fire abilities. Ubel jumps from the viewing platform, hands thrown out in front of him, planning to use an ability that I can only guess at.

Torren sees him first, draws steel with brutal speed, and then he and Ubel collide amid the chaos.

I hear a screech that grabs my attention, then I scream, "There are more!"

The final gates open. All the remaining Cryptfiends flood the arena.

It becomes a war, and several things happen simultaneously.

Jet nulls entire waves of fiends, leaving them twitching and powerless, ready to be slaughtered.

Zeke coats the sand in ice spikes, turning the arena floor into a death field.

Zane breathes fire—draxon fire—incinerating anything that gets too close, his skin glowing like embers.

Nathan teleports in bursts of flame, cutting through enemies with brutal efficiency.

Oren summons lightning from the sky, calling it down and striking the Cryptfiends dead where they stand.

And Torren…

Torren fights like he was made for war—matching Oren strike for strike, killing as fast as the others, his eyes never leaving me.

"Where the hell did Ubel go?" I whisper to no one. Did Torren kill him? Was I delusional?

Selene calls for reinforcement.

Archers aim carefully.

And then Jet raises both hands.

For a heartbeat, nothing happens.

Then every guard in the arena—every archer, every mounted soldier—loses their power all at once. Their weapons clatter. Their abilities fizzle. Nothing better than human now.

I hear a scream of protest, then grab my head in pain.

Fucking Kristine.

I drop to my knees, eyes squinting in pain, and see her and her men drop onto the sand.

She approaches, smirking, my men too busy to notice her.

"It's time to end you, bitch." She motions to Evan, and I know I only have seconds.

Her eyes widen as I drop my hands from my head and stand with ease. "It's time for someone to die, but it's not going to be *me*."

I'm too powerful for her ability to touch me now. Four streaks of fire ripped from the palm I raised in their direction. The first three hit each of her Faction before they even had the chance to scream, bodies igniting, skin splitting, then poof—gone—nothing but drifting ash.

"This one's for Jet," I muttered as the final flame found Kristine. She briefly met my gaze, a quick succession of shock, disbelief, and fear crossing her face. Flesh blistered, hair curled away, her shriek swallowed by the roar of heat until she crumbled into falling gray dust.

"I guess I was too hot to handle," I smirk, wishing I had the time to piss on her ashes.

I hear a massive roar, and turning, I see Zeke and Zane transform into massive Draxon.

I'm in complete shock, and by the crowd's reaction, I don't think I'm the only one.

Ice and fire collide.

Stone ruptures.

Pillars crack.

Walls buckle.

The coliseum starts to collapse.

"MOVE!" Oren shouts, grabbing me around the waist and slinging me in Nathan's direction.

He teleports us to the lower arch as Jet and Oren scale the wall to meet us. Zane melts an exit through the wall. Zeke freezes the ground behind us, slowing the armored guards.

Torren falls in at our backs, defending us as stone begins to fall like rain.

We burst out into the night—and the entire coliseum implodes behind us.

Bellona shakes.

The stands crumble.

Cracks split the earth.

Flames light the night sky.

I can't believe it. I'm finally free of that place.

Zane laughed, chest heaving. "One star, would not recommend."

Nathan grinned wickedly. "I'd give that a solid ten stars on the 'creative destruction' scale. Although I am disappointed that we didn't get to sewer surf."

"You would be disappointed about that." Zane gagged.

Sewer surfing? What were they talking about?

Jet wiped blood from his mouth. Then grabbed me from Nathan and hugged me so tight I had difficulty breathing.

After only a few seconds, Oren pulled me into his arms and buried his face in my hair. His voice was barely a whisper, shaking with relief. "You're safe now, baby."

I wasn't sure if he saw me kill Kristine, but I felt like I needed to say something. After all, she was his stepsister.

"I killed Kristine." I stared intently at his face, looking for any signs of grief. "I'm sorry."

"I'm not. That bitch deserved worse." He kissed me hard on the mouth. "Let's get the fuck out of here."

Over his shoulder, Torren stood at the edge of the group, sword still in hand.

Eyes still on me.

Expression unreadable.

He fought beside them. He saved my life. But I really didn't think my men were going to be happy about his presence.

And I still don't fully trust him, even after today.

By the time we make it deep enough into the woods that the glow of Bellona fades, my legs stop cooperating—the ground tilts. My knees give.

Oren catches me before the ground can. One arm under my knees, the other around my back, holding me like he's afraid gravity might try to steal me next. He pressed his forehead to mine, breath ragged.

"You're okay," he whispered, voice cracking. "You're *okay*. I've got you." His arms shake.

Nathan crouched in front of me and carefully took one of my hands, inspecting the burn marks and brushing soot off my skin as if he could erase what happened in that arena. "I want to kill every last one of those fuckers again," he says softly, then sighs. "That's the last time we'll be apart, even if I have to stitch us together."

By the look in his eyes, I wasn't entirely sure he was joking. My psycho was absolutely capable of it.

Jet knelt on my other side, thumb wiping blood from my cheek. "I don't know how to exist in a world where you're not in it."

Those words from Jet stole my ability to breathe.

Zane dropped to his knees behind me and slid his arms around my waist, pressing his forehead to my shoulder. "I'm going to kill everyone who held you here," he murmured. "Never again will I be without you. I swear it."

Zeke's hand went to the back of my neck, grounding, gentle. "We should never have let them take you."

Then out of nowhere, my beautiful Pantar appeared and wedged his enormous body under my free hand, rumbling protectively, tail thumping the ground. *I was at the ready in case the men you've picked for your Faction did not measure up. They are on probation after letting you be taken in the first place.*

I'm surrounded.

Smothered.

Loved so fiercely it hurts. And for a moment, I let myself melt into them.

Oren's fingers shake against my cheek as Nathan kisses the back of my hand.

Jet's nose brushes my temple.

Zane squeezes me tight enough to steal breath, only letting go when Zeke cups my jaw and whispers, "We've got you, precious."

I smile, shaky. "I missed y'all so very much."

Five sets of hands tighten at once.

Then Oren's entire body goes still. "Someone's behind us."

The men unfold around me in a heartbeat—Jet in front, Nathan and Zeke flanking my sides, Zane rising slowly with fire crawling up his arms.

Oren disappears in a blink.

I twist around.

Torren stands at the edge of the clearing.

Stormcutter lowered.

Bloody.

Breathing hard.

Watching me.

Not the men. Me.

Oren reappears in front of me, voice low and lethal. "She's safe now. *Leave.*"

Torren's gaze flicks to Oren—measured, cold. "You're welcome."

Nathan scoffs. "Welcome for what? We were the ones to get her out."

Jet grabs the knife at his waist. "We don't know you."

Zeke's eyes narrow to icy slits. "We don't trust you."

Zane just grins, enjoying the tension.

Torren doesn't flinch. "I don't need you to."

He was either the bravest man I knew or the most arrogant. I suspected it was a little of both.

I stepped between them, heart racing. "He saved my life. Let's all take it down a notch."

Five voices combust at once, all in protest of my statement.

My mouth opens. "He helped—"

Oren's voice slices the air. "We won't take the chance." He took a deep breath and narrowed his eyes at Torren. "We do appreciate that you were there when we couldn't be, but we've got her now."

"We were coming," Jet growled, not appreciating Oren's words.

"We always will," Zeke added.

I swallowed hard. "I *know*, but he helped when he didn't have to. That should earn him at least a little trust."

I really didn't know why I was fighting so hard for him because there was no doubt I didn't fully trust him, either.

Torren lifted his chin slightly. "She wouldn't have survived long enough to get to the coliseum without me."

I didn't know about that, but at this point, I wasn't going to protest his statement.

Nathan's smirk is dark. "Maybe, but my Nexi is strong, and even without you or us, she would have found a way." His smirk shifted into a sweet smile as he looked at me. Then he turned back to Torren. "So kindly fuck right off."

The tension was about to go from a small flame to a wildfire out of control—then a twig snapped.

Everyone turned.

Chloe burst out of the trees, Oliver, and (is that the guy from the dining hall?), breathless and pale and covered in ash. "What *the fuck*, you assholes? That wasn't part of the plan at all!"

"Chloe?" I murmur. Not really believing my eyes.

"Reverie!" She screamed, sprinting towards me.

Before any of the men could move, Chloe threw her arms around me, sobbing against my shoulder. "You're alive—*you're alive*—I thought—you badass bitch—don't scare—"

Zane picked her up mid-hug to get her off my bruised and battered body. "Careful. She's just been through a battle of epic proportions."

Chloe ignored him completely and pulled out of his arms to kiss my forehead. "I will buy you a cake, a new minion bra, and get tickets to the fucking Catalina Wine Mixer if you promise to never scare me like that again."

"I *knew* that it was you who sent him to deliver a message to me." I nodded in the direction of the guy from the dining hall.

She smirked, "He's my other Faction member, Deshawn. Two and counting." She waggled her brows.

Oliver exhaled, "I aged ten years tonight." He frowned at my men. "Why make a plan if you're just going to do what the hell you want to anyway?"

Deshawn walked up to me and held out his hand. "My dad speaks highly of your parents."

"*Damien?!*" I snapped my fingers. "You look just like Damien." Deshawn jumped at my enthusiasm and then grinned.

"There *is* a slight resemblance." He suddenly grabbed his shoulder and fell to his knees, followed closely by Chloe.

"She has earned a Faction through her loyalty as your Aegisseer."

Chloe pulled her shirt down, revealing a beautiful Nexus mark that looked very similar to my mom's. Deshawn stared at her in awe, then pulled his collar aside and saw the tree of life surrounded by a circle.

"Now we match." He mumbled to his Faction, clearly in shock.

Oliver dropped to his knees and put his arms around them both. The rest of us were too stunned to move.

After a few moments, Chloe stood and pulled me into her arms, and when her eyes met mine, they were glassy and fierce all at once. "You just made me whole. Ancestors help anyone who tries to hurt you—because they'll have to go through us first."

Oliver and Deshawn echoed the vow, then pulled their new Nexus back into their arms, not wanting to lose the connection to her for a second.

"You have Aegisworn?" Torren asked, clearly stunned by what had just happened.

Before I could reply, Oliver, Chloe, and Deshawn glanced at him, only now noticing his presence.

"Who's the tall, sketchy guy? Do I need to kick his ass?" Chloe examined him from head to toe, then grinned at me. "It would be a pity, though—he's quite the snack."

Both of her men growled.

Oren stepped between Torren and the others, shoulders broad, voice lethal and calm. "He's leaving."

Torren looked at me. *Only me.* "The forest won't stay safe. They will come looking for you as soon as they regroup."

No threat or fear.

Just the truth as he saw it.

Oren's voice dropped to a whisper lined with steel. "Don't stare at my Nexus. We decide as a group whether you stay or go."

Chloe leaned near my ear, "Say the word and we'll bury him. Ride or die. Your choice, bestie."

Torren's voice remained steady, not wavering at all. "I'm staying."

Silence snapped through the clearing.

Oren stepped forward, shadows slithering around his body. "You don't make that decision."

Torren's eyes lock onto Oren's stare without a blink. "You don't know this forest. I do. They'll send everything they have to find you. They'll set fire to this entire forest to smoke you out." He glances at me—just a quick flicker of connection, brief and careful. "I know where the old tunnels are. I know which rivers flow deep enough to hide tracks. I know which cliffs won't support weight. You *don't*." He smirked slightly. "And I know where there might be a portal that's open."

Pantar stepped up to him at his full height and growled low. *"I can take his head for you."*

"That won't be necessary." I smoothed my hand down his side.

Jet's eyes narrowed. "So, you're volunteering to be our guide?"

"No," Torren sniffed. "I'm far from a lowly guide."

And there was the arrogance.

"But I'm not leaving, so you might as well use my knowledge to keep your Nexus safe."

Zane spat on the ground. "You're really asking to die tonight, huh?"

Nathan rolled his neck as his hands burst into flames. "I'll help."

Oren's jaw flexed, hands twitching with barely contained power. "We can keep *our* Nexus safe. We don't need anything from you." Shadows began slithering around his body. "You can tell us the way."

"I'm not here for you." Torren showed no concern despite Oren's display of power. "And you won't be able to find it without me. I'll make sure of that."

A ripple moved through the group—anger, shock, disbelief.

Then he looked at me—*only* me. "You're not safe yet, Reverie. So, I stay." He turned to my men. "They saw what I did in that arena, so they'll kill me on sight, anyway."

My heart was pounding so loudly, I swear they could all hear it. Not once did he mention that he's my Potential.

It was nice that he waited for me to start that conversation.

Oren steps half an inch in front of me, voice low, lethal, final. "You don't touch her, ever."

"Not unless she asks," Torren said with zero inflection.

Every man in the clearing froze.

But Torren turned and smiled gently at me before quietly sitting down at the base of a tree, sword across his lap, back straight, eyes on the darkness beyond us— protecting us as if he belonged there.

Like he'd done it a thousand times.

"I'm not leaving, so you might as well get a few hours of rest."

Oren snarled. "This isn't over."

Torren nodded once. "I didn't think it was."

And for a brief moment, so short that I couldn't be sure... I thought I saw a malicious gleam of satisfaction in his eyes.

CHAPTER 21
REVERIE

The morning tastes like smoke.

Not the sweet kind from campfires—this is the burned metal ash of the coliseum still dying behind us. The sky is a washed-out purple, like even dawn isn't brave enough to shine here.

I push myself up on my elbows, and for a heart-stopping second, pain flashes up my side—then fades. Gone. Skin smooth, muscles knitted, blood vanished as if I hadn't fought for my life last night.

Aurathion healing.

Fast, relentless, and efficient.

My men rouse with me, each immediately alert. Jet takes the lead, examining the corners of the fallen hunting cabin. Thanks to Torren and his annoyingly practical knowledge of Bellona's secret structures, we managed to find this place.

Zeke rubbed his face, his voice gravelly. "How long have we been asleep?"

"Two, maybe three hours," Oren said, already armed and ready to go.

Chloe yawned. "Feels like six minutes."

Zane scoffed. "Be thankful you got to sleep. I spent two hours being Reverie's mattress."

I slapped his chest. "You volunteered."

He kissed the tip of my nose. "I did no such thing. I was forced by destiny, gravity, and the need to have those incredibly perky boobs smooshed to my chest."

Nathan sulked, "And the fact that your Draxon wouldn't allow any of us to get near her."

We laughed briefly, none of us able to forget the danger we're in for long. If caught, none of us would survive. I could accept my death, but I couldn't bear the deaths of the people I love.

Jet catches my gaze. "You healed?"

"Seems like it." I touch the spot where the Cryptfiend bit deep enough to scrape bone. Nothing. Not even a scar. "Faction perks?"

Zeke huffs a laugh. "Perks? More like blessings from the Ancestors."

Across the cabin, Torren pushed off the wall, obviously annoyed. "We need to move. Selene and Seamus were in the coliseum when the explosions started. Ubel too. They'll be screaming for your return."

I shivered at the thought of what that would mean. But it also reminded me of his strange fight with Ubel. Why did it seem like I was the only one who noticed? And why hadn't I mentioned it to one of my men yet?

Silence cracked through the room like lightning.

Oren turned slowly, his entire aura sharpening. "You saw them alive?"

Torren nodded. "Hard to miss the people screaming orders to capture or kill the girl who just slaughtered their prized monsters."

The temperature in the room dropped ten degrees as Zeke and Zane went still—too still. That Draxon edge beginning to bleed through their eyes.

Nathan's voice sounded full of delight. "And now they're ready to go on the hunt for the soon-to-be dead fuckers."

"Every warrior in Bellona will be looking for you," Torren continued. "Including the ones who won't bother taking you alive."

Zane rolled his shoulders, cracking his neck. "Let them fucking try."

Jet leaned against the broken window, peering at the tree line. "How much time do we have?"

"Not enough," Torren said. "But the cabin is hidden. You're safe for now."

"For *now*," Oren echoes, voice like steel. "We leave this minute. What's the plan?" He reluctantly directed the question to Torren.

"At this point, all known portal access has been terminated. We must distance ourselves from Bellona as much as possible. From there, we might locate the one I've heard about. If it's damaged, you still have an advantage. He looked at Pantar, who was curled up in the corner. "It's fortunate that you have a Fellat bonded to your Nexus."

Oren nodded, "We leave immediately."

Everyone began packing what little they had, checking weapons, and grounding themselves for another run. I stand easily, no pain, no weakness: the bite, the bruises, the agony from the fighting… all gone. Aurathion blood is fast—but my healing has evolved since the voices have made themselves known.

Zeke watches me with something like awe. "You heal quicker than us."

I hadn't mentioned the voices yet, but in my defense, it may be a while before we can settle enough to have some of the discussions that are needed.

"Probably because my body is used to it." I winced, realizing that my statement would remind them of some of the things I went through.

Zane snorts. "New rule: no torture or almost dying."

I smiled, grateful that he brushed it off for now. The things done to me can't be unpacked in a few minutes, and honestly, I might decide never to unpack them. I knew they would feel that everything was their fault, and I didn't want that for them.

Chloe slung her bag over her shoulder, eyeing Torren. "If he's coming, someone has to babysit him to make sure he's not going to stab us in the back."

Nathan lifted a brow. "Dibs."

Zane raised his hand. "No, *no*, I want to babysit the mysterious man who looks at my Nexus like she's a Snickers bar."

"Careful. I bite." Torren smirked. "And if I wanted to stab you, I had plenty of opportunity last night."

Zane growled deep.

Jet stepped between them. "Enough. We need to move."

Oren opened the cabin door. Cold, sharp morning air poured in. Behind the trees, Bellona's glowing skyline rose—a mix of orange and black, resembling a funeral pyre.

Oren stepped out first.

The rest of us followed.

Torren fell into step behind us, silent and watchful.

I heard a bird shriek overhead, then watched as it landed on Nathan's shoulder.

"I was wondering where you were. Nexi, meet Dale." Nathan grinned. "I named him with you in mind."

"I like it." I stepped closer and ran my hand down his soft feathers.

Pantar butted me with his head. *"Time to get moving. You can pet the chicken later."*

Seems my men weren't the only ones with a jealous streak.

I whispered with a smile, "Let's get out of here then."

The forest quickly swallows us with towering trees that resemble pines, thick underbrush, and a silence that feels like it's holding its breath. Bellona smolders behind the trees, sending thin gray ribbons of smoke into the sunrise, but each step forward feels like we're peeling away chains.

I'm oddly eager to see this land that might have been my home if circumstances had been different. I was captured and brought directly to the coliseum, so I haven't seen any of the countryside.

Pantar pads beside me—massive, sleek, black fur

rippling with every step. His tentacles curl slowly and cautiously as he scans the woods. Not even the men breathe too close to him. One growl from Pantar last night convinced everyone that I am *his* person, and he is very willing to enforce that. He only deferred to Zane when his Draxon appeared, reassuring Pantar that I was as safe as when I was with him.

We travel quietly for a while—there are too many shadows among the trees, and too many sounds that don't belong in the forest. Zeke and Zane continue partially shifting, nostrils flaring, eyes flashing, ensuring nothing gets close without their knowledge.

Every few minutes, Torren points in a new direction, guiding us through terrain only someone from Bellona would recognize. The men don't trust him—and even after everything, neither do I—but he's useful. *Infuriatingly* useful.

Oren raised his fist.

Everyone freezes.

Pantar crouched, muscles coiled, growling low.

Zane murmured, "There are two scouts."

My heart rate soared, and my breathing became uneven. I would *not* go back.

Nathan moved to my side, voice soft. "Look at me."

His hand cupped the side of my face, thumb brushing just beneath my lips. There's no teasing in his eyes—just rage, fear, and want. The forest faded, danger faded, everything narrowed to the heart of him.

"You're scared of being recaptured." He murmured. "I'll never let that happen."

"I'm fine." I averted my eyes, unable to meet his gaze as I lied.

He huffed a breath—half annoyance, half desperation—and then he kissed me.

Not gentle or careful.

Hungry.

His mouth crashed against mine, his other hand slid to the back of my neck, and he pulled me in. The world tilted—heat, breath, teeth, the taste of smoke, adrenaline, and him. He kissed like he was trying to steal the memory of every hurt that was done to me while I was here. Like he's staking his claim all over again.

My fingers twisted into his shirt, pulling him closer. The fear, the exhaustion, the chaos—all of it melts under the heat of his mouth.

When he finally pulled back, his forehead rested against mine. His voice is a rough whisper. "Don't do that again."

I was confused and asked, "What?"

"Lie to me."

Zane cut in, grinning, "I enjoyed the show, but Nathan's technique could use some improvement." Nathan flipped him off. "The scouts are nearing, so wrap it up, Loverboy."

Nathan pressed one more quick, fierce kiss to my lips and stepped back, fire sparking at his fingertips. Then he motioned Dale to go scout.

"I'll follow the chicken. I do not trust his skill." Pantar grumbled and then disappeared.

Oren gestured sharply. "Move. *Now.*"

We slip further into the woods, fast and quiet, shadows clinging to us.

Torren is the only one who looked completely calm. "There's a cave up ahead. Hidden by rockfall. It'll buy us a few hours."

Zeke muttered low. "Convenient knowledge."

"Yes," Torren said dryly. "That's why I mentioned it."

Whether we trust him or not, every step brings us farther from Bellona's reach. And with Nathan's kiss still burning on my lips, I suddenly feel very, very alive.

The forest felt wrong.

Too quiet. Too still. Even the wind seemed to hold its breath as we picked our way toward the narrow stone opening Torren swore would lead to an old mining tunnel. A half-collapsed cave mouth yawned ahead, gnarled roots curled over it like skeletal fingers.

Nathan still had his hand on the small of my back, guiding me like I was made of spun glass instead of someone who'd just taken down Cryptfiends and a coliseum full of psychopaths. Zane and Zeke flanked us, eyes burning gold as their Draxon senses sifted through every scent and heartbeat in a mile radius. Oren walked ahead, invisible—just his voice flickering through our minds when needed.

Jet stayed close, one hand hovering near me, the other curled in a fist that kept clenching and unclenching. We had a lot to work out. I knew he felt responsible for my capture, and that just wasn't so. He'd done all that he could at the time, and I was determined to make him realize it.

Pantar padded quietly beside us, glaring at Dale from his perch on Nathan's shoulder.

We were almost to the cave mouth when he stopped dead, ears flattening. A low, rolling growl vibrated from deep in his chest. *"Something's here."*

Fire ignited across Nathan's palms.

Torren took a single step back, voice barely audible. "He… followed."

The trees to our left shuddered. Bark splintered. Leaves burst from branches in a thousand frantic spirals.

And then he emerged.

The Varruk. Vee.

The same towering, obsidian-furred beast from the coliseum—horns curling into the shape of a crown, snout with fangs bared, talons carving the earth as he slowed to a halt. Eyes locked onto me first… then flicked to Pantar… then to the men surrounding me.

Zane's fire roared to life.

Zeke's ice crackled across his forearms.

Oliver and Deshawn stepped protectively in front of Chloe.

I smiled in welcome, happy to see my friend.

Nathan frowned at my expression.

"*No.* Absolutely not. We are not adopting another monster," Nathan said firmly.

"Look how much Pantar has brought to this Faction." Jet nodded in the Fellat's direction.

"Pantar is different. He's classy and fierce. Like a murder-panther thingy with extra limbs." Nathan explained, making absolutely no sense.

Pantar preened, as if he were being paid the highest compliment. *"He has always been my favorite."*

I heard a snort somewhere to my left. Oren had gone invisible in case we needed a surprise attack.

The Varruk ignored the commentary and lowered himself—massive body folding, claws tucked in, head bowed toward me.

Submitting.

"Khal' Sira... I tracked your scent. You freed me. I still owe you a death."

Zeke froze. "What the hell does he mean by that?"

"He doesn't mean it the way it sounded. I killed for him, and he's honor-bound to kill for me," I explained quickly. "At least, that's how he put it."

Nathan muttered, "Khal-what now?"

I ignored Nathan and looked at Vee. "You followed us?"

His head lifted. That monstrous snout almost brushed my hand. *"Debt must be paid. I know where a portal is that you seek."* The air snapped with shock. *"I have not traveled there in many years, so I can't know its condition. But it is near to us."*

Oren materialized suddenly, voice low and dangerous. "Why help us?"

The Varruk rose to his full height—nearly seven feet—muscles coiling, teeth flashing. Looking like a monster from nightmares, but there was intelligence behind it—something ancient, wounded, and bound by his own code. "Because she did not kill me when ordered." His gaze swept over my men. "Because they would kill her, and that cannot be allowed."

Then his eyes landed on Torren.

Hard.

Knowing.

For the first time, Torren didn't look like the confident, arrogant man he usually presented. Neither spoke, but something important passed between them.

Nathan's hand tightened around my hip, voice low. "Reverie… are you sure he can be trusted?"

There was a warm, instinctive certainty in my chest. "He's not our enemy."

Pantar moved to Vee's side, enormous heads inches apart. The Fellat didn't growl or try to attack. Instead, he reached out with one tentacle and slowly touched Vee's shoulder.

Nathan blinked. "Are they fucking bonding?"

Zane laughed, "Looks like it. This Faction just leveled the fuck up."

Vee turned, pointing a claw toward a rocky ridge behind the cave. *"The portal is close. But others hunt it. They hunt you."*

Jet stepped beside me, voice tense. "Reverie, if he knows the route, he might be our only chance."

Oren nodded once. "We move with him. Quietly. Quickly."

Vee crouched, lowering himself as if he expected—Ancestors help me—to carry someone.

Zane whispered, "No way. No. Absolutely—"

Nathan shoved him toward Vee. "Shotgun. Enjoy."

"REVERIE!" Zane shouted, shoving back at Nathan.

"Man the fuck up, brother." Chloe laughed so hard she was leaning on her men to keep from falling.

I couldn't stop myself from laughing. Even now—dirt in my hair and an army hunting us—my men were chaos mixed with love.

We headed toward the portal with a monster who owed me his life and a Fellat who trusted him enough to bet *our* lives on it.

And somewhere behind us, I hoped Selene was sick with stress, worrying that the girl she tried to break... was coming back with an army of nightmares to finish what she started.

CHAPTER 22

KHAROX

They did not hear the forest the way I did.

The trees whispered of hunters.

The earth trembled beneath heavy boots.

Blood-scent rode the wind like a warning.

Yet they walked, tired and hopeful, toward the stone arch nestled in the ridge—a broken thing. And still… they hoped.

Khal' Sira walked among them.

Small. Soft. *Strong*.

But she had freed me.

Her scent was fire and ancient power. Her spirit unbroken. Untamed.

A queen without a crown, yet the world bowed when she breathed.

I approached the dead archway. Stones collapsed in places, roots crawling where magic once lived. My claws pressed into a shattered glyph. Energy sparked—weak, fading—then died like a dying star.

Not enough.

The portal would not hold.

They gathered behind me—her warriors.

Protective.

Suspicious.

Afraid.

The fire-handed one—the snarling male—glared as if they might kill me. The Draxon-possessed twins watched with predatory focus. The shadow-wielder poised, ready to strike.

I could break them all.

Yet I bore no fangs.

My debt was to her.

I turned, towering above them. My voice slid into their minds, heavy and rough. *"I am called Kharox."*

The fire-handed male blinked. "Carrots?"

The one called Chloe elbowed him so hard his breath left his lungs.

Good female. Sharp. Deadly.

We reached the broken archway, roots strangling ancient stone. The air tasted wrong—old magic and dust. I pressed a claw to the glyph. Blue sparks crawled up my arm, then died.

Dead portal.

The pack reacted as Aurathions tend to do—voices, panic, questions. But I watched Khal' Sira.

Her breath stuttered.

Her face filled with disappointment.

She feared losing the others on the far side—her family, her tribe.

"Can we fix it?"

"Not tonight." I pointed out where the damage had been done.

Chloe's voice was tight. "That was done recently."

Deshawn's grip tightened on his weapons. "They waited until she escaped. They wanted to funnel us here."

The shadow-male, Oren, swore under his breath. He turned to the liar with accusation.

"I couldn't have known. I'm sorry." He ducked his head, but I alone saw the slight smirk on his face.

I would kill him, but I knew he had a purpose.

I looked to Khal' Sira. *"It's a trap."*

Oliver moved closer to Chloe, shielding her with his body. Deshawn shifted beside her, jaw clenched.

Good pack.

Protective.

Smart.

"If you try to open it, they will feel it. They will come with chains and blades and fire."

Reverie's voice cracked. "We have to get Chloe and the others home."

I stepped into her path and lowered my head until my snout rested inches from hers. Her scent trembled—fear, fury, love, all bleeding together. *"Stay. Fight. Kill those who hunt you. Then cross when the way is safe."*

Chloe looked between us, her eyes shone with fear and defiance. "I wouldn't leave without you, anyway." She turned to me. "What if they find the portal on the other side first and attack from there?"

"Then we kill them there too," I growled. *"I follow you through worlds if I must."*

The forest screamed a warning—snapped branches, distant shouts, metal on stone.

Hunters.

Dozens.

The fire-male snarled. "Reverie, they're close."

"Too close," Oren, the leader, bit out.

Oliver slipped forward, blades drawn. Deshawn rolled his shoulders, ready for blood.

Chloe whispered, "We can do this."

Khal' Sira looked at every one of them, including me.

Her voice broke open with something ancient. "*We make our stand here.*"

I roared so deep the ground around us vibrated.

Good.

Let Bellona learn what it means to hunt monsters now that our queen has returned.

The first hunter broke through the trees with the stench of fear and sweat.

Then another.

And another.

Dozens.

They thought numbers would matter.

My claws slid free with a soft metallic whisper. Pantar beside me did the same, tentacles coiling like living blades.

Deshawn stepped forward, voice low. "Here we go."

Oliver crossed one blade over the other in silent promise. Chloe pressed her back to his, chin lifted. Small, but unbreakable. When their abilities appeared, they would be legendary, as the queen's Aegisworn should be.

The fire-male—Nathan—laughed darkly and lit his hands like torches.

The twins—Zeke and Zane—exhaled smoke, eyes glowing with the shift they barely controlled. Their scales rippled beneath their skin.

And Khal' Sira... she stood in the center of them all.

Too fragile.

Too scared.

The hunters charged.

I met the first with a swipe that opened him from collarbone to hip.

Pantar tore through two more.

Oliver moved like a whisper of knives, and Deshawn fought like a man who had lived his life on the battlefield.

But the enemy did not tire.

More poured through the trees.

Archers.

Blades.

Shackles.

Shackles meant for *her*.

Khal' Sira's breath quickened. Trapped. Surrounded. She lifted her hands—but not with fire. Her eyes unfocused, pupils dilating. Something ancient stirred in her blood. In the air.

The world went silent.

Even my heart paused.

A voice—not hers—spoke from her throat, layered and echoing through bone and soul. *"She is ours. We stand."*

Her hair lifted on a wind that did not exist.

The air rippled.

Every Ancestor who had worn her blood ignited inside her.

Hunters that had been lunging stopped mid-stride.

Frozen. Mid-air. Suspended as though time itself bowed.

Khal' Sira's hands spread, and the light around her turned white-hot, ghostly, shimmering like a thousand spirit hands overlaying her own. A spectral Queen rose behind her—tall, crowned, made of smoke and stars.

Pantar's fur stood on end.

This was no Aurathion ability.

"You do not touch what is ours." the spirit-voice echoed in every skull.

The hunters hung—choking, clawing, terrified.

Reverie whispered, voice her own again, but filled with command. "Drop."

Every enemy slammed into the ground at once—like the earth itself had called them home. Dead before they hit the ground.

Silence.

Even the forest held its breath.

Her knees wavered—body shaking under power too significant for her bones—but her men caught her before she fell. Nathan's fire dimmed. Zeke's claws gentled. Jet and Oren stepped in protectively. Zane stood at the ready to defend her if needed.

I lowered myself—not in weakness.

In recognition.

Khal' Sira.

The Reborn Queen.

Last child of the bloodline.

And I made the sign of loyalty. Crossed arms, claw dragged down my sternum.

They didn't want her dead.

They wanted her contained.

Because if she rose…

The Dark Faction could not cage her.

I moved to her side, towering over her, growl vibrating the earth. *"You did well, little queen."*

She looked up at me, not frightened. Not horrified in the least by what she'd done.

Just steady.

"Did I?" she whispered. "I'm not even sure how I did it."

CHAPTER 23

REVERIE

We had won.

At least, it looked like we had.

My pulse was still racing, breath sharp in my chest. Stunned by the ability that had taken over my body.

"Please tell me that was all of them," Nathan complained.

"No. There will be more." Jet whispered.

The air turned cold, sharp enough to sting. A ripple of dread crawled up my spine.

Zane flicked blood from his blade. "If that was their best—"

"That I very much doubt." Deshawn shook his head.

A slow clap cut through the clearing.

Ubel Brummond himself.

He looked at the bodies scattered across the earth with mild disappointment. "Well," he sighed, "that was faster than expected."

Zane's nostrils flared, fire rippling across his palms. "Come closer. I dare you."

Ubel barely looked at him. His eyes were on me. "Aurathion healing kicking in... bond restored... and somehow you still survived the Varruk." His smile sharpened. "You're evolving."

My stomach twisted. "Go straight to hell."

"Don't worry, little Hawthorne." He smiled evilly. "It's not as though you killed them."

He lifted one hand.

Just a flick of his fingers.

The fallen soldiers began to jerk.

My breath caught.

One by one, corpses rolled to their knees—armor scraping, bones cracking. Eyes that should have been shut for good snapped open, milky and wrong. A man whose throat had been slashed open gurgled as he stood, head lolling at an impossible angle, sword hanging from limp fingers.

Jet stumbled back. "What the fuck?!"

Chloe whimpered, and Oliver stepped in front of her at the ready.

"They don't need breath to serve," Ubel murmured. "They only need me."

He twitched his wrist.

The dead charged.

Not human. *Fucking* zombies.

Pantar lunged, knocking the first one back. Zane roared and half-shifted, wings ripping open the air. Zeke's ice exploded outward in jagged shards. Kharox slashed with teeth and nails.

I should have attacked, too.

But something inside me locked on the dead—something ancient and furious.

They didn't want to fight.

They wanted to be released.

And suddenly, I could feel it.

Not their bodies.

Their *souls*.

"Reverie!" Nathan grabbed my wrist. "Stay behind us—"

He should have known better.

Power slammed through me, white-hot and electric, like a thousand voices whispering the same command through my blood.

"Not his to control."

The earth trembled. Light flared under my skin. The dead froze mid-lunge—swords inches from my face—turning rigid as stone.

Ubel's smile finally cracked. "What did you just do?"

My voice shook, but it didn't break. "I broke your hold."

The corpses stood motionless, caught between his command and mine—no longer puppets, but not yet free.

"And I'm not done."

Ubel's expression darkened. "Interesting," he whispered. "Trent will want to hear about this." He glanced in Torren's direction with a smirk.

And before Nathan's fire could reach him—Ubel vanished into shadow.

Leaving us in a clearing full of unmoving corpses…

And a power burning in my veins that didn't come from any Aurathion ability I'd ever heard of.

❧ ⚛ ☙

The clearing was full of flesh-and-blood statues.

Dozens of bodies stood frozen mid-strike, swords inches from their targets, eyes wide and cloudy. They weren't breathing. They weren't bleeding. They weren't alive.

But they weren't dead either.

Not really.

I could *feel* them, like whispers pressed against the inside of my skull. Fear. Confusion. Pain that didn't belong in bodies that should have been at rest.

Zane lowered his flames, chest rising and falling hard. "What... what *is* this?"

Nobody answered.

Because every gaze was locked on me.

Chloe started forward, but Deshawn laid a hand on her arm, stopping her.

I didn't remember deciding to move, but I stepped forward anyway. My fingers brushed the chest plate of the nearest soldier, cold metal slick with soot.

His eyes that were soulless a moment ago, shifted just enough to find mine. A plea. The kind that didn't need words. Not my enemy anymore. Just a soul seeking absolution.

Nathan's voice was rough behind me. "Nexi... what are you doing?"

"I don't know," I admitted, my voice trembling while my hands stayed steady. "But I can sense them."

They were trapped—hooked on tangled threads of magic, tied to Ubel's will. They couldn't move. They couldn't rest. They couldn't leave.

My throat tightened. "They don't want to be here."

Jet's face went pale. "Reverie, how do you know that?"

"Because I can hear them."

Kharox made the gesture he'd made several times since we first met. Arms crossed, then running a single claw down his sternum.

A shiver ran through the clearing.

I closed my eyes.

A warmth bloomed behind my ribs, soft at first—like someone touching my heart with gentle hands. Then sharper. Older. The feeling of standing in the footprints of a thousand warriors before me.

Female voices rose—not loud or harsh. Whispered. Reverent.

"Let them go."

Light rippled from my palms, pale and bright as starlight. It sank into the soldier under my hand, then spread through the others like a breath of wind.

Their bodies relaxed.

Swords dropped from stiff fingers.

Helmets tilted back.

And one by one, those cloudy eyes cleared. Not physically, but in a way that made my chest ache. Every soul trapped inside them exhaled at once.

And then—

They fell.

Not like puppets cut from strings. Like men finally allowed to sleep.

Armor hit the earth with dull, final thuds. Grass shifted beneath them. The air tasted lighter. Cleaner.

The magic holding them was gone.

Nathan approached me carefully, as if I were fragile. "Reverie… what did you just do?"

I swallowed hard. My voice came out small. "I freed them."

Torren stared like he'd seen a ghost. "Only one other ever had that ability."

My heart stuttered. "Who?"

"Queen Lilibet."

Silence swallowed the clearing.

Pantar pressed against my side. Zeke looked at me in concern. Oren watched me like I was a storm about to break.

Kharox reverently whispered, *"Dhal' Sira."*

That wasn't the term he'd used earlier. I really needed to find out what he was calling me, but at the moment, I wasn't sure if I was even breathing.

Because Ubel didn't just send soldiers to kill us.

He sent them to test me.

No one spoke at first.

The only sound was armor settling as the bodies finally rested.

My hands were still glowing faintly—soft white light fading slowly like dying embers. I curled my fingers tight to hide it, but everyone had already seen.

Nathan was the first to move.

He stepped close, cupping my face in both hands,

searching my eyes like he expected to find someone else staring back. "Reverie... you just—"

He didn't even have words.

Jet finally found his voice, but it came out thin and unsteady. "You unmade Ubel's magic. Have you ever heard of anyone being able to do that?"

He directed the question to Oren.

"Not in all of my studies." He replied, still staring at me in awe.

"It didn't hurt them," Zeke said, staring at the fallen soldiers. "It released them."

Torren dragged a hand through his hair, "Ubel has the ability of necromancy. I've fought people with that ability, though it's rare. This wasn't that. She didn't control them —she freed them."

Oren stood a few paces back, lightning flickered across his knuckles, like he didn't trust the air around us anymore. His voice was quiet, but dangerous. "We need to move. Ubel didn't leave because he was afraid. He left because he's calling for reinforcements."

Torren nodded hard. "There's another portal, older and unmarked. But the Dark Faction has probably begun searching for it. After this..." He waved a hand at the bodies. "...they'll come in force."

Nathan pressed his forehead against mine, just for a moment. "We're not losing you. Not after all this. We move now."

Pantar rumbled at my side, tail flicking, ears forward. Even he felt the pressure in the air—like the forest itself was waiting to swallow us.

Zane stepped forward, voice low. "Precious girl… what did you feel when you did it?"

I swallowed. "Their fear. Their pain. They didn't want to be trapped inside their bodies anymore."

Zeke's breath stuttered. "That's not an Aurathion gift."

"It is now," Oren said fiercely. "And we protect her until she figures out why."

Torren looked at me with something that wasn't fear—something that was a mix between guilt and reverence. "Whatever you woke up… Ubel won't stop. Trent won't stop. And Selene will tear the world apart to get her hands on you."

Jet's jaw flexed. "Then we don't give them the chance."

"We'll try the portal first, but if it's being monitored, our only chance may be the resistance," Torren mumbled to himself.

A cold wind rushed through the trees—like Aurathia herself agreed.

Oren's jaw clenched. "Portal. Now. We'll discuss that if and when it might become necessary."

No hesitation.

No argument.

They didn't understand what I was turning into. Hell, I didn't either. But they closed ranks around me like a shield, weapons raised, powers humming, senses stretched to the limit.

We were running again—for *now*.

I lifted my chin in determination. I was going to learn how to use these new abilities. These men and our friends were worth everything I had to do from this point forward.

The portal was our only chance…

…and Ubel would be back with more than corpses.

I had a feeling Selene would be with him, and that was someone I would like to avoid at all costs. But if they backed me into a corner this time, it might be them running.

CHAPTER 24

REVERIE

We traveled well into the night. The forest swallowed all sound as we moved.

No birds.

No wind.

Just the steady crunch of leaves beneath our boots and the low growl of Pantar somewhere ahead, scouting with ears sharp and muscles coiled. Every few steps, someone glanced behind us, expecting Ubel or Selene to materialize from the shadows.

The adrenaline from the fight faded, replaced by exhaustion that we felt deep in our bones.

Each of my Faction was struggling in their own way and I knew we all needed to rest before we collapsed.

Torren cut through the underbrush, jaw tight, eyes scanning the dark. "We're half a day from the portal—less if we move fast. But traveling at night is dangerous. The Dark Factions know this territory better than we do."

Oren didn't slow. "We're not stopping unless it's safe."

"If we keep going without rest, safety may be the least of our issues." Nathan glanced meaningfully in my direction.

My legs trembled, though I'd never admit it out loud. Nathan was right. My healing worked fast—usually—whatever had just awakened in me, left a deeper kind of fatigue. Not physically, but soul deep.

We traveled for another hour, and I knew it was time to let my men know, my pride be damned. "We need rest. *I* need rest." I murmured.

They all stopped.

No argument and not the least bit of hesitation. Their concern for me outweighed anything else.

Zane ran a hand through his hair. "We'll find something. A cave. Abandoned cabin. Anything with walls."

"There is a place right ahead that may do," Kharox growled into our minds.

Pantar suddenly froze, ears pricking, tail stiff.

Nathan tensed. "What is it?"

The Fellat turned, eyes glowing amber, and nudged me with his head—firmly—before padding deeper into the trees, silent as shadow. *"Come, Nexus, I found the place the Varruk spoke of."*

We followed.

Branches parted to reveal a narrow cut of gorge, stone walls rising on either side like ancient teeth. A thin river ran along its base, glinting under the moonlight. And carved into the rock, half-hidden by vines and moss, was a dark opening.

A cave.

Natural, but deep enough to hide us.

Oren exhaled. "We stay here until dawn."

Nathan led me in first, one hand warm at my back. The air inside was cool and dry, smelling of old earth and stone. Zane lit a small flame in his palm, revealing smooth walls curving inward, wide enough for all of us to sleep and guard the entrance.

Oren and Deshawn checked the perimeter, shadows flickering at their boots. Zeke and Zane shifted back fully, exhaustion weighing them down. Jet extended his hand to check for lingering abilities in the air.

And finally—finally—everyone exhaled.

Chloe sat beside me, brushing the hair from her face. "How are you holding up, bestie?"

I just wanted to say it's fine, or everything's all good here. But lying didn't feel right with this strong woman who'd traveled worlds to help find me. "I don't know what's happening to me."

Her shoulder leaned into mine. "Whatever it is, we'll face it together." She turned her wrist over. "See this mark, this means I will always be here for you, no matter what."

I felt tears fill my eyes at the sight of the tree of life inside a circle that marked her. "I didn't mean to do that."

"I'm glad you did. It helped me find you. Oliver and I are honored to be marked by our future Queen." She smirked, "Deshawn was so jealous until you made him part of the club. He even threatened to take my best friend status."

I bumped her shoulder with mine. "That'll never happen." I waggled my brow. "But I bet he does give good foot rubs."

"Girl, you have no idea!" We both started giggling.

Oliver crouched near the entrance, voice low but firm. "Get some sleep. We need to move at first light."

I saw Kharox join him and settle down to watch over us while we rested.

The cave settled around us—warm bodies, dim firelight, the rhythmic breathing of my men, and Pantar sprawled protectively near.

Just before I drifted off to sleep, I felt Jet lie down beside me and pull me close.

I stood in the middle of a battlefield.

Not mine.

Hers.

The sky was the color of blood and lightning, torn open by magic. The air shook with the roar of creatures and steel. Bodies lay scattered across cracked earth—soldiers twisted in unnatural shapes, arrows jutting from armor, ground torn apart by power.

My heart pounded, but not in my chest.

In hers.

Lilibet's.

Her hand clenched around a sword etched with runes that glowed when she breathed. Flames spiraled along the blade— familiar, yet older than any fire I knew how to call.

Dust gusted past. Screams. War cries—the thunderous beat of wings overhead.

And there, at her back—her Faction.

Ambrose, bloodied and staggering, lightning crackling, unstable along his arms.

Merritt, one leg limp, is defending Ambrose with impossible fury.

Bren and Zenon, slashing through enemies twice their size.

Larkin, teeth clenched, summoned earth and stone to shield them.

Five men.

Not six.

Kratos wasn't there.

And something inside me—inside Lilibet—felt that absence like a wound.

She spun, slicing through an armored beast that roared as it split apart. Power surged through her veins, painting the world in white-hot clarity. She was unstoppable.

Until a scream ripped through the air.

Merritt.

He fell to his knees, an arrow lodged deep in his side.

"NO!" Lilibet's voice roared out of my mouth, power shaking the ground around her.

Ambrose caught Merritt before he collapsed fully, lightning flickered uselessly across his skin—his ability was gone, drained from battle or blood loss. Their eyes met, raw and terrified.

Zenon and Larkin rushed to cover them, blades flashing, but too many enemies surged forward.

Lilibet's hands burned—light exploding from her palms—magic tearing upward like a detonation. The ground cracked open in a shockwave, and bodies flung into the air.

Her breath heaved, vision shaking, but she reached for Merritt. "Merritt, stay with me. Stay with me!"

His hand came up, trembling, stained in his own blood. "I'm here, My Queen."

But his voice flickered like it was fading.

Behind us—behind her—I could feel it: Kratos should have been there.

He wasn't.

The hole his absence left was jagged and wrong.

Lilibet's heart broke with that realization. Not because she thought he was dead, but because she could feel him alive... and separated from them.

Ambrose looked up at her, desperate. "He can't hold on much longer."

Merritt's breath hitched. Blood soaked his armor. "It's... alright. You have to protect them."

"NO," Lilibet cried, voice cracking into something feral. "I will not bury another one of you!"

Fire erupted from her hand, searing the arrow to ash. Her ability poured into him—healing, stitching flesh, forcing his heart to keep beating. Her power was fury and love and refusal to let fate steal him.

Merritt screamed, but his eyes stayed open.

He lived.

Barely.

Lilibet lifted her head, tears cutting through ash on her cheeks, and whispered, "Where are you, Kratos?"

But the battlefield only answered with thunder.

Her scream of rage ripped me awake.

I shot up in the cave, heart racing, breath shattered into pieces.

Jet stirred beside me, his hand reaching for me instinctively.

"Reverie? Angel—hey, what happened?"

But I couldn't answer, still feeling the echo of another woman's grief in my chest.

Still hearing Lilibet's voice.

"Where are you, Kratos?"

And deep in the cave's entrance, Kharox lifted his head, ears pricked—because he heard it too.

It felt like I'd only been back asleep for a few minutes when I felt Jet shake me gently awake. "Can we talk for a minute? I found a private spot deeper inside."

I rubbed a hand across my face, trying to wake up. "Of course."

Pulling me to my feet, we walked silently deeper into the cave until we reached a small body of water with steam rising from it.

I couldn't hold back my squeal of excitement, but Jet quickly covered my mouth with his large hand, almost concealing my entire face. "Shhh, angel, I don't want the others to come looking for us."

I nodded, and he removed his hand, "Sorry, I haven't had a bath in days, and that water looks wonderful."

"It's safe. I checked it over before I woke you." The big man suddenly looked bashful. "Do you want to take a dip with me?"

"Hell, yes, I do." I started stripping off my torn, bloody clothes. When I saw he was just standing there, I looked at him, questioning. "Aren't you coming in?"

He nodded, then said with reverence, "I've just never seen anything as beautiful as you."

I blushed. I hadn't thought about this being the first time for him to see me fully nude. I'd been too excited about the bath. "I wish you could've seen me before I had all of these scars."

He walked over and pulled me into his arms. "Those scars tell a story of your bravery and strength. Before you were a stunning girl, now you're an amazing woman, and I couldn't be prouder that you chose me to stand by your side."

I didn't plan to kiss him.

But when his mouth brushed mine—just barely—something inside me unraveled.

The first touch was soft. Warm. Cautious. Like we were learning what the other liked. His lips moved against mine slowly, gently, tasting the moment. His hand slid to the back of my neck, fingers threading through my dark hair, and heat bloomed through me in a slow, sweet wave.

I kissed him back.

Tentative at first.

Then deeper.

His breath hitched, and something in him snapped loose. His arm wrapped around my waist, pulling me closer until there was no space left between us. The kiss grew hotter, hungrier. The kind of kiss that stole thought and breath and everything else. Steam curled around us, and the spring hissed softly.

Jet pressed me lightly against the warm stone, not trapping me, just holding me with an unfathomable need. His lips parted mine, tongues brushing in a slow, devastating slide that made my knees weak. His hand cupped my jaw, tilting my head up to deepen the kiss, and I tasted every ounce of restraint he was trying—and failing—to keep.

He kissed like he wanted to memorize me.

Like he'd feared losing me.

Like he'd never be parted from me again.

When we finally pulled apart, foreheads still touching, breath mingling in the warm air, his voice was rough. "It's my fault you're here."

My hand found his chest, feeling the wild beat beneath my palm. "That's not true. It's *their* fault, never yours."

He leaned in again—just a whisper of a kiss, softer, almost reverent. "They're going to die for that."

"Yes, my love, they are."

Jet's thumb brushed my bottom lip once more, like he wasn't done tasting me—or deciding if he wanted to take this further.

He must have reached a decision, because he quickly stripped off his clothes and then offered me his hand.

I took it while trying to pick my jaw up from the ground at the sight of his ripped body. Damn, this man was *fine*—muscles upon muscles and a face that would make angels weep.

His *angel* just might if he didn't touch me soon.

The water was scorching, almost too hot, enveloping my skin as I dropped into the spring beside him. The heat sank into my bones, easing the pain in my muscles and the tremor in my hands. Jet stepped in front of me, his body just close enough that every tiny movement caused the water to swirl between us.

For a moment, neither of us spoke.

He was watching me. Carefully. Hungrily. Like every breath I took might pull him apart.

"You're staring," I whispered.

His voice dropped into that low, unguarded place he rarely let anyone hear. "I've been staring since the moment I met you."

I didn't have time to breathe, much less answer, before he crossed the space between us. His hand slid beneath the water, fingers curling around my waist, guiding me toward him. Heat flared everywhere his skin touched mine.

His mouth found mine again, and this time, there was nothing slow about it.

The kiss hit hard—urgent, deep, all tongue, breath, and need. The water splashed softly as he pulled me close, my legs brushing his beneath the surface. Jet kissed as if he'd waited too long. His restraint had finally broken.

His free hand cupped the back of my head, tilting me into him. The other held my hip, dragging me flush against his chest, and I felt every hard line of him under the water. My fingers curled into his hair—wet, soft, perfect—and he groaned against my mouth, low and rough.

The heat of the water was nothing compared to him.

He kissed me more deeply, his lips parting mine, tongues tangling in slow, powerful strokes. Breathless. Dizzy. Hungry. Every time I pulled back for air, he chased after me—lips finding mine again, as if neither of us needed air to breathe.

"Jet," I gasped against his mouth.

He kissed his name away. Then he pressed his forehead to mine, breath ragged. "Tell me to stop," he whispered, voice shaking with how badly he didn't want to.

My fingers slid down his chest beneath the water. "That's not going to happen."

That was all it took.

He lifted me, water slicking our bodies, my legs instinctively wrapping around his waist. The kiss deepened, harder, needier—his mouth claiming mine like he'd been drowning and only now could breathe.

We weren't gentle anymore.

We were like fire in the water.

Heat and hunger and breathless want.

When he finally broke the kiss, both of us shaking, his lips brushed my ear. "I will never get tired of this," he murmured. "Of you."

And in that hidden spring, under stone and steam, I kissed him again—because the world outside was falling apart, and this was the one thing that felt unbreakable.

CHAPTER 25
JET

I couldn't believe I had her in my arms after everything that had happened. She said she didn't blame me for being taken, but I blamed myself. The first step in fixing the situation was to smear the blood of those son-of-a-bitches all over my skin. Maybe then I could start forgiving myself.

The feel of her pussy pressed directly on my aching cock broke me out of my thoughts. I'd been waiting for this moment ever since I saw her in the office with a pink crown sticker on her forehead.

"You feel so good, Angel." I raise her to sit on the rock ledge, then lower my head to her warm slit, inhaling deeply.

She smelled like the sweetest desert, and it was all mine... at least for this moment in time.

My angel had the most beautiful pussy that I'd ever seen, and my cock became impossibly harder just looking at it—plump, pink, and glistening with her desire for me. I could gaze at her for hours if she would allow it.

I had to prepare her because I was a larger-than-average man, and that included every part of me. I wanted this first time to be incredible and painless—we could save the pain for when I had more time to spend with her.

"Fuck, I love how swollen and wet you are for me. Now lean back and let me taste you." I growled the last part, already lowering my head.

She lay back on the stone and spread her legs wide for me. "Such a fucking *good girl.*"

I threw her legs over my shoulders and sucked her pretty clit into my mouth. Her legs started to shake, and I could feel the goosebumps erupt all over her thighs.

I barely had time to insert my fingers in her sweet pussy before she came all over my face. "My sweet Angel needed me more than I thought."

She whimpered as I pulled her back into the water and kissed her swollen lips where she'd bitten them in her moment of passion. "I'm going to need you to do that again."

"What?" she asked, looking dazed.

"Cum." I plunge two fingers in her tight pussy, stretching her open even more than before, hoping against hope she can take my large cock.

As I plunged my fingers in and out of her, I searched for that magical spot deep inside. I knew when I found it because she let out a moan and started to move, trying to bring my fingers even deeper.

"*Fuck* Jet, that feels so good. I need you inside me *now.*"

Reverie grabbed my face and pulled my bottom lip into her mouth and bit down, less than gently.

I pressed her clit with my thumb, and she moaned in pleasure, letting go of my lip. Her eyelids fluttered closed as I felt her walls spasm, and she let out a scream that I swallowed, cumming a second time.

I pulled her legs back around my waist and dragged her down onto my swollen cock. Even though I'd prepared her as much as possible, it was still a tight fit, and I groaned at the feeling of her walls squeezing the head of my cock tight.

"Fuck, if you keep doing that, this isn't going to last long." I closed my eyes and groaned as she squeezed me again.

I slapped her thigh, and startled, she slid down further on my cock. "I told you not to do that. Be a good girl, or you won't get to cum again."

My Angel narrowed her eyes, but quickly closed them again, moaning as I worked my thumb back and forth against her clit, relaxing her even more so I could slide deeper into paradise. We both groaned, and I saw stars, the pleasure almost too much.

I didn't know where she ended, and I began.

I started to move, using my strength to slide her up and down on my shaft, my movements becoming more frantic as the pleasure intensified. She started rotating her hips and moaned out her approval as we both approached orgasm.

I felt her walls begin to flutter; I knew she was there, and I wasn't going to be far behind. Throwing my head back, my vision blacked out, and I came harder than I ever have before. I squeezed her to my body tighter than I knew was comfortable, but this moment was everything I needed to feel whole again.

I buried my head in her neck and kissed her throat, *"I love you more than you could possibly know."*

"I love you too." The words felt too sacred to speak out loud.

We murmured sweet endearments to each other as we bathed, then Reverie kissed me and stepped out of the water, cheeks flushed, hair dripping down her shoulders, steam curling off her skin. I followed right behind her and raised a hand to brush the droplets from between her breasts—then froze.

Right there, on her skin—where Selene had cut it away—something pulsed beneath the surface. Faint at first, like a memory of color. Then brighter. Stronger.

A crimson shimmer.

My mark.

My shield.

The one Selene tried to erase, ripped off Reverie's body as if the mark was disposable. I felt that loss like my ribs were cracked open.

But now—

It flared.

Deep red, metallic, like molten ruby poured into flesh and bound by blood and love. The shape sharpened, defined—not a wound.

A mark.

My mark.

The mark that showed the world she was mine to protect, even if she didn't need protection.

The moment it solidified, power burned through my chest. The bond surged so hard that I had to grab the rock beside me just to stay upright.

Reverie followed my stare, fingers brushing the glowing mark. "Jet… is that—"

"Yeah," I whispered, voice cracking. "It's back… at least partially."

She looked at me with something soft and fierce and a little broken. Selene didn't just fail—she had forged us into something more substantial… stronger than before.

Reverie didn't get the mark back by luck.

She took it—*we* took it… together.

Something ancient woke up inside her—and it called my shield home. The crimson glow softened into her skin, pulsing once, twice, like a heartbeat syncing with mine.

I moved before I could think—hand covering the mark, thumb brushing the edges of it. It was warm. Alive. Part of her again.

"Selene could try to remove it a thousand times," my voice was rough. "But it will always find its way back to you."

Reverie swallowed, eyes shining in the lowlight. "It never really left."

I tilted my head in question.

"When the skin healed, I saw my Nexus mark sink into my skin, as if it was being protected until the right time to reveal itself again."

I leaned down, my forehead touching hers. "I think I know why it never left."

"Why?" She touched her lips softly to mine.

"Because *you* are the bond. The mark is always there, whether we can see it or not."

And for the first time since we'd arrived in Aurathia, I didn't feel fear.

I felt certainty.

She wasn't breakable.

She was becoming unstoppable.

And my shield wasn't just a mark anymore—it was a promise the universe itself had decided to honor, whether Selene liked it or not.

Reverie's fingertips touched the crimson mark like she was afraid it might disappear if she blinked too hard. I should've been focused on her—on the flicker of awe in her eyes, the heat still drying on her skin, the bond that pulsed between us like a living heartbeat.

But something scraped against stone behind us.

A shift of weight.

The feeling of being watched.

I tilted my head just a little—enough to see without appearing like I was looking.

There he was.

Torren.

Half-shadowed against the cave wall, arms crossed loosely, expression unreadable. Assessing. Like the return of my mark wasn't unexpected—but rather confirmation of something he'd already suspected.

A part of me wanted to lunge at him—demand what he knew, why he was watching her like she belonged to him. But Reverie leaned closer, brushing her lips along my jaw, soft as a sigh, and I swallowed the instinct to bare my teeth. He better be glad I'd draped her in my shirt earlier, or I would've had to kill the fucker.

She didn't see him.

And that was the only reason I didn't move and confront the suspicious bastard.

Torren's eyes flicked to the crimson shield on her skin. There was something in his stare that felt like calculation… and a hint of fear.

Not of *me*.

Of *her*. Maybe of what she was becoming.

He realized I'd spotted him. Instead of stepping back, he held my gaze a second too long—silent warning or silent understanding, I couldn't tell which—then vanished deeper into the cave, soundless as smoke.

Reverie rested her forehead on my shoulder, and I wrapped my arms around her, tucking her close. She didn't notice the tension winding through me.

I kissed her temple, keeping my voice even. "Get some sleep," I murmured. "We have a little time before we have to leave."

As I held her, heat still rising from the spring and the shield pulsing steadily beneath my palm, a quiet certainty settled in my chest; Torren was waiting for something.

Maybe for her.

Maybe for a moment, she wasn't surrounded by us.

Maybe for a part of her power to surface that even she didn't know she had.

I didn't tell her.

Not yet.

Because whatever Torren was playing at—whatever he

knew—Reverie deserved one night where she wasn't looking over her shoulder.

So I gently kissed her hair and watched the shadows instead, just in case they moved again.

When Reverie finally slept.

It took a while—her breathing was shallow at first, like even unconsciousness couldn't quite pry her away from the world—but eventually her body gave in. She curled into my side, one hand resting over the crimson shield on her skin.

I waited until her breathing became steady before I carefully slid out from underneath her. Pantar had found us a few minutes earlier and stayed close enough to share his warmth. He lifted his head, watching me with glowing eyes, but said nothing.

Oren stood just beyond the glow of Zane's small fire, keeping watch with that unnatural stillness only he could manage—his shadows roaming the mouth of the cave.

I stopped beside him.

He didn't look at me, just kept his gaze fixed on the cave entrance. "Couldn't sleep?"

"No," I muttered.

He didn't comment. Oren was many things, but blind wasn't one of them.

After a moment, he spoke quietly. "You got something on your mind, or are you here to gloat?"

"I saw Torren watching us," I growled. "Watching her."

Oren didn't flinch. "How long?"

"Long enough to know he wasn't checking for threats. He was checking on her. Waiting for something."

Oren exhaled through his nose, slow and irritated. "Of course he was."

"So you know something's off?"

His jaw tightened the slightest fraction. "I knew it the moment he followed us."

I stared at him. "Why didn't you say something to her?"

His eyes finally cut to mine—cold, sharp, fire beneath ice. "Same reason you didn't. I won't trouble her until I know what's going on with him. She has enough on her mind."

He read me too easily.

Oren turned back to the entrance. "He's hiding something. Maybe a lot of somethings. And you're right—he's waiting for her to change. To become something else."

I swallowed, "You think he knows what's happening?"

"I think he has an idea, but I doubt he knows the whole truth."

My stomach twisted.

"You trust him to have her best interests in mind?"

Oren snorted. "*Fuck no.* I barely tolerate him." He shifted his weight, shadows curling around his hands like smoke. "We watch him. We stay between him and her. And if he tries anything—" Lightning crackled across his knuckles, sharp and silent. "We end him."

I didn't smile. But something in my chest loosened.

"Good," I said. "Because I'm not letting anyone—*anyone*—take her away again."

Oren nodded once. "Get some sleep. You look like death."

"I should look satisfied."

"That too, you lucky bastard."

We didn't laugh, but the tension in the air eased slightly.

We kept watch together—silent, alert, a united wall of teeth and magic and fury.

Torren might be playing a long game, but he better watch out; Reverie didn't only have one protector.

She had *five*—more than that with the inclusion of Pantar, Kharox, Chloe, and her men.

And every one of us was willing to burn the world to keep her safe.

CHAPTER 26

REVERIE

The forest thinned as we neared the ridge.

The air grew colder, sharper. Even the birds had gone silent.

Torren lifted a hand to halt us. "The portal's less than half a mile ahead. Stay sharp."

None of us needed the reminder. After everything that had happened, trust was a fragile thing. Even the silence felt threatening here.

Zane's fire flickered over his fingertips as he scanned the trees. "I don't like this quiet."

Pantar's low growl rolled through the air, deep enough to make the ground hum. *"Something comes."*

Oren turned, electricity and shadows dancing faintly at his fingertips. "Where?"

Before Pantar could respond, an arrow hissed through the air and embedded itself in the ground between us.

Kharox placed himself directly in front of me, teeth bared.

Nathan flared with fire instantly. "Ambush!"

"Hold!" The voice came from the tree line—a deep, commanding shout with a hint of desperation behind it.

A man stepped into view, hands raised, blond hair catching sunlight like a halo of gold. He wasn't much older than thirty—fit, battle-scarred, eyes bright and alert, but shadowed with something that looked like guilt.

Razor.

I couldn't be more excited to see him. I'd been afraid he'd been injured when the coliseum fell. Except why was he here? Now?

"Razor! You son-of-a-bitch! I'm so glad to see you again!" Nathan approached him and gave him a bro hug.

Razor's grin was quick. "Still a little too touchy-feely, I see."

Deshawn stepped forward and offered his hand. "You saved my dad's life. I can't tell you how much my mom and I appreciate that."

"Believe me, he's saved my ass too many times to count. He's the reason my Faction wasn't dismantled." He said earnestly. "Now listen, time is short. The portal ahead —it's a trap. Selene and Ubel are waiting for you to attempt to use it."

Torren stiffened. "You're sure?"

Razor looked puzzled at his presence before answering. "They fortified their position overnight. Once you step inside, the circle closes. You'd never have the chance to make it through."

Kharox's heavy form moved beside me, his voice deep and certain. *"The man speaks truth."*

Razor's eyes widened slightly at the sound of it.

"Ancestors above," he breathed. "That's a Varruk. The one you helped escape, I assume?"

"Yes, his name is Kharox. He's the reason we've come this far." I wasn't surprised he'd figured out it was me behind that whole incident.

Razor studied him for a long beat, then nodded respectfully. "Then I owe him as well."

"What's your plan?" Oren asked bluntly.

Razor turned to him. "Nyberie."

Zeke looked at him with surprise. "That's Draxon territory."

"Yes, but it's the best shot you've got. At this point, you're out of options." Razor looked at us all in expectation.

Chloe exhaled, "He's right. We can't risk the portal. Nyberie's the smarter move."

Deshawn grunted. "Smarter doesn't mean safer."

"No," Razor agreed. "But it's hope. And right now, that's more than what's waiting over that ridge."

The group went silent.

Every face turned to me.

Kharox lowered his head, golden eyes meeting mine. *"Your choice, Khal' Sira. I will follow."*

My chest ached at the weight of it—so many lives balanced on what I said next.

I nodded. "We go to Nyberie."

Razor's relief was sharp but brief. "Then we move now. There's a river trail about a mile west that feeds into an underground passage. Once we cross the threshold, we'll be under the Draxon border and safe from Ubel and Selene."

Oren gave a slight nod. "Lead the way."

Kharox rumbled, *"If this is the path to survival, then we run."*

And we did.

Through fog and darkness, we chased after Razor—the forest receding behind us, with Nyberie's promise ahead.

The sound of the river deepened as we descended, echoing off stone walls like a heartbeat. Razor walked ahead, guiding us along a narrow path cut between dark cliffs. The air shimmered faintly—Nyberian energy, old and heavy, bleeding through the cracks between realms.

No one spoke for a long while. The only sound was the splash of boots through shallow water and Kharox's low, steady rumble echoing down the gorge.

"How did Tanya get to Nyberie? The last time I saw you, she was still being used to bind Factions together." Nathan and I started tussling over my pack, but he won out in the end and slung it over his shoulder with a smug look in my direction.

"I got her out when your Faction blew up the coliseum." He glanced in Oren's direction. "Thanks for that, by the way."

Oren gave him a nod. "How much information did you get about their plans before you left?"

"Not much. I was too busy getting my Faction to safety." Razor turned to me. "I did overhear Selene telling Seamus that she wanted you brought to her alive, no matter what it took."

I felt chills run through my entire body. I knew I was more powerful than Selene, but I needed more time to prepare. Hopefully, in Nyberie, I'd get the chance to practice and improve these new abilities.

"Tanya can't wait to meet you. Maybe it'll distract her from kicking my ass. She was less than happy I came alone to find you."

"I hope not. I love to watch a good ass-kicking." Zane walked by and pinched my butt. Before I could retaliate, Nathan teleported behind him and set fire to his pants. "Don't touch my Nexi's ass without permission."

"She's not just *your* Nexi, you selfish bastard! And I'll touch *my* precious girl's ass anytime I get good and ready!" He tried to turn and see the hole in the seat of his pants. "You better be glad that I have an excellent ass, or I'd be pissed that you did that. Now it's only Reverie you'll have to deal with when the women of this world won't leave me alone."

"I somehow think she'll get over it," Zeke smirked.

Jet walked even with me and took my hand, shaking his head at their antics. Since last night, he'd spent most of the day touching me in some way.

Chloe drew even closer to my other side. "I heard some suspicious noises coming from deeper in the cave last night. I was going to investigate, but Deshawn said it sounded like two cats mating, and it might be dangerous." She side-eyed me. "Did *you* hear anything?"

Before I could answer, Razor slowed and held up a fist. Ahead, carved into the jagged face of obsidian stone, loomed the tunnel entrance—a colossal arch etched with faint, glowing sigils. The edges were reinforced with crude metalwork and weapon racks, signs of habitation.

The Resistance lived here. Looked like we were joining their ranks after all.

Two armed figures emerged from the shadows as we approached. "Identify yourselves," one demanded, his voice deep enough to vibrate in my ribs.

Razor stepped forward, steady. "It's me, Turner."

I heard a gentle, feminine voice say, "Razor?"

I saw his breath catch—the first crack in his composure since we'd begun this journey. "It's Tanya," he said softly.

A glow flickered from the tunnel mouth, and then Tanya appeared. Her steps were sure but quick, her braid swinging over her shoulder. She had dark hair and eyes that tilted slightly at the corners. Her beauty was exotic and memorable.

"You made it," she breathed, relief breaking through her voice.

Razor's lips curved into a tired smile. "Told you I would."

We were all stunned when she slapped the shit out of him before pulling him into a tight embrace. Her words were muffled against his chest. "Don't ever leave like that again!"

When she pulled back, her gaze shifted to me—and the others. Jet at my side. Chloe and her men behind us. And then her eyes found Kharox.

The guards immediately moved, weapons half-drawn. The Varruk stood motionless, his red-tinged eyes catching the torchlight like warning beacons.

"Stand down!" Tanya barked, holding up a hand. "He's with them."

Her stare returned to me. "You're the one who brought down the coliseum."

I didn't flinch. "Not alone. But yes."

For a heartbeat, her mouth twitched into something that almost looked like a smile. "Then you and yours are welcome here. The Resistance owes you that much."

Behind her, the tunnels stretched into darkness lit by scattered campfires. I caught the scent of oil, smoke, and steel. Distant hammering echoed down the stone halls—proof of life, and of war.

"Come inside, I have a surprise for you," Tanya said with a grin.

"Do we know anything more about the DF's movements?" Oren moved to my side and put his arm around my waist.

I kissed the underside of his jaw and squeezed him close. This man was powerful and used that power to keep his Faction safe. Just one of the many reasons I loved him.

Side note: his tight ass and shadow-daddy vibes were among the other reasons.

"The Dark Faction's been moving troops through the lowlands. We know that much." Tanya smiled gently. "You'll be safe here—at least for tonight."

Kharox's growl rolled low beside me, his voice brushing my mind like thunder. *"Safe is a fragile word."*

I met his gaze, then looked back at Tanya. "Then let's make it stronger," I said, and stepped into the tunnels.

The tunnel air was cold, still, humming with faint Draxon energy. Crystals glowed along the cavern walls, lighting the path Tanya led me down. Her fingers are woven tightly with Razor's. Pantar was padding at my side with a soft, warning growl every time a shadow moved.

I kept expecting another ambush—maybe another Cryptfiend or another assassin from the Dark Factions.

Tanya squeezed my hand and whispered, "You're all safe. I promise."

My chest tightened. *Safe* stopped feeling real weeks ago.

We turned a corner, and I stopped breathing.

Three figures stood in the center of a bioluminescent cavern, silhouettes carved by blue-white light.

A woman.

Two men.

And behind them, a broad shadow leaning on the wall —scarred, feral, familiar in a way that punched the breath out of me.

My voice cracked. "…Mom?"

Adelaide turned first.

Her eyes filled with tears so fast she didn't even try to blink them away.

"Reverie?" She whispered, like she was afraid saying it too loud would make me disappear.

My legs moved before I even realized it. Zane began to reach for me, but Chloe caught his wrist—this was my parents' moment—a reunion long overdue.

I collapsed into Mom's arms, and she held me as if she could make me safe with just her will. I couldn't breathe. I couldn't think. I started crying before I even realized I'd begun.

Grumpy and Pop wrapped around us, their arms

strong yet trembling. I felt their heartbeat pounding against mine.

"We thought we'd lost you," Pop said into my hair.

"You were just gone," Grumpy added, voice breaking. "Vanished where we couldn't reach you."

Dad walked over and pulled me into his arms, squeezing me tightly. "I'm so sorry for everything."

"Why would you be sorry? None of this was your fault." I hugged him and breathed in his scent.

"Selene may not have fixated on you if it wasn't for me." He grumbled.

"Sly! I've told you repeatedly this wasn't your fault. She's hated me from the first moment we met, but I recognize true evil doesn't need an excuse." Mom pulled us both into her arms. "Now's not the time for self-flagellation. Let's just be glad we're all together."

I pulled back, wiping my face uselessly. "H-how are you here? How—"

A low rumble vibrated through the cavern.

Mira.

She sat like a shadowed sentinel near the wall, tentacles curling protectively around her sides. But her eyes— those huge, telepathic, ancient eyes—were on me.

Her voice pushes into my mind. *I opened the last echo of the rift your men tore through. Their Faction bond left a scar in the veil. I pulled your family through before it closed.*

Adelaide nodded shakily. "She said that our world needed to be set right. That you needed us to do that."

"We weren't supposed to stay behind," Sly spoke up quietly. "The DF halted all attacks almost immediately because of you."

I blinked. "Me?"

Jesse's jaw tensed. "When you escaped Aurathia—when you vanished from their control—the Dark Factions stopped attacking Earth entirely."

John nodded grimly. "They redirected everything. Every resource. Every soldier. Every creature."

"To hunt you," Sly finished. "And the men you're bonded to."

A suffocating wave rolled through my stomach.

Chloe cursed under her breath. Zeke and Zane exchange stiff, tense glances. Oren went rigid beside them, shadows crawling across the ground like snakes. Jet's hand twitched, hovering above the dagger at his waist. Nathan stepped behind me, palm warm between my shoulder blades.

"They're all hunting us," I whispered.

Adelaide cupped my face gently. "They're terrified of you."

I swallow hard. "Why?" I knew the answer at least partially, but didn't want to admit it out loud.

Mira answered before anyone else could. *"Because you shook the curse awake. Because you are the first heir to stand in centuries. Because your Faction is forming without Dionysus's wine. Because the throne remembers you."*

"They know about how our Faction formed?" Oren looked horrified.

"I'm afraid they do now." Adelaide nodded. "We're not sure how they found out, but the council knows."

The cavern seemed to shudder around me, and my knees weakened. Zeke caught me by the waist immediately, holding me upright with a soft, "Breathe, my Treasure."

I looked at my parents—really looked at them—and they're all staring back at me with this mix of terror and pride that makes my heart ache.

"I'm forever grateful that you're alive," Mom whispered, brushing hair out of my face. "So glad you escaped that *bitch*. So happy that your men found you."

Razor cleared his throat softly. "There is more to tell. But not all at once. Not tonight."

Tanya nodded. "You all need rest."

But something cold and sharp slid up my spine. A feeling I couldn't explain, almost like a warning.

Torren.

My eyes darted around, heart stuttering.

He's not here, and he should be.

Zeke noticed instantly. His hand tightened around my hip. "What's wrong?"

I swallowed. "Torren. He… disappeared."

Oren stiffened violently, eyes narrowing. "When?"

I shook my head, confused. "I-I don't know. I didn't see him leave. It's only a feeling."

Pantar's voice rolled through us like thunder. *"His thoughts are not quiet."*

The hair on my arms stood up.

My parents look confused.

My men look angry.

And somewhere deep in the tunnels… a shadow listened.

CHAPTER 27

TORREN

I shouldn't have followed her.

I know this.

I know it with the same certainty that I know how to kill a man in the dark without leaving a sound.

But for me, knowing something and following it are never the same.

She walks ahead of her men toward the darker fork in the caverns, her shoulders tight with the weight of everything she's just learned—her family alive, her world no longer hers, the Dark Factions hunting her relentlessly.

Power clings to her skin like starlight, just like a fucking beacon.

And I… I am drawn to it like a starving man.

Her reunion with her parents is still echoing in my skull. I watched the way she crumbled into their arms. Watched her men form a perimeter around her without needing a word. Watched her cry, breathe, break—and survive.

And something inside me hurt. Something I shouldn't feel.

I stepped out of the shadows before I could stop myself. "Reverie."

She flinched and turned sharply to face me. Her breath caught, and her eyes remained glassy from crying. The light from the crystals cast a soft blue and rose gold hue over her.

She looked like a memory I couldn't quite grasp and a future I can't have.

"What do you want, Torren?" she breathed, voice shaking slightly and full of suspicion.

I should tell her the truth. That I want things I have no right wanting. That I'm dangerous. That I'm unraveling.

Being near me is a mistake she'll regret.

Instead, I lie the way I always do. "I wanted to be sure you were alright."

Her eyes soften a fraction, which is worse.

So much worse.

"Everyone keeps watching me," she whispered, "but I just... I needed a second."

I act before I think—instinct taking over. The serum I was given warping my emotions. My control is slipping more and more as the years go by.

I close the distance.

Slowly.

Carefully.

Like approaching something sacred or, in her case, possibly feral.

I leaned one hand against the stone beside her head,

blocking her escape without completely trapping her. Her breath quickened.

"You shouldn't be alone," I murmured.

Her throat worked to swallow. "I don't think you should be here either."

"I know."

But I don't leave. I can't.

She doesn't retreat. The small gap between us gets hotter, sharper, and electric.

"You don't look okay," she whispered.

"No." My voice broke in a way I can't hide. "No, I'm not."

Her fingers trembled at her sides. I can see the moment her resolve snaps—the moment she stops thinking about danger and prophecy and Factions and everything she should fear about me.

"Torren..."

I don't let her finish.

I kiss her.

It's wrong.

It's reckless.

It's the single most catastrophic thing I could do.

And I do it anyway.

Because the second her mouth meets mine, the noise in my head—the screaming, the curse, the fractured magic —all goes silent.

Completely silent.

Her hands clutched my shirt. My palm cupped her jaw. I kissed her as if I'd been drowning for years, and she's the first breath I'd taken since our last kiss—since a fucked-up childhood I had no control over.

And then—

I feel power detonate beneath her skin.

A pulse.

White-hot.

Ancient.

Her power slammed into me like a brand, searing through my shoulder, my ribs, my throat. I choked on the shock of it, stumbling into her with a gasp I couldn't control.

A mark flares across my skin in blazing gold.

Her mark.

Her Faction.

The bond snapped into place so violently that my vision fractured.

I see her.

Feel her.

Feel her heartbeat as if it's inside my own chest.

Oh Ancestors. *No.*

No —no-no.

I stagger back from her, tearing away like I'm ripping off my own limb.

Reverie reached for me, eyes wide and terrified, "Torren—are you—did I hurt you?"

"You can't—" My voice cracked. "You don't know what you've *done.*"

She froze. "I marked you?" she whispered.

I can't answer that. If I do, I won't leave. And if I don't go—everything I've built, everything I've hidden, everything I've fought the serum and this curse and myself over will fall apart.

"I can't stay." My voice is barely human.

"Torren—"

"I can't stay with you." I rasped out.

It was my confession—my punishment.

Her breath trembled. "Why?"

Because I'm dangerous.

Because I'm a lie.

Because I'm losing pieces of myself every day.

Because I want her too much.

Because the bond changes everything.

Because her enemies will know.

Because I will break her.

Because she just made me hers, and she has no idea what that means.

Instead of confessing all of that, I whisper the only truth I can and survive. "You deserve someone whole."

And I run.

I run before she can stop me. Before her men feel the mark through her veins. Before I lose the small part of myself that still remembers how to walk away from what I want.

I run because I'm already hers. And that is *unforgivable*.

This time, I don't look back.

As I push deeper into the tunnels, the burning intensifies—not fading like a Faction mark should, but sharpening and spreading, crawling over my skin like molten metal.

I grit my teeth, rip my sleeve down to expose the mark—

And freeze. "Oh… Ancestors…"

It's not what it should be.

Her other men carry clear symbols—simple, strong,

direct. I've seen them many times because they love to display them, so proud of their Nexus and the marks they bear.

But mine—it begins as a crown, glowing gold under my skin, carved in flawless ancient lines.

Then—

CRACK.

A jagged fissure splits it down the center.

The broken crown pulses—once, twice—syncing perfectly with her heartbeat.

My pulse stumbled, and a choked laugh escaped me—broken, humorless, and terrified.

"Of course," I whisper. "Of course it would be this."

A crown.

A broken one.

A symbol of a throne that is no more.

A curse I was never meant to be a part of.

A bond I was never meant to share.

It shouldn't have happened. No heir had ever marked someone outside their Faction… and survived.

I shouldn't have stayed this long, letting my curiosity about the prophecy guide my decisions. I'd only wanted to witness what she was becoming.

The crack burned brighter, like a warning.

"I can't stay," I breathed.

The mark pulsed again— a white-hot throb that burned my flesh. I pressed my hand over it, fingers trembling violently.

"I can't stay near her. I'll ruin her. I'll destroy everything… and part of me craves that pleasure." I gasped in panic.

And for the first time in years—not because of what was done to me, not because of my brother's cruelty, not because Ubel and Selene had twisted me into something unrecognizable—

But because I cared—I felt fear.

Cold.

Real.

I staggered to my feet. "I have to leave before they see this."

The crack pulsed again.

I shudder. And then I run.

CHAPTER 28

REVERIE

Tanya waits just inside the narrow passageway when I return—arms folded gently, eyes soft, the crystal above casting lavender light across her dark hair.

"There you are," she said quietly. "Your parents are settling into their space. Come on—let me show you where your Faction will be sleeping."

My Faction.

The words hit differently now.

Heavier.

More complicated and infinitely confusing.

Tanya touched my shoulder—warm, steady—and led me deeper into a branching tunnel. It widened into a room half-lit by glowing crystal clusters embedded in the walls. Bedrolls have already been laid out—supplies stacked in neat bundles.

All five of my men are there.

Waiting.

Nathan rose first, his expression shifting from cautious to alarmed the moment he saw my face. "Nexi—" he breathed, quickly crossing the space.

Jet pushed off the wall behind him, eyes flicking over me in a clinical, terrifyingly quiet assessment. Oren's shadows are already curling around his ankles, restless and sensing something wrong. Zeke and Zane look like they're halfway shifted, jaws clenched, pupils narrowed.

Chloe stood off to the side with Oliver and Deshawn—but Pantar lifted his head, growling low, then nudged Chloe hard.

She blinked. "Oh—uh… right." She made a gagging noise, then she grabbed Oliver and Deshawn and whispered, "We'll… give you a minute," before Pantar herded them out the opposite passage.

The door flap fell shut behind them.

I briefly wondered about Kharox and where he's staying, but the room filled with energy, and I put my focus entirely on my men.

Dangerous.

Electric.

Every single one stared at me.

Nathan reached me first, his hands slid to my waist as if he was terrified I'd disappear if he didn't hold on. "You're shaking." His voice sounded rough. "What happened?"

"I'm okay," I lied.

Jet moved closer, eyes dark. "That's not an answer."

Zane inhaled sharply, his gaze snapped to my neck. "She smells… different."

Zeke's voice dropped. "Adrenaline. And something else."

Oren's shadows lashed the floor. "Who touched you?"

My breath stuttered. "I—"

But Nathan pulled me in, cradling the back of my head, his forehead pressed to mine. "Tell me you're not hurt," He murmured, voice shaking with barely controlled fire.

"I'm *not* hurt."

Just haunted.

Changed.

Jet's fingers brushed my arm—light, but a spark shoots down my spine like a live wire, as I remembered what it felt like to have his mouth on me.

"Someone kissed you." He bit out.

My breath caught.

Zane growled quietly under his breath. Zeke instinctively reached for me but stopped himself, jaw tight. Oren's shadows whipped so fiercely that the crystals flickered.

Nathan lifted my chin gently. "Reverie… *who?*"

Heat flashed through my cheeks. Through my whole body.

"Nathan—"

He cut me off with a kiss.

Not soft by any stretch of imagination and definitely not soothing.

Claiming.

His mouth took mine in a hot, hungry rush that stole the ground from beneath me. My knees weakened, and he caught me, slipping an arm around my lower back as if he's been waiting—aching—for an excuse to hold me like this.

A sound escaped me—desperate, helpless—and the others reacted instantly.

Jet's hand clenched my hip tightly. Zeke moved behind me, his fingers lightly brushing my neck. Zane's touch on my spine sent a warm rush to my stomach. Oren's hand rested on my wrist, and he pressed his lips to my pulse, checking that I'm alive.

Nathan pulled back just barely, lips grazing mine, breath shaking. "Tell us what happened…" he murmured, voice a low, dangerous promise…

"… *after.*"

His mouth crashed into mine again—and the world dissolved into heat, breath, hands, shadows, fire, lightning, ice.

And I fall into all of them at once.

Nathan doesn't kiss me softly. There's nothing gentle or sweet about the way his mouth claimed mine—it's all heat and desperation, more of a collision than a meeting.

His hand fisted in my hair, tipping my head back just enough that his lips crashed against mine with bruising intensity.

His tongue swept into my mouth, deep, hungry, tasting me like he'd been starving for years. He groaned against my lips—a low, rough sound that vibrated straight through me—and the sound breaks something open inside my chest.

I kissed him back just as fiercely.

I missed this man… *all* my men with an ache that encompassed my entire soul.

My fingers gripped the back of his neck, pulling him closer, dragging him down into me, and our teeth clashed —sharp, electric—sparking a jolt of pleasure so sudden it tore a soft sound from my throat.

He growled at that… actually *growled.*

His other hand moved to my jaw, thumb stroking once before he positioned my mouth just how he wanted it, deepening the kiss until it felt like he was trying to breathe me deep inside him.

I felt a nip on my neck, and another hand unbuttoning my shirt and pulling it away from my body.

Nathan's tongue tangled with mine—slow at first, then harder, urgent, needy. His breath mingled with mine, hot and unsteady, as he devoured every inch of my mouth like it was a promise he's waited too long to claim.

He bit my lower lip—sharp, deliberate—and I gasped again.

He answered that gasp by catching my mouth in another fierce, consuming kiss, so full of teeth and tongue and unrestrained want that my knees buckle—

—and he held me up as if he'd never let go.

A warm hand slid up my side—Jet. His touch is slow and deliberate, tracing the curve of my waist as if he were mapping out where he wanted to hold me next. His breath brushed my ear, sending a shiver through me.

"You're trembling," he murmured, low and rough. "Let us steady you."

Before I could answer, Oren's shadows curled around my ankles like a dark caress, and then his hand wrapped gently around the back of my neck. He tilted my head, forcing Nathan to break the kiss for a heartbeat.

Oren's aqua eyes held mine—fierce, possessive, melting.

"You come back to us shaking and smelling like another man," he growled softly. "We're not letting you slip away again."

His thumb stroked my pulse, and the touch is so intimate it makes my knees buckle.

Zeke caught me from behind, strong arms banded around my waist, pulling me back against his chest. His breath hit the side of my neck—cold, hungry, Draxon-dark.

"You're ours, little queen," he whispered. "Don't forget that."

Zane joined him, warm where his brother is cold. His fingers brushed my hip, then slid around to cradle my stomach. Their matching energy traps me between them—heat and ice, danger and devotion.

Nathan growled softly and dragged me back toward him, lifting my chin with two fingers before crashing his mouth into mine again. This kiss is different—deeper, reckless, full of tongue and teeth and desperation.

Jet's hand slid up my spine, fingers splaying between my shoulder blades. "Breathe, Reverie," he whispered against my jaw, placing a slow kiss there. "We've got you."

Oren's lips brushed my temple, soft yet trembling as if he's barely holding himself together. "Don't run," he whispered. "Don't *ever* run... because you won't like what that brings out in us if you do."

Zeke pressed a kiss to the base of my neck. "Or maybe she will." He's careful, reverent even, but I can feel his need to bite down.

Zane's mouth found my shoulder, warm and hungry, his breath sent a pulse of heat across my skin. Even as Nathan's kiss grew rougher, stealing my breath, my thoughts, my balance. His tongue tangled with mine, sharp and consuming.

All of them.

Touching.

Grounding.

Claiming.

Surrounding.

Hands on my waist.

Fingers tracing my hips.

Lips brushed my jaw, my neck, my breasts. Bodies pressed close, heat and magic vibrating in the air.

Their breaths mixed with mine.

Their abilities hummed against my skin.

Their presence became a physical force—tightening around me until I'm drowning in them.

Nathan broke the kiss with a soft scrape of teeth against my lower lip, leaving me dazed, trembling, breathless.

He rested his forehead against mine.

"Are you ready for us?" He whispered, voice wrecked with hunger.

I can only nod as he gently lays me on the bedrolls someone has pushed together.

Jet reached behind his head and pulled his shirt off one-handed. Damn! That man is sexy as fuck. His abs have abs.

"I love it when you look at me like that." He growled out. "Like you'll die if you don't touch me."

I hear clothes falling around the room, and I know things are about to get serious. I have a brief moment of doubt, wondering if I can handle all of these men, before I get distracted by Orens' shadows, which have snuck into my pants and underneath my panties.

Zane cupped my breasts, his thumbs stroking my nipples, and my back arched to give him more access. I feel Zeke slide behind me and position me where I'm leaning against his chest as he begins to lick my neck and shoulders with his tongue.

"Jet told us about his mark reappearing, precious girl. I expect mine to appear shortly." Zane's smile was pure filth as he traced the place where his mark still rested under my skin.

I close my eyes in pleasure as he takes my nipple into his mouth, almost cumming immediately when I open my eyes to see Nathan kneeling on my other side, with his mouth on the opposite nipple.

Oren's shadows must feel like they're losing my attention because they start moving over my clit in what I can only describe as a sucking motion. Between that feeling and two men at my breast and one at my neck, I began moaning and writhing with pleasure.

I hear a grunt and open my eyes to see Jet holding his massive dick in his hand, stroking himself as he watches his brothers pleasure me, the sight driving me higher still.

"That's the way, baby. Cum on my shadows. Cover them in your delicious cream before I put my cock deep inside you." Oren's voice is low and deep.

I feel a pinch on my clit and gasp as pleasure rockets

through my body, almost causing me to pass out with the intensity of it.

"She's so responsive. We're lucky men." Zeke moaned against my neck as my movements caused his dick to harden even more against the small of my back.

I feel hands pulling my pants off and see Nathan kneeling in front of me with his beautiful cock jutting out proudly. "I need you, Nexi."

I pull him into my embrace as Zeke supports me by holding the backs of my thighs and widening my legs, providing Nathan with better access.

Nathan entered me in one hard thrust, and I gasp at the sensation of him filling me so completely. A movement over his shoulder grabs my attention, and I see Jet stroking his cock in slow, smooth movements, squeezing the head before he starts all over again... never taking his eyes from me.

Oren walked over, and his shadows grabbed Nathan and pulled him off me. "What the fuck?"

"You still haven't learned to share." Oren grabbed my hand and pulled me up from the floor.

"Fuck off, Shitstorm. What the fuck would you call all of this, if not sharing?" Nathan growled at him.

I'm too weak with desire to join their argument and follow where Oren leads me. I'm a little surprised when he pushes me to my knees, but then I understand what he wants when he kneels behind me. I moan as his dick fills me.

"You can have our beautiful Nexus' mouth." Oren groans out while pounding deep into my pussy.

Nathan huffs but wastes no time kneeling in front of me. "Is this okay, Nexi mine?"

I nod because the ability to speak is beyond me. Nathan feeds me his cock and throws his head back in pleasure as I begin to suck on him, then open my throat to take him deep.

I hear the other men shuffling around the room and wish I could please all of them at once like Queen Lilibet did in my dream, when suddenly I hear a yelp.

"What the fuck, Oren!" Zane yells. "Get your fucking shadows off my dick."

Oren halted what he was doing, and I groaned out in protest. "I wouldn't touch your dick with someone else's shadows!"

"Then what the fuck is this?" Zeke growled out.

We all pause in our activities, and I see shadows curling around Jet, Zeke, and Zane.

"Get them *the fuck* off of me." Jet glowered at Oren, looking murderous.

"I'm telling you motherfuckers that... is... not... me!" He was pissed.

"I think it might be *me*," I whispered, guiltily, before things get out of hand... so to speak.

I thought about what I wanted the shadows to do, and Jet groaned as they wrapped around his dick and started to squeeze.

"Yep, it's me." I giggled, which turned into a moan as Oren surged back inside me.

"Well, that's all right, then. Get busy pleasuring me, Shadow Momma." Zane's comment ended in a moan as I did exactly that.

Soon, the room is filled with filthy noises and moans as we are all overwhelmed by the pleasurable sensations.

Oren let out a growl. "*Fuck, baby.* I'm going to fill you up with my cum."

Nathan groaned, "I'm cumming too, and I want you to swallow *every single drop.*"

Both men cum simultaneously, and I soon followed, but didn't have a moment to recover before Zeke took Oren's place. I groaned as he entered me in one smooth thrust, then winced as it felt like his dick grew exponentially after he entered me. His dick was so thick that it stretched me to an uncomfortable level. Then I realized I felt a knot.

"What the hell is *that?*" I moaned out as it rubbed against my G-spot.

"I'm not sure, but you feel fucking *amazing,*" Zeke growled, around a moan of pleasure.

I mewl at the stretch and the sensations I'm feeling, a strange warmth spreading through my entire body.

Suddenly, Zane is in front of me and begins to strum my clit with two fingers, even as he moans and snarls in pleasure from the movement of my shadows around his red and throbbing cock.

Zeke pumped in me three more times before I feel the hot jet of his cum bathing the walls of my pussy, and I scream as it sets off another orgasm.

Jet has fallen to his back and is writhing on the floor as my shadows run over his entire body, and it isn't long before he and Zane find their pleasure, cum spurting from their cocks onto the eight-pack abs they both have.

The room is filled with warmth from everything we've just done, and a sense of contentment fills the air.

My breathing is slowing, but my body feels light, boneless, like the world melted a little around the edges. My thighs are shaking, lips still tingling, magic gently humming under my skin.

And they're all still there.

Close.

Quiet.

Soft in a way they aren't with anyone else.

Nathan is the first to gather me up, lifting me as if I weighed nothing. Zeke protests briefly, but Nathan ignores him as he presses a soft kiss to the top of my head, his earlier wildness softened into something warm and protective.

"You alright, Nexi?" he murmured against my hair.

I nod, sinking into his chest. "More than alright."

A low sound rumbles in his chest—proud, relieved, affectionate.

Jet stepped to my side, brushing my hair back from my face with slow, careful fingers, as if he's smoothing the chaos right out of me.

"You scared us," he whispered. "Come here."

I reach for him, and he takes my hand, squeezing gently—a promise, not a demand.

Oren crouched in front of me, shadows curling lazily around his feet now, no longer snapping outward. He studies my face as if he's cataloging every detail to make sure I'm okay.

"Let me see you," he said softly.

I cupped his cheek, and his eyes warmed instantly. He leaned into my touch just enough to tell me what it meant to him.

Zeke and Zane settle on either side of me, shoulders brushing mine, body heat steady and comforting. Zane nudges my knee with his.

"You're glowing," he teased with a grin.

Zeke rolled his eyes, but he was smiling too. "She always glows. But… yes. More than usual."

Zane waggles his brows. "Must be from the Draxon knot. I can't wait to experience that with you." He side-eyed Zeke. "I bet my knot is bigger than yours. At least a *quarter inch.*"

Zeke punched him in the arm. "Shut the fuck up, asshole."

"*Knot* right now, boys." Nathan grinned, "You're both being total *Knotheads.*"

I laugh—a real, soft, unguarded laugh—and it makes all of them smile and visibly relax.

Nathan adjusted me in his lap, wrapping his arms around my waist, holding me as if the world outside this cavern can't touch me here.

"You were amazing," he whispered into my neck. "In every way."

"Especially mastering those shadow abilities. It took me years to learn that kind of control." Oren's chest puffs out with pride at my accomplishment.

I blushed. "Thanks… I guess."

"No. Thank *you*, precious." Zane smirked, "*Big Sly* appreciates it."

My eyes widen before I remember the conversation from back at the academy with Nathan. "Shut up. Or my love castle is closed for business."

The twins and Nathan began laughing, but Jet and Oren looked confused.

"Your dick is named after one of her dads?" Jet's complexion was green.

Nathan stopped laughing briefly. "If you know, you know."

That made us laugh again. It felt good and right to be with them like this.

Jet sat beside us, his thigh pressed to mine, and Oren stretched out a hand, brushing it over my arm with feather-light comfort.

Zeke leaned his head briefly on my shoulder and yawned. "Tomorrow I have a gift for you, don't let me forget."

I smiled softly. "I won't let you forget."

Zane sprawled against my other side, fingers absent-mindedly tracing little shapes on my knee.

For the longest time, none of us talked. We just breathed together.

Five different heartbeats.

Five different kinds of touch.

Five different ways of holding me steady.

The fire of what just happened cools into something more profound— a warm, steady pulse of connection that anchors me in a way I didn't know I needed.

Nathan kissed my shoulder.

Zeke squeezed my hand.

Zane nudged me with his chin.

Jet's thumb strokes a soft circle over my wrist.

Oren leaned his forehead against mine and whispered, "You're safe with us. Now, tomorrow, and always."

And Ancestors help me—I believe him.

<h1 style="text-align:center">CHAPTER 29
REVERIE</h1>

I woke to heat.

Not the comforting, post-ecstasy warmth with my men wrapped around me like a living blanket, but something deeper, sharper—like a strand of molten gold being pulled straight through my sternum. A hiss escaped from my lips before I could hold it back, my hand shooting to the spot between my breasts.

The mark.

It was burning under my skin.

No—it felt like it was *awakening*.

Jet jerked up beside me, hair a dark snarl, eyes already flaring with heat. "Reverie?" His voice was rough, deep, and so ready to wreck anything that would harm me. But the moment his gaze dropped to my chest, his breath stuttered.

The others begin to stir.

Zane growled in satisfaction, "I knew it!" even as he scrambled closer.

Zeke blinked sleep out of his eyes, freezing when he saw the light pulsing beneath my fingers. Nathan was already kneeling behind me, palms warm on my shoulders. Oren was the last to move but the first to *understand*—his whole body went still, shadows around him thinning as if they too were holding their breath.

The glow built.

White-hot.

Beautiful.

"Reverie," Zane whispered reverently, his voice dropping into that deep rumble Drakk used when the Draxon was too close to the surface.

I pulled my hand away.

And the world shifted.

My mark—my triquetra with the tree of life spiraling through its heart—was no longer the soft shimmer it had always been.

It was *alive*.

The lines glowed like heated metal, curling and shifting under my skin as if drawing breath. Tiny roots stretched outward, reaching toward the individual symbols of my Faction as though eager to claim them anew.

Nathan's dagger flashed first—emerald and sharp, the green so intense it looked carved from a star.

Zeke's moon pulsed a bruised, royal violet, casting gentle arcs of icy light across my skin.

Zane's sun flared next, burning gold so bright I swore I could feel Drakk's heat radiating beneath it.

Oren's bolt wasn't just red—it was raw, pale-crimson lightning, writhing as if it wanted to leap into his hands.

Each symbol was pulled toward the center, toward me, toward the Nexus of the triquetra.

"Reverie…" Jet's voice had dropped to a hush. "Something's different."

He wasn't wrong. Because right there—above the interwoven knot, just touching the top of the tree of life—another shape began forming, as though carved by invisible hands.

A crown.

Simple lines at first.

Not regal, but raw.

Older than Aurathia's history, older than the memories whispering in my bones.

But as it sharpened into clarity, the room fell silent.

A crack split the crown clean down the right side.

A mark of a broken sovereignty.

A mark of someone torn between two identities.

A mark of a king who'd splintered himself in two.

A mark that belonged to Torren, and whoever he really was beneath all the masks.

My breath caught.

Zeke was the first to speak, voice barely a whisper. "Reverie… what's going on?"

Oren swore under his breath, shadows twitching like startled birds. "It's a crown… and it's fractured."

Nathan leaned closer, eyes narrowing. "This is Torren, isn't it?"

Jet's jaw clenched. "He's part of this Faction?"

My heart slammed against my ribs. Because even though I should have been terrified—furious—betrayed…

The crack in that crown pulsed in time with my heartbeat.

"Claim me," it whispered. *"Remember."*

My voice came out barely audible. "He didn't want this. *I* didn't want this. I don't think he had any idea it would happen."

Zane cursed softly. "We need to talk to the fucker."

Zeke's voice darkened, Frynn taking over, "Starting with what he's hiding."

Oren's eyes locked onto mine. Steady. Unwavering. "I think you *did* want it, baby. Somewhere deep down. But there are questions that need answering. The first being why the crown on your chest looks like it's begging you to fix the missing piece."

The cracked crown was still throbbing against my skin when the memory of last night hit me like a blow to the ribs.

His mouth on mine. Hard. Desperate. That first brutal press of lips turning into teeth and tongue, the kind of kiss that rewired the bones in my spine.

Torren hadn't kissed me like a man giving in to temptation. He'd kissed me like a man breaking.

And then—He'd torn himself away and stumbled back as if he'd scorched his hands on my body and whispered something jagged—something that sounded like "I shouldn't"—and then bolted down the tunnels, as if the shadows of hell itself were dragging him.

That image hit the present with a clarity that took my breath away.

No.

Not an image.

A *connection.*

The cracked crown throbbed once more.

Jet's head snapped up. "Reverie? What is it?"

I swallowed hard. "Last night… when he kissed me." My voice shook. "He ran like he was terrified. And I—" I pressed a hand to the crown. "I think he's doing it again."

Zeke's brow shot up. "Torren kissed you, then ran?"

Zane let out a sharp, low whistle. "Well, that explains why his mark decided to wake up pissed. It's attached to the dumbass that ran from the best fucking thing that ever happened to him."

Nathan leaned in, eyes darkening. "I know this is rich coming from me, but did he force you?"

"No," I whispered. Heat crawled up my neck. "He more… ruined me for a second and then panicked."

Jet's jaw clenched like he wanted to break something on Torren's face. "He *ran.* What a dumb fuck."

"Yes." I knew my worth. I considered his running more of a him problem than anything to do with me.

Oren exhaled once, slowly. "And the bond flared tonight to tell you why."

I looked down at the fractured crown, faintly glowing. "Maybe, maybe not." I shrugged. "There are a few things I need to talk to you about. Maybe together we can figure out what it all means."

Oren nodded, then abruptly straightened, muscles tightening. "He's leaving. *Right now.* I can feel it creeping through your connection."

Nathan moved for the exit instantly, fire licking faintly along his fingers. "Then we're not waiting."

Jet grabbed one of his blades. "I'll bring him back."

Zeke's eyes flickered frost-blue. "I can't guarantee in what condition."

"Before we go chasing after someone that doesn't want to be caught—didn't you say you had something for me?" I looked at Zeke.

I wanted to figure this out with Torren, but Zeke was right here. Always the first to ensure everyone else was taken care of. I wanted him to know that he was just as important to me as anything else happening right now. Being away from these wonderful men for all those months made me appreciate them even more, and I wanted to put them first, just as they always did for me.

He blushed, and I felt my heart melt. "We have more important things to worry about right now. I can give them to you later."

"Nope. Nothing is more important than you at this moment." I walked over to him and leaned my head back for a kiss.

Zane slapped him on the back. "Don't be modest, bro. Show her what you made."

Zeke kissed me again before walking over to his bag and pulling out two of the most beautiful things I'd ever seen.

"Holy shit!" I rushed up to him, barely able to contain myself. "Are those really for me?"

"Who else would they be for?" He grinned at my enthusiasm.

He handed them to me, and I laid them on a natural ledge that jutted out from the wall near me, so I could examine them closely.

They were both about twenty-two inches long,

matching the exact length of the blades I'd used in the coliseum, but that was all they had in common. These two blades were far superior. Both were slightly curved, but each looked different from the other.

The first blade appeared to be composed of smoke-colored steel, absorbing the room's light. Pale crimson veins streaked across it, resembling trapped embers within the metal.

The second blade gleamed with a faint silvery shine, resembling a layer of frost. Sharp, irregular patterns similar to ice fractals were carved along its edge.

Zeke cleared his throat, "I call them Ashfang and Frostbane. But you can call them whatever you want."

I couldn't take my eyes off them. "That's perfect." I reached behind me and took his hand. "Thank you, I love them."

Zane walked up beside me. "Turn around."

I turned without hesitation, still overwhelmed by my stunning gift. I felt the cool, supple leather brush against the back of my arm, as if frosted. He raised the piece so I could see, and I gasped. Two smooth sheaths formed a perfect V against the harness of pale, shimmering leather that gleamed softly in the light.

"Zane," I breathed, reaching back to touch it. The material was smooth but firm, reinforced with subtle inlays that glowed faintly blue. "You made this?"

He snorted softly. "Of course I did. I couldn't have you only wearing something my brother made." He leaned in and bit my ear, whispering, "It also has my initials on it. Wait until Nathan finds out."

I burst out laughing. "Thank you, it's stunning."

"I call it the Frostflare Harness," his tone deliberately casual. "Flare for me. Frost for him." A faint smirk tugged at his mouth. "The harness is almost too fancy for these blades."

"The hell you say!" Zeke growled out.

"Just fucking with you, bro." Zane laughed, and the rest of us joined in.

Zeke slid the blades into the harness. They crossed upward behind me like wings of fire and frost—Zeke and Zane both wore an expression of pride and possession.

"I hate to break up this moment, but we need to get back to the topic at hand." Oren paused at the tunnel opening, his shadow-threaded voice softer than the others. "Tell me exactly what happened before he ran."

I sighed and met his gaze, and the truth burst out in a single breath. "He kissed me—and the bond surged. I felt something pull at me. Like a mark trying to form. Then he saw it—just a flash—and he freaked out."

Zane muttered, "It probably spooked him. The man clearly didn't run because of you. There isn't a more beautiful woman in any world. But marking a member of a Faction isn't something normal. The Nexus is usually the only one with a mark."

I pulled him in for a kiss. "I don't think it was fear. I think he was terrified of what the bond meant."

Jet nodded slowly. "The claim."

Oren's voice dropped to a low, dark murmur. "He's done running from this."

I pushed myself to my feet, the men immediately circling me without thinking—protective, ready, furious on my behalf but so very careful with me. I loved them each with a ferocity that came from deep in my bones. And I felt their love for me.

All but one.

What I felt from him wasn't love but obsession.

The cracked crown pulsed once more. Faint. But insistent.

A tug.

A direction.

"He's not far," I breathed. "The bond is… pulling."

Zane grinned with wicked delight. "Good. Then we hunt."

And with that, we ran.

～☙～

We found him in the ribbed aquifer tunnels—stone arching overhead like the skeleton of some ancient beast. Torren stood at the end of the corridor, chest rising fast, hands curled like he didn't trust what they might do.

The moment his gaze cut to me, something vicious and haunted flashed through it. "Don't," he rasped. "Stay where you are."

Zane snorted. "You kissed our girl and ran like a scared little shit. You don't get to give orders."

Torren's jaw flexed. But it wasn't fear this time. It was fury. Cold, sharp, beautifully dangerous fury.

"That kiss was a mistake. Both of them," he said sharply. "Your mark appearing was a mistake." His voice dropped to a razor's edge. "I don't belong in your bond."

The cracked crown pulsed in response—an unmistakable throb beneath my skin.

Torren winced as if the bond itself tore into his ribs. His eyes suddenly snapped to mine.

He wasn't looking at me like the shy, damaged man who fled last night. He looked at me like a predator who'd accidentally grown attached to the one creature he meant to kill.

"Reverie..." His voice dipped low. "You weren't supposed to mean anything."

Something in me stilled.

Jet stepped forward, fire in his eyes. "You don't speak to her like that. I'll cut your dick off, motherfucker."

Nathan laughed cruelly. "He's done it before, so I'd take him at his word."

Torren's mouth curled into a twisted smirk. It wasn't gentle or vulnerable, but rather cold and cruel.

"There are lines you don't cross," he said. "And I crossed one by letting myself touch her."

The air around him crackled—wrong, unstable, the way lightning behaves before it shatters into a storm.

Nathan snarled, "Just admit the bond chose your unworthy ass, and we'll go from there."

"No." His laugh was cold. Sharp. A sound meant to cut. "It didn't choose *me*. It chose the illusion."

Zeke's eyes narrowed. "Illusion?"

Torren's gaze shifted away, jaw tightening—then the bond slammed through both of us again. The cracked crown flared as if it were tearing open. Pain shot through my chest.

And Torren—

He stumbled.

A strangled sound tore from his throat, half fury, half something dangerously close to grief.

He spat the words like venom: "I SAID NO!"

The air distorted.

His form blurred.

White-blond hair darkened—melting into ink-black. Shoulder-length became waist-length. Hazel eyes bled into an emerald so vivid it glowed. His face sharpened— aristocratic angles, the kind that made you want to step back… or step closer.

His entire posture changed.

Cold.

Commanding.

Elegance refined through cruelty.

He looked so similar to Oren that I felt my breath catch.

Oren appeared stunned, but not in the same way as the others—there was no fear or shock, or perhaps not *only* shock.

Recognition.

"Uncle?" The word tore out of him, hoarse, disbelieving.

Nathan snapped his head toward him. "What?"

Oren didn't look at us. He couldn't take his eyes off the man in front of us.

"That's Trent Storm," he whispered. "My father's brother. The one who vanished during the war."

The blood drained from Zane's face. Zeke tensed, frost crawling up his arms. Jet looked like he wanted to rip the world apart.

Me?

I stared at the stranger who now wore my mark. And he stared right back—no hesitation, no fear, no hiding.

Only cruelty.

And something else.

Something he couldn't kill, no matter how hard he tried.

Fascination. Obsession.

"Reverie," he murmured, his voice blending velvet with steel. "You really shouldn't have been so trusting..." A dangerous smile formed. Sinfully arrogant, meant to destroy. "...then again, your naivety was quite delightful."

My pulse roared in my ears.

Oren growled, stepping forward. "How in the hell did you disguise yourself?"

Trent tilted his head, the picture of patient wickedness. "The serum gifts... many things. Things you'll never understand with your small mind."

His gaze slid to me. But there—there was the betrayal—the crack in his cruelty. "You were supposed to be a game," he said softly. "You made yourself a problem."

Then he lifted his hand. Reality twisted.

A force slammed outward—warping the stone, bending the air, throwing my men back even as they fought against it.

He held my gaze.

Not with regret.

With an almost affectionate cruelty. Like a man admiring the bruise he left behind.

"You shouldn't want me in your bond, Reverie," he said. "You shouldn't want me anywhere near you."

My chest ached with the bond's pull. The cracked crown burned.

"Too late," I whispered.

For a split second—one heartbeat—his expression cracked.

Not soft or tender.

Just *real*. And so very haunted.

Then he vanished in a ripple of warped light. Leaving the echo of a broken man, a lie, a monster—and a bond that refused to let him go.

CHAPTER 30
TRENT

The warp-drop slammed me to my knees.

Polished obsidian tile met my palms first—cold, smooth, flecked with silver veins. My manor. My domain. Walls of black stone and dark walnut rose around me, lit by flickering torches that never smoked.

Home.

Or was Reverie my home now?

Reverie.

Her heartbeat pulsed once—steady, treacherous—and I snarled, pressing my fingers into the tile until it cracked.

"Silence," I hissed at the bond that shouldn't exist. "You don't get to claim me."

The bond didn't care what I wanted. Of course it didn't.

The doors thundered open.

Selene swept in first—like the bitch owned the place—silver silk, blond hair braided with steel rings, her expression an elegant sneer carved with cruelty. Ubel followed behind her like the wannabe ruler he was.

Both stopped when they saw me.

Selene tilted her head, a faint, sharp smile on her face. "My king... that was a dramatic entrance."

She was the only one who ever called me that. Ubel wouldn't do it under threat of death. I smirked. Today might be the day I insist on it.

I stood slowly, letting the obsidian dust fall from my palms.

Ubel stepped forward. "Your appearance... are you done with the games?"

"Are you tired of the games?" I asked softly, "You want me to play with you?"

He shut up.

Good.

Selene circled me like a serpent admiring a kill. "You look like yourself again," she murmured. "No more of that... pale Torren imitation."

I didn't react. She had always wanted me, but she would never make a move because she liked to hold the power in a Faction.

Torren had been a mask. True. But Reverie had looked at him as if he were still someone worth saving.

Reverie again.

Damn her.

Selene moved closer. "Did your little hunt in the tunnels succeed?"

I almost laughed. Neither of these, *oh so powerful Aurathions*, knew what had happened.

"You seem... unsettled," she added, eyes narrowing. "Did the girl do something?"

My jaw clenched. The bond pulled again—a phantom tug in my ribs.

Selene's lips curled, delighting in the thought. "She is Adelaide's daughter after all. That alone makes her a curse." She smirked, "Didn't you have a crush on Adelaide for a bit?"

A cold stillness slid through me. "Careful," I said quietly.

Selene froze.

I moved closer to her, taking small, deliberate steps. "You speak of things you know nothing about, like you think you have the right."

Selene's chin lifted in defiance. "Adelaide was insufferable. Arrogant. Favored. The academy adored her." A hiss curled into her voice. "She deserved everything she lost."

Images flashed behind my eyes—Adelaide laughing in the winter courtyard of Emberhold—Adelaide's defiance. Adelaide trying to shield Sly from the very fate Selene forced on him.

The memories of her didn't affect me now. A young guy, she was much too busy to notice at the time.

When I first saw Reverie, I realized that what I felt for Adelaide was simply a boy's crush on a girl he never had a chance with. My feelings for Reverie were the kind that could build kingdoms... or tear them down. The feelings a man felt for a woman.

My hands curled.

Selene mistook my silence for permission. "And her

daughter? That girl reeks of the same naïve purity. I loathe her immensely."

The bond roared.

My vision snapped sharp—feral, electric, dangerous.

I moved before she realized—one moment across the room. Next, my fingers are squeezing her face.

Selene stiffened.

"You hated Adelaide," I murmured, my voice smooth as silk over steel. "So you stole her lover." A cruel smile twisted my mouth. "You dragged Sly into your Faction. Broke him. Tortured him. Made him kneel to you. But he never loved you, wouldn't even answer to his name. Made you call him Hayes."

"He deserved it," she spat.

"Tell me," I whispered, "does Reverie remind you of the woman you could never outshine?"

Her breath caught.

"Does she make your skin crawl because she looks like the one person who was everything you wished to be? The daughter you'll never have with Sly?"

Ubel flinched in the background at my tone.

Selene's eyes filled with hatred—but also fear.

Good.

I dropped her face, stepping back.

"You forget yourself," she snapped, voice shaking. "We built this kingdom with you."

I chuckled quietly—dark and amused. "You built nothing."

Ubel straightened, gathering what little courage he owned. "Surely you see the benefit of our influence. Our—"

"Influence?" I repeated. The torchlight dimmed. The shadows thickened around me.

I stalked toward him. "You think you *influenced* me." My voice shook the very air. "You think you shaped me. Directed me. Controlled me."

I reached out and placed two fingers under his chin.

Lifted.

He trembled.

"You mistake proximity for power," I said softly.

Selene's voice cracked. "We are your allies—"

"*No.*"

The word struck like a sharp blade.

"You are the tools. And I'm done pretending I need you."

The manor itself seemed to exhale in relief. Recognizing its master.

Selene swallowed, her voice barely audible. "What... changed?"

Reverie's kiss.

Her heartbeat.

The cracked crown binding itself to me.

"Nothing you deserve to know about," I said.

Ubel dared a step closer. "Then what are your orders?"

I turned my back to them—because it was the greatest insult I could offer—and walked toward the massive window overlooking Bellona.

Winds tore across the sky, lightning flickering in distant sheets.

"My orders," I said, clasping my hands behind my back, "are simple."

Silence clung to every corner of the room.

"Do nothing unless I command it." I let my voice darken. "And do *not* touch the girl."

Selene's breath hitched in fury. "Why do you care what happens to her?"

I smiled at the window. "I don't."

Another lie.

An easy one.

One that would keep her alive.

"I simply don't like others playing with my toys." I stared at them both, letting the insanity I usually kept hidden show in my eyes.

Ubel bowed instantly—deeply terrified. "As you command."

Selene's bow came slower. Trembling but resentful.

Good.

Let her hate the girl. Let her fear me.

Both truths served me well.

⌥

The manor felt too quiet.

My manor was usually a sanctuary—constructed of cold stone, colder air, and silence that soothed me.

Tonight, it felt like the walls were listening.

I paced across the chamber, boots hitting the obsidian tile with sharp, precise rhythm, my breath steadying only when I ripped away the last remnant of Torren's shirt and finally saw what I'd been avoiding.

My arm.

The mark burned there like a bruise drawn in molten gold—a cracked crown carved cleanly across the inside of my left forearm.

It glowed faintly.

Mocking me.

I dragged my fingers over it, nails pressing until my skin split and blood rose.

It didn't fade.

It only pulsed.

In time with her heartbeat. The only rhythm it seemed to know.

I slammed my arm against the stone wall. The entire section cracked, dust raining down like ash.

"Damn, you," I hissed—not at her, never at her—but at the bond that dared to think I deserved this. Something like her.

And then—The next pulse hit harder.

Not soft. Not steady.

A flicker of emotion that wasn't mine.

Warm hands. Masculine voices. Her name whispered like a prayer.

Her men. What the fuck?

I froze.

The bond didn't show visions. It wasn't supposed to. But my bond seemed different. It whispered secrets of skin against skin and of claiming hands that weren't mine.

Nathan's warmth against her. Zane's teasing murmur. Zeke's quiet protectiveness. Jets intensity. My sniveling nephew's devotion.

My jaw clenched hard enough to crack stone.

They were close to her now.

Comforting her.

Touching her.

The bond didn't show details, only impressions—but that was enough.

I growled under my breath, pacing again, the resentment old and savage. Those men had something I didn't even want—shouldn't *want*—and yet the idea of their hands on her skin made something feral inside me lunge.

"Pathetic," I spat at myself.

Wanting what belonged to others was beneath me. Being tethered to them through her was an insult.

Each man left a mark on her chest—symbols shaped by their bond.

Selene had taken it from her. I didn't know about that until it was already done. At the time, part of me delighted in her cruelty. Now I wanted to slit her fucking throat.

But the mark was back. I'd seen it in the tunnels. I'd seen their devotion. Their certainty.

They would burn the world to keep her safe.

And there was no doubt she loved them back.

I hated that.

Not the love—I didn't give a single shit about that—but the security of it, the inevitability. That ironclad devotion that wrapped around her like chains.

They didn't fear what she could become. They didn't fear what she could destroy.

They didn't fear *her*.

And they sure as hell didn't fear the bond.

Fucking morons.

I flexed my hand, watching lightning-like energy

crackle across my palm—part of the immense power my injections gave me.

"I am not one of them," I said aloud to the empty room.

I wasn't part of their little brotherhood. I wasn't their ally, their friend.

I wasn't someone she would ever welcome.

The bond pulsed anyway. I nearly laughed.

Her men had spent time with her, protecting her, earning their marks—each one tied to her heart. But *my* mark had carved itself into me in seconds. Violet, instinctive, undeniable.

It infuriated me.

They earned their right to her.

I did not.

They were chosen.

I was claimed.

Their marks were symbols of love, loyalty, devotion.

Mine was a scar. A warning. A mistake.

And still—the bond pulsed again.

Stronger.

Hotter.

As if reminding me she had felt something when I kissed her—something she shouldn't have.

I dug my fingers into my hair until I could barely breathe. "This ends." My voice calm. Final. Cold.

I would not be another man orbiting her. I would not fall into the same trap countless men before me had—destroying themselves for a woman they could never have.

And I sure as hell wouldn't let the bond control what I do.

But then—

That damn heartbeat brushed mine again.

Channeling through the cracked crown. Through the bond. Through the mistake etched into my arm.

Soft.

Steady.

Unbroken.

I hissed out a breath and leaned back against the stone pillar, eyes closing. "I will not want you."

A lie.

I felt the bond answer. *We'll see.*

My eyes snapped open. No, this was not happening.

I pushed away from the pillar and strode to the far edge of the manor hall, the night wind slamming against my back.

If her men thought they could keep her safe—

Good. Let them try. Let them all stand between us. I wouldn't cross that line again. But if one day she came close—If she stood before me with those eyes—If she whispered my name—Trent…

My breath stuttered.

I slammed my fist into the wall again.

"No," I growled. "*Never.*"

But the bond pulsed. Relentless.

I closed my eyes. And for the very first time in years, I didn't feel like the hunter.

I felt hunted.

CHAPTER 31

REVERIE

I wake up in a tangle of blankets and half-mended feelings, the faint hum beneath my skin telling me before I even sit up that it's still there.

My Nexus mark.

The men left to get breakfast, giving me the privacy I needed this morning to get my head around everything that happened last night. Zeke made me promise to meet them and eat (of course, he did) before we decide what our next move will be.

I feel like all of this is my own doing—not consciously, but I felt the truth the moment my mark flared into existence.

Something inside me knew all of them—even Trent, beyond this lifetime.

Something ancient.

The voice in my dreams—the one who whispers through Queen Lilibet's memories—murmured one word in the moment before I fell asleep and then woke to the pain.

"Restore"

And my body seemed to have obeyed a little too well, making Trent Storm a member of this Faction right along with the rest of them.

I knew I had to suck it up and get dressed. My guys were just as upset about this shit as I was. We needed to face this together, and my bestie would help me handle it too. She always knew how to make me see things differently.

This bond with Torren—*shit*—Trent was not something I asked for, even knowing he was a Potential. And to be fair, I don't think it was something he wanted either.

My abilities and forces that I wasn't entirely sure about did this.

The voice takes that exact moment to whisper, *"We warned you, bonds are permanent... unless broken by truth."*

I don't even know what the hell that means. "Why do you speak in riddles?" I mutter aloud, aggravated with everything this morning.

"Why does who speak in riddles?" My mom asked, standing beside my bedroll, Mira at her side.

I jumped, not hearing her come in the room. "What the hell, Mom? You scared the crap out of me."

She laughed, "Sorry, baby. I saw your men heading to breakfast, and they told me you were still here.

My brain isn't functioning right this morning. "What time is it?"

"Early." Her eyes flick down to my bare shoulders, then lower, and I remember—too late—that I fell asleep in one of Nathan's shirts last night, the neckline loose and gaping. I started to tug the blanket up out of instinct, but she reached out and stopped me.

"Don't," she whispered, voice oddly reverent. "Let me see it again."

My heart gave one hard thud.

The mark.

My mother sighed and hung her head.

"You know what it means?" I tilted my head in question.

Her silence is answer enough.

"Torren," I whispered.

"Trent, you mean." She corrects me. Her jaw tightened around the name, hatred, and history flickering in her eyes.

Mira let out a low growl. *"He should be dead for the things he's done."*

I let out a slow breath, the memory of his touch flaring in my mind—his mouth, that reckless kiss in the tunnels, the sharp crackle of something binding between us before he tore himself away. The way my skin burned afterward, like my body was trying to decide if it wanted him or wanted him dead.

"I didn't mean to do it," I murmured. "The marking, I mean. It was different from what I did with my men at the academy. It *felt* different, I can't really explain how."

"Did it?" Mom asks quietly. "Did *she* have something to do with it?"

The voice.

The one that curls through my dreams with smoke and starlight, threading visions of my past life through my veins. The one that sounds like a chorus and a single woman all at once. My Ancestor. My queen. Myself.

Last night, just before I woke with my chest on fire, I'd seen something—a man standing in the dark with two faces. One was soft, almost boyish, eyes bright with that crooked fascination I'd seen in Torrens's gaze. The other was harder, cruel, a stranger made of edges and shadow.

One man. Two faces. Both are looking at me.

I explained what I'd dreamed to my Mom.

"I don't think the Ancestors did this to me," I said slowly. "I think… they let me do it. Or I did it with their *permission*. Like they opened a door and I walked through without realizing." I stopped talking and stared at her for a moment. "How did you know about the voice?"

Mom's fingers tighten around the blanket. "There are things we know that we can't tell you," she whispered. "We want to *desperately*, but it might harm the order of things."

"I understand, but it's extremely frustrating," I mumble.

Her gaze softened. She leaned down and pressed a kiss to my temple, then stood, her leather pants creaking softly in the quiet. She reached into her jacket and pulled out a small, time-worn note. I felt my body grow hot. I recognized that piece of paper; it was the note from Professor Lee.

"I know you recognize this," she whispered, eyes searching mine with something close to fear. "He said you were only to read it when the man with two faces appeared." My breath stalled. Her hand tightened around mine, steady and sure despite the tremor beneath it. "Reverie… It's time."

I started to open it, and she stopped me.

"Get dressed," she said. "You need to read the note. But not here."

"Where then?"

"Breakfast," she said solemnly. Mira nuzzled her in comfort. "With everyone. And then, you and I will have our own conversation. About Trent. About that mark. And about the fact that the sign of the man with two faces has finally shown up on my daughter's skin."

I blink. "You understand what all of this means?"

She hesitated. "Later, sweet girl. Get ready. Your men are already up, and Chloe's threatened to eat your portion if you don't show."

"That *monster*," I mutter. But my chest is too tight to joke properly.

She and Mira left, and I dragged myself out of bed, the chill of the cave air making me shiver. The makeshift sleeping quarters were carved out of Nyberie's tunnels—smooth stone walls, low ceilings, and the faint glow of bioluminescent moss painting everything in muted blues and greens. Voices echo down the passage, low and familiar.

My parents brought me some clothes from home, and Tanya filled in the gaps—Aurathion leathers and modern Earth fabrics—a strange mix, just like everything else in my life right now.

I stared down at the small piece of paper, a feeling of dread in my gut.

Best to get it over with. I knew there was nothing I couldn't face with my men at my side.

M y chest tightened as the words left my mouth:

"Rue lives. But if Trent is not with you when you find him...you both die."

The table fell silent.

Mom was the first to react. She gasped and pressed a shaking hand over her mouth.

Pops let out a strangled breath and stood to gather Mom into his arms, Grumpy jumping out of his seat to rush to her side.

Dad just sat there in shock, not saying a word. He'd searched for Rue for years and never found him. Suffering Ancestors knew what, at the hands of Selene, Ubel, and Trent.

That bastard, Trent—I couldn't believe I was connected to the guy who caused my family so much pain. And now, the only way we got Rue back was through him? This had to be a damn joke.

Dad startled me out of my thoughts when he slammed a hand down on the table. "Fucking *Lee*, my daughter isn't going to go to *fucking* Trent Storm for help. I'll find Rue without him!"

My mother left the comfort of Grumpy and Pops and went to sit in his lap, holding his face in her hands. "Sly. Stop."

He didn't look at her. Couldn't. His gaze stayed on me. "Reverie... Rue was the bravest of us. If he's alive—if he's trapped—" Dad's voice broke for the first time since his return, even after everything he'd been through. "We get him back. But you won't go it alone. I'll drag Trent by the balls if I have to."

Grumpy wiped a tired hand down his face. "Precognition or not… Lee wouldn't have written this unless every other path led to losing both our daughter and our brother."

My throat tightened. "I'm not sure I'm meant to bring anyone else with me."

I barely had time to inhale before my men went *full* apocalypse.

"I have to go *alone*," I repeated firmly.

And that was it.

That was the match.

Zane didn't just drop his fork. He hurled it at the wall so hard it stuck in the stone like a tiny Excalibur.

"You think you're walking up to *Trent Storm* by yourself?!" he shouted. "NO. No, you are not. I will physically hold you down until you change your mind!"

Nathan didn't stand.

Nathan teleported beside me, wrapped his arm around my waist like I was a misbehaving child, and stormed toward the door.

"NATHA—"

"No talking," he snapped.

Zeke didn't say a word. Not one.

Then Zeke ripped his chair in half with his bare hands and muttered, "I'm so tired. So fucking *tired* of you being in danger! How the hell am I supposed to take care of you when every *fucking* body keeps sending you into harm's way?"

I didn't think he wanted me to answer that.

Oren and Jet were the scariest because both fell silent as they followed behind us to our room.

Nathan sat me down, and I was facing all five of them.

"NO." Jet growled. "If you try to go to Trent without us, I will help Nathan tie you down. I'm done with being separated from you."

Before I could share my opinion on this, Oren walked up to me and took my hand in his. "You say you need to go alone," he absently stroked his long, elegant fingers over my knuckles. "And what I hear is you don't want us."

My stomach twisted. "Oren—no, that's not—"

"It *is* how I hear it," he stepped closer, shadows curling against the floor. "You're ours. *We* are yours. And you think we would let you walk into the den of the man who has tortured countless Aurathions? A man whom I know has killed more men and women than any other, even Ubel and Selene."

Zane gasped dramatically. "OH, MY ANCETORS! SHE DOESN'T WANT *YOU*—" He leans in and whispers to Zeke, but of course, we all hear him. "Cause I know how much she wants *me*."

Zeke cuffs him on the head, "Now's not the time."

"Guys," I brush my hair back and take a deep breath. "This is my father we're talking about. He could die."

"And WE ARE YOUR HUSBAND-ISHES," Zane declared, waving his arms. "Your Faction... we are IMPORTANT."

"Are you on something?" Jet asked him.

"No," Zane glared his way. "I'm making a point, Jolly."

I facepalmed.

Zeke ignored his brother. "Reverie, listen to me. I love

you. I *adore* you. I would *kill* for you. But the one thing I can't do is let you walk into Trent's presence without backup. I won't allow it."

Zane slapped Zeke's back. "Exactly what I meant." He turned to me, "Now that that's solved, how about a repeat of last night? Shadows activate… or however you got them to work before."

"Zane," Jet snapped, "shut the fuck up, or I'll null your vocal cords."

He pouted but then winked at me. I knew he was trying to lighten the mood. I also knew that if I even thought about heading toward the door, he'd be on me before I moved.

Oren grabbed my chin, eyes burning, shadows swirling like storm clouds. "You walk in alone," he whispered, "and Trent will kill you just to break the bond."

"I won't let him—"

"No," he cut in sharply. "*We* won't let him."

Shadows wrapped around my waist, soft as silk, firm as iron. "You go," Oren murmured, "and we go with you. Trust us to help you with this." His voice dropped into a dark, hungry growl. "I'll get to your father and keep you safe, even if I have to kill every last one of the DF to do it."

It was the first time since we met that he scared me a little.

It was hot, in a shadow-daddy, being firm kind of way.

Zane leaned in. "Tell her, Oren. Tell her about the plan."

"What plan?" I wrinkled my brow.

Nathan teleported out of the room, then came back seconds later, handing Zeke and Jet something.

Zeke held up a rope. "Plan Rope."

Jet held up what I assumed to be sedatives. "Plan Sleep."

Nathan lit his hands on fire. "Plan Force."

Oren's shadow brushed over my cheek. "Plan Don't You Ever Say 'Alone' Again."

My voice cracked. "You're all insane."

Zane gasped. "We're in love." He winked again, "And maybe just a little insane."

"I love y'all too! So very much, but that's not the point. I really believe if I'm alone, Trent will listen." I tried to reason with them, but the room became a hurricane at my words.

Zane lost all his playfulness and started pacing in circles, with Drakk clearly in charge, smoke billowing from his nostrils. Zeke was muttering curses in three languages I didn't even know he spoke. Jet was staring at me so intensely that I could feel the heat on my face. Nathan had that look he wore before I admitted my feelings to him, and Oren looked like a living shadow.

"Please listen to reason—"

The door blasted open so hard it ricocheted off the wall and nearly decapitated Zane.

Chloe burst in first. "What the hell? Everyone can hear you four tunnels away."

My parents strode in next with Pantar and Mira behind them, both showing their teeth to everyone in the room, including me—Kharox prowled in, the caboose of this shit train.

Adelaide strode to the center of the room. "Reverie Hawthorne," she snapped, "are you screaming at your men or are your men screaming at you? Because the acoustics don't make it clear."

"All of the above," I frowned down at the floor.

My fathers fanned out behind her like an intimidating parental wall.

Grumpy pointed at the broken chair. "Who did that?"

"Zeke," we all said in unison.

Zeke lifted his hands. "It was an emotional moment!"

Dad stared at the scorch marks on the floor. "And that?"

Nathan coughed. "Also, an emotional moment."

Zeke frowned at him, then turned to my mom. "Reverie feels it would be better to meet with Trent alone. We stringently disagree."

All three of my fathers turned to me as my mother's eyes went nuclear. "Absolutely not. No. That's not going to fucking happen."

"Adelaide!" Grumpy admonished.

She rolled her eyes. "Now's not the time, John. We just found out Rue is alive—" She choked up for a moment, "and our baby girl is the one who needs to take Trent to find him." Mom took a deep breath, "We don't even know where Rue is, so I think the first step is more information. Reverie. You tell us everything you're thinking. Exactly why you want to go alone."

I swallowed. "Because I think... if everyone came... Trent is less likely to listen. And I don't want to lose Rue before I even get to meet him."

Oren walked over to me and took me into his arms.

Zane stepped toward us. "Precious girl, we understand

how you feel, but don't shut us out. We *are* stronger together."

Pops put his arm around Mom. "We want Rue back, but not at the cost of our child." He smiled slightly, lost in memories. "Believe me, Rue wouldn't want that either."

My mother nodded. "We'll come up with a plan. Together. But we do it smart. Strategically. No rash heroics. No suicide missions."

Kharox had been very quiet since we'd come to the caves, but chose this moment to speak. *"The two-faced one will not run... if he believes she chooses him."*

Every man in the room went rigid.

My mother pinched the bridge of her nose. "Let's... table that comment for now."

Chloe sidled up to me and whispered, "This is going to be a long day."

I exhaled, shaking.

But for the first time since reading the note...

...I didn't feel alone.

CHAPTER 32

TRENT

Our headquarters on Earth smelled like smoke, power, and lies.

Perfect.

"Trent."

My brother's voice echoed through the hollow chamber—cold, impatient, oil-slick smooth. Remus Storm stood at the center of the obsidian table, flanked by the three pretenders who helped him poison the Factions that had found a home on Earth.

Sylvester, Claudia, and George, all high-ranking DF operatives. All of them *cowards* pretending to be someone important.

I sprawled in my seat, annoyed that I had to be here when I could be in Bellona, tormenting the warriors in— well, not the coliseum—since it was destroyed by she-who-shall-not-be-named. Instead, the battles were taking place in the new-old-school arena (a dirt circle). My

Cryptfiends had been undefeated so far, but today was a new day, so anything could happen. I needed some entertainment because the injections weren't effective enough to keep the voices at bay. Torren was supposed to be just a means to an end for torturing—you know who—but lately, he had found his voice and was torturing me daily.

"Trent!"

"What?" I blink, snapping back from my thoughts.

Claudia folded her hands. "The attacks on Earth have ceased."

"Randall had a lot to do with our defeat at Langley. I think our control over him is slipping. Especially since Adelaide has gotten Sly back. You know, he and Sly were friends back at Emberhold." Sylvester added nervously.

Remus continued to stare at me, "I gave up my position on the council to help stop suspicion falling to me." He frowned. "Now with my own son tied to that bitch's daughter, I'm sure he's given them any information he has. And with you playing childish games with the girl, things seem to be unraveling."

Oh, here we fucking go.

I smiled—sharp enough to draw blood. "I don't expect you to understand, but the information that I retrieved from those 'childish games' was invaluable."

"You sound defensive," George muttered.

"I sound bored," I corrected.

But the truth was it was hard to concentrate with this connection to *her*. Burning through my veins like wildfire.

The fucking serum wasn't dampening the bond like I hoped it would. I think it was actually making it worse.

Torren's voice clawed my brain, causing a headache I couldn't seem to get rid of.

My vision flickered. For a heartbeat, the room tilted sideways.

Remus's eyes narrowed. "Trent. Focus."

I straightened, power crackling at my fingertips. "The attacks failed because your Cryptfiends are incompetent."

George bristled. "You gave us use of those Cryptfiends."

"Exactly my point. So, the failure belongs at your door." I smirked, loving the mad hatter act I had going on. These dumb fucks were getting on my nerves, and I had more important things to do.

Sylvester swallowed. "We need her back."

I froze.

Claudia leaned forward. "Reverie Hawthorne must be recaptured. The DF cannot progress without her."

Torren snarled in my mind.

I didn't bother holding it back.

"No," I whispered.

Sylvester blinked. "N-No?"

"She is not to be touched without my say-so." I stared them down.

George scoffed. "We command you to bring her to us."

Shadows erupted beneath my feet as my chair scraped violently against the floor as I stood. "You command nothing."

Lightning forked up the walls.

The chamber lights flickered. And with a slash of my hand, George's head rolled across the floor.

Claudia gasped, grabbing the table to steady herself.

Remus finally spoke, voice calm but edged with anger and a hint of fear. "Trent. Control yourself." His jaw tightened. "You're going to clean up that mess." He grimaced in distaste at the pool of blood growing on the floor. "She *is* a threat, and without her, we have no control over Adelaide's Faction."

"She is MINE!"

Silence.

Pulsing.

Heavy.

Terrified.

Remus was the only one who dared meet my eyes. "Is the serum working? Is the bond still strong?"

That *motherfucker*. I'd told him to keep that confidential. I should have known he'd not abide by my wishes. He still thought his control of me was absolute and that Ubel and Selene were holding my chains."

"No."

Claudia's lips thinned, and she squeaked out. "Then take more."

"I have," I growled. "Every damn hour. It makes it worse."

Claudia trembled. "Worse how?"

I stalked toward her. "Worse, like I can feel her screaming at someone right now. Worse, like the bond wants to rip out of me. Worse, like Torren is clawing at the edges of my skull."

Claudia backed away until she hit the stone wall. "I—I didn't mean—"

"I know," I said sweetly, "because you don't think."

She slid down the wall, hyperventilating.

Remus's expression didn't change. "Then we accelerate the plan. Find her. Bind her. Use her."

Something inside me snapped.

Lightning exploded outward. The table split down the middle. Claudia shrieked. Sylvester dove under a chair. Even George's body twitched on the floor.

I didn't give a fuck.

Turning to Remus—my brother—the man who thought he owned me. "You cannot bind her," I growled. "You won't touch her unless I allow it."

"You *are* losing control. Everything we've worked for will be destroyed if you don't pull yourself together." Remus spoke softly.

I grinned—feral and fractured. "*Finally.*"

"Finally, what?" Remus was confused.

The bond surged—

Hard.

Violent.

Electric.

She was coming.

Reverie was coming for me.

And Torren purred inside my skull, *Ours…*

I dragged a hand through my hair. "The attacks will begin again. But this time they will be aimed at the resistance."

Sylvester squeaked from under the table. "Why not here?"

I smiled, teeth bared. "Because she needs to see that

insubordination will not go unpunished and the best way to do that is to target the ones she loves."

Claudia whispered, horrified, "And what happens when she reaches you?"

The shadows coiled around my throat like a lover's hand. "I stop pretending to be sane." I smirk, "And everyone learns just how much I've been holding back."

⟿ ⟐ ⟾

I stalked back into my chambers, bloody and exhausted. I decided to fight with my Cryptfiends and destroyed quite a few of the warriors hoping to find Factions.

Ubel had been pissed, but *fuck him*. If they were this weak, then we didn't need them.

I lay back on my bed and closed my eyes. I'd get cleaned up in a moment. The headache had come back and was blinding me with pain.

One instant, I was thinking about my plans to attack the tunnels in Nyberie.

The next?

A blinding flash of white.

Then gold.

Then blood.

Then her. Lilibet. The Queen.

Crowned in starlight, gown rippling like living magic, bare feet on the marble floor of her throne room. She turned toward me slowly, as if she had been waiting for this moment across centuries.

"Kratos," she whispered.

And the world split open.

My knees nearly buckled. "No... no, don't call me that—"

"You were always Torren Kratos," she said gently. "And you have always come back to me."

Her voice carried memories—

Mine.

Hers.

Ours.

A violent pulse cracked through the dream, and the throne room dissolved—

—becoming a battlefield of shattered marble.

—torches blown out.

—abilities screaming in the air.

—and five men lying at Lilibet's feet.

Her Faction.

My brothers.

Broken.

Dying.

Because of me.

I staggered back. "No—NO—I didn't do this—"

"Yes," she said softly. "You did."

A younger version of me—Kratos—kneeling in front of her, begging her to run.

Another flash—me raising a protective ability that wasn't natural.

Another—the Ancestors screaming warnings I ignored.

Another—

A prophecy carved into the wall: "One life must be given to save the realm."

Lilibet's life.

The Ancients' balancing law required her sacrifice to prevent all Aurathions from losing their abilities.

The other five Faction brothers fought with me at first to change her mind, but then eventually gave in and chose to die with her.

They loved her, as I did, but the difference was that I refused to believe this was the only option.

The rest of the Aurathions in the realm could go fuck themselves as far as I cared. I wanted to live out my life with her now.

I loved her more than I loved the realm.

More than I loved fate.

More than I loved my own soul or those of my brothers.

More than she loved herself.

Kratos gripped her arms. "I won't let you die."

Lilibet cried softly. "Kratos... we were chosen for this together. Please—don't fight it."

I watched myself refuse.

Kratos cupped her face desperately. "I would burn the realms to keep you breathing."

Then he used an ability that was forbidden, one that he'd kept hidden until this moment. He forged a shield meant to redirect the will of the Ancients and force it onto the Faction instead.

To save her.

It detonated.

The whole of Aurathia seemed to scream.

The bond convulsed.

The air cracked like a dying star.

The other five Faction members' marks shattered—not by design, but by the backlash.

Ambrose died instantly.

Merritt and Bren fell gasping.

Zenon and Larkin crawled to her, reaching—and collapsed.

The realm trembled.

Lexith, Cassian, Viktar, and Soren crumpled to the floor trying to reach their queen. Her faithful Varruk warrior and Fellat dying before they could stop me.

The ancestral tether broke.

My attempt to save her went horribly wrong.

Lilibet hit her knees, face streaked with tears. "Kratos," she whispered, touching the bodies. "You killed them."

"I tried to save you," he pleaded. "I did it for you."

She looked up at him with a heartbreak so deep it carved itself into my bones. "Kratos... love was never the realm's enemy. But your fear was."

He—I—reached for her.

She stood. Her abilities rising around her—silver, cold, holy.

"Then curse me," he said, choking. "If it keeps you alive— curse me."

Her lips trembled. "I don't curse out of hatred," she shook her head, tears pouring down her cheeks. "I curse out of knowing."

Lightning cracked overhead, shadows writhing on the ground. She placed her hand over his heart. "You will return in every lifetime," she spoke softly. "You will remember me too late. You will find me only in rebirth. And the girl who carries my soul—"

The dream trembled.

Her face blurred—

Reverie's face phasing through it like a ghost.

"—will see all of it when the time is right."

My breath caught.

"And Kratos," she finished, tears still falling, *"When she remembers what you did... only will a great sacrifice make things right."*

The dream shattered—

And I woke up screaming.

This changed everything. I knew what needed to be done.

CHAPTER 33

REVERIE

We rode hard through the forest, mist curling low on the ground, Mira leading the way with Pantar by her side, their tentacles waving around, scenting for danger. Kharox followed in silence, hulking, protective, terrifying to look at but calming in his presence.

My men stayed close.

Too close.

Nathan kept glancing at the shadows. Zane nearly rode backwards in his saddle half the time to keep an eye on me. Jet never took his eyes off me, insisting I ride with him. Zeke was half-shifted into his Draxon form, feeding me snacks from his saddlebags now and then.

And my Oren was more stressed than all of them combined, shifting his gaze between me and our surroundings, never relaxing his guard for a second.

Ahead, Tanya, Razor, and Malik joined our formation, ready to help execute whatever plan would get Trent alone without any of us ending up dead. Razor had insisted on coming because he knew the ins and outs of Bellona along with my father, Sly.

Speaking of my fathers... they traveled at the back of our group, surrounding my mother. Each of them was edgy about having her and me exposed like this. But on the other hand, they understood that if they wanted Rue back, all of this was necessary.

I tried to keep my breathing steady. I'd ridden horses my whole life, but these animals were huge, and I was still a little hesitant around them.

One minute I was gripping Jet's waist, and the next... the world tore away.

A cold voice whispered inside me. *"Remember, child of my blood."*

I didn't have time to scream before the vision hit.

White stone. Silver banners. A queen's heartbeat.

I wasn't me.

I was her.

Lilibet.

Standing in her throne room with magic pulsing through my veins like starlight. The six Faction marks burned bright across six chests. Mine glowed at the center.

Love.

Unity.

Power.

Destiny.

And then—

The prophecy.

A voice like thunder cracking inside my skull. "One life must be given to save the realm."

I felt the truth settle like a stone.

It had to be me.

The Ancestors demanded the queen.

My Faction—my heart—knelt before me one by one.

"We'll support your decision," Bren whispered.

"We tried to find another way, but we understand now." Ambrose's deep voice spoke loudly, filled with assurance. "Our sacrifice will be rewarded, and we'll live again together."

Each man nodded in agreement, their face full of grief, but hope shone brightly beneath it.

Except for one.

Kratos.

He stepped forward, shaking, furious, eyes burning with a wildfire devotion that terrified and warmed me at once.

I was aware he had difficulty with this. His struggles had split our Faction, leading to numerous internal conflicts. Still, I had hoped...

"No," he shook his head. "You will not die."

I touched his cheek. "Kratos—my love—"

He grabbed my wrist with trembling hands. "I won't lose you. Not for prophecy. Not to the realm. I WON'T!"

He kissed my palm—desperate, shaking.

I reached for him. "I need you to stand with me—"

"No," he whispered. "I will stand AGAINST the Ancestors."

An ability I didn't know he had, one forbidden to use, surged at his fingertips.

"Kratos, STOP—"

"Let them take the realm," his voice was cracking. "Let the world burn. Let all of Aurathia become powerless. I won't let them take you from me."

And then—

He let his ability free.

The air shattered like glass.

I screamed.

My Faction screamed.

The bond, once pure and golden, warped into something monstrous and jagged. I felt five hearts seize in unison.

One died instantly.

Two fell broken.

Two crawled toward me before their marks flickered—flickered—faded—

"No—NO, NO KRATOS WHAT HAVE YOU DONE—"

He collapsed to his knees, sobbing. "I saved you."

"I didn't need saving," I whispered. "I needed you with me."

The realm trembled. The Ancestors were furious. The dark seed of corruption had seeded itself in the wound he had opened.

I felt my own soul crack.

And as I knelt with my dying Faction, I touched Kratos's face one last time.

"Beloved," I whispered, "your love was never the realm's enemy. But your fear destroyed everything."

His agonized scream echoed through centuries. "I'm sorry—I'm so sorry—kill me—"

"No," I mourned, grief eating through every bone. "No, Kratos. That would be mercy."

I laid my hand on his heart, my magic trembling and broken. "I curse you to remember. Life after life. Era after era. Until she—the girl who carries my soul—sees the truth."

My voice cracked as the mark flared.

And until you understand what true love requires... You will always be too late.

I came back to myself screaming.

Not figuratively. Actually screaming.

My men jerked their heads toward me—each of them going feral in an instant, searching our surroundings for danger. Jet pulled me in front of him and clutched me to his massive chest in desperation.

"Nexi, what the fuck is going on? Did you see something?" Nathan shouted.

"She's hurt. She's broken. I feel it." Zane babbled, jumping off his horse and pulling me from Jet's death grip.

"Her mark flared," Jet rumbled. "I saw it. I FELT it."

Oren pulled me away from Zane and held me tight enough to hurt. "Baby, look at me—breathe—just breathe."

My fathers ran over, each of them confused but ready to defend my invisible enemy.

Only my mother seemed to understand. Her face, filled with heartbreaking concern for me, gave me the strength I needed to overcome the panic.

Tanya jumped off her horse, eyes wide. "Are you okay?"

I could still feel the blood. The broken Faction. Kratos's desperation and Lilibet's heartbreak.

Oren cupped my face. "Reverie. Say something. Anything."

My voice trembled. "I saw Lilibet."

Everyone froze.

"And… Kratos."

Oren's voice deepened. "Kratos? As in the Ancestor who—"

"No," I stared into his eyes intently. My chest hurt like I'd been stabbed. "Not an Ancestor."

They all stared.

I swallowed. "Kratos was part of her Faction."

"Like us?" Zane took one of my hands in his.

"Yes," I choked.

"And he…" Zeke hesitated. "He betrayed her?"

My throat closed.

Oren brushed a tear from my cheek with shaking fingers. "Baby… what exactly did you see?"

I looked at him.

At all of them.

Then whispered, "Trent was him."

They all went still.

Completely, terrifyingly still.

Pantar moved to my side, *"Nexus, there is a purpose to everything. Do not despair. The Ancestors always set things right."*

Kharox nodded his head, then made the sign he'd been doing since the moment he met me. *"Your Fellat is wise, Khal' Sira."*

Pops frowned. "If Reverie knows… then I would bet Trent knows too."

I shivered because the bond pulsed once.

Hard.

Like Trent's soul had responded to his statement.

Nathan started pacing. "You should have told us about these dreams sooner."

I sighed. We'd had this argument multiple times already. "Maybe, but what difference would it have made? We were running for our lives. There wasn't time to try and figure out what it all meant anyway."

I squeezed Oren tight, then dropped my feet to the ground and went to my Psycho. "I know all that, but I don't like feeling helpless. Maybe Zane and I should teleport to him and kill the bastard. Even if we don't make it, at least you'd be safe."

Zane cackled, "I love that idea. Nothing says romance like being covered in the blood of my precious girls, enemies."

"No, you will *not!*" I screamed, "What happened to living for me, asshole?"

I pushed his chest, furious at the very thought of anything happening to him or Zane. Especially with my vision still fresh and Lilibet's pain when seeing each of her men fall dead.

He didn't move.

"Nate," I whispered.

He inhaled sharply at the nickname I hadn't used since we were little kids. I'd hoped it would soften him, but tonight he didn't soften.

Tonight he was a storm.

His eyes glowed like embers. "No. I don't want to lose you. Not again."

"Nathan—"

He grabbed my wrist. Gentle, but the kind of gentle that barely contained something feral underneath.

"I think this is our cue to leave." I heard my mom say, and my dad's grumbled as they followed behind her.

"Say it again."

"Nate."

He exhaled like I'd punched the air from his lungs. Then he hauled me in. There was no warning. No hesitation. Just heat.

His hand slid up my spine, gripping the back of my

neck as his mouth crashed against mine—hungry, angry, desperate. His body pressed me back against one of the thick tree trunks close to us, pinning me there with all that fire and pent-up terror.

I gasped, and he took advantage—deepening the kiss, teeth catching my bottom lip, growling into my mouth like he needed to taste my heartbeat.

"Nathan—" I breathed against him. My blood heated from the intensity of his kiss.

His thumb brushed my jaw, tender for half a second—

Then he tilted my head, angled his mouth over mine again—

And kissed me like he wanted to claim every thought I'd ever had.

My knees buckled. He held me up effortlessly.

Heat flared with every sweep of his tongue against mine until I felt like I would combust. His chest trembled against me, his breathing harsh, furious, and terrified.

When he finally tore his mouth away, he pressed his forehead to mine, panting.

"Just know that nothing has changed if he comes for you," his voice was like molten steel. "I will burn the Ancestors themselves to ashes."

My whole body shivered.

He cupped my face with both hands, thumbs brushing my lips as if memorizing the bruise he'd left there. "I'm not gentle, I'm not calm. I'm not rational. I'm *scared*, Nexi. I'm so fucking *scared*."

"Okay, not to interrupt Nathan's emotional crisis meltdown—"

"—but the rest of us are dying too!"

Before I could respond, Zeke approached me like a winter storm on legs, eyes fixed on me with a hunger I felt deep in my spine. "Nathan got to go first," voice low and rough. "But don't think for a second I'm going without touching you myself for a second longer."

Nathan snorted. "Nathan has been first right from the start—in everything." He waggled his brow obnoxiously.

I smiled softly just as Zeke cupped my jaw with one hand—cool, steady, grounding–and kissed me with precision that made my pulse stutter.

But the moment my fingers slid into his hair, he broke —just a little—pressing his forehead to mine. "You scare me," he murmured. "Please don't let this shit take you from us." His thumb brushed my lower lip right where Nathan's bruise was, possessive and soft at once. "Next time you dream, I want to be there."

Jet stepped forward next, quiet but burning behind the eyes. He touched my cheek with his massive hand, as if asking permission.

I nodded, eyes never leaving his.

He picked me up then kissed me like a secret he'd been waiting to confess—slow, deep, needing. His breath trembled against my mouth.

When he pulled back, he didn't look away. "I'm not losing you," he growled. "Not to a prophecy. Not to a past life. Not to him."

My chest tightened. "Jet—"

He lowered me to my feet. "I'll do whatever it takes. That you can count on."

Zane didn't ask. He never did.

He swooped in, grabbed my waist, and dipped me like

an overdramatic hero in a romance novel—except his kiss was nothing like those simpering heroes.

It was messy.

Hungry.

Possessive. A little reckless.

And so very Zane.

He pulled me upright and rested his forehead on mine. "I love you. Don't go Lilibetting off into danger without me."

I laughed, but then stopped when I noticed that my men had fallen silent.

The reason for that was still sitting in the shadows, watching me with those deep, unreadable eyes.

He rose slowly.

Deliberately.

Like he was keeping his power from spilling everywhere.

When he reached me, he didn't touch. Not at first.

He just looked through me, into me, like he was searching my soul for cracks... or others that might be occupying my body. "Come here."

I went.

He wrapped an arm around my waist and pulled me in gently, cautiously, then kissed me with a careful reverence that made something inside me shatter wide open.

He kissed me as if he were afraid I would vanish. Then, as if he were afraid *he* would.

When he finally broke the kiss, he rested his forehead against mine, breathing hard. "You are the center of everything I'm trying to hold together," he whispered. "Don't ever forget that. My family isn't allowed to destroy that."

My eyes stung.

He brushed his knuckles down my cheek. "And if Trent ever touches you…" His voice deepened, darkened. "…I will ruin him."

We chose to camp at this spot, and as we all settled down, there was no pushing or crowding. Instead, they formed a circle around me—one by one, each gently pressing a kiss to my forehead, temple, hair, shoulder, and hand.

And as I drifted toward sleep, surrounded by their warmth, their breath, and their bodies draped like shields—

I had no idea it would be the last peaceful moment before Trent's shadow swallowed us all.

CHAPTER 34
TRENT

The forest slept.

The Aurathions in it did not.

I could feel her pulse through the bond—wild from the dream, shaken raw and aching in a way that made something inside me turn animal.

She'd seen it.

The throne room.

The blood.

My sin.

Kratos.

The name hissed through my skull like poison.

She knew.

She *knew*.

And before she could run from me—before her men could hide her away—I moved.

I *slipped* between shadows the way Torren used to, when he was still just a mask I wore to torment her and not a fracture in my mind.

The camp came into view, fires low. Everyone is quiet. Bodies still.

Reverie slept between her men with Tanya, Razor, and Malik, Chloe, and her men arranged like wolves guarding a queen.

Like Aegisworn.

Her parents slept curled together, trusting Mira, Pantar, and the Varruk to keep watch.

Unfortunately for them, I had an ability that none could withstand, not even a Fellat or a Varruk.

I exhaled.

Then let the ability loose.

It spread outward like a dark mist—soundless, formless, a psychic hand closing over their minds.

Unconsciousness rippled through the camp.

They all succumbed except Oren, who tried to fight it, shadows curling around him like claws and sparks coming to his fingers, recognizing what it was too late. He managed to whisper. "Rev—. And then dropped.

I almost admired the big bastard. Maybe if things had been different, we could have been friends.

I stepped into their sleeping ring.

Reverie's breathing hitched—she felt me even unconscious.

Her mark glowed faintly under her shirt, broken crown pulsing like a heartbeat.

Mine answered.

Violently.

I knelt beside her.

"Reverie," I whispered. "You shouldn't have seen that."

She didn't wake—

My ability held too tightly—but her fingers twitched toward me, as if her soul knew mine.

Tanya stirred beside her, brow furrowing. She wasn't strong enough to break free… but she resisted.

Good. I respected her more knowing she was a fighter.

Razor and Malik had the same faint tension—warriors with instincts too sharp to succumb fully.

I brushed a hand above their foreheads. "Sleep," I commanded.

And they obeyed.

I slipped my arms under Reverie and lifted her against my chest. Her long dark hair spilled down my arm and onto the ground like ink.

She felt… right.

Too right.

A centuries-old ache softened in my ribs—

Kratos reaching across time,

Torren whispering "mine",

My heart is pounding harder than it should.

"No more running," I murmured.

To her.

To myself.

To the curse.

To the past.

I know how to fix this.

Transporting them was effortless. The ability that rendered people unconscious also let me move through space—not teleportation, but a slipping between shadows that bypassed physical distance.

One moment, I stood in the camp. The next—stone,

cool air, and the soft hum of the wards I'd created years ago.

My stronghold.

My sanctuary.

Her prison. At least for now.

I placed Reverie gently on the cot in the center of the room. Her hair mixed with mine, falling like dark fire on her pillow.

Tanya, Razor, and Malik, I arranged in the adjoining chamber—close enough to control, far enough that they couldn't interfere.

I activated the sigils on the floor.

Light spiraled around the room—soft blue, locking them in, locking us in.

I felt the curse thrumming beneath my skin and realized it had always been there. I just hadn't understood exactly what it was.

I felt Kratos whispering, *"You failed her before. It's time to redeem yourself."*

Torren sighed, *"This isn't the way."*

My own voice muttered out loud, "I won't lose her again."

I sat at the edge of the bed and brushed a strand of hair from her cheek. "Reverie," my voice cracked. "When you wake, you'll hate me. But I promise this is the only way."

The bond pulsed painfully—no, not hate.

Fear.

Confusion.

Grief.

I closed my eyes and bowed my head. "I don't want to be him."

Kratos.

The man who chose love so fiercely that he destroyed everything.

I'm smarter than he was, and I believe I can break this curse. Restore Aurathions to their former glory without the evil my brother spread through our people like confetti. I wasn't ignoring my part in it; this would make everything right.

Make me worthy of a queen.

After all, every king should have a queen. I was the most powerful Aurathion alive, and I could keep her safe — from herself, the Ancestors, and even myself when it was called for.

Tanya was paramount to my plan. But I knew she wouldn't do it without me holding something important over her head. Thus, I took both of her men.

I paused in my thoughts—Reverie was starting to move.

Her breathing shifted—she was waking.

The bond yanked tight—violent, electric, inevitable.

Her eyes fluttered open.

And the first word she spoke, "Torren." broke me cleanly in half.

CHAPTER 35
REVERIE

The stone ceiling swam above me.

Cold air.

Wards humming.

Magic pressing against my skin like a warning.

And then—

"Reverie."

His voice. "Torren."

I jolted upright.

Trent sat at the edge of the bed, elbows on his knees, hands clasped so tightly the veins stood out. Shadows clung to him—shifting, restless. His jaw was clenched hard enough to crack teeth.

The man was beyond attractive. Long hair, as dark as my own that spilled down his back to his waist. He had to be at least Oren's height at 6'5, with green eyes that could pierce your soul. Nothing like the man I had fallen half in love with.

Torren.

His eyes lifted.

Ancestors.

They were burning. And no sanity whatsoever shone from them.

I pushed myself back against the wall. "You—you took me, my family, my—my friends—"

"They're all alive," he smiled. "I even brought Tanya and her men here with you."

"Why?" I snapped. I knew there had to be a reason.

He flinched.

I wasn't expecting that.

Trent Storm did not flinch.

"To keep you company." The sly smile he displayed suggested something else entirely.

I blinked. "I can't trust you."

His jaw ticked. "You shouldn't."

"What?"

"You shouldn't trust me," he repeated, softer. "Not after last time. Not after… before."

Before.

Meaning:

Before this life.

Before Reverie.

Before the curse.

Lilibet.

Kratos.

My throat tightened. "I saw it."

He closed his eyes, as if the words physically hurt him. "I know."

"You killed your Faction."

His breath hitched. "I didn't mean—I didn't want—"

"You defied the Ancestors and caused misery for thousands of years!"

"And I would again," he whispered, voice breaking. "That's the problem."

Something inside me stuttered.

He looked away—shame, fury, longing, and madness flickering across his face like a storm. "You don't know what it's like," he ran a hand down his face. "To suddenly understand that you're the one who ruined an entire population. Lost the one person you were born to love."

His voice cracked into something jagged. "You don't know what it's like fighting off insanity every day and being split three ways." He pressed a palm to his temple as if he could physically hold himself together. "Part of me wants to shield you from everything." His hand trembled. "Part of me wants to run before I hurt you again." His eyes lifted—shattered, feral, terrified. "And part of me—the part you saw in the vision—" His breath shuddered. "That part wants to burn anyone who looks at you."

Silence.

Heavy. Crushing.

I swallowed hard. "Which part brought me here?"

A bitter laugh slipped from him. "All three."

Then his expression shifted—just slightly—into something darker. "But if you're asking which part wanted to keep you close..." He lifted one hand, stopping inches from touching my cheek. "Kratos."

My heart hammered.

"I'm not asking you to trust me," he pushed his silky hair off his face. "But right now? The only one who can lead you to Rue—" His eyes flicked upward, savoring my surprise, pupils shrinking to a thin, inhuman ring. "—is the monster you're afraid I still am."

I swallowed. "Are you that monster?"

He smiled.

Sad.

Beautiful.

Terrifying.

"Yes," he whispered. "And I'm trying to find a way to be *your* monster."

Something inside me cracked open.

"How did you know about the letter?"

"Through the bond, how else?"

But before I could answer—

A distant thud echoed in the fortress.

A shout.

A Draxon's roar… two Draxon to be exact.

Trent's head snapped toward the door, expression darkening into the predator he tried to bury. "I guess they woke up. Seems they're stronger than I gave them credit for."

I stood.

"I'm sorry, little Bellator, but they're not part of my plan."

That word sparked a memory, but it was gone before I could hold on to it.

～☖～

C old stone touched my cheek.
My eyes snapped open.

For one breath, I didn't know where the hell I was.

Then everything slammed back at once—

Trent. Shadows. A hand over my mouth. The world tearing sideways.

I sat up too fast, head spinning. My wrists were bound by thin metallic cuffs that hummed faintly—null cuffs. They didn't tighten, didn't bruise, but they swallowed my abilities whole.

Tanya was slumped beside me, still unconscious, Razor and Malik on either side of her, wrists cuffed to the same black stone table I was.

Torches flickered along walls that looked carved from the rare shimmering stone used only in ancient ruling halls—silver flecks of crushed crystal rippling through the surface like starlight trapped in rock. High-tech and archaic at the same time.

My heart hammered.

Shadow-travel. He used shadow-travel on all of us.

That ability wasn't normal.

It was far from ordinary.

It wasn't even supposed to exist outside myth.

Only Kratos and the old royal Factions were believed to hold it. Oren mentioned it to us one night while we were relaxing together.

I swallowed hard.

Trent wasn't just skilled. He wasn't just powerful. He had Lilibet-era abilities.

Just like me.

My breath left my body.

Where are my men? My parents?

Footsteps echoed from outside the chamber.

And then he walked in.

Trent.

Hair loose.

Eyes sharp.

Shadows curling around him as if they adored him.

"My darling Reverie," he lowered his voice, silky and wrong, "awake at last."

I jerked away as far as the restraints allowed. "You kidnapped us… again."

He didn't deny it.

The fucking crazy man actually smiled. "Only temporarily."

Razor lunged, metal clanging. Trent barely flicked two fingers—and Razor froze, breath choking in his throat.

"Don't," Trent said pleasantly. "I prefer to keep you alive."

Tanya burst out, voice shaking, "Please—don't hurt him!"

Trent sighed, genuine irritation flickering across his features before he smoothed it away. "I'm not here to harm anyone. I'm here to save someone."

He stepped behind me and the temperature in the room dropped.

A ripple of shadow rolled outward like a black tide, forming a sphere of void in the center of the chamber.

The hair on my arms rose.

The shadows tore open—

And Rue fell out.

My father.

Alive.

I only recognized him from photographs; he was older now and looked like he'd lived a thousand lives since those were taken, but it was him.

"What the *hell*?!" I whispered, unable to believe my eyes.

"Stay calm, little Bellator. There is no need to be angry with me. I'm here to help." He strolled to my side of the table and leaned down to kiss my cheek.

He was weak, bruised, and barely conscious. But he was ALIVE!

He collapsed onto his hands and knees, shackles smoking around his wrists, ability-disrupting cuffs cracked from Trent's interference.

"Rue—Rue!" I screamed, fighting the restraints.

Rue lifted his head, his beautiful blue eyes glassy but trying—trying—to focus on me.

"Adelaide…?" His voice was racked with pain.

I lost my breath. This man knew nothing about me. He hadn't even known my mother was pregnant with me before they were separated.

"Not Adelaide…I'm your daughter… Reverie." I spoke in a quiet voice, knowing just what a shock this was going to be to him, and frankly, he looked like he'd been through enough.

Trent stood over Rue like a proud magician revealing his final trick. "You see?" he whispered, crouching beside him. "Alive. But not for long unless she comes with me."

"We don't have a choice, Reverie." He turned to Tanya.

She shook her head violently. 'No, this is wrong—this is—"

"If you don't," Trent said softly, "Rue dies on this floor.'

Rue swayed, wheezing but never taking his eyes off me. "Reverie… my sweet baby—" The look on his face was pure loss and devastation. "My life isn't worth anything he's asking of you."

Trent trailed a finger down Rue's spine, shadows sparking beneath his touch.

Rue arched with a groan.

"STOP!" I shouted.

Trent grinned and winked at Tanya, "If you don't do this, I'll end your men. You know how effortless that would be for me."

Tanya sobbed, looking between Razor and me with complete sorrow, and I couldn't stand to see it. "Do it. You can't lose Razor."

The green glow began to form in her hand. "I'm sorry…" she whispered as a tear fell down her cheek.

Trent came back around to me and reached out a finger, dissolving my cuffs.

I took the opportunity to call fire to my hands, but when I started to burn him, my ability just fizzled out. It was almost like now that we were bonded, I couldn't hurt him. I brought up my knee and threw a punch at his throat simultaneously, but neither landed.

He threw back his head and laughed. "I do so love your spirit, little Bellator." He grabbed me around the waist. "Now, Tanya, I don't want to wait any longer."

"Please forgive me." She raised her hand and closed her eyes. The green glow spread from her palm and enveloped us both.

I felt my heart break, and I knew things would never be the same. Too late, I connected this to the dream I'd had months ago, never realizing it had been a warning from the Ancestors.

A BOOM shook the chamber.

The torches guttered.

The shadows recoiled like something huge had just stepped into the room.

Tanya's magic flickered out.

Trent went rigid.

The door blasted inward—

—Ubel Brummond stormed in with six Dark Faction guards behind him, blade drawn and crackling with energy.

"TRENT!" Ubel roared. "WHAT HAVE YOU DONE?!"

Right behind him, Selene, pale hair wild, eyes glowing with lethal fury. "If you think we're letting you undo years of containment of that man—" she hissed, pointing at Rue. "—you've finally gone insane."

Trent straightened, shadows coiling around him like living armor. "Oh," he smirked in amusement, "I've been insane for a very, very long time. His serum saw to that." He motioned at Rue, who looked horrified at everything taking place. "But no worries, I've found my Nexus, and together we're going to fix everything wrong with our world."

Selene flicked her wrist—and the guards surged forward, weapons drawn.

Ubel's voice thundered: "SEAL THE ROOM! GET HIM AWAY FROM HER!"

Trent stepped in front of me. Shadows rose behind him like wings. "Try it," he whispered.

And the whole room exploded into chaos.

CHAPTER 36
OREN

Something ripped me out of sleep.

Not a sound.

Nothing had moved.

It was a lurch in my chest—like the bond had been punched.

I sat up sharply, heart hammering.

The campsite was still dark, embers glowing faintly. Chloe curled up between Oliver and Deshawn.

I sat up so fast I nearly knocked into Zane beside me.

The camp was still.

Too still.

The space where Reverie had been curled? Empty.

A chill bolted through me.

"Oren?" Jet whispered, rubbing his eyes, instantly alert when he saw my face.

Before I could answer, Nathan jolted upright with a ragged gasp, flames blooming across his arms as instinct overtook sleep. His kestrel, Dale, took to the sky in distress.

"She's gone," he growled.

Zeke and Zane both sprang up at the exact moment, every muscle tensed. Beasts flashing in their eyes.

"Not just her." Jet looked around the camp, noting what I had missed in my panic.

I scanned the clearing—

Tanya's bedroll: empty.

Razor's gear: untouched, but he was clearly not here.

Malik's coat near the logs: no Malik in sight.

Four missing.

The question was: Why?

Adelaide bolted awake next, eyes sharp as blades. John jerked up behind her.

"Who's missing?" Adelaide demanded.

Jet's voice shook. "Reverie, Tanya, Razor, and Malik. All four signatures vanished at once."

John's face drained of color. "Shadow displacement."

I snarled low in my throat. "Trent."

The air itself seemed to recoil at the name.

Zane breathed fire onto the dying embers to help warm the air. "Why would he take them *too?*"

Jet frowned. "What is Tanya's ability?"

"Fuck!" Jesse growled, then changed into a massive tiger and started shredding his sleeping gear.

"What?" I directed my question to John, more than a little startled by Jesse's loss of control.

John began to walk toward his twin, but Adelaide stopped him and went that way herself. "She can bind things together, whether it's a person, animal, or object." He answered distractedly.

"Okay, but he's already bonded to her. So why would her ability matter to him?" Nathan looked relieved at John's answer, but I waited for the other shoe to drop.

Adelaide replied from within the circle of Jesse's arms, him having transformed back into a man. "She can also break existing bonds."

You could have heard a pin drop.

Then Zane ended the silence. "That dead motherfucker!" His pupils elongated, and I knew he wasn't far from his Draxon taking over.

"Get it the fuck together." Zeke grabbed his brother's shoulders. "She'll fight with everything she has, so we can't fall apart at what-ifs. Now suck it up and let's use our abilities to find her."

Jet closed his eyes, reaching for any lingering echo of our Nexus. His breathing hitched. "I can't feel her. Not even a flicker." His hands fisted.

I reached for Reverie, "He's right. The bond is silent."

"He can do that?" Chloe whispered, standing by Kharox, who had drifted closer during our panic.

Adelaide's voice turned low, bitter. "Trent can silence anything he touches. Power. Memory. Bond. He developed that, among many others after he was injected with the serum."

John took her in his arms till he and his brother surrounded her.

Zane cracked his knuckles. "So, we hunt him."

Zeke nodded, Frynn's icy presence humming under his

skin. "We don't wait. We don't rest. We don't think. We go."

"No," I corrected quietly, standing. "We go—but we think like Trent." The others stilled. "Because he didn't just kidnap Reverie," I frowned. "He took the one woman who binds abilities, the man who steals them, and the third who is their anchor."

"What else is he planning?" Jet mumbled to himself, not expecting a reply.

A sharp *pulse* hit the back of my mind—fast, urgent, unmistakably Fellat.

Pantar. I hadn't noticed he was missing. Neither he nor Mira was here.

My eyes snapped wide.

"Oren." The telepathic voice was rough silk, deep and edged with panic. *"Wake. Now."*

"I'm awake," I hissed under my breath.

The others froze, sensing the shift in me.

Jet glanced over. "Pantar?"

I nodded once, already rising.

"He took her," Pantar growled into my mind. *"And the Binding One with her Faction."*

Nathan surged forward. "Do you know where they went?"

Pantar's voice trembled with fury and something like fear. *"Trent. He masked his scent—but not well enough for a Fellat. Mira and I followed him as soon as I awoke."*

My heart slammed into my ribs. "You're tracking them?"

"Yes. Through the trees. Through stone. He went to holding

cells beneath the mountain—outside of Bellona." I repeated this information out loud.

"I know where those are located." Sly moved silently into camp.

"Where were you?" Adelaide untangled herself from Jesse and John and threw herself into his arms.

We hadn't noticed him missing either.

He seemed defeated by life, but his face lit up when he held his Nexus. "I woke up and realized Reverie was missing. I hoped she had just woken early and was checking out our surroundings. Sadly, I saw no sign of her and came back this way."

"Do you know how to get in?" I asked Sly, not giving a shit as to where he was.

"No. I can get us there, but they were closed years ago. Or at least that's what I thought." He kissed the top of Adelaid's head. "Maybe that's where Rue has been held all these years. Selene knew I'd been searching for him, and I'm almost positive it was Beatrice who mentioned that the Resistance had destroyed those chambers."

A cold feeling twisted in my gut. "Pantar—are they all alive?"

There was a long, terrible pause. *"Yes. Our Nexus is fine. The Binding One, too. Though her men are frantic."* He growled low. *"Trent smells more unstable than before."*

Nathan swore softly. Stroking the kestrel who had landed on his shoulder.

Zeke stepped closer to me, Frynn humming under his skin. "Pantar—can you lead us to them?"

"We can. But not alone." His voice shifted—lower, protective, ancient. *"Danger coils there. A predator older than*

your wars sleeps in those tunnels. Even two Fellat cannot defeat it without help."

Before I could respond, a second voice rumbled behind Chloe.

Kharox.

The large Varruk emerged from the shadows like a rising mountain, his eyes glowing like embers. *"Reverie is touched by the Ancestors—no creature bound to Aurathia will ignore the call to help her."* He looked deadly in that moment. The urge to kill was evident on his face, with sharp teeth ready to rend and tear flesh from bones.

I knew the feeling.

Oliver drew Chloe away from him and into his arms. Deshawn placed himself subtly in front of her.

Kharox continued, his gaze on me. *"I will summon others of my kind. Varruk, who still honors the old oaths. Some will answer. Some will come hoping to regain the favor of a queen once more."*

"How fast?" Zeke asked, his voice echoing slightly as Drakk surged closer to the surface.

Kharox lowered his head, listening to something none of us could hear. *"The signal has been sent. They will be waiting in the forest surrounding the mountain."*

Nathan paced like a caged storm. "We can't delay for them. If they're not waiting, I'm going in."

"We won't," I nodded in agreement.

Pantar appeared at my side, fur bristling, tentacles twitching with distress. He pressed his broad head against my chest—a gesture he hadn't used since he was much younger. *"Hurry, Oren. Hurry before all is lost. He knows not what he's doing, and the Ancestors won't allow another betrayal."*

Everyone froze.

Nathan's voice was barely a whisper. "Betrayal?"

Pantar looked at him, eyes burning amber. *"He has one chance to put everything right, or Aurathia will be no more. Mira has stayed behind to monitor them, but we must hurry."*

My blood went cold.

Kharox growled, teeth flashing like scythes. *"Then we do not delay. We prepare, we gather strength, and we strike with every creature that answers the call."*

I straightened, feeling the bond roar back to life for the briefest of moments—even silenced, it fought. "Then we move," voice steady with purpose. "It's time to end this once and for all."

CHAPTER 37
REVERIE

Trent slammed Selene into the stone so hard that the wall cracked around her outline, dust pouring down in sheets. Already, he had killed every last guard they brought with them in one fell swoop. Ubel's lightning strike grazed Trent's shoulder, causing him to spin sideways, but he didn't fall. He twisted in mid-air, shadows wrapping around his arms like living serpents, and landed between them and us.

He was breathing hard now. Not from exhaustion—from fury.

"Tanya—just give me a second—" I muttered through my teeth, wrenching at the cuffs that bound her. I was trying to reverse my Aegisseal ability to get them off, but so far, I wasn't having any luck.

"Reverie—leave me—" Tanya gasped, trying to push me away with bound wrists.

"Not happening."

A crack split the stone near my head as Selene threw a bolt intended to decapitate me.

Trent's shadow shield ate it mid-air.

He didn't even look back at me. Trent was entirely in predator mode—the façade gone, the restraint gone, and the honest Torren/Trent standing in front of me like a weapon sculpted by something ancient.

Ubel laughed—a broken, wild sound. "You can't protect her forever. When I kill her, you'll be destroyed along with her, and I'll take control of everything."

He raised both hands—his ability condensed into a single spear of white-hot annihilation—the kind that shatters souls.

"Watch out!!" Rue croaked, trying to drag himself upright.

"Stay down!' I begged him.

Ubel turned the spear toward *me*—

Trent moved without thought.

He moved to protect me with absolutely no hesitation.

He blurred into the spear's path, no time to shield himself.

"NO!" I screamed. Loving and hating him at the same time.

The blast hit him square in the chest.

His body bowed backward, shadows exploding outward in violent arcs. He staggered, slamming into the far wall. The shadows tried to hold him together, knitting smoke into flesh, but Ubel's magic burned through every stitch.

He dropped to one knee.

Selene froze.

Not in shock, but in horror. Because she felt it, they both did.

The curse that had enslaved Aurathia for centuries? That forced all Aurathions to rely on a ritual to access their abilities? That kept our people weak and dependent on finding a Nexus?

It snapped like a rope held too tightly.

A ringing filled the chamber—metallic, ancient, holy.

The torches blew out.

My breath vanished.

Light erupted beneath me—the Ancestors howling in my ears. Golden lines crawled outward across the floor, weaving into a coronation circle.

"Impossible," Selene whispered, backing away.

"Not impossible," Rue whispered, clutching his chest as tears slid down his face. "Destiny."

Trent looked up at me through smoke and blood. His voice broke on a whisper.

"I never meant to hurt you, Bellator… I only ever wanted to love you."

Selene staggered, a momentary crack appearing in her facade of hatred.

Ubel swore under his breath. "He took the entire strike for her—why—WHY would he—"

Trent turned his head toward them, shadows crawling weakly along his ribs where the blast had ripped him open. "Because she…" He coughed, choking on smoke. "…she was always mine to protect. Even before I knew her name."

And then—

The world split open.

The Ancestors erupted upward in a cyclone of light—gold, silver, deep blue, storm red—wrapping around me, lifting me off my feet. My body arched as centuries of lives poured through me like tidal waves breaking in reverse.

I saw them all.

Lilibet, fierce and sorrowful.

Seraphine, the queen who commanded storms.

Maera, who fought the First War with a Fellat at her side.

Isara, crowned in starlight.

Callida, whose fire melted mountains.

Dozens.

Hundreds.

Every queen I had ever been.

The Ancestors spoke with a thousand voices:

"THE SACRIFICE IS ACCEPTED."

"THE LINE RESTORED."

"THE QUEEN RETURNS."

My back arched, my mouth opened in a silent cry as light sealed itself along my sternum—the broken crown burning into brilliance, no longer fractured.

A completed crown.

A sovereign mark.

Selene and Ubel fell to their knees, unable to breathe, unable to move under the weight of divine recognition.

Tanya's cuffs shattered.

Malik gasped as light hit him and healed the wound on his ribs.

Rue bowed his head, overwhelmed.

Trent collapsed fully, body giving out—but his eyes

stayed on me, shining with something raw and terrified and reverent.

And then—

The chamber bowed.

Not the people.

All of Aurathia bowed.

As I hovered in the air, wrapped in ancestral fire, every life I'd lived whispered through me the same truth: I was queen not because I reincarnated.

I reincarnated because I was queen.

The Ancestors' light dimmed, and the chamber settled. Selene and Ubel were both silent in shock against the wall as Tanya and her men stood over them.

But none of that mattered.

Because Trent—Trent was dying.

He lay on the shattered stone; one hand pressed weakly to the smoking wound Ubel had carved through him. Shadows leaked from the edges of his body like spilled ink, evaporating before they touched the ground.

His eyes found mine.

Not as Trent.

Not as Torren.

But as the man he had been before any of those names.

Kratos.

I stumbled toward him, falling to my knees. "No—no, please—stay with me. Trent—"

He let out a trembling laugh. "Finally, you're saying my name as I always wished you would—now, when it doesn't matter anymore."

My vision grew blurry. "It *does* matter."

A faint smile touched his lips. "Reverie… Lilibet… gods, I don't even know what to call you anymore."

I cupped his face with trembling hands. "Call me whatever you want to."

His breath hitched—a soft, broken sound—because he remembered. The past life memory flickered between us: Lilibet in her golden armor, Kratos tugging her hood down to kiss her forehead before a battle. A moment stolen, a moment frozen in time.

"*My heart.*" He whispered.

The name struck me like lightning. I had forgotten it—but Lilibet hadn't.

Tears spilled down my cheeks. "You saved me, Trent."

He swallowed hard, pain shuddering through him. "In every life, I failed you. I betrayed you. I betrayed all of them. I was supposed to protect you—but instead, I doomed you."

"I saw it," I said softly. "In my dreams. I know what you did."

He flinched. His eyes closed as if the memory physically hurt.

"But this—" I pressed my forehead to his, voice shaking, "—this was your choice. Not Kratos's. Yours."

His breath trembled. "There was no other choice. The moment I saw Ubel's attack—"

"I know, my love," I whispered, kissing his forehead.

"—I thought only that it couldn't hit you. Not in *this* life. Not *any* life."

My chest caved with a sob.

His hand lifted weakly, tracing the side of my jaw with a touch that felt like it belonged to centuries. "You were my queen then… and you're my queen now. But this time… I loved you the right way."

"You can't leave me," I breathed. "You just broke the curse. We just—"

"That's why I can leave." His thumb brushed my lip, a trembling, tender touch. "You're free now. No more dying young. No more heartbreak. No more fighting just to live a life with your Faction." His pupils flickered—a flash of gold from Kratos, a swirl of shadow from Trent. "I don't get a second chance," he whispered. "This was my second chance."

"No," I said fiercely. "No, you stay with me. We can fix this. We—

He coughed—dark blood staining his lips. "Reverie… I don't deserve your forgiveness. I've done too much."

"But you earned it," I cried.

His eyes softened in a way that gutted me. "You were always the bravest of us," he murmured. "Even more than Ambrose and the others…even more than the men in this life."

"Please stay with me. I love you." I buried my face in his neck, inhaling the scent that had called to me as much as it had repelled me.

"I'll love you for eternity, and I'm glad…" he murmured, fading fast. "That in the end… I died doing one… thing… right."

His fingers slipped from mine.

The shadows around him dissolved.

The Ancestors' light sank into the stone.

And the man who had once destroyed me—who had once betrayed me—who had once doomed a queen—an entire race of people—died while saving the woman I had become.

I bent over him, shoulders shaking, the silence thick and suffocating.

Rue dragged himself over to me and put his arm around me in comfort.

And that's when I sensed it—a ripple—a change in the air behind me. The cold that only comes from hatred.

Selene's snarl sliced through the grief. "Get away from him."

I turned just as Ubel ripped himself free of Tanya's restraints, eyes glowing with murderous zeal. "She's weakened!" Ubel barked. "Finish it now—while her power is still settling!"

Selene's face twisted with feral rage. "He chose her," she spat, voice breaking. "He *chose* her over us. Over *me*."

She raised a hand, pointing her ability straight at my back. Ubel raised a second attack, white lightning coiling like a spear in his fists.

Both powers aimed to end me.

Right above Trent's body—the man I loved in a past life and would never get the chance to love in this one.

I lifted my head, something ancient and furious rising behind my grief—something that didn't feel entirely like me.

And for the first time, I didn't feel alone inside my own skin.

I felt Lilibet, Seraphine, Maera, and every queen who had ever breathed through my soul.

Their abilities hit me—but they didn't touch me.

Light exploded outward from my spine, my sternum, my palms—a crown-shaped blaze of ancestral fire.

It slammed Selene and Ubel back against the far wall, pinning them like insects in amber.

The chamber shook.

Tanya, Razor, and Malik shielded their eyes. Rue fell to the floor.

And I felt every queen inside me—not passing me power, but *joining* me.

My feet lifted off the ground.

My hair whipped around me like a storm.

The crown mark burned gold, no longer broken, no longer fractured by curse or betrayal.

A voice boomed through me—the voice of every life, every queen, every Ancestor. "YOUR QUEEN RISES."

The chamber walls cracked outward as the energy burst through the mountain.

And that's when my family arrived.

CHAPTER 38

REVERIE

Oren burst through the shattered stone first, blackened wings of shadow spreading behind him without him even realizing it. It brought a tear to my eye how similar he was to his uncle in ability and temperament.

Nathan's flames died the moment he saw me—replaced with awe so raw it made my chest ache.

Zeke and Zane skidded to a halt beside him, their Draxon eyes glowing like Starfire.

Jet whispered, voice hoarse, "Holy shit... she's... she's crowned."

All of them looked like they'd been in a horrible battle. Clothes torn and blood covering them.

Mom entered the chamber with Grumpy, Pops, and Dad circling her protectively.

And when she saw Rue, Mom froze.

She was wearing the twin swords Zeke had gifted me on each side of her hips. They'd been lying beside me before Trent took me. Her eyes found Selene pinned to the wall by my power.

A tremor went through her. Not fear but of pure, unadulterated hate.

Selene hissed, "Adelaide—you bitch—don't—"

Mom didn't hesitate. She stepped forward, and my fathers stepped back, giving her room.

I lowered my power just enough for her to approach—the queens inside me humming in approval.

Mom stopped inches from Selene, looking her dead in the face. "For my daughter and my Sly," she whispered.

Then she pulled Ashfang from its sheath and drove it straight into Selene's throat in one clean, unflinching strike.

Her skin cracked first, thin glowing fissures racing across her throat and jaw. Smoke curled from the wounds, followed by a low, rising hiss as if the fire inside her had been waiting for this exact moment to breathe. She clawed at the blade, but her fingers blistered instantly, flesh blackening before our eyes. Heat shimmered around her, the air bending and buckling.

Then she ignited.

Flames roared out from the wound, swallowing her neck, her hair, and her scream. Her body arched, burning from the inside out, edges collapsing into glowing embers that drifted away on the air like falling stars. The last thing to crumble was her glare—still hateful, still locked on Adelaide—before it disintegrated into ash and scattered across the floor.

Ubel screamed, but Zane's fire and Zeke's ice hit him

at the same time, pinning him helpless until Oren's shadows wrapped around his wrists and throat.

Mom cleaned her blade with a steady hand. She spoke, voice not trembling in the least. "Thank you, my queen. I've waited a long time to end her."

The Ancestors whispered through me, satisfied.

The chamber settled.

The light dimmed.

My feet touched the ground again—but the power didn't vanish.

I walked forward, glowing, part goddess, part woman.

All queen—and everyone bowed.

I approached Mom and drew Frostbane from its sheath. Then turned and slid it into Ubel's chest with a sound more like shattering glass than tearing flesh, the blade's icy magic racing ahead of the steel. His breath hitched—one sharp, shocked inhale—before a plume of white mist burst from his mouth, frosting the air between us. The cold spread violently, spiderwebbing across his skin in jagged crystalline patterns, freezing him from the inside out.

He tried to speak, but his lips had already turned blue, then pale, then translucent as the frost consumed him. A heartbeat later, the ice surged outward in a brutal snap, encasing his entire body in a glassy shell. Cracks formed instantly—hairline fractures shooting through him like lightning—until with a final, brittle gasp, Ubel shattered.

He broke apart in a burst of glittering shards, scattering across the stone like crushed diamonds, the remnants of him dissolving into drifting frost that vanished before it touched the ground.

"That's for killing one of *MINE!*"

I turned, tears rising again, as the ancestral glow softened around Trent's still form. Handsome beyond belief even in death.

"Rest now," I whispered. "I'll see you when this life is done."

And I could swear I heard him reply, *"Live well, little Bellator. I'll be waiting."*

⌒ ⚜ ⌒

We carried Trent's body as we walked out of the chamber—Rue leaning heavily on Sly, Mom at my side, my men surrounding me like a shield.

I was shocked to see a giant creature I thought was a myth, dismembered and dead, right outside the room.

I looked to Oren in question, and he just smiled that arrogant smile that filled my heart with love. "A small problem we had to get through to reach you."

I arched one brow, "I'd like to hear the whole story at some point."

"You absolutely will since I'm the hero of the tale." Zane puffed out his chest.

Zeke rolled his eyes, "Of course you were."

We stepped out into the open air, just as dawn was breaking across the mountains.

And all of Aurathia seemed to be waiting.

Fellats—dozens of them, summoned by Pantar and Mila—bowed low, tentacles rippling like banners. Pantar pushed forward, giving a deep, reverent rumble.

The Varruk warriors, towering and fearsome, slammed their fists to their chests the moment they saw me. Kharox—the one who had chosen me first—stepped forward and bent one knee, then ran a single claw down his sternum. All of them looked as if they'd been involved in a battle of epic proportions. It seemed I'd missed some things while I was in the chamber.

"My queen," he growled.

Behind them, warriors from the caves of Nyberie gathered in ranks, eyes shining with awe.

My people.

My realm.

My birthright.

A sound broke the moment—

"Bestie!" Chloe ran through the warriors like a hurricane, throwing her arms around me and sobbing into my shoulder. "What the fuck? Why didn't Trent take me too? Doesn't he know we're ride or die besties, sisters from different misters, bound for eternity by our love for Dale and Brennan?"

Nathan grunted, clearly irritated, but for once, he kept his mouth closed, smoothly stroking his hand down Dale's feathers.

I laughed through tears, hugging her tight.

Behind her, I saw Mom and my fathers embracing Rue, tears streaming down their faces. Their Faction was whole again for the first time in years. I gave Chloe one last squeeze before letting her go and approached them.

When Rue saw me coming, he met me halfway. I nearly collapsed into his arms.

"I can't believe I have a daughter." His voice was thick

and broken. "My girl…a queen." He lifted a strand of my hair, then ran a finger over my cheek. "I've missed so much, and all of this was my fault."

"No!" I hugged him tight. "You tried the only way you knew to fix things. The Dark Factions were the ones to pervert your cure."

He whispered nonsensical words as he rocked me in his arms, and the rest of my parents joined him. After a few minutes, they took him away to be alone, away from the crowd, where they could comfort him and each other. I knew they had a lot of time to make up for, and I was beyond happy for them.

I felt the warmth of them surround me, tired of waiting for my attention. Each of them touching me, somewhere: a hand on my waist, a shoulder, a cheek, a kiss pressed to my hair.

For the first time since my very first life—

I was ready to embrace my men and live the life Kratos/Trent/Torren had given *his* life for us to have. The name didn't really matter; it was the soul that gave everything to me.

A ripple of wind swept across the mountain as every creature, every warrior, every soul bowed.

The Ancestors whispered one final time through the echo of dawn: "*A QUEEN WITH SIX HEARTS. A REALM RESTORED.*"

I stepped forward, my men flanking me, Chloe crying, Deshawn and Oliver fussing over her, my parents radiating joy, the Fellat and Varruk roaring their allegiance.

The sun broke the horizon.

And a new reign began.

EPILOGUE
REVERIE

The castle looked nothing like the crumbling ruin I remembered from dreams. It rose from the mountain like it had been grown from the stone itself—white marble threaded with gold veining, banners fluttering from tall spires, windows blazing with light.

The Ancestors had restored it when they restored me.

Inside, music hummed like an echo from past lives—low drums, strings that vibrated in bone-deep resonance, voices humming ancient song.

My people were gathered in the great hall—Fellat prowling the upper balconies like the sacred guardians they were, Varruk standing like statues flanking the entrance, Aurathion warriors lining the aisle in armor newly blessed by ancestral magic. Most had found their Faction, now that the ritual wasn't needed with the curse broken.

And my parents.

Adelaide stood near the dais, her face glowing with joy

and love. All my fathers were gathered around her, smiling proudly at me, except Grumpy, who was scowling at Nathan and Zane as they strutted beside me when we entered the hall.

At my entrance, every creature—Aurathion, Fellat, Varruk—lowered themselves in reverence.

The crown etched onto my skin burned warm, as if Trent approved and was with me in spirit.

Nathan pushed Zane and stepped to my side, grabbing my hand, always possessive and not always willing to share.

Jet took my other hand and gave Nathan a disapproving look. Oren, Zeke, and Zane fanned behind me like the points of a star. Zane, not in the least bit subtle, stuck his middle finger in Nathan's face from behind.

"Zane!" his mother gasped as we walked past, and he quickly pulled his hand back, stuffing both into his pockets and adopting an innocent look that no one was deceived by.

My Faction.

My heart.

My line.

The joining ceremony wasn't rushed—it moved like a living thing, a tradition older than even my previous lives.

A circle of ancient silver was engraved into the floor—a replica of my Nexus mark.

We stepped inside together.

The air shifted instantly.

The Ancestors were close—I felt them at my back, brushing their presence against my shoulders.

Adelaide stepped forward first, carrying the ceremonial bowl of water, glowing faintly with Ancestor fire. Her hands were steady, no trace of the viciousness they had contained when slitting Selene's throat.

She looked at each of my men with something like awe. "You love her," she said softly. "Each of you. Truly.'

Nathan nodded confidently, his love for me clearly visible. Jet remained stoic, offering only a faint smile. Zane smirked and gave her a thumbs-up. Zeke and Oren met her eyes, their love shining through.

Adelaide smiled and dipped her fingers into the glowing water. She drew a line across my forehead. My skin ignited in light—not with pain, but belonging.

The next part was for my men. One by one, they stepped forward before me—their marks blazing.

Nathan cupped my jaw, thumb trembling. "I would burn the world if you asked," he whispered. His kiss was fire tempered by a promise.

Jet stepped forward and pressed his forehead to mine. "You are my quiet in a world gone crazy, and I want to be your safe space too." His kiss was soft, reverent, and grounding, everything that he was.

Zane grinned, but it was shaky—and brushed my cheek with a knuckle. "Guess we're official now, precious girl." His kiss was heat and mischief with a devotion so pure that it stopped my heart.

Zeke lifted my hand, pressing his lips to the center of my palm. "You're my center. I'll take care of you for all the days of my life." His kiss was slow, deep, melting me into a puddle at his feet.

Last but never least, Oren stepped up to my side, shadows rising behind him like a cloak. "You are my queen," he murmured low so only I could hear. "In every life. But in this one most of all." His kiss stole my breath. It always did.

When his kiss ended, the ring erupted in color—six marks blazing into the floor at equal points around mine.

Our energies braided together, weaving emerald, purple, yellow, crimson, ruby red, and lastly a beautiful gold into a radiant cord that hovered above the ring.

The sound that followed wasn't music. It was acceptance.

From the Ancestors.

From the land.

From the realm itself.

Mom stepped back, tears streaming down her face. Each of my fathers surrounded her, Rue's hair shining like gold, with a smile I thought I would never see.

The Fellat roared their approval—Pantar and Mira in the lead. Kharox dragged a claw down his sternum, and the Varruk bowed as one, fists pressed to their chests.

Oren reached for my hand. Nathan for my waist. Jet for my back. Zeke and Zane stepped closer, surrounding me.

The Nexus cord sank into our skin like warm starlight.

Our Faction sealed.

Our future was so very bright.

Sadness filled my heart for the one who wasn't here, but I knew we'd meet again someday.

The castle roared with celebration.

Finally, we were all together. There was still plenty of work ahead. Oren had plans for his father and the corrupt council. The guys were ready and willing to help.

Jet had his branding iron warm and ready, and Nathan kept muttering something about adding to his collection… I was smart enough not to ask any questions.

Lots of things to correct and reverse. Fortunately, together, I knew we could accomplish anything.

EPILOGUE

REVERIE- FIVE YEARS LATER

EMBERHOLD ACADEMY, BELLONA-

Emberhold Academy no longer existed in a pocket dimension.

It stood in Bellona now, rebuilt atop the shattered remains of the coliseum that had once taken lives for spectacle. Where blood had soaked into the sand, gardens now bloomed. Where cages had stood, classrooms had taken their place.

I had insisted on that, and my men had made it so.

Those ghosts deserved to be buried beneath laughter.

Avery Cleopatra sprinted across the large lawn, blond curls flying, light flaring uncontrollably around her hands as she shrieked with delight. She was only four but utterly convinced she was invincible.

Emery Lilibet followed at a slower pace, shadows clinging to her heels like a loyal hound. She was always watching, calculating everything.

Both of my daughters, named after great queens and loved by all, looked identical from head to toe, except for their eye color. Avery had Nathan's green eyes, while Emery had Jet's warm brown ones. Both inherited their grandmother's white-blonde hair.

Emery had a combination of Zeke and Oren's personalities; she cared for everyone but was also a bit bossy. Avery had the free spirit of Nathan and Zane, and unfortunately, their sense of humor.

Since the curse was broken, children had begun exhibiting their Nexus status earlier every year. My girls were going to be the most powerful Nexus this world had ever seen.

Don't ask me how I knew this—I just did.

I rubbed my slightly rounded belly—only the Ancestors knew what traits this one would inherit.

"Avery! If you don't come here *right now*, there won't be any rides on Frynn later," Zane said, trying to sound stern. However, even at her young age, she knew that her fathers rarely enforced punishments. Both of our girls were spoiled.

"I'll bring her back," Bennet spoke softly.

Blaze rolled his eyes but made his way over to Emery's side, where he bounced around playfully trying to get her to join in.

Blaze and Bennet—five years old, identical smiles, and terrifyingly competent—were Chloe, Oliver, and Deshawn's sons, instincts as sharp as both of their fathers combined.

Both were large for their age. Inheriting their size from Oliver, their skin tone and good looks from

Deshawn. The only thing they got from my bestie was their piercing blue eyes.

Neither boy was ever far from my daughters, already very protective. I wouldn't want to be the men competing for their Faction.

Chloe stood beside me, arms crossed, her expression equal parts pride and long-suffering amusement. "They've decided they're the girls Aegisworn," she said dryly. "I've given up trying to convince them otherwise."

"I don't doubt that if my daughters have their way, they will be." I smiled.

She snorted. "True that."

"Isn't Razor and his Faction coming to visit y'all for Christmas?"

"Yes, they're excited to experience snow for the first time," Chloe smirked. "Deshawn has a snowball maker and plans to welcome Razor vigorously."

I laughed. "Ohio is beautiful this time of year. Wait till I bring them to Texas and introduce them to Bluebell ice cream and Tex-Mex."

She groaned, rubbing her rounded stomach. "Don't even start with that ice cream. I've made Oliver portal twice this month alone to pick up a half-gallon of butter pecan. I can't get enough of the stuff." She narrowed her eyes at me. "And we know whose fault that is."

I guiltily changed the subject. "I love to hear Deshawn tell the story of how Oliver's ability made itself known."

"Don't remind me. Do you have any idea what it's like to be sexted up against the shower door one minute, then fall butt naked into Bellona's market square the next?"

I threw my head back and laughed so hard I snorted. "Stop… you'll make me pee!"

"*You* stop with that stupid laugh, or I'll pee!"

We clutched each other, our legs crossed, gasping for air. After we stopped cackling, we finally noticed Deshawn signaling to Chloe.

She scowled. (The mood swings were no joke.) "I swear, if he's calling me over to rub my belly, I'm going to kick his ass. He goes at it like he expects a genie to pop out."

I giggled as she stomped off, glancing in Oren's direction when I heard him barking orders to a line of older students, looking annoyed as usual.

I admired his body in the tight leather pants he wore. The man was even sexier than when I first saw him walking across the gym floor all of those years ago.

"I despise this job." He muttered to me when I joined him.

"But you're so excellent at it," I smirked as I sent one of my shadows out and copped a feel of his ass.

He raised an eyebrow, his face set in his usual haughty expression, which softened when he pulled me into his arms. "That isn't behavior befitting a queen."

I waggled my brows. "I have a new decree concerning that very thing."

"Is that so?" He grinned.

"Yes, it is. Every queen from this day forth is allowed to grab the amazing asses of each of her Faction at her discretion." I spoke in my most queenly voice. Although I was pretty sure the Texas twang I had ruined the tone I was going for.

He grinned, "I like it."

"I was sure you would." I stood on tiptoes and kissed his beautiful lips.

Oren couldn't fool me. I knew he loved torturing the students at Emberhold as he ran them through their paces. The man had a bit of a cruel streak… but who didn't like a bad boy?

Nathan, lounging nearby, with Dale resting on his shoulder, grinned. "Give it up, Shitstorm. We know you love lording it over the students. It's the lesson plans you hate."

Now, the instructors at Emberhold rotated. All of my men took a turn and spent part of the year as instructors. Jet assisted Instructor Lee in battle strategy. Nathan helped Oren. Zeke and Zane handled draxon studies and controlled shifting. (It was now more common since our Factions were able to form without the ritual due to the curse being broken.)

I taught a legacy course. I kept the classes small but thought it important to remember our past queens as the wonderful rulers they'd been. The crap the council had taught generations of Aurathions was a massive pile of steaming bullshit.

Nathan waved me over, and I snuggled into his lap. He gently rubbed my belly, and I smirked, thinking of what Chloe had said earlier. Zeke appeared beside us and sat, pulling my feet into his lap, rubbing them firmly, making me moan. Jet and Zane made their way over, each of them touching me in some way.

I was more than content.

The council had been disbanded, and Oren's father

stripped of his abilities. We hadn't known it was possible, but with Rue's help, it had been done. He hadn't been imprisoned per se, but Tanya had bound him to his estates. Mira and Pantar popped in and out to make sure he was behaving himself.

Mom and all of my fathers thrived here. She was head of Faction restoration and ensured that the Factions formed through the ritual were strong and healthy.

It took a long time for Poppa (Rue) to recover, but with time and patience from Mom and my other fathers, he improved. I credited his granddaughters with most of his recovery. He worshiped the ground they walked on. I believed that my mom killing Selene the way she did also helped put all of their demons to rest.

I smiled as I saw all five of them walking out of the main building. Pops smacked Mom on the butt, and Grumpy put him in a headlock. Dad smiled in approval as Poppa took the opportunity to tuck Mom under his arm.

Life was damn near perfect.

We spent part of the year here at Emberhold, living in the house the academy built for us. (Honestly, I loved it more than the massive structure the ancestors willed to me.) For the rest of the year, we're either at the castle, dealing with the politics of my position, or on Earth, working on strengthening our relationship with humans. I loved Aurathia, but I was born on Earth, and that helped me relate to their concerns. Jet had also been a tremendous plus in that endeavor.

The spy planted in Aurathia turned out to be one of his friends from basic training, Nathan Sterlings, who had tested positive as a passive. So far, he hadn't found his Faction and liked to fuck with my men, pretending he was my potential. He screwed with Nathan the most, calling him an imposter and a placeholder for the much more superior Nathan.

My Nathan hated his guts.

Chloe and I had a bet on how long it would take all of them to realize that Nathan Sterling batted for the other team.

Avery's laughter echoed across the green. Emery was right behind her, shadows curling around her shoulders. Blaze and Bennet weren't far behind—more like older brothers than cousins.

My parents, my bestie, and my men are all nearby. The battle is won, but we know better than most how quickly things can change. Pantar, Mira, and Kharox have taken it upon themselves to travel between Earth and Aurathia, ensuring the DF never rises again.

This—*this*—is what winning looks like.

And the future?

It's already here.

One resting gently in my belly, the others:

Barefoot.

Laughing.

Guarded closely.

Answering to the names—

Avery.

Emery.

As I sat surrounded by my men, my two sweet babies' laughter ringing in the air, I knew it was all worth it.

Every bit of the pain and suffering we'd endured. This life was worth fighting for, and the Ancestors better take mercy on anyone who tried to take it from me—because I would not.

410

The End

Okay, for those of you who want the villain to have his happily-ever-after, here's an alternate ending for you. I'll admit I started to fall a little in love with Trent and just couldn't leave it like that.
If you liked it as is, then feel free to skip it.

SURPRISE

Trent collapsed, smoke still rising from the wound in his chest—the wound meant for me.

But as the Ancestors lifted me, as their power surged and the curse shattered into embers, a thread of gold snapped downward, shooting into his broken body.

I heard a gasp—his—low, strangled, shocked.

He wasn't dead.

Not quite.

The Ancestors whispered through me: *"The betrayer becomes the bound. The betrayed becomes the tether. His life is no longer his own."*

I dropped to my knees beside him as the light lowered me, and his eyes fluttered open—no sign of the madness that had shown in them before.

They were gentle and brimming with love. "Reverie..." his voice was hoarse and filled with awe. "I thought... I believed this was how I atoned."

Tears stung my eyes. "You don't get to choose dying as your apology."

His lips twitched. "Stubborn. In every life."

"And you're still impossible," I breathed, touching his cheek.

He closed his eyes under my hand—like Kratos once had, all those lifetimes ago, before betrayal, before curses, before kingdoms drowned in blood.

"I remember," he whispered. "All of it. Lilibet. The oath I broke. The Faction I destroyed. The curse that followed."

"And yet you still saved me," I said softly. "You broke it."

His voice shook. "How can you forgive me?"

"I don't know," I stared at him, tears sliding down. "But I can't lose you again."

His breath hitched.

Then the chamber erupted.

Selene and Ubel, desperate and furious, broke free of Tanya's bindings with a scream of betrayal and lunged straight at me—but this time I didn't need Trent to shield me.

I was the shield. The crown. The queen.

Golden fire burst from my palms, blasting them across the chamber. Walls cracked—the floor split.

The Ancestors' voices thundered through me. "SHE IS SOVEREIGN."

Selene crumpled, too overwhelmed to stand, and Ubel crawled backward, trembling.

My family suddenly burst in, and as soon as my mother—Adelaide—saw Selene, she stepped forward. She was wearing my daggers at her waist, Ashfang and Frostbane.

Mom stopped inches from Selene, looking her dead in the face. "For my daughter and my Sly," she whispered.

Then she pulled Ashfang from its sheath and drove it straight into Selene's throat in one clean, unflinching strike.

Her skin cracked first, thin glowing fissures racing across her throat and jaw. Smoke curled from the wounds, followed by a low, rising hiss as if the fire inside her had been waiting for this exact moment to breathe. She clawed at the blade, but her fingers blistered instantly, flesh blackening before our eyes. Heat shimmered around her, the air bending and buckling.

Then she ignited.

Flames roared out from the wound, swallowing her neck, her hair, and her scream. Her body arched, burning from the inside out, edges collapsing into glowing embers that drifted away on the air like falling stars. The last thing to crumble was her glare—still hateful, still locked on Adelaide—before it disintegrated into ash and scattered across the floor.

The chamber went silent.

～☘～

When we emerged into the daylight, trembling, raw, and reborn, the world was waiting.

Fellats lined the cliffs, massive beasts bowing their heads, eyes glowing reverently.

The warriors Kharox summoned knelt, fists over their hearts as he made the gesture that now warmed my heart.

My men moved beside me—Oren anchoring my right, Nathan burning at my left, Zeke and Zane flanking behind, Jet gently brushing my fingers with quiet awe.

They appeared both shattered and relieved, completely and utterly in love. And I returned the emotion tenfold as was evident on my face when I looked at them.

Chloe flew into me, crying, hugging me so tight it felt like my ribs might break. "Don't ever do that again, asshole, or I'll refuse to include you in any new activities."

I laughed into her hair. "No promises."

My mother and fathers pushed through next—Adelaide covering my face in frantic kisses, John, Jesse, Sly, and Rue pulling me into an embrace. The Hawthorne Faction is complete… finally.

My heart almost burst.

Trent stepped out into the sunlight behind us, swaying but alive. He'd stayed behind to deal with Ubel. I was reasonably sure he wouldn't be a problem anymore. Trent was still a monster at heart, but now he was my monster. He had a lot to atone for, but I knew he'd get there.

The Fellats rumbled low.

The Varruk bowed once again—not just to me.

To us.

To all of us.

The castle was rebuilt through ancestral magic—walls rising from stone, banners unfurling, ancient sigils glowing like stars returned to the night sky.

The ceremony took place in the Great Hall, beneath a canopy of floating crystal lanterns.

My men stood before me, marks blazing, growing brighter as I approached.

One by one, they placed their hands over my heart, speaking their vow—ancient words the Ancestors put in their minds when the curse broke.

"My queen, my Nexus, my sovereign bond. In this life and every life to follow."

When I spoke mine back, power exploded through the hall, binding us as a Faction not of convenience…

…but of destiny.

All six of my men standing together.

Trent is more than prepared and eager to make amends for the many wrongs he's done in this life. As his Nexus and queen, I couldn't ask for anything more.

BUT WAIT...

Keep turning the page for a second Epilogue... I mean, how can it end with Reverie never getting to visit the bone zone with Trent?

BONE ZONE

TRENT

I should've left the moment the shadows settled.

That was the plan—slip out, lock the night behind me, and pretend she didn't make my pulse skyrocket. But Reverie stood there in the moonlit quiet, watching me like she could read every secret I'd spent years burying.

Since the ceremony, I'd made sure to be available to every member of this Faction. Answering questions and helping get information from council members. Not letting myself be alone with my queen.

I wasn't worthy of her yet.

I knew it, and each one of my Faction brothers knew it.

Reverie's parents despised me for holding Rue captive all of these years, and I didn't blame them. They were trying for their daughter, and I was doing everything I could to show them that I'd changed.

Ever since the bonding ceremony, I'd slowly become more stable, and so had my abilities. I still had most of them, but my shadow ability had become my favorite. Oren wasn't a fan of sharing his shadow daddy title, but that was just too fucking bad.

It didn't help that Nathan and Zane loved to fuck with him about it on the regular.

You'd think that being his uncle and part of the same faction would be awkward, but it wasn't, probably because we were pretty much strangers, with me having been in Aurathia for his entire life.

What I hadn't done was allow myself to be alone with my Bellator. She was a temptation I didn't trust myself to resist. I wasn't fully reformed, and if I'm honest, I probably never would be. Denying myself wasn't something I enjoyed. I was trying for her, but hearing my Faction brothers enjoying her night after night was wearing down my willpower.

I'd made a point never to be alone with her. Obviously, she tricked the great Trent Storm tonight. I smirked at how far I'd fallen. This girl made me stupid, and I was here for it.

"Going so soon?" She smiled innocently, then dropped her wrap, revealing the pale pink nightie beneath.

Dangerous girl.

Dangerous to me, most of all.

"Reverie," it emerged more as a moan than the warning I intended.

She stepped closer.

Her fingers brushed my arm—light, curious, trusting.

She didn't realize that one simple touch nearly broke down the last of my restraint. I felt my composure crack, like glass under too much pressure.

I lifted a hand to the back of her neck before I could stop myself.

Warm.

Soft.

Mine, whispered something feral inside me.

Her breath mingled with mine, her lips hovering a hair from mine, her heartbeat walking its delicate rhythm right into my ribs. I half-expected her to pull away.

She didn't.

Of course, she didn't.

"You have no idea what you do to me," I whispered—truth torn from a man who never gives any.

She closed the remaining space.

The first touch of her lips hit me hard. Not gentle, not hesitant. Desperate. Real. Her hands clenched in my shirt's fabric, pulling me toward her as if she needed me just as much as I'd spent nights pretending I didn't need her.

I kissed her back, and the world narrowed to the heat of her body and the exquisite agony of finally touching what I'd been denying myself.

She tasted like temptation and redemption. Everything I wanted but shouldn't take.

But Ancestors, I wanted.

I pulled her hard against me, a sound escaping me— half groan, half surrender. I felt her answer it with her whole body, felt her melt into me like she belonged nowhere else. Every instinct screamed to take more. To claim. To let the shadows close around us and keep her with me, away from the others who had no idea how fragile she was, how powerful she was, how much she could break me.

At some point, I pressed my forehead to her collarbone, sucking in a breath that didn't steady me at all.

"If I stay," I murmured, voice unsteady, "I won't be able to pretend I don't want this. I won't be able to pretend you're not mine."

She tilted my chin up—Ancestors, the boldness of her—and held my gaze like she could see the war waging behind it.

"Then don't pretend."

Those words detonated something inside me.

I kissed her again, harder this time, hands sliding along her back, pulling her closer as the restraint I clung to finally came undone. She answered every touch, every hungry breath. And though the night swelled around us— heated, tangled, breathless—I kept myself just this side of losing control completely.

Not because I feared her.

But because I feared what I'd do to the world for her.

Of course, my little Bellator wouldn't accept that. She wanted everything and was determined to make me give it to her.

Taking my hand, she placed it on her breast, and I could feel the point of her nipple through the satin of the nightie.

Something deep inside me broke.

With a growl deep in my throat, I grabbed her and

pressed her body to me as I took her mouth in a kiss that was more teeth and tongue than anything else. Too blinded by my want for her to be gentle.

I picked her up and carried her to the large bed in the center of the room. Leaning back on her headboard, I arranged her so she's straddling my legs, pressing her center to my raging hard-on.

She's soft where I'm hard, and the feel of her is going to be imprinted in my brain until the day I die.

My fingers wove through her long black hair, its silky strands slipping through my hand. I used it to pull her head back and take possession of her luscious mouth once more. Enjoying her taste on my lips.

She pulled free, and I think she's changed her mind until she stands and pulls the nightie off her shoulders, letting it fall at her feet in a puddle of pink silk.

I think my soul left my body as I took in the milky white of her skin, framed by all of that thick midnight hair. Pink nipples pointed and stood proud, not ashamed of her desire for a monster like me.

"Don't you think you're a little overdressed?" Reverie smirked at me like I was some blushing maiden.

Fuck it, if I'm doing this, I'm going to show her that being a villain in bed might not be such a bad thing.

I stood, then reached behind my neck and pulled my shirt over my head in one smooth motion.

I saw her lick her lips while staring at my chest, and I smirked as I reached for the ties on my leather pants, loosening them and letting them drop to the floor. Stepping away from them, I stand there with my dick at full attention, allowing her to admire what belongs only to her for all eternity.

"This is your last chance to back out." I stared into her eyes with all the love I have. "I'm willing to wait as long as it takes to prove that I've changed."

She approached me, hips swaying, with those beautiful amber eyes glowing slightly. "We're connected, Trent. I know your heart as well as I know my own. I never wanted perfection. I just wanted honesty, and you've given me that. I'm tired of waiting. Now, man the fuck up and give me what I want."

I grinned, then used my shadows to pick her up and throw her on the bed hard enough that she bounced. The lady asked for honesty; the least I could do was give it to her in the bedroom.

I climbed onto the bed and lay flat on my back beside her, with my arms behind my head. She looked confused for a moment, then got up on her knees and crawled over me, straddling my thighs.

"So, you're a lazy lover. I should've expected as much." She narrowed her eyes and smirked.

I raised a brow. "Not lazy, just seeing what the other members of this Faction have taught you."

My Bellator looked pissed for a brief moment, then resolve took over.

Damn, this might have been a bad idea. I didn't want to embarrass myself. And with the desire I felt for her, that was entirely possible.

My hands stay clenched at my sides, even as she placed my hand on her breast once more and whispered, "Touch me."

I pulled her down until I could suck her nipple into my mouth and lick it with my tongue, biting down gently. She sucked in a breath even as she lowered herself down on my large cock, so tight she had to stop halfway. I reached down and rubbed her clit with my thumb until she became wet enough to take me inside her completely.

"Fuuck, that feels so good, my queen." I moan as she starts to slide up and down my length slowly.

She threw her head back and moaned my name as my shadows encircled her hips, enabling me to go deeper and savor how her body constricted around me. Her velvet walls seem to strangle me, eliciting growls and grunts from me that sound animalistic.

I want this to last, so I lift her off me and stand. Using my shadows, I raise her high and then position her on her knees at the bed's edge. Without delay, I thrust back inside her, making her shudder and moan as my pace quickened.

"Please, Trent, let me cum," my sweet girl moans as I let her get close, then slow my pace, trying to prolong this moment.

I can't deny her anything, so I reach around, running two fingers over her clit, gently. Not using my shadows because I want to feel the evidence of her desire on my fingers.

I can't resist the urge to taste her, so I withdrew and flipped her onto her back, burying my face in her sweet pussy, licking and sucking as I pumped two fingers inside her. I can't help the obscene noises I'm making because this is the best thing I've ever had in my mouth. Sweet, with just enough tartness to make it enjoyable. Just like her personality.

She began to twitch and moan and grabbed the back of my head, pushing me even deeper. It's not long before I feel her tighten on my fingers, and her pussy gushes with her release.

I licked up every last drop, then flipped her over. She's boneless and gives no resistance as I thrust into her so hard I have to use my shadows to pull her back to me and hold her still. As my movements sped up, she started trying to push back against me, desperate for another orgasm.

"My greedy girl. You love it when I fuck you, don't you?" I stop my movements when she doesn't answer.

"Yes, fuck, yes. Please don't stop." She moans out, desperate for my cock.

I resume my thrusts, my dick so hard that I could drive nails. I feel her body tighten as her back arches, and I know my control is done.

My cock erupts, and I black out, never having come so hard in my life, collapsing on her back. We both lie there in silence, just enjoying the connection.

Finally, I find the strength to clean both of us up, then wrap her in my arms before starting all over again, unable to get enough of this extraordinary woman. I doubt I ever will, even when we're old and gray.

Hours later, when the fire had softened into something deeper—hot, steady, grounding—I held her close. Her breathing was slow against my chest, her body warm in my arms.

This should have been a victory for me… or maybe a disaster for her.

Instead, it was exactly what she asked for…honest.

"This changes everything," I whispered into her hair.

And for the first time in a very long time… every part of me hoped it would.

The End

Afterward

Thanks to everyone who made this series possible.

Adaira and Hayley—thank you for being my calm in the chaos, my sounding board for wild plot twists (that I don't always go through with). And most of all, thank you for patiently guiding me through the wilds of social media and all things computer-related, despite my repeated questions and impressive ability to forget things five minutes after learning them.

Thanks to my ARC readers. It blows my mind that you want to take time from your busy lives to give your feedback. You rock!

Thanks to my Mom for being my biggest fan and showing off my books to everyone who walks through her door (and letting them take center stage on her coffee table). I love you very much.

Thanks to my wonderful husband for always giving me his unwavering support. (and help with the laundry!) I love you!

And as always, I love you, Frank James. You were the best father a girl could have, and I'll miss you for the rest of my life.

ALSO BY FRANKIE JAMES

ABOUT THE AUTHOR

Frankie James is a brand-new Indie author. She's been an avid reader all her life and decided to try her hand at creating her own stories. She raised her babies in a small town in Texas. After they left the nest, her husband decided to take a job traveling. They bought a fifth wheel RV and haven't looked back. Seeing this beautiful country gave her all the inspiration she needed to put pen to paper. When not reading or writing her favorite things are loving on her grandbabies, cooking, and hanging out with her husband. Come hang out with her at page or Join her group . Instagram: @frankiejamesauthor Tiktok: @frankiejamesauthor